To sleep: pe

The old Osraed loo
course, it's good to see you looking so happy."

Daimhin took another sip of the sweet, thick wine. "I am happy. And I'll tell you why. The cannon is ours."

Ruadh raised his glass to his cousin in silent applause, but the Abbod could only stare vacantly and murmur, "Cannon? What cannon?"

"The one that's going to blow the doors of Haligliath to the skies."

"What?"

Now the old boar was clearly dumbfounded. Daimhin was both amused and irritated. "I've convinced the Deasach to lend us a marvelous new machine of war. A cannon—three horses in length—that fires explosive ordnance. With it, I intend to go up to Nairne and, by fear or force, bring back Cyneric Airleas."

Ladhar's full lips puckered mutinously. "And Taminy-a-Cuinn?"

"I intend to bring her back to Creiddylad and drown her. She should never have escaped the Sea in the first place; she will not do it again."

The large Osraed took a deep, noisy breath. "I'd rather see her burned. It's more certain."

"Abbod, there is in the depths of Mertuile, a chamber which admits the Sea. There is always at least one hand's width of water covering the floor and, as the tide rises, so does the depth of the water in the cell. When the tide is high, sea water fills the chamber to a depth of four feet."

"Four feet of water," said the Abbod, "will not drown a woman who is over five feet tall."

"Everyone must sleep, Abbod. Even the wicked."

BAEN BOOKS BY
MAYA KAATHRYN BOHNHOFF

The Meri
Taminy
The Crystal Rose

THE CRYSTAL ROSE

BAEN

THE CRYSTAL ROSE

Copyright © 1995 by Maya Kaathryn Bohnhoff

A Baen Books Original

Baen Publishing Enterprises
P.O. Box 1403
Riverdale, NY 10471

ISBN: 0-671-87648-1

Cover art by Darrell K. Sweet

First printing, March 1995

Distributed by Simon & Schuster
1230 Avenue of the Americas
New York, NY 10020

Typeset by Windhaven Press, Auburn, NH
Printed in the United States of America

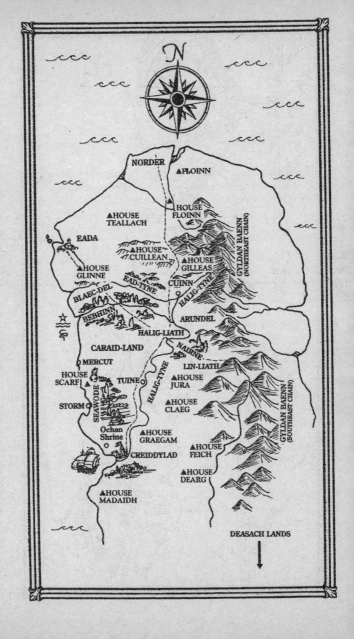

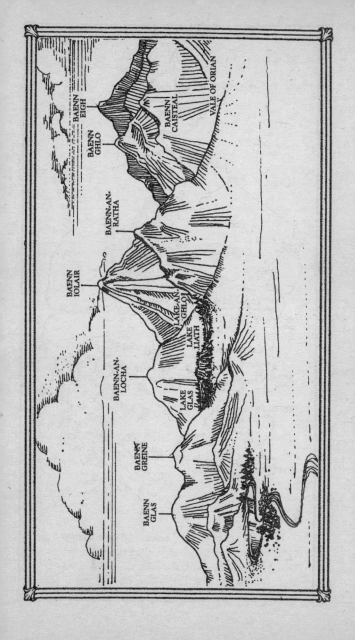

PROLOGUE

The mystic Beloved, before concealed by the veil of words, is now revealed to the eyes of men.

I bear witness, my friends, that the benediction is complete, the testimony fulfilled, the proof demonstrated, the sign given. Let all now see what your efforts in the path of the Meri will unveil and accomplish.

Divine grace has been bestowed on you and on all that dwell in the Lands of Shadow and Light. Sing duans of praise to the Spirit of All Worlds.

—from the Testament of Osraed Bevol

✧　　　✧　　　✧

Blood thundered in his ears. Daimhin Feich listened, heeding its siren call. He wondered at the strange visceral elation he felt just strapping on this sword. He had never worn one, save for ceremonial purposes, and this was no ordinary sword—it was a Malcuim sword, worn, so legend said, by the Malcuim himself. It was a sword intended for fighting, and Daimhin Feich had every intention of putting it to that use.

He strode the corridors of Mertuile with a new vigor this morning. A vigor the black banners and bundles of dead flowers that festooned the halls could not dampen. He was Regent to Airleas Malcuim, Cyneric if Airleas failed to take the throne. Dark joy bubbled in his breast, threatening to make him laugh. That would be inappropriate now, with Mertuile in mourning; he would laugh when he stood before the Stone and felt the Circlet on his head. A Feich on the throne! He began to whistle a tune, but

Mertuile's empty interior threw it back at him misshapen. He stopped whistling.

In the lower hall, the Abbod Ladhar met him, along with his own cousin, Ruadh, commander of his fighting force. One was dressed for travel, the other for battle.

The Abbod's face was screwed into a disapproving mask and he glowered fiercely. "Why do you insist that I accompany you on this war crusade? My place is here."

"To comfort the mourners?" Daimhin asked. "To pray for the soul of your poor dead Cyne? His soul is wherever it deserves to be, Abbod. With the souls of other men who have taken their own lives. Your place is with those living, those who will march to free the Cyne's heir from the clutches of the Taminist evil. Your place is beneath the banner of the Meri, facing that evil. Or do you fear facing it?"

"I fear no man, nor woman, nor Wicke. But the period of mourning is not passed. It has barely begun."

"Mourn on the road, Abbod. Now, we ride to Haligliath." He passed through the door his cousin held open for him, out into the morning Sun that slanted over Mertuile's landward wall. The gates to the outer ward were open and, through them, he could see the ranks of horses and men that were now at his command. He smiled, letting his earlier elation rise to a boil within him. Sensual, it was. He felt heat fan out from his groin and listened, again, to the song of blood in his ears. A quest. A crusade. And it would end at Halig-liath.

It was not Airleas Malcuim he thought of as he and his hundreds rode east, but she who had taken him—Taminy-a-Cuinn, Wicke.

The Feich forces were arrayed before the gates of the Holy Fortress. Daimhin Feich rode at their head with Ruadh Feich at his side. Behind them, the Abbod Ladhar glowered from the back of a sturdy horse, the Malcuim standard fluttering overhead. Beside it, on a second staff, the Star Chalice was borne aloft. It was a bit of grandstanding that did not sit well with the Abbod, but to

Daimhin Feich, it added a twist of historical irony to his crusade. Centuries before, another army had rallied to face down another Malcuim heir, using the same holy relic to confound his forces. And now, as then, hundreds had rallied. Not only Feich, but Feich allies—southern Eiric, for the most part, to whom the Osraed were a nuisance and the idea of supernatural intervention, an anachronism. For the Feich it was a return to the glory days. The days when the great House was a thorn in the side of whatever Malcuim happened to sit upon the Throne.

Daimhin Feich, Regent and would-be Cyneric, turned to glance up at the standards aloft behind him. He would tear down that Malcuim emblem soon, replace it with his own. But for now, the Feich crest appeared only on the arm bands of the troops massed behind him.

He moved his mount forward, all the way to the shadow of Halig-liath's gates. The heavy oaken doors were open, but the portcullis was down. The Ren Catahn, leader of the Hillwild, stood behind it, the Chief of the House Claeg at his side. Feich spoke to the lowland Chief. "A twist in history, this, old friend—that Feich and Claeg face each other across defenses."

"Aye, well, it was inevitable. The Claeg do what they believe is right. The Feich do what they think is profitable."

Feich chuckled. "Barbed words, Claeg."

"May they draw blood."

"I must speak to the Cwen Toireasa and the Riagan Airleas."

From behind the sill of the gate, Toireasa Malcuim heard the words and shivered. Grasping her son's hand, she willed her feet to move her forward. They behaved as if rooted to the cobbles. Someone took her other hand, flooding her with strength. She smiled. *Oh, to feel this strong and resilient, always.*

With Airleas on her left and Taminy on her right, she went out to face Daimhin Feich. His eyes gleamed when he saw them, and he dismounted, coming to stand before the portcullis.

"This is absurd," he said. "I merely wish to reason with you, mistress. Can't we do without further barriers between us?" He gestured at the heavy wood and iron grille that separated them. "Your men have their bows aimed and ready. What could we do against them?"

Taminy turned her head and glanced behind her. The portcullis rose ponderously.

"Thank you." Feich dropped his gaze to Airleas. "I bring you sad news, Airleas. Your father, Cyne Colfre Malcuim, is dead. You are now Cyneric of Caraid-land."

The boy's face paled, but he showed no other sign of emotion. "We know," he said. "We felt him die."

Feich moved his narrowed eyes to Toireasa's face, fighting the urge to look at Taminy. "I regret to say that he died by his own hand. Your desertion destroyed him, madam."

The Cwen shook her head. Her gaze on him was hard and cold. "I destroyed nothing, Daimhin Feich. It was you who destroyed him. You who deserted him. You who passed him the cup of betrayal. This——" she nodded toward the soldiers arrayed behind him "——this is forever and always what you have wanted, is it not?"

Feich's insides cooled at her words. What did she know of a "cup of betrayal"? He only just kept his eyes from seeking Taminy's reaction. "You mistake me, mistress. I had nothing but the good of my Cyne at heart. And the good of Caraid-land. That good can only be served by the return of the Cyneric Airleas to Mertuile to be set before the Stone."

"Under whose regency?"

"Under my own. By the Cyne's decree. Ask Osraed Ladhar, if you don't trust me. He witnessed the act and counter-signed the document. For the sake of this land, which we both love, I beg you, Cwen Toireasa—let Airleas return to Creiddylad with me. Let him be set before the Stone as is his right."

Toireasa smiled wryly. "Ah, Goscelin's dilemma. To be parted from her child, or to hold him fast to her side."

"Goscelin had no choice, mistress. You do. I offer it to you."

"And the alternative?"

Feich gazed around him at the hills above, the town

below, the long slope, meadows and woods behind. "This land is divided, torn by dissension and strife. Blood flows. Lives are lost. Mistress, Airleas is a symbol of Caraid-land's unity. If he is not at Mertuile, Caraid-land is a headless corpse, thrown to merciless eaters of carrion."

"Then let him return to Mertuile with me. Let Taminy Weave her will in Caraid-land and let its wounds be healed. Let Taminy complete her purpose—to renew and unify Caraid-land as it has never been unified before."

Feich did look at Taminy now and the hatred that had collected in him over the weeks roared for release. Her face blanched as his eyes touched it, and he knew without doubt that she could feel the black emotion roiling within him. Something else sprang to join it, something that burnt its way up from his groin, scorching him. Self-disgust followed—disgust that his own body could betray him so thoroughly. He knew what she was—anathema. "She will Weave her will in chill hell and nowhere else."

"Then you return to Mertuile empty-handed."

"You deny your son—Colfre's son—his birthright. He is a Malcuim—"

"Yes, and so am I. And I shall behave like one. Cowardice ill-befits a Malcuim Cwen. I will not give my son and Colfre's into your hands, Daimhin Feich. In your hands he would become a pawn . . . as Colfre was."

Beside Toireasa, Taminy stirred, returning Feich's gaze. His innards squirmed. "Then you shall be declared outlaw—all of you. Heretics like her." He pointed at Taminy, and sought the faces of those behind the trio in the archway. "I'll have you declared Wicke. You'll be hunted down like vermin wherever you go. Fed to the waves or the flames. You'll watch your husbands and wives and children die horribly before your eyes. Is that what you want? Cyneric Airleas, is that what you want for your mother?"

The child twitched as if Feich had poked him. He glanced from his mother to Taminy, then set his eyes on Feich's face. "If we deny Taminy-Osmaer, we'll *live* horribly. A Malcuim does not poison himself."

"Your father did. Day by day his soul writhed in torment

because he believed in *that*." His finger pointed at Taminy again. "It tore him asunder in the end." He glanced at the Ren Catahn, standing just behind the three. "Perhaps it was the Hillwild blood in his veins that made him susceptible to pagan goddesses—that made him weak of will and shallow of mind."

"Or perhaps it was having a fox for a Durweard," Catahn growled.

"My father worshipped power," said Airleas. "That's what made him weak. And you knew it. I don't care if you call me a Wicke or a heretic. I love Taminy and I love my mother. I won't leave here no matter what you say. Go away, Durweard Feich, and leave us alone. You can have the Throne and the Circlet if you want them so much." He looked up at his mother. "Can I go now? I don't want to talk to him any more."

Toireasa smiled into Daimhin Feich's face. It was a smile fierce with pride. "You've heard the Malcuim. Leave us."

She turned her back on him then, and prepared to usher Airleas away. Desperate, he leapt forward. "Airleas! Come to me! These women deceive you! They've poisoned your mind. Your father made me your Regent. Trust me, Airleas, and come to me!"

Airleas turned back to give his father's Durweard a scathing look. "You stink," he said.

Feich made a move to draw his sword and follow the royals into the courtyard. Before he had tightened his grip on the hilt, the portcullis crashed down again, digging its sharpened tines into the earth. Feich jumped clear, swearing. When he regained his poise, the Cwen and Airleas were gone and only Taminy faced him from the other side of the grille, Catahn hovering warily behind her.

"You—!" Feich moved forward again. He stopped at little more than arm's length from her, the portcullis bars creating a thick frame about her head and shoulders. "You are a dagger in the heart of this land."

"And you are the man who directs the blade. Stop this now. Let Airleas and Toireasa return to Creiddylad free. Let me pursue my mission in Caraid-land and the wound will quickly heal."

He gazed at her a long moment, then nodded. "All right. I see that what you say is true. My actions are a determining factor in what happens here. Yes. You may return to Creiddylad a free woman."

Taminy smiled while, behind her, the Ren Catahn laid a hand to his sword hilt. "I have changed since we last spoke, Daimhin. Then, I was caught at a crossroads, stranded in a state of transition. Powers ebbed and flowed, awareness informed me only fleetingly. I am past that now. And because I am past that, I know that you lie. If Airleas were to pass into your hands, Regent Feich, he would become, as his mother said, a pawn. As it seems his father was, as you intended me to be. There is still pain in that memory. How close I came to allowing my purpose to be consumed by yours. And for what—a flash of white heat, a touch of warm flesh? That was an ordeal by fire, Daimhin. And I still ask, 'Did I pass?' Or did Osraed Bevol rescue me?"

Feich jerked. "Bevol? Bevol is dead."

"After a fashion. And yet, he lives, after a fashion. You wouldn't understand." She shook her head and he felt her sigh rush through him like a cool breeze. "I want so to appeal to your spirit. I want so to speak to your conscience. But by all the powers that vibrate in this great rock, I cannot reach either."

Talk of spirits and consciences made him squirm. "Enough nonsense. I have no choice but to return to Creiddylad and have myself declared Cyneric."

"You already think of yourself as that."

Feich hurled himself against the barricade. It rattled only slightly, though he threw his whole weight into the motion. "Bitch! Stop pretending to read my mind!"

Catahn's sword was out as he came to Taminy's shoulder, ready to run Feich through—if Taminy would allow such a thing, which she wouldn't.

"Afraid of me, Wicke? Does your trained bear dance attendance because you fear me?"

"Lady?" Catahn's intent was clear in his voice. He wanted to put an end to Daimhin Feich. Yes, of course—he wanted to keep the Crystal Rose for himself.

"I'm not afraid of you," Taminy said, and Feich scoffed.

"Then send your bear away."

Taminy knew Feich's demand posed no mortal danger. She looked up over her shoulder into Catahn's dark face. "It's all right, Catahn. Stand down. He can't harm me." *I must be certain he can't harm me.*

Reluctantly, the Hillwild removed himself from Taminy's side, fading into the shadows beneath the arch. Taminy moved close to the portcullis.

"You feel nothing for me, Taminy?"

"I feel pity."

"Prove that. Give me your hand."

She put her left hand, palm up, through the grille. The star there, golden, gleaming, shone at him. He started to take it, hesitated, and jerked away when their fingertips brushed. His face burned red and he wriggled as if ants crawled upon him.

She withdrew the hand. "Now who is afraid?"

"I will return to Creiddylad and I will, myself, be set before the Stone."

"While Airleas lives? Then you will be Cyne of a land divided completely. Your only chance of maintaining Caraid-land's unity is to have Airleas at Mertuile."

"Half a country is better than none at all. I *will* be set before the Stone, and the Throne and Circlet shall remain in my possession and be passed down to my sons. The Osmaer Crystal will be in the hands of Feich from this day forth. And no Malcuim shall ever take it from us. And as for you, dear lady, I shall hound you and yours until I have eradicated every last one of you. These hands—" he held them up before him "—these hands caressed you and drew such passion from you not that long ago. Today I would cheerfully use them to strangle you. But I think you're worth more to me alive. The people love you, Taminy-a-Cuinn."

"And I love them."

Calm—she was too calm. He spoke to her with passion threatening to tear itself loose and devour him, and those green eyes gazed back with the coolness of sea water. He quaked with the effort it took not to scream at her—not to thrust his hands through the grille and tear at her throat. *Why did she not love me?*

"You can't receive what you refuse to give," she murmured, and there was nothing left to do but stare at her, hating and wanting, until he could make himself turn away from her gaze and return to his horse.

When he was Cyne, he thought, as he turned his troops about, things would change. He would hold the Crystal and, with Ladhar's help, he would learn to wield its power. He had always been fey, though he'd kept it well-hidden. Then, as Cyne—no, as more than that, as Osric—he would let that Gift come to the fore. Caraid-land would find itself possessed of a very powerful leader. First, the Taminists would be eradicated, then the Deasach would be made to tremble.

He turned in the saddle just before the trees obscured the gates of Halig-liath from sight. She still stood there, watching him, looking small and vulnerable and absurdly young. Heat licked up his spine, irritating him. He dug his heels into his horse's flanks and rode to the head of the long column.

Taminy felt Catahn's presence at her side as a spot of soft warmth in the cold, iron shell about her. She allowed the shell to melt away into the earth and sagged back against the Hillwild's comforting bulk.

There was a creak of leather and one large hand came to her shoulder. "He will return, Lady."

She nodded, thanking the warmth that spread from his hand to suffuse her. "He will return when he realizes that Airleas is Cyne of Caraid-land's heart and that to possess that heart, he must possess Airleas."

Catahn snorted. "He'll be happy enough with the body for a while."

"Not long."

"And when he returns, will he find us here?"

She shook her head. "No. With us here, the people of Nairne are in danger. We must be elsewhere when Daimhin Feich revisits Halig-liath."

She turned and re-entered the courtyard, Catahn maintaining his place beside her. She ignored the questioning faces that greeted them for a moment, and paused to gaze up and over the high eastern walls. Five of the seven peaks of the Gyldan-baenn marched away toward the south. Far and away, she could see the snow-capped thrust of Baenn-ghlo, for once not wrapped in the mists that gave it its name. The smaller summit of Baenn-an-ratha stood out in stark relief against its bright, massive flank. Somewhere among those crags and forested passes Catahn's stronghold, Hrofceaster, snuggled in near-inaccessible safety. It would be a difficult place for those used to milder climes to winter, but there they would be safe, and there they would not be subject to sudden siege.

Catahn had followed her gaze to look lovingly and longingly on those same peaks. "Shall we begin preparations for travel, Lady?"

She smiled and squeezed his hand where it still rested on her shoulder. "Thank you, Catahn," she said and moved to where Cwen Toireasa and Airleas waited in the midst of a cluster of other believers.

Catahn watched her till she was absorbed by the group, then pulled his eyes back to the Gyldan-baenn. His heart swelled with a surge of something big and fine and warm. He would go home soon, and he would bring the Lady of the Crystal Rose with him.

CHAPTER 1

*An oration by Abbod Ladhar regarding Taminy the Wicke;
given at the Cyne's Cirke in Creiddylad, Autumn, Year of
Pilgrimage 605*

Children, as I gaze out at you this morning, my heart fails
me and my soul weeps. Your faces, so full of confusion and
fear, are turned to me for solace, for certitude. I have no
solace to give. And the only certitude I can offer is this: Our
world is in chaos. Is there one here whose life has not been
savaged by it? One who does not wonder why our streets
are full of terror and noise? Why our government is in turmoil and our ruling House empty? Listen, children, and I
will tell you what has happened—what has brought these
things upon us.

Last Solstice, the Osraed were compelled to allow a cailin
to leave Halig-liath on Pilgrimage. Compelled, I say, because
this girl, Meredydd-a-Lagan, was ward of the Osraed Bevol,
Apex of the Osraed Council. I hear your murmurs; you wonder how such a man—foremost among the Meri's Chosen—
could contrive such a thing. Could go so far as to lead the
girl through her heretical quest himself. The answer is simple
. . . and terrible. Meredydd-a-Lagan was no ordinary girl.
She was one of a succession of Wicke so powerful that their
rising causes the Sea of Revelation to boil and the entire
creation to weep like a lost child. These Dark Sisters, these
evil women, have as their collective goal the subversion of
our religion and the annihilation of your souls.

At the end of her dark Pilgrimage Meredydd-a-Lagan
stepped into the Meri's Sea and disappeared. Those who
were wise rejoiced at this, but the danger was not past. In

11

Meredydd's stead, Osraed Bevol brought back with him a second Wicke—a wheat-haired child who, with her beauty and winning ways, coerced the youth of Nairne to love and worship her. She secretly taught them Wickish ways and performed miracles for them—going so far as to slay one of them so she might resurrect the child to prove her powers. Then, when she had won the hearts of the people of Nairne, she made a claim so blasphemous as to deafen the ears of the righteous. Her claim (can you not have heard it?): That she and the Meri are one and the same.

Some of you have not heard this. You quake and gasp, but there is more. She claims that as she was the Meri's vessel for the past hundred years, so her wicked sister Meredydd is the Meri's vessel now. And she has arrogated to herself the title Osmaer—Divinely Glorious—while in her contempt-ible hands, she claims to proffer a new covenant to the people of Caraid-land. What she truly offers is a covenant with chaos, with corruption, with death.

Children, the pages of history are not mute. They show what occurs whenever a woman has the temerity to go to the Sea, seeking what she has no right to seek. There have been Cusps before, during the reigns of Bitan-ig the Preserver, of Readanor Fisher, of Earwyn, of Liusadhe the Purifier, of Thearl the Stern. We survived those times. We weathered those storms. Can this one be any different?

Yes! It can be and is. This Age is unique; this Cusp like none before. For now, Evil has found form, and clothed itself in a pleasing guise. It walks among us in the shape of Taminy-a-Cuinn. Many of you have seen her perform what you took to be miracles. Some of you have met her, spoken to her, taken her to be lovely and kind and generous. But those things are lies, as Taminy herself is the greatest of lies. She seeks to charm you, to seduce your sons and win your daugh-ters even as she won the children of Nairne—a village now damned by its ignorance.

Be warned, daughters, for Taminy will tell you your birth-right is great. Be warned, for she will whisper to you of tal-ents and powers that might be yours if you but take up her cause and follow her. Be warned and guard your hearts against pride, for the Wicke of Nairne reaches out her starred hand to snatch your souls—every one—into damnation complete and eternal. Just as she snatched the souls of our Cyne, of the most learned of Osraed, of the lost children of Nairne. In the shadow of embattled Halig-liath, whose halls echo with the prayers of the damned, mothers and fathers wail and despair for those poor, lost children.

Do not be like them, People of the Jewel. Believe in the Spirit and His Child, the Meri. Resist this Evil—this vile deceiver who calls herself Taminy-Osmaer.

CREIDDYLAD

"Damn you! Damn you to icy hell!" The goblet left Daimhin Feich's hand and hit the closed door with a solid, metallic clang. Wine stained the wood like blood spreading, sudden, from a wound. "A dagger, next time, *friend*."

The applause of a single pair of hands mocked him. "Bravo, cousin. An affective speech. A shame the object of your invective wasn't around to hear it."

"Pissant," growled Daimhin Feich, but he smiled. He would tolerate a certain amount of mockery from his uncle's youngest son; Ruadh was easily his favorite relation. "He *will* hear it . . . in my time."

"In *your* time? Hardly. And that's Feich hell, isn't it cousin—to need the Claeg."

"Hell, indeed. But where the Claeg go, so go the southern midlands."

"You've already lost old Iobert Claeg to the pretty Wicke. He'll no doubt take a large share of his House with him. And more, if you can't convince one of the other Claeg elders to take his seat on the Privy Council."

"The Privy Council is the least of my worries." Daimhin Feich lifted himself from the throne—the Malcuim throne, he reminded himself bitterly—and paced to the near door of the audience chamber. There, he bent and picked up the goblet he'd flung, holding it up to the light that fell, bright and clear, from the high, slanting windows. The Sun found tiny pathways of silver and gold in the delicately incised bowl and made them rivers of radiance. "Things, Ruadh. I have gotten from the House Malcuim its riches, its belongings, and as much of its territories as Feich forces can hold from these walls. But I do not have its *people*. If Colfre Malcuim—God damn his spineless soul—had dropped this cup, it would not have reached the floor but a servant's hand would have caught it and whisked it away. Except for a mercenary few and the folk you brought from Feich, this castle is a spacious, luxurious tomb. You heard the young Claeg just now."

Ruadh crossed arms over his chest. "Oh, aye. 'The throne at Mertuile has always held a Malcuim. I doubt it will suffer itself to be sat upon by a Feich ass.'"

Daimhin gritted his teeth so hard they hurt. "His exact words. How kind of you to recall them for me."

"Welcome. And you didn't drop that cup, you hurled it. Even a Feich servant would think twice before answering that summons."

"We'll bring in more servants. Perhaps we can hire from the poor neighborhoods of Creiddylad. There should be plenty of those after Colfre's years of excess."

"Aye, and we can bring more Feich men, and hire more mercenaries, I wager. But never enough, cousin. Never enough to hold Caraid-land by force. Unless this castle is all you aspire to, we *do* need the Claeg and as many of the other Houses as they can bring to us. But I fear Saefren Claeg is right; a Feich on the throne of Caraid-land is not something the Houses will tolerate. If not for loyalty to the Malcuim, then for envy alone."

"The Malcuim is dead . . . and I have the Stone of Ochan."

Ruadh smiled wryly. "Ah, no. The Malcuim is a twelve-year-old boy hunkered upriver with a pack of apostates. If Colfre had died childless, you might rally the Houses to you. But he didn't. Airleas Malcuim exists, and as long as he exists beyond your control, the Osmaer Crystal is useless to you. You can't set him before it, nor can you use it to place yourself on the throne."

Sour, that thought, but true, and Daimhin Feich knew

it. Airleas Malcuim was the key to winning Caraid-land out of its present chaos and into his hands. Even now, mobs rallied in the streets of Creiddylad, roiled beneath the castle walls. Their voices and torches kept him awake nights. Their voices, especially, reached him wherever he lay his head. They cried for Cyneric Airleas, they cried for Feich blood, they cried for Taminy-a-Cuinn, Wicke—or Taminy-Osmaer, Seeress, Prophetess.

Bitch.

He hated her. Passionately. And yet, when he finally slept, his dreams informed him of a different passion. Daimhin Feich was a man in conflict where Taminy-Osmaer was concerned.

He was hunting. Flying over the ground on a fantastic black horse so powerful, thunder rolled from beneath its hooves and assaulted the sky. He gripped the reins in both hands, feeling the tension of the animal's massive neck, the superb, nervous lightness of its mouth on the bit. Between his legs the broad, muscular back rippled with unimaginable power.

Sensual. Heat invaded his belly, wrapping hot fingers around his heart. He tightened his hands on the reins, his thighs on the horse's barrel. The animal responded with a forward surge, its hooves leaving the ground as if in flight.

He laughed in complete delight and the horse turned its great head to look at him. An eye as pale as his own fixed him, sending a chill up his spine. In that reckless moment he understood that he was both the horse and the rider of the horse. The animal was an extension of Self; it was he who held the reins and he who breathed fire and struck lightning from the earth.

Beyond exhilaration, he soared, barely taking in the world around him—an aislinn world, he now realized. Shapes flickered past, looking vaguely like trees, rocks, brush. A hunt. Of course. He hunted. And the Object of that hunt lay somewhere ahead in this strange and wonderful realm.

His gaze strained ahead now, to where the path opened into a corridor of giant trees, light falling like golden snow through the dense lace of branches. The end of the corridor was indistinct, dark, a mysterious destination that resisted approach. He willed himself to reach that dark forest heart and it began to grow before him. Deep green, it was, emerald, like a spot of night in the depths of a daylight wood. Less and less sunlight filtered through the trees as he rushed toward it and a veil of mist rose to obscure his way. And though he knew he still rushed forward, he felt time stretch like a lazy cat, drawing his senses out, prolonging each moment, underscoring each hoof/heart beat.

He was upon it then—in a breath, in an eternity. The emerald deep swallowed him whole. It was a distorted place of shadows and glimmers of light that danced just beyond the eye's grasp.

He was drawing near the Hunted. Hard by the end of his quest. He could feel her, smell her, taste her. He reached up over his shoulder and found the crossbow there. Fingers met cold metal and smooth, hard wood and he chilled at the touch.

But no, this was wrong. He hunted with a longbow. His hand tightened on the curve of ash wood, felt the notch where the bowstring lay, taut. Yes.

He dropped the reins, knowing the horse to be obedient, and pulled the bow into his hands. A quiver of arrows lay along his left thigh. He took one up and notched it, eyes roving ahead. In the deep a soft light quivered—a fitful flame. There! The Prey. He couldn't see her, but he knew she was there at the heart of the flame. He could feel her through the thick air, smell her on the wind, taste her on the tip of his tongue.

How impersonal a bow seemed in the face of that intimacy. A sword would be better. No, a dagger. He looked at the thing lying across his palm, blade sharp, glittering. Yes.

With a crack like close thunder, time ceased its stretching and lunged, hissing, into a blaze of light. The Universe roared and the great, black beast he rode spasmed beneath him. He took up the reins again. Fought for control. But the horse's mouth no longer responded to his touch. The

*Universe reeled, roaring crescendoed, light blinded. And
then it all winked out—snuffed like a candle flame between
fingers—leaving an echo of light and sound and sense, a
nightmare afterimage.*

His breath left his body in a gasp; he sucked it up again
on a sob of frustration and lay sweating in his bed, blankets tangled around his limbs, his fist clenched painfully
on nothing.

He disentangled himself, shivering—not an ember
glowed in the huge hearth—and moved to light a lamp.
His hands stopped short of their goal and, for a moment,
he feared the dream had followed him. Before him in the
black night of his bed chamber hung an image. It moved
where his eyes moved as if burned into them: A crystal.
A face. No. A crystal, and within the crystal, a face. *Her*
face—sweet, beautiful, treacherous.

A sigh slipped between his lips before he could drag it
back. The hand that reached for the lamp now quivered
toward the mirage; fingers grasping . . . nothing.

Sudden hatred wrung a howl from him. He swung at
the black air, hitting the unseen lamp and sending it to
the floor in a spray of broken glass and fragrant oil.

Stunned to silence, he trembled, listening for the movement of his guards in the corridor, struggling to rein in
his rage.

The door rattled. "Cousin?"

Ruadh. He dragged in a cleansing breath. "It's all right.
I've only broken a lamp."

"Shall I call a servant to clean it up?"

Stupid brat, I said I was all right. "No. It can keep.
Leave me."

There was a moment of silence, then the soft scrape of
leather on stone.

He was cold now, his shivering born of chill, rather than
rage. He flexed his fingers, still tight from gripping the
aislinn reins. When next he hunted, he promised himself,
he would control his mount. He would choose the right
weapon. He would finish the Hunt.

CHAPTER 2

A dissertation on Taminy-Osmaer by Osraed Tynedale, given at Halig-liath, Autumn, Year of Pilgrimage 605

Beloved, welcome. Today I shall speak again of the wondrous Event we have witnessed. I shall give tell of a door that has opened before us.

The Corah, our holiest book, tells us that we cannot perceive God directly. Is this so strange? Is it possible that our eyes could fathom the brilliance of the physical Sun? That our feet could walk its blazing surface? Even while standing firmly upon the earth, to comprehend the Sun is impossible and the attempt foolish. Our puny senses cannot grasp it; even at so great a distance, it overwhelms us.

So it is with God.

Yet, God in Its mercy gave birth to a Glorious Child that certain ones among us might see and become enlightened. That Child is the Meri, Whose glory, though less than Her Divine Parent's, is yet so great as to stun all but the most pure.

Once in a generation One arises whose purity of spirit allows Her to mirror forth the splendors of the Divine. This, we have come to understand, is the Osmaer—the Divinely Glorious. It is this soul—this dear, human soul, daughter of man and woman—who enfolds the Meri and who is enfolded, who embraces Her and is embraced, who makes the Spirit Child of the Creator sensible to us. For the Meri is spirit without form, an emanation from the Divine, and it is the Osmaer, the Chosen Daughter, who gives Her form.

Through the ages, when our young men went as Pilgrims to the Meri's Shore, seeking to become Osraed, it was the

18

Osmaer they in truth saw, Her voice they heard. Meanwhile, we Osraed, ignorant that one of our daughters was the Vessel of the Meri, denied all other females access to Her. For that we can only beg Her forgiveness.

In a single generation, many Pilgrims arrive at the Meri's Shore, seeking Her. Few attain Her Presence and return as Osraed, anointed with the Meri's Kiss. Most are sent away empty. And as time passes fewer are chosen; fewer are worthy.

A century has come and gone since the last Cusp and our spiritual eyes have grown dim. Solstice past, the Meri chose another stainless soul to house Her Glory and changed form for form, giving back to human life what She took. Even as is revealed in this lay penned by Our Lady, herself:

> One walks upon the Shore;
> One glides beneath the Sea.
> In the water meet the twain
> Who never met and meet again.
> In the water they combine
> The human soul and the Divine.
> Humanity is glorified,
> Divinity personified—
> The dance of glory to and from
> One to return, One to become.
> One glides beneath the Sea;
> One walks upon the Shore.
> —The Meri Song, Book of the New Covenant

We will teach our children this song, hoping they will understand its meaning. Yet, do we understand it? This is the Cusp. The Change. A time of great promise and great peril. We have seen the Change in ages past and sorrowed at it because we had no understanding of what it meant. But this Age is unique. In this Age we have been led to see that the Cusp is a time of renewal—renewal of the Meri's Vessel, renewal of Her religion.

In ages past when the Meri gave the Osmaer back into the world of men and women, that One was forced to live apart, to hide herself from the eyes of others behind a cloak of cleverness, to conceal her true nature from us. But now, in this unique Age, she does not hide. She stands among us, the embodiment of God's Covenant with the World of Form and Shadow: Taminy-Osmaer, risen from the Sea of Revelation.

Now, beloved, we must understand the substance of this New Covenant. It is this: That we renew our spiritual pact, not with a body of men, nor with institutions, nor with the government that now exists or fails to exist in Creiddylad, but with the Meri and the Spirit of the Universe. And that we do this through Taminy-Osmaer—our Lady of the Crystal Rose.

✧   ✧   ✧

HROFCEASTER AT AIRDNASHEEN

The room was grey this early. Though murky light entered through the three tall windows along the northern wall, it was not strong enough to bring the rich array of tapestries, arras and carpets to vivid life. A row of light-globes sat above the east-facing hearth, two more hung on either side of the fur-covered couch opposite the windows. All were unlit and the hearth was cold.

On the threshold, Taminy took in the empty chamber with something like relief. She raised her hand, palm out, to the dark globes. They lit, blue-gold flames dancing, seemingly suspended in whorls of mist. On the walls, furniture, and floors, colors leapt from sleep; golds, reds, verdant greens—all the colors of midland foliage. All the hues Taminy would have left behind in coming to Hrofceaster, were it not for Hillwild artistry; were it not for Catahn.

Taminy smiled at the thought of the Hillwild lord. He was easily her fiercest supporter, her most imposing ally and her most ardent devotee. It had taken her weeks to break him of bending the knee to her. She had yet to teach him not to call her 'Glorious Lady' with every other breath. And as he treated her, so did his people.

As if I was Cwen, she thought, moving to the firebox by the hearth. But that was Toireasa Malcuim's station, not hers. It was a station she could not imagine growing accustomed to.

"They'll always treat you that way."

Hands full of kindling, Taminy turned. "Skeet. Will you help with this fire or just stand there pecking at my thoughts?"

The boy moved from the doorway, face unsmiling, unboyish. "You're more than Cwen, Taminy-Osmaer. Catahn knows that. His elders know that. Toireasa is Cwen of Caraid-land; you are its soul."

Taminy bent to arrange the kindling, not caring to look into Skeet's eyes. She knew he was right, the little old man. Knew that in her hands was the fate of the House Malcuim and, through it, of the Caraidin people. "And Airleas is its spirit," she said. "I feel for the boy—to have his childhood end so suddenly, so cruelly."

"If he'd grown up here, his childhood would've been over long since. In Creiddylad, he'd've stayed a child past time. Colfre was a young man; were it not for Daimhin Feich, he'd still be on the Throne. Maybe Airleas is better off here."

Taminy smiled, rising from the hearth to brush at her skirts. "Pov-Skeet, you know as well as I do the truth of that. He may not see it now, but Hrofceaster is no mean place to become a man."

"If the Ren Catahn is any measure," Skeet added.

Taminy turned to look at him. "Such a sly tone. Don't you like Catahn?"

Skeet's dark eyes widened. "Why, Mistress! I should say I like him very well, indeed. He's a prodigious man."

The observation coaxed laughter from her throat. It felt good to laugh.

"Mistress! What are you doing? God-the-Spirit, the fire! Now, now—you oughtn't touch that!"

The Eldress Levene scuttled into the room like a fretting hen, bobbing and clucking, while Taminy, errant chick, scooted away from the hearth, dropping the log she'd been holding. Skeet cackled.

"You really mustn't do for yourself, dearest Lady," chided

the older woman. "Where's Eyslk? She should ha' been here to start this. Not like her to be so lazy—"

"Please, Eldress, you needn't curtsey. And I came early today. I didn't ring for Eyslk. I rather intended to be alone for a while . . . in the quiet."

Eldress Levene paused in her fire-making and blinked at Taminy. "God's Breath, Lady! It never came to me that you'd like to be left alone in the mornings."

Taminy's hands flew out in reflexive apology. "Oh, please, Eldress, I didn't mean— It's only that occasionally I like to come here and meditate. It's a lovely room."

The other woman's face suffused with pleasure. "Why thank you, Mistress. It was done all for your joy. . . . Now, now, where's the tinder box?" She poked along the rough mantle piece, looking for the box of flints.

"Eyslk usually asks me to start the fire," Taminy said.

The Eldress was aghast. "Eyslk *asks*—?"

Taminy laughed. "Please don't fault Eyslk. She caught me at it one morning. I admit it's a guilty pleasure of mine." She moved back to the hearth as she spoke and held her hands out to the pile of unlit wood as if a fire was already there to warm them. In a moment, a red glow appeared among the kindling. In another, flames leapt—gold and white—to consume the wood. "You see, it's really much easier for me than for poor Eyslk with her flints."

The Eldress nodded, eyes casting back the glow of the flames. "A good, practical bit of Weaving, that." She shifted her eyes to Taminy then, head tilted questioningly, asked, "Would you like me to leave you a bit, Lady? I can return in your time."

"Not if you've some business for me, Eldress." Taminy retreated to the couch from which she now "held court" as Skeet put it. She preferred to think of it as consultation and had even convinced Catahn that the couch, which had once sat on a raised platform, be on a level with the other furniture in the room.

Eldress Levene approached her (curtseying again) and seated herself in a facing chair. "If it please my Lady . . . Taminy," she corrected, when Taminy would have reminded her, "the Aeldra have consulted this past eve and have raised some questions."

Taminy gestured with her left hand, bidding her to continue. The Eldress's eyes followed the gesture, seizing on the blessed mark—the *gytha*—glowing from the palm like a tiny flame.

"We have certain rites, Lady Taminy, which have been held in the heart of these mountains since time known. We are born and named, cross from childhood into adulthood, marry, give birth and die. All these things we mark and celebrate. And in between, we plant some and harvest some and mark the passing of the seasons. We revere the Gwyr, too, as you know, and celebrate Her rare appearances. We lay before you these things, these rites and ask . . . " The Eldress paused, glancing aside at the silent Skeet. She was troubled, clearly. "These are ancient rites—"

"And sacred," said Taminy. "They remind you that you are the Hillwild and that these things have shaped you, nurtured you, become part of your relationship with the Spirit."

The Eldress's relief was evident. "You'd not have us give them up?"

"No, Eldress. Why would I?"

"Some have tried to persuade us that these things are superstition. That we should leave them and worship as do the people of the lowlands."

"They worship as they worship; you worship as you worship. The Spirit isn't interested in the form of your worship, but in its sincerity."

"They say the Gwyr is a heathen spirit, unrelated to the Meri and Her God. They say our God is not their God."

They. "The Osraed, you mean?"

"Aye, and others."

"The Gwyr is a window to the world of the Spirit. There is only one Spirit. There are many windows through which to see It."

The Eldress considered that. "Yet, each window offers a different view. How does one see the Spirit entire?"

"One finds a Door and enters it."

The Eldress nodded. "You are the Door."

Even now, Taminy could feel a part of herself shrinking from that truth—but it was truth. "Here, now, for you, I am the Door."

Eldress Levene slid from her chair to her knees, bending her forehead to the floor. "Blessed Lady! Last night I dreamed of a doorway filled with light. I see it again this moment."

"Rise, please," Taminy murmured, uncomfortable with the open adoration. "Rise and look at me. You have another question."

The woman raised her head, but remained huddled on the carpet, her wool pantaloons billowed about her like grey cloud. "The Council of Elders also wishes to know if it should continue to guide the affairs of Airdnasheen."

"And what other body but the Aeldra would shepherd the community?" Taminy asked in return. "Who else would be qualified? You know the people's needs. There's no reason why the Aeldra should not continue to elect the Ren and mind the affairs of his people. I didn't come here to govern the Hillwild, Eldress Levene, but to renew a Covenant."

The Eldress nodded, looking thoughtful. "And to ready the young Malcuim to govern. He's a good boy, that one, but rash, stubborn, fox-clever . . . for boon or bane."

The absent Eyslk chose that moment to put in her appearance. It was Eldress Levene's pleasure to tease her gently for her cleverness in lighting the fire without a tinder box. While the two bantered, Taminy's gaze roamed to the fire. Boon or bane, indeed. The Eldress had no way of knowing that in describing Airleas, she had also described his father. Colfre Malcuim's cleverness had connived to disaster and his rashness had made him a willing puppet for Daimhin Feich. Taminy could only pray Airleas had something his father had not—strength of will.

The narrow outer corridor was empty and Airleas Malcuim congratulated himself on that good fortune. His arms wrapped around the long, swaddled package, he scurried the length of the hallway, down the narrow stone steps at its nether end, and out into the small, dark courtyard. It was a little-used yard; he knew that after several days of careful watching. Its only other access was from the rear of the main kitchen and it occasionally hosted the kitchen crew's after-dinner chats, but little more than that.

Alone, Airleas laid his treasure out on a rough wooden bench and unwrapped it, a smile hovering at his lips.

"Airleas! A sword! Oh, wherever'd you get tha'?"

He jumped and swore, twisting his head toward the kitchen entrance. "Gwynet Alheart, you little weasel! How dare you sneak about like that? And keep your voice down."

Gwynet's eyes were two pools of reproach. "I'm sure I'm not a weasel, *Cyneric* Airleas. Nor was I the one sneaking. And my voice *is* down. . . . Where'd you get the sword?"

Airleas sighed. "I found it. In a leather satchel at the bottom of a grain bin in the stable."

Gwynet's nose wrinkled in curiosity as she came down the short flight of kitchen steps to hover at the bench. "What were you doing in a grain bin?"

"I was pretending to hide from marauding Feichs, if you must know. Learning the ways of a Hillwild warrior."

Gwynet glanced again at the sword. "Surely it belongs to somebody."

"Surely it doesn't. The bag was so old it was rotting away. Whoever put it there must have forgotten all about it. So it's mine now."

"But why, Airleas?" Gwynet touched the freshly polished blade gingerly. "Why should you have a sword at all?"

"You said it, Gwynet. I'm *Cyneric* Airleas. A Malcuim. *The* Malcuim, now. If anyone is going to retake Mertuile and pry the Stone out of Daimhin Feich's hands, it must be me. I *have* to do that, or I'll never be set before the Stone."

"Do you know how t'use it?"

"Of course. I've had lessons in swordplay." He didn't add that they were with a much flimsier sporting blade, a blade that weighed about a quarter what this one did. "Besides, I watched the Claeg's men practicing at Halig-liath. They gave me some pointers, too. . . . Here, I'll show you."

Clutching the sword in both hands, Airleas moved to the center of the little courtyard. There, he closed his eyes. The mountain fortress dissolved away and he stood in the Great Hall of Mertuile beneath the House banners. That was a fitting place to face Daimhin Feich, for it was here that his father's treacherous Durweard had taken up a cross-bow with the intent of murdering Taminy-Osmaer, while Colfre Malcuim, who should have been defending her with his life, cowered behind his throne.

But Airleas Malcuim would not cower, would not run, and would defend Taminy-Osmaer to his last breath. He brought the sword up, saluting his imaginary foe, then swung it in a circle over his head. The blade caught air and sang. It was a magical sound to Airleas and his blood rose in harmony. He danced and bobbed, following the blade around and around.

In moments, he had Feich on the run and was backing him against a wall. Good thing, too, for his found weapon grew heavier with every swing. Slash! He caught the flat of Feich's blade and ripped it away. Now, in for the kill.

Airleas lunged, his feet sliding on the stone foundation at the bottom of the kitchen steps. Over-balanced, he pitched face first onto the stone risers, releasing the sword in a desperate effort to catch himself. He sprawled on the steps, bruising body and spirit. He heard Gwynet squeal, but the sound of the sword striking stone never came. What he heard, instead, was laughter—loud, ribald laughter.

He scrambled to his feet, rubbing his bruised elbows. Another boy stood above him on the kitchen steps, shaking with laughter, the sword propped carelessly on one shoulder.

Bristling at the open mockery in the tawny eyes, Airleas gathered his Malcuim dignity and held out his hands. "May I have my sword back?"

"*Your* sword? And where would a midge like you come by a weapon like this?"

"It's mine."

The boy lowered the sword and gave it a careful glance. "This is a Hillwild blade, midge. Made at Moidart, by the crest." His thumb brushed a design worked into the blade just below the hilt. "No one gives a boy a weapon like this. I'll just take it back to the armory where it belongs."

Stung, Airleas lunged, his hands grasping, but the larger boy was also quicker. He leapt from the steps, landing behind Airleas in the yard . . . still laughing.

Airleas spun on him. "Give me the sword! It's mine. I found it."

"You'll never make a decent swordsman if you give up your moves in your eyes like that. That ogre you were play-fighting almost got the best of you, midge. You're lucky I came along."

"It wasn't an ogre. And I only lost my footing. Give me back the sword."

"Sorry, midge." The boy turned to go, the sword flung over his shoulder as though it weighed nothing at all.

"Don't you know who I am?"

The boy paused. "Ah, let me guess—you're the Ren Morgant of Moidart in disguise. I'd pictured you as a larger man, Ren . . . and older."

"I'm Airleas Malcuim—Cyneric of Caraid-land. Head of my House. Son of Cyne Colfre Malcuim and Cwen Toireasa. And you will give me that sword." He put all the authority he could behind that.

The taller boy merely looked amused. "So, you're the Malcuim brat. Well, *Cyneric*. All the more reason for me to keep this dangerous toy. I'm sure our good Ren Catahn'd be madder'n a treed catamount if one of his royal guests got nicked up." Chuckling, he resumed his journey cross-court toward the covered flight of narrow steps Airleas had descended earlier.

Uncertain, Airleas glanced aside at Gwynet. She still stood by the bench, her face radiating amazement. His pretensions to Malcuim dignity evaporated. Gwynet was the only person he knew who looked up to him. The only one in all of Airdnasheen who treated his station as if it mattered. To look foolish before Gwynet . . .

The young Cyneric launched himself at his adversary's retreating back, catching him not quite unawares. The boy flung the sword away and met him face to face, falling beneath him in a grapple of arms and legs. Gwynet squealed again and was silent.

Airleas knew more of wrestling than he did of sword-play, which was fortunate, because the enemy was a strapping lad who left the young Malcuim only the advantages of quickness and flexibility. He used them as best he could, managing to trip his opponent and get a lock on his neck before superior strength sent him flying end over end.

Snarling and snapping like wild foxes, they met again, struggling and straining one to fell the other, ending up again in a scrabble of arms and legs. Airleas got another neck hold and wove his legs with the other's, pinning him. It gave him a moment of respite in which to wonder how one determined a winner in these affairs.

A hand on his collar rendered the quandary academic. Airleas found himself dangling well above the ground, glaring into his adversary's dunnish eyes. The two boys were at once separated and connected by the same things—a pair of huge arms and a broad expanse of chest.

"Hold, both of you!" The roar of the Ren Catahn's voice was enough to rattle Airleas's teeth. "What in the name of all holy are you about, Broran Hageswode? Have you no idea who you're scrapping with?"

Airleas's feet touched down, but the hand on his collar stayed.

"Says he's *Cyneric* of Caraid-land," snarled Broran, trying to shake hair from his eyes.

"Happens, he *is* Cyneric of Caraid-land," Catahn agreed. "A cousin of yours, too, a few dams removed. It won't do to assassinate your blood relations." He set Broran down. "Now what's this about a sword?"

"Here, master. This is the sword."

Airleas and Catahn both turned. Behind them, Gwynet stood, the Moidart blade clutched in two hands. Its point dug into the dirt between her feet, the sword was taller than she was.

"Airleas found it in an old leather bag in the stable, master. He wanted to use it to retake Mertuile."

Catahn was surprised into a sharp laugh, Broran sniggered, and Airleas thought he would sink into the earth.

Still smiling, the Hillwild Ren fetched the weapon from Gwynet's hands, lifting it easily with one of his own. "Well, Cyneric Airleas, I once had similar thoughts about this sword. Oh, not that I'd take Mertuile with it, but that it'd prove I was battle-ready. That I was a man just in the having of it. But I stole it, you see, so it proved nothing of the sort."

"You *stole* it!" repeated Airleas.

"Aye. I was much of an age with you boys, head full of tales I'd heard about the Battle of the Banner, aching to prove myself a hero. Round about that time, we had a bit of trouble with the Deasach. My Aunt, who was Renic then, took me over to Moidart to a Council. And while I was there, at loose ends and looking for trouble to get at, I saw this sword. It belonged to the daughter of the Ren Gaineamh. Her name was Geatan. She was thirteen and she'd just celebrated the Crask-an-bana. I thought her the most beautiful, brave and wonderful woman I'd ever seen.

"I snuck the sword from her room, leaving a thistle-rose in its place, and I thought of a grand scheme. With Geatan's sword, I'd take up arms against the southern harriers and become a hero to my people. Then I'd be worthy to take the Crask-an-duine and then, once I was a proven man—*then* I'd ask young Geatan to marry me. And, of course, I'd make a grand gesture of returning her sword."

"But you didn't," Gwynet observed.

"Well, the theft was noticed, which should've been no surprise to me, and the talk of her parents about it chilled me so, I decided I must try to put it back. But I couldn't. There were guards everywhere I turned that night and the next morning we were bound for Airdnasheen. I carried the sword home, knowing I'd never be able to use it, and feeling an idiot. I buried the damn thing at the bottom of that grain bin twenty-three years ago. I figured never to see it again."

"Might she forgive you if you returned it now?"

Catahn's eyes seemed to lose their focus momentarily.

"Oh, that lady's long dead, Gwynet. She died when our daughter was twelve years old. And I never did tell her about the sword, though she might've known, she was that fey. I suppose Desary should have it, now."

Airleas's heart sank. "But, what would Desary do with a sword?" he asked.

Catahn's brows rose. "Fight, if the occasion arose. Of course, she already has one of her own. . . . "

Airleas took his eyes from the weapon only long enough to let them plead with Catahn.

The Ren ignored him, glanced from one boy to the other and asked, "Why were you fighting over this?"

"He," said Airleas, glaring at Broran, "tried to take it away from me."

Catahn turned to Broran. "And why did you do that?"

"He was like to have killed himself, lord. He was dancing all over with it, slash and bash, and barely able to hold it up. I was afraid he was going to hurt himself. I was coming to bring it to you when he jumped me."

Catahn grinned. "Yes, and it appeared Gwynet brought me none too soon. The Cyneric had you at a loss. Now, I'll be taking this sword with me. And I want no more fighting between you boys. Broran, I'm sure you've got duties. Airleas and Gwynet, you'd best attend to your studies."

Catahn left the courtyard with the sword in hand; Airleas followed it with his eyes until he could no longer see it. Nor was his longing lost on Broran. Grinning, the Hillwild brat dusted off his jacket and saluted Airleas with a mocking bow.

"Pardon, Cyneric Midge, but as my lord says, I've duties."

Cyneric Midge. Airleas wanted to rage and make Broran take back the taunt, but at the moment, it was all he could do not to cry.

✧   ✧   ✧

I feel I should speak of time, but time has lost its meaning. So, I will not say we have been here for so many days, weeks, months. (Can it have been months?) But the seasons progress here, and that has meaning.

Autumn in Nairne meant crisp mornings and evenings, balmy-cool days, the smell of sun-drying leaves and harvest. There is little to harvest here and the trees never lose their glossy needles. Here, there is only the pulling to of shutters and the delicate, chilled fragrance of pine. The wind howls up the passes below Airdnasheen and whistles through the spires above the Ren Catahn's fortress, and I hear winter in the song.

Of what do I write first? Do I give the Tell of our escape from Creiddylad? Do I record that harrowing, magnificent moment when Taminy-a-Cuinn stood in the Cyne's Great Hall and declared herself Osmaer—by the Grace of the Spirit, mediator between man and Meri? Do I tell of how she stunned all with her claim that she had, herself, been the Vessel of the Meri for the past one hundred years and that Meredydd-a-Lagan of Nairne, whom I loved, was that Vessel now? With those claims we began our flight, first to Halig-liath and Nairne, now here, under Catahn's devoted protection.

Do I report that our Cyne is dead? Yes, I must. Some suppose he was murdered. I, unhappily, know he was, because Taminy knows. I am grateful not to be endowed with her Sight. Our Cyne is dead and his heir, fled from the murderer, is among us. That murderer will come to our mountain eventually. I pray not before spring.

But there is a tension in us that urges to preparation. It is a strange preparedness we seek, having nothing to do with armaments or fortifications. God knows Hrofceaster, on its craggy scarp, has enough of both. Instead, we learn duans and practice Weaves that must provide a different sort of bulwark against Daimhin Feich. He will no doubt come with more than an army. The Regency Cyne Colfre bestowed upon him is meaningless without Colfre's lone heir. So, he will come to us.

I wish to say something of this place and its people. There is a wild beauty to the environs of Airdnasheen, and the fortress of Hrofceaster is as different from Halig-liath as that hallowed place is from the Castle Mertuile. Yet, there is a spirit here that brings Halig-liath to mind. I am bereft and consoled at once. Will we ever go home?

I ask that, yet realize that for me, for the others who

accompany Taminy into exile, she has become home. Even familiar, beloved Halig-liath would be exile without her. In her presence the loss of Osraed Bevol, my mentor, is eased, though I still grieve. Where he is, only Taminy knows and only she can reach him.

In this new home, we live among people who treat us all as royalty. We are Taminy's first disciples, *waljan*, they call us—chosen—and marvel at the star-shaped marks we each carry in our palms—marks Taminy put there. They have a name for those too: *gytha*, meaning "a gift." The word refers to more than the mark.

I discover many shades of meaning in the words of the Hillwild. I once dismissed these people as simple, imagined them warlike and rude. The truth is, they speak plain words, but those words often carry elaborate meanings. They perform simple tasks of which every movement is freighted with significance. They are a religious people, though there are no Cirkes in their settlements. And they are, almost to a person, devoted to Taminy.

As are we, her First, her *waljan*.

    —*Osraed Wyth Arundel, Hrofceaster; Autumn, YP 605*

Osraed Wyth set his seal to the journal entry and sat back to rub his aching fingers. It was early, but he'd been up already for hours, writing—letters, mostly. Then, he'd opened his journal for the first time since they'd fled Haligliath. The words had finally come. And were wholly inadequate.

His chamber door rattled sharply and he rose to answer it, realizing, as he did, that the Sun had risen to pour watery amber light into the grey mists of Airdnasheen. The Sun itself would not be seen for some time; it had yet to clear the eastern crags of Baenn-iolair.

Outside his chamber door stood a Hillwild lad a bit older than Airleas and considerably brawnier. He scrutinized Wyth with bold, tawny eyes, then handed over a bound leather folio. "You'd be Wyth," he said. "This is for you. From Creiddylad."

"From Creiddylad?" Wyth took the folio and eagerly flipped the leather latch. There was a letter inside from Lealbhallain-mac-Mercer. Wyth hurried to lay it out on his writing table, glancing at the date. Nine, no, ten days ago.

"This is likely the last you'll see from lowlands."

Wyth turned. The Hillwild boy had followed him into the room and stood watching, thumbs crooked casually through his belt.

"The last?"

"Aye. Storms're coming. Passes'll be closed soon." The boy's eyes were far from casual. They assessed Wyth from stem to stern, lingering on his hands. "You're one of them, aren't you? *Waljan?*"

Wyth nodded.

"Is it true what they say—that you've got the Star in your hand?"

In answer, Wyth opened his left hand and held it out. The stellate *gytha* shimmered a vivid green that hovered on the edge of invisibility—like a shadow cast through translucent glass.

The boy put out an inquisitive finger and rubbed across the mark as if he thought it might smudge or come off. "Huh. Can't feel it." The dunnish eyes moved to a similar golden mark on Wyth's brow. "You've been Meri-Kissed, too."

"Yes."

"This Taminy did that?" He poked again at the *gytha*.

"Yes."

"Hurt, did it?"

"No, it didn't hurt. It felt . . . wonderful. Like cool fire."

"Some sort of Wicke, is she? Or a paeri? I don't believe in paeri."

Wyth closed his hand. "She's Osmaer. The Meri sent her."

"Raised her from the dead, I heard."

"No. Not . . . not exactly. She was—"

The boy grinned suddenly, displaying even white teeth. He reminded Wyth of a mountain cat showing a playful bit of fang. "No need to waste your time explaining that spirit stuff to me, Osraed. I figure, Wicke or not, she's the Ren's business not mine. Airdnasheen's agog with her, is all. Just thought I'd sniff a bit. I'm a curious lad."

The curious lad left then, affording Wyth the barest whisper of a bow, and Wyth, bemused, hurried to read his letter.

"The streets are not safe for us, now, and Creiddylad has become an alien place of warring factions. All Osraed have been ordered to carry papers affirming their loyalty to the Covenant established by Ochan and to the House Malcuim. To be caught in the streets without these papers is to be labeled a Taminist. That can lead to a harsh questioning and some time in the dungeons of Mertuile. Several of our number have disappeared within the last week and we fear that's where they are.

"The rest of us have given up the wearing of Osraed garb, but there is no way to disguise the Meri's Kiss against close inspection. Osraed Fhada tried tying a black scarf around his head, but the Kiss shone through as if lit from within. So, we wear our forelocks long and affect scarves and hats and cowls, but this only brings suspicion on us among those who style themselves Loyalists or Covenanters. Loyalist men go about hatless, regardless of the weather, so as not to be taken for Taminist Osraed—'burn brows' they call us. There is an actress named Siusan among us. She has brought us theatrical paints to drab the Kiss. Osraed Eadmund has used it well enough to be able to stay at Ochanshrine right under Abbod Ladhar's nose.

"Meanwhile, the rumor is spread that Cyneric Airleas has been kidnapped by Taminists. No man or woman can help but have strong feelings about that. Even the non-Osraed in our number must carry themselves carefully in public, for there is no way of telling if the person standing next to you in the market square is Taminist or Loyalist by leaning. Regent Feich has not seen fit to quell these rumors; suspicion and fear are rampant and easily erupt into violence, as every word a man or woman speaks in the street is seized on by those who hear it.

"The Cirke is full to bursting these days and those who do not attend worship find themselves the focus of suspicion, as well. Devotions are largely given over to warnings about us, condemnation of Taminy and harsh words against the wayward women who have allowed themselves to be seduced by lust for unnatural power. The Abbod Ladhar delivered an impassioned message this past Cirkedag, casting Taminy-Osmaer as Evil incarnate and seeking to turn the people's fear into hatred of her. He had especially harsh words for the women of Caraid-land. I am happy to be no man's daughter in this time, for to be female is to be suspected of all manner of filth. I'm happy *she* cannot hear what they are saying about her here.

"I think it must have been like this in the days of Cyne Liusadhe and I fear that Creiddylad quivers on the verge of apocalypse. The death of the Cyne, the disappearance of the Cwen and Cyneric, the fighting in the streets, the general disorder—all this is laid at Taminy's feet. I think Daimhin Feich intends to use rumor to rewrite history, giving a different tell of what happened that day in the Great Hall. Those who were there know these rumors as lies, but the many who were not must rely on hearsay. To counter the lies with truth is to incite suspicion and anger. It seems we can only wait and pray and rejoice that Taminy, herself, is safe with you."

Wyth looked up from the page to Taminy's troubled face. "Shall I stop, or would you hear more? He speaks of the situation at Ochanshrine. . . . "

She nodded, her eyes fixed on the mullioned windows behind him. "Please, go on."

Wyth cleared his throat. "Abbod Ladhar is still strongly in control of Ochanshrine and Wyncirke. The ranks there have dwindled, though; a number of the Brethren have come to us here in the city, though one or two stay behind as spies, pretending loyalty to the old Order. The Stone of Ochan is silent and dark, they say, and Osraed Ladhar frets over it as a mother over a sick child. Ladhar is often with Daimhin Feich and has stepped quietly into the role of Apex. The fact that you, Wyth, were appointed to that

position by Osraed Bevol, himself, means nothing here.
You are apostate—no, worse—you are a heretic, as much
a Wicke to them as they believe Our Lady to be.

"But as to the Stone—the Osmaer Crystal: Ladhar brings
it into the Cyne's Cirke every Cirkedag and displays it there
under brilliant lights, so the congregation might not notice
its darkness. I think it is the Crystal that convinces the
people Ladhar has a right to his position at the Apex. It
has become a rallying point, and in the streets, you will
hear people swear by the Stone of Ochan. I swear, too,
that it is the only thing that holds Creiddylad together and
keeps her from falling to complete chaos.

"We, here, are desperate for some word of Taminy. Is
she well? Please ask her to pray for us and to guide us to
the Meri's will. Your friend, Osraed Lealbhallain-mac-Mercer."

Wyth folded the letter and returned it to the folio. "The boy
who brought me this says it may be the last post we'll receive
from Creiddylad. To lose touch with them now . . . "

Taminy was shaking her head. "If Leal only knew it, he's
capable of staying in touch with us at a thought. He has
the capacity, but not the discipline." She looked up at Wyth.
"If one of you went back to Creiddylad you could instruct
them, and in the meantime, you could keep in contact
with me."

"Are you thinking of me, in particular?"

The expression on his face drew a chuckle of amusement from her. "No, not you, in particular . . . Not you,
at all. Your place is here. But one of you must go, I think.
And soon."

"How? How will they get there? The high passes will
be closed soon and it's a dangerous journey at the best of
times."

Taminy rose from her couch and moved to the windows.
Through the thick diamond-shaped panes she could see
the multiple distorted images of the oblong courtyard below,
in sunshine now, the coming and going of small figures
repeated over and over. One figure stood out among them
as it crossed toward the residence; taller, broader, it seemed

to collect more of the Sun's fickle rays. Catahn. Warmth curled in Taminy's breast.

"Maybe the Ren Catahn could spare some men as an escort," Wyth said from behind her.

"Dangerous," Taminy murmured. "The Hillwild would only be a target for Feich's rage." Even as she spoke, a sharp image formed in one of the tiny panes before her eyes. Mounted men struggled upward through a mountain pass the Hillwild called the Cauldron. Horses danced along the narrow, wind-whipped trail that circled the rim, while below them a curving expanse of gleaming black rock fell away into the mist-filled bowl. A banner bearing a sword-cleft rock on a red field snapped above the standard-bearer. The Claeg.

Taminy turned away from the window. "I think an escort will be provided," she said.

Wyth merely nodded. He was well-used to her sudden pronouncements by now and did not question them. "Is there anything else we can do?" he asked.

"We can wait. And pray. And be ready."

Wyth shifted restively. She'd said that often since they'd come here—be ready. And he no longer asked, "Ready for what?" She had no answer to give him yet, but she knew things were ever changing and that an answer would be soon in coming.

CHAPTER 3

In this Cusp, whatever is hidden in the souls and hearts of all people shall be discovered. This is the Day of which the Osraed Gartain prophesied: "In that Day, the piercing gaze of the Meri will bring every dark secret to light, though that secret be as tiny as a dust mote. The deceiver shall deliver up what is in his breast and lay it bare before the Eye of God. Nothing can escape Her knowledge."

—Osraed Tynedale, A Commentary on the Golden Cusp

Daimhin Feich came to Ochanshrine by boat, docking at the private wharf below the Abbis. To leave the castle by any other route would expose him to the rabble that seemed to mill endlessly in the streets without the walls, ready to pelt visitors with rotten produce and pebbles.

Abbod Ladhar, watching him debark at the little jetty, would rather he had stayed barricaded in Mertuile. Ladhar had never dealt well with ambiguity. Now, it was marching up the steps and right into his face. Part of him wanted nothing more than to retire to his chambers and pray until things were normal again. But normal, they would never be and here, if he looked at it right, was not disaster but opportunity. Cyne Colfre's death had left in its wake a welter of dependencies. Daimhin Feich was not in complete control of Caraid-land and could not be without two essentials: Airleas Malcuim and the Osmaer Crystal.

The Crystal was close enough at hand, physically, but removed from the new Regent across the estuary and within the stronghold of the Shrine at Ladhar's broad back. More than that, the Stone was removed from him by subjects who would as soon see him dead as set before it. His threat to Cwen Toireasa that he would take the Throne in her son's stead amounted to bluster. Such a move was the surest way of forcing the Houses to open rebellion, which the House Feich, populous and powerful though it was, could not withstand alone. Among the twelve other Houses of Caraid-land, allies must be had and, just now, the Chieftains and elders of those Houses were being singularly tight-lipped about their loyalties.

The Stone, sitting on its pedestal within Ochanshrine, could not be drawn upon for aid without the intervention of someone capable of wielding its power. Daimhin Feich needed the Osraed. Or what was left of them, Ladhar mused grimly. The irony was that he needed them to an end that could ultimately prove their undoing—if . . . if he shared Colfre's dislike of the Osraed, of the Hall, of anything that diluted the power of the Throne. He claimed he did not, for all he was brutally honest in his disparaging of things spiritual. Another irony. Daimhin Feich was a puzzle, and the last thing in the world Abbod Ladhar wanted was another puzzle.

Feich reached him, breathing hard, as were the two armed guards behind him. Ladhar's eyes fell on the guards' colors with bemusement. They were not Feich.

Catching the Abbod's look, Daimhin Feich grinned. "We have allies, Abbod. The House Dearg has fallen into our column."

The two men strolled toward the Abbis; the guards remained to keep an eye on the boat and the bank of the estuary.

"And will this suffice to take Halig-liath?" asked Ladhar.

Feich shook his head. "Not and hold Creiddylad. Ruadh assessed Halig-liath's fortifications and defensibility while we were there last. We had over a hundred men with us, but my cousin informs me twice that number would scarcely be enough. Between the forces of Ren Catahn and the Claeg they could easily defend the ridge. And the ridge is our only point of assault . . . unless, of course, we teach our horses to fly." He shot Ladhar a sideways look. "What do you say, Abbod? Does the power of the Crystal run to flying horses?"

"It has never been tried," said Ladhar dryly. He was weary of Feich's constant teasing.

"Hmm. Well, then too, we'd have to be able to guard our flank from rearward attack. That ridge would make a dandy trap. No, we need to field a large enough force to secure the town. And we need enough men skilled with heavy weaponry to be able to take out Halig-liath's front gate."

He paused for a few strides, tilted his head and said, "Or we need a miracle. Is the Stone up to a miracle?"

Ladhar had once had a raven drop onto his window sill and fix him with a gaze like that one. He'd thrown a walnut at the raven. Today, his pockets were empty. "The Stone was much abused by that Nairnian bitch. I don't think it has quite recovered."

Feich seemed amused. "Abbod, your language shocks me! 'That Nairnian bitch,' indeed."

They stepped into the Abbis and made their way along the curving outer corridor toward Ladhar's chambers.

"By the way, Abbod, that was a fine address you delivered last Cirkedag. Taminy-Osmaer as Evil incarnate—very clever. I don't think even I could have dreamed that up. A few more speeches like that and every able-bodied man in Creiddylad will volunteer to take Halig-liath."

Ladhar snorted. "Perhaps you've not noticed the make-up of our congregation these days. Able-bodied men are a conspicuous minority. My addresses are delivered, for the most part, to old men and women and their minor children and grandchildren. Every last one of them terrified. Every last one of them seeking familiarity as insulation against change. Now, if it's able-bodied young *women* you want, we've no shortage of those. Parents drag them in by the score to hear my dire warnings, while they cower on their benches, afraid Colfre's Wicke will get them. No, Regent Feich, the only army you'll raise among that lot will carry canes and distaffs, not swords."

Feich heaved an exaggerated sigh and came to a halt before the entrance to the Abbis's inner sanctum: The Shrine of the Osmaer Crystal. "Abbod, for a religious man, you are surprisingly negative. Where's your faith?"

Heat rose in Ladhar's bowels. "What do you know of faith?"

Feich glanced aside through the carved and filigreed doorway. "That I have it in abundance. Faith in myself, first of all. Faith in my fellow Caraidin."

The Abbod chuckled. "And which Caraidin might your faith reside in?"

"The fence-sitters, Abbod. Those who wait. For the past weeks, rumors have been circulating that the Taminists forcibly abducted Riagan Airleas from Mertuile."

"Rumors you started."

Feich inclined his head. "I think it timely to acknowledge those rumors. Yes, the whole story must come out; Cwen Toireasa, seduced by your walking Evil, Taminy, handed her own child and Colfre's heir over to her. Our poor Cyne, the Wicke's unwitting champion, was so smitten by guilt at his own culpability that he took his life."

Feich wandered to the Shrine's doorway and peered down the long aisle into its sacred heart. "Now I, Cyne Colfre's last friend and his heir's Regent, propose that every man with any loyalty to the Throne arise to aid me in retrieving our future."

A frisson of inexplicable anxiety shivered its way up Ladhar's spine. "A noble speech. Just how do you propose to 'acknowledge' these rumors?"

"I propose to post bans; I propose *you* shout them from the altar."

"I never shout, Regent Feich."

Feich grinned at him. "You will now. There is a sea of passion awash in Caraid-land. We must harness it."

"And to what end? Do you really intend to put Airleas Malcuim before the Stone? He's a Taminist."

"He's a child. And do I really have any choice? Imagine, for a moment, that Airleas were to perish while in my hands. What do you think would become of me?"

Ladhar had considered that, of course, but wasn't sure Daimhin Feich, in his strange and intermittent passion, had considered it. When they'd returned from Halig-liath he'd been fired with the notion that he could simply declare Airleas delinquent or heretic and set himself before the Stone of Ochan to accept the Circlet and Throne. Confronted with harsh reality, his fire had been forced to cool, but that feverish light had not quite left his eyes and it made Ladhar queasy. "I doubt your life would be worth much under the circumstances," he said.

"My life and that of every other male Feich. Even after all that's happened, the Claeg are leaning toward Haligliath and I've no idea how many other Houses have similar attitudes. They're tight as a pail of clams. But if they thought for one moment that I was responsible for harm coming to that boy, they'd wipe out the House Feich to a man."

"So you're content to rule from behind the Throne?"

"Or from beside it as Durweard. But no, not content. Not forever."

"Ah. And how do you propose to make the transition from being Regent to being Cyne without leaving yourself open to deadly outrage?"

"There are any number of ways. They all take time. Once I have Airleas in hand, I'll have enough of that."

He turned back into the Shrine, then, stepping through the arched doorway onto the uppermost level of the circular room. Below him, the broad, shallow tiers fell away to its lowest point, where the Osmaer Crystal sat on its ornate wooden pedestal. The perfect facets of the Stone winked at him through the semi-gloom of the dimly lit chamber. "Tell me, Abbod, do you intend to bring the Stone to Cirke again this week?" His steps continued to carry him closer to the heart of the Shrine.

Ladhar hurried to catch him up, his spine a-quiver again with uncomfortable static. "It's an important symbol in these chaotic times. I believe it comforts the people."

Feich's pale eyes flicked sideways to the Abbod's flushed face. "And reminds them where the real power lies, eh?"

I only wish I knew, Ladhar thought, *where the real power lies.* He was immediately contrite. But, God, the Stone seemed so dim. Aloud, he said, "We'll be more comfortable in my offices, Daimhin."

Feich stopped halfway down the aisle, his eyes still on the Crystal. "The fire seems to have gone out of it."

Ladhar's face flushed even hotter. "I told you, Daimhin, it was sorely abused by the Wicke."

"Drained? Is that what you're telling me—that she *drained* the power from the mighty Stone of Ochan?"

"The Stone of Ochan," Ladhar said, as if instructing a first year Prentice, "has no power of its own. It is merely the purest of channels."

"Which she defiled."

"Yes."

Feich fixed him with wintry eyes and asked, "How do you propose to cleanse it?"

"That is a matter for the Osraed to consider, Regent. It can be of no concern to you."

"Oh, but it can."

"You, sir, are an unbeliever. You've taken great pains to make that apparent. The Osmaer can surely be no more to you than a chunk of ancient rock."

Feich smiled. It was a saintly smile—insidious, charming. "I meant only what you said before: The Osmaer is a symbol of the Covenant. If the Caraidin believe in it, adhere to it; if it helps hold this kingdom together, then it damn well must concern me." He gave the Stone a last glance. "Shall we retire to your chambers?"

Ladhar moved quickly to usher him from the room, sparing the Crystal a backward glance. A trick of light made him think he saw a ruddy light pulse deep within it. A trick that made his heart leap in his breast.

He heard Feich draw a hissing breath and realized that he had seen it too. *Good,* he thought, *perhaps now he'll cease his scoffing.*

"Now," said Taminy softly, "here is the next aislinn." A picture filled her mind, moved, sounded, breathed aromas.

For the next several moments, the only sound in the small, candlelit room high on Hrofceaster's massive flank was the faint rustle of fabric, the flutter of flame. Taminy watched the row of faces rapt in concentration. She knew they were seeking to clarify the multi-sensory image, calling up whatever duans they thought might aid them, clutching their crystals tightly. Too tightly.

"Relax," she murmured. "Sing the thought through the stone, don't try to push it through with your bare hands. The crystal responds to the *aidan*, not brute strength."

Along the row of meditative *waljan*, fingers loosened self-consciously.

"Good. Now, breathe. Send the *aislinn* out with the air . . . and focus."

In relaxed hands, the crystals glowed softly or intensely as the nature of the owner dictated. Then, in the center of the row, a stone took quick fire. Above the flare of light, Aine-mac-Lorimer's face displayed a triumphant smile. Then she caught up the slate that lay on the braid rug before her crossed legs and scribbled hasty words.

One by one, the others in the row echoed her as their crystals flared and pulsed—Gwynet, Iseabal, Eyslk, Phelan Backstere. When the last scratch had been made on the last slate, Taminy called the light-globes in the room to full flood. Then she turned her thoughts to the next room where five more *waljan*, in Desary Hillwild's charge, sat in similar contemplation.

In a moment, the chamber door opened and Desary, herself, appeared, trailing Wyvis and Rennie Lusach, Cluanie Backstere and Airleas. They hurried to find themselves places on the large braid rug, clutching their slates. All eyes turned to Taminy.

"Aine," she said, "you were the first to finish. Give tell."

Aine's face flushed with pleasure. She whipped a lock of bright hair behind her ear and glanced at her slate. "Well, the aislinn I got was about the Osmaer Crystal. I saw the Crystal on its pedestal in a dark, circular room—a room like a shallow bowl. And I heard rainfall and a Wardweave being sung and I smelled incense and roses. The aislinn seemed to say that the Stone needed protection." She glanced aside at Taminy. "I don't understand that part. But then I touched Rennie Lusach and sent the aislinn to him. And he sent back . . ." Here, she glanced at the slate, now reposing in her lap. "A small host of mounted men coming through . . . a bowl? And marching under a banner of red with a black . . . glob of some sort."

"It's a rock!" wailed Rennie and his sister, Wyvis, whin-nied laughter.

Taminy hushed them. "And the meat of the message?"

"That one of the Houses marches on Hrofceaster." Aine blinked, hazel eyes fearful. "Is that so, Taminy?"

Taminy smiled and spread her hands. "Can someone else shed light on this dire aislinn?"

Iseabal-a-Nairnecirke spoke up. "The message to send was right . . . or at least, it was the same one *I* got. But, of course, the Stone needs protection, Aine. Cusps always seem to put it in dire jeopardy of being taken off by folks—like Buchan Claeg during the reign of Kieran the Super-stitious."

"Well, you'd more chance to study history than I, Isha, being an Osraed's daughter. A Lorimer's girl doesn't get those opportunities."

Taminy halted the argument with a thought. Both girls jumped and looked up, guiltily. Taminy nodded at Iseabal who cleared her throat and went on.

"I sent to Airleas. His message was that Iobert Claeg was leading his men through the Cauldron pass to bring news and more pilgrims to Hrofceaster. It was clear as day, Taminy." She gave Airleas an appreciative glance. "I saw the Claeg banner snapping on its standard and the color of the Claeg's eyes and I swear I could count the whiskers in his beard. I smelled wet wind and stone . . . and pine."

One by one, the others reported as well, with varying degrees of success; Gwynet and Eyslk had done well—Phelan, not so well. Meanwhile, Taminy and Desary lis-tened closely—and did more than listen.

When all was accounted for and the students sat cupping varying degrees of satisfaction or disappointment in their hearts, Taminy dismissed everyone but Aine and Iseabal into Desary's hands to work at their Weaves. The two girls curled, expectant, by the hearth. Taminy joined them on the great braided rug, crossing her legs carefully beneath her. She glanced from one to the other, making them fidget, then said, "Aine, summon Wyth to us, please."

Aine blushed and smiled simultaneously, then closed her eyes and sat in perfect stillness. To Taminy her thoughts were bells pealing out a summons. Melodic, they were, but forthright, even demanding. They tolled a message that would no doubt take its recipient by surprise and sheer force. Taminy smiled wryly and hoped Osraed Wyth wasn't handling anything delicate at the moment.

Aine's eyes opened and she flushed a deeper red—her face competing with her hair for vividness. "I got him!" she whispered. "He's coming. He was just down the hall in his study. For just a second, I saw the room *through his eyes*." She pressed her hands to her face. "Will I ever get used to being able to do this?"

Taminy laughed. "Someday, I suppose. Although I hope you'll always marvel at it. I do."

"*You* do?" Aine shook her head. "How can that be?"

Taminy gazed down at her entwined fingers. How, indeed. "I live between two worlds—this and That. The world of Form and Shadow and the World of Light. When I'm pulled into That world, it seems as natural as . . . as breathing. When I'm in this, I stand amazed that I ever knew That, at all."

"Do the two worlds never . . . merge?" asked Iseabal, and Taminy felt her concern as a warm stole about her shoulders.

"Oh, more and more," she said, smiling reassurance. "Day by day."

The chamber door opened just then, admitting a damp chill and a startled-looking Wyth Arundel. Wide-eyed, he all but tiptoed across the floor. "Did I . . . ? Did you . . . ? Did *Aine* summon me?"

"Well, don't sound so surprised, Wyth Arundel. Why might I not be able to summon you?"

Wyth gave the girl a wary glance, then perched himself carefully on the edge of a chair. "What did you want, then, Aine?"

Aine stopped just short of tossing her head. "Nothing at all. It was Taminy bid me call you."

"There's a Claeg force arriving from lowlands," said Taminy. "They're bringing us about a dozen more pilgrims. We'll need to make arrangements for them. Catahn and the Aeldra will find them lodging, I'm sure, but it means the classes will expand and I think you'll have to teach some yourself."

Wyth sat back in his seat. "But Mistress—Taminy . . . I thought you were training these girls to be teachers."

"I was, but, well . . . of the group, only Aine and Isha are quite ready to teach and I need them elsewhere, now. That is, if they're willing to go."

Both girl's heads snapped about as if tugged by puppet strings.

"What? Where, Taminy?" said Iseabal and, "Needed where?" asked Aine.

Taminy rose and began to pace the braided pathways beneath her feet. "Winter's fast coming and the passes will be all but closed. We'll lose touch with Creiddylad and with Nairne, as well, unless someone there can Weave a strong enough Speaking rune. Leal could. Fhada could. I can reach them in their dreams, in their unguarded moments, but to get word *from* them, well, they need to be taught the discipline. It's a lost skill among the Osraed these days—or all but lost. Even in my days at Halig-liath, a boy was thought to be a prodigy if he carried a strong enough Gift to Weave images as you girls did today. And only if that spark showed early, was it fanned."

She stopped pacing and faced them. "Well, you *are* prodigies, but more than that, you've now got the discipline to make your Speakweaves consistent and clear. And you can teach others. Iseabal, I'd like you to go back to Nairne to teach your father and anyone else who dares to learn. And Aine, I'd like you to go to Creiddylad to instruct the believers there. Most especially Lealbhallain and Fhada."

Aine's eyes flickered to Wyth's suddenly ashen face while Iseabal cried, "*Leave* you, Taminy? Leave you? How *can* I?"

Taminy dropped to her knees before the distraught girl and took her hands. "Anwyl," she said, and let the endearment carry her love between them. "It wouldn't be forever. And you've family there, so you wouldn't be alone. And you and I will always be able to touch somewhere above and beyond this." She squeezed Iseabal's fingers. "But your poor, dear father has only his dreams. Of the Osraed at Halig-liath faithful to the Meri, only Tynedale has a great Gift for the Speakweave, and he's half-forgotten how to use it. Through you, I would be able to speak to them, and once they've learned to discipline the *aidan*—"

"Then I could return?"

Taminy nodded. "Then you could return. Will you go to Nairne, Isha?"

"I'll attempt anything you ask, Taminy. You must believe I can do it."

"I believe you can do anything that needs to be done," Taminy told her. She raised her head to regard the other two, very much aware of the tension skittering between them. It was no more than she expected. "Well, Aine, will you go to Creiddylad?"

Aine flushed. "Surely you can't mean for *me* to instruct *Osraed*."

"Well, there are no doubt things they can teach you, as well, but yes, that's just what I mean for you to do."

"But Creiddylad . . . it's so far away. I'll be among enemies, strangers—"

"Now, Aine. Leal-mac-Mercer is hardly a stranger to you."

"But I'm sure I couldn't send a Speakweave that far or receive one."

Taminy shook her head. "Distance makes no difference. You know that. Aine, I know I'm asking you to do a hard thing, but I must ask. There's no one else to send."

Aine bowed her head, trying to hide her expression. That, she might hide from Taminy, but not the fears and anxieties and disappointments that lay behind it, filling her eyes with tears. "I know. And I understand why someone's needed there, it's just . . . I'm sorry. Of course I'll go."

Wyth cleared his throat noisily and said, "You'll want them to leave with the Claeg, then."

"I hope he'll agree to take them. I thought he could head north to Nairne and leave Isha with her family, then ferry Aine to Creiddylad."

Wyth nodded, his eyes, for a moment, seeming unable to focus. Taminy knew his thoughts had similar problems of late.

"Is there something wrong, Wyth?" she asked softly.

The large, dark eyes snapped to sudden clarity. "Ah, no, Mistress. I was just meandering."

Aine, her tears abandoned, clambered to her feet. "Well, that's that, then. I'd best go pack my gear."

A sonorous tolling began outside, bringing Wyth to his feet, as well. "That will be the Claeg coming in. I'd best consult with Catahn. How long do you think he'll stay?"

Taminy regarded him soberly, knowing she made him want to twitch. "Some days, I imagine. His men will be weary."

He nodded. He glanced at Aine. "I'd best go, then."

Taminy got to her feet, bringing Iseabal with her. "You girls, too. Aine's right. You'd best start packing; make sure you've got good warm traveling clothes. If you've not, tell Eyslk or Eldress Levene."

Iseabal gave her a kiss on the cheek and left quickly; the others lingered for a moment more as if caught in an invisible eddy, then scurried to the door, nearly colliding on the threshold. Aine, seeming near tears again, shrugged through first and ran off down the hall.

"Wyth." Taminy halted him before he'd quite gotten himself back in motion, and came to him at the door. "What is it, Wyth?"

He closed himself up for a second, then hesitated, then opened himself, revealing a thick stew of confusion and not a little embarrassment. He said, "Must you send Aine?"

"Must I send Aine," she repeated, laying subtle stress on the name.

"I've grown fond of her." He searched her face, eyes direct. "But you know that, don't you?"

Taminy smiled. "Most people wouldn't have noticed. But you do scrap a lot."

He blushed. "I suppose we do. It's uncertainty, I guess. We've not spoken of it, even to each other. Most of our conversations, as you've obviously noticed, seem to be Aine thrusting and me parrying. She's a strong willed girl."

"Like Meredydd."

Wyth could hide neither his surprise nor his wistfulness at the mention of that name. "I . . . In some ways, yes. She is like Meredydd. Though she's more sure of herself than ever Meredydd was. . . . No. I'm wrong in that, aren't I? Meredydd knew what she wanted. . . . It wasn't me. It couldn't have been me. She was destined for the Meri. She . . . " He shook his head.

"It's still difficult for you to talk about."

He took a deep breath. "Some days. Some nights. Some moments. Yes. Meredydd is still with me. And when the Meri speaks to me, it's Meredydd's voice I hear."

"You asked if I must send Aine. The answer is 'yes, I must.' Listen," she insisted, when he opened his mouth to protest, "and I'll tell you why I must." She glanced past him into the hall. "Please, close the door and come back to the fire."

He did as bidden and they sat before the great stone hearth, knee to knee; she, holding his elongated hands; he, trying to read her eyes.

"I didn't lie when I said Aine and Iseabal were the most ready."

"I didn't mean—!"

"Shush! Now, Airleas has a powerful Gift, and Gwynet and Eyslk are purer channels. But Airleas must stay here with me, and Gwynet is too young for this task, and Eyslk is just discovering her Gift."

"There's still Phelan."

"Phelan lacks the native talent. He'll do his best work for you in the academics when he's fully trained."

"What about Skeet? I know he Speakweaves as easily

as he speaks aloud. He seems as comfortable with the Art as you do."

"Yes. But Skeet must also stay here—for my benefit," she added when his lips moved to ask why. "The only other people I could send would be Desary, who would draw immediate suspicion in Creiddylad . . . and you."

"Me?"

"You've the Gift and the power and the discipline. Do you wish to finish your work in Creiddylad?" Now, she knew, he wanted to look away and could not. She held his eyes tighter than she held his hands.

"But . . . but, Taminy—Mistress. The Meri, Herself, made me Weard to the Covenant."

"Aye, she did."

"You are the Covenant. The embodiment of it. To leave your side would be an act of betrayal. Nor can I complete my work apart from you. The collection of the ancient texts is all but finished. What I commit to writing now must fall from your lips."

"This is all true," she agreed. "So you see, I'm left with Aine and Iseabal."

He grimaced and nodded. "I do see."

She smiled at him. "Go to Catahn," she said. "He's looking for you. He's in your study just now."

When he was gone, she wondered if she might have been just a bit more honest with him. Aine was a good choice for Creiddylad, but Desary was better. She was more disciplined, more comfortable with her *aidan*, which was unusually strong, and she was more confident in her ability to use it. And it really wouldn't have been too difficult to disguise the Hillwild girl to pass among lowlanders. She already knew and had used a Weave that changed the color of her startlingly black eyes; she knew, also, how to lose her Gyldan accent.

But, of the two, it was Aine who reminded Wyth of his lost Meredydd, and Wyth who reminded Aine that she was only a Lorimer's daughter.

"Airleas!" Gwynet caught him up halfway down the corridor from their "classroom." Desary had let them go for the mid-day break. In the afternoon, Osraed Kynan would give them their lessons in the more mundane arts of reading, writing and history. Now, Airleas fled as if pursued by demons instead of a bright-eyed little girl.

Gwynet fell into step beside him. "Airleas, whatever was wrong, just now? You looked as if you'd gone to sleep with your eyes wide. Didn't you hear Desary? You knew the answer, why didn't you give tell?"

"God-the-Spirit, Gwynet! Do you stop to *breathe*? I was just . . . daydreaming."

"Daydreaming? You? Oh, Airleas, you *don't*. You *never*."

The hallway ended in a cross-corridor with deep window embrasures set along its outer wall. One lay just before them, streaming pale light over the chill stone floor. Airleas moved to the embrasure and leaned out toward the iron-framed panes, peering into the courtyard below. Through the faceted glass, he could see only a portion of the hectic activity around the Airdnasheen gate. Claeg warriors were everywhere and their banner was even now being run up the fortress standards to flutter and snap beside the Hageswode pennant of white stars on a a dark blue field. Airleas pulled himself up into the embrasure and curled there, chin on knees.

Gwynet stood and watched him for a moment, then crawled up into the casement across from him.

After a moment of brooding silence he said, "Why Aine and Iseabal?"

Gwynet puzzled. "Why Aine and Iseabal what?"

"Why did she keep them by her and send the rest of us away?"

Gwynet shrugged. "I reckon she wanted to talk to them privy."

"I did as well as either of them."

Now he'd lost her. "What does the one have to do with th'other?"

"She's got a mission for them. Something special she wants them to do."

"How d'you know that?"

He gave her a half-sly, half-abashed look from under his thatch of black hair and shrugged.

Gwynet narrowed her eyes and peered at him with all her senses. What she read made her gasp. "Airleas! You were listening in! To *her*! *That's* why you'd no ears for Desary's questions. You were trying to—to pick their thoughts! How *could* you?"

He had the good graces to look guilty. "I wanted to know what was going on. I knew it was something important."

Gwynet shook her head fiercely. "But it's *wrong*, Airleas. To listen on *anybody*, leastwise *her*."

"Well, I wasn't listening on *her*; I can't. She's different. She doesn't . . . leak. I was listening to Aine and then Wyth when he came into it. Aine leaks a lot," he added, as if that excused him.

"It's still wrong," Gwynet said and eyed him warily. "Was it something important?"

"She's sending them away."

Gwynet's heart turned over uneasily and she gasped.

"Aye, it's true. She's sending them to teach the *waljan* in Creiddylad and Nairne. They'll be leaving with the Claeg." His eyes moved back to the glass diamonds. "I wish she'd send me to Creiddylad. Why didn't she send me, Gwyn?"

"What nonsense, Airleas! You're Cyneric, now. And Daimhin Feich is likely lying for you like a hungry cat. You'd be in such danger."

Airleas sat straight up and leaned toward her. "Why? In these clothes" —he tugged at his leather jacket— "I look just like any other Hillwild boy. And my grandfather used to disguise himself and travel among the people to see how well or poorly he was thought of. I could do as much. It's not as if I've a brand on my forehead that says, 'Look! Here's a Malcuim!' No one would even know me, Gwyn. I'd be just another Gyldan youth out to see the real world."

"But why? Where would you go? What would you do?"

Airleas's eyes caught fire. "I'd go to Creiddylad, like I said. I'd free the Stone of Ochan from Daimhin Feich's foul hands. And then, I'd avenge my father."

Gwynet was stunned to sudden tears. Grasping Airleas's forearms, she looked right into his amber eyes and said, "Airleas Malcuim, how can you think of venging *here*? There's more importful things than your Malcuim pride. She's brought you here to *teach* you how to be the Meri's own Cyne. Learning, *tha's* your task, not risking all to be your own hero. Listen to Taminy, Airleas. Don't listen to your proudful voices."

"But it's not *fair*, Gwynet! It's not fair that my father is dead and my mother is forced to run away and live in this poor, cold, hateful place. Meanwhile, the man that put her here roosts his behind on my father's throne—on *my* throne."

"Airleas, your father betrayed Taminy." Gwynet was surprised to hear those harsh words leave her lips.

Her companion seemed equally amazed. "No, it was Feich. He betrayed them both. He *used* my father."

"It comes to the same end, so there's no use you rewriting the tell. We're here and Feich is there and right now, tha's as should be."

Airleas glanced away again to the window. "You don't understand. You *can't* understand."

Gwynet gazed at him for a moment more, then pulled her hands away and levered herself out of the window embrasure. "I'm hungry. I'm going down to the refectory and get my dinner." She turned on her heel and walked away from him down the right-hand corridor without once looking back.

The atmosphere in Taminy's audience chamber was somber. Somber, too, the hardened face of the Claeg as he gave his report to Taminy and the Ren Catahn.

"Feich has not yet set himself before the Stone and knows he dares not while Airleas lives. He talks of his duty to the Malcuim and seeks allies now among the Houses. Still, I've no doubt the Throne is all he thinks about."

Seated beside his uncle, Saefren Claeg watched Taminy digest his uncle's tell, his eyes never leaving her face. She always surprised him; seeming so young, looking so serene, speaking as if she knew the inside of everyone's head. He was always struck with the delicacy of her. *A woman like that should waste away and die up here*, he thought, *yet she thrives*. There she sat on her couch, wearing, of all things, a youth's breeches, twyla shirt, and long leather vest, her nearly white hair bound into a fat plait that hung over one shoulder.

"Most of the Houses are indecisive, my Lady," Iobert Claeg continued. "They wait for signs, for portents, for intelligence about you and the Malcuim. I've spoken, myself, to the Gilleas and the Jura. Both Houses pledged themselves to the Meri's service, but they sought surety, Lady, that your service and Hers were one and the same."

"Aye," added Saefren, "they grilled Uncle long and thorough—and their own Chieftains and elders as well."

"And?" The Hillwild Ren seemed edgy—like a cat too near water. But then, he always seemed on the verge of leaping or roaring.

Uncle Iobert smiled. It was rumored he never smiled, but the truth was his smiles were simply lost beneath the steely coils of his facial hair. He turned his eyes to Taminy. "They are yours, Osmaer. And I think, too, we may count on the Cuillean and the Graegam. I'll make certain of them on our trek westward. But the others—" He shrugged eloquently. "They must be courted before they can be counted."

"Damn the fickleness of the animal!" swore Catahn. He pushed out of his chair and paced around the room beyond the hearthside circle. "Did I not hear the Chieftains of these so-called *noble* Houses swear fealty to Taminy-Osmaer in the Great Hall at Mertuile? They heard her claims and proofs, saw her miracles—"

"Miracles," said Taminy quietly from her couch, "are transient things. Like dreams, they seem vivid at first flush, then fade to translucence."

"Aye," agreed the Claeg, "there is that. And, too, what a Chief may pledge, his elder kinsmen have a right to challenge. Many of those elders were absent that day. And they're a stubborn lot." He leaned forward in his chair, grey eyes on Taminy. "They wait, Lady. They wait for a Sign. From you. You've disappeared from sight, their Cyne is dead and his heir has vacated the capital. As you say, they were willing to pledge to you at first flush, but now they waver. I speak to them of you, but I can only offer them words."

Taminy nodded. "You wish to carry away some direct message from me. Some . . . token."

"Aye. Exactly that."

"When you leave, I'll have something to send to each House. Will you deliver these tokens, sir?"

Iobert bowed his head, submissively, making his nephew twitch. "Chill hell take me if I don't, Lady. I'll see that the tokens are delivered."

"Will that be dangerous to you and yours, sir?" Taminy asked, and seemed genuinely concerned. "I think of Daimhin Feich. He must surely suspect where your loyalties lie."

Saefren's ears pricked up at this. It was the first time he'd heard the Golden Wicke indicate there might be minds she couldn't fathom. He caught his uncle's eye, but the older Claeg gave no indication that he was thinking similar thoughts.

"He may suspect all he wants," Iobert said, "but he won't press me, because he doesn't want to make an enemy of the Claeg. Feich would like to believe Colfre's death and your flight has changed everything up—that it's his game we play."

"He may be more right than we're ready to admit," observed Saefren, trying to rein in his uncle's unbridled enthusiasm.

"I prefer to think," said Iobert, slanting a fierce scowl at him, "that things are at least even. Our greatest enemy is, as the Ren Catahn so aptly puts it, the fickleness of the animal. That may also be our greatest asset."

"We've had reports from friends in Creiddylad," Taminy said, "that things there are . . . tense."

Saefren Claeg grimaced. "An understatement. The place is a powder barrel, needing only a spark to set it off. I've no guess as to how many Taminists there are to Covenanters in the city—it's not something you can get a man to discuss with you on the street—but your burn-brows are under cover."

Iobert Claeg glowered. "Saefren Claeg, your brattish tongue is going to damn you. Speak with respect of the Lady's Osraed."

"Sorry, Uncle," said Saefren, and was not the least bit contrite. Taminy smiled at him, surprising him to the core. Could she not sense his doubt, his skepticism?

She said, "If you've no objection, sirs, I've a special favor to ask of you."

"Ask, Lady," said Iobert before his nephew could pass comment, "and consider it done."

"I've special 'tokens' to send to Nairne and Creiddylad. With winter coming our only way of communicating with the believers in those places will be the *aidan*—the Gift. I need to send two of my *waljan* to be with them. Iseabal-a-Nairnecirke must go to Nairne and Aine-mac-Lorimer to Creiddylad. Are you willing to take them?"

Iobert Claeg bowed to her in acquiescence for the second time that day, but his nephew wasn't willing to be so accommodating.

"Women? You want us to take on a couple of *women* in such harsh weather?"

"Cailin, actually," said Catahn, returning to his seat beside Taminy. "But older girls; seventeen or eighteen. Healthy, hardy . . . and exceptional."

"And not afraid of inclement weather," added Taminy.

Saefren fancied his glower was almost as intimidating as his uncle's. He gave Taminy the full force of it. "The trip down the mountain is vicious. Cold, biting winds, chilling mists, rain. They'll be expected to sleep on freezing ground—"

"They know," said the Golden Wicke. "They had to come *up* the mountain to get here."

Of course they had. Saefren could have kicked himself for his over-reaction. Now his uncle was scowling at him and the Osmaer woman was grinning at him and Catahn's great hands were flexing.

"If you object to my request, Saefren—"

"He does *not* object!" roared Iobert. He came to his

feet, quivering with suppressed rage. "That a kinsman of mine should utter such mealy words—should dare to speak in sly opposition—!"

Taminy threw back her head and laughed. It was a girl's laugh, light, carefree, delighted. "Please, Chieftain Claeg, don't flog your poor nephew for his doubts. He's entitled to them. After all, he wasn't in Creiddylad with you this summer. He didn't see what you saw. He only heard about it after the fact."

"He should trust what he hears from his elder kinsman!"

I was wrong, Saefren realized, *my glower is nowhere near as intimidating as Uncle's.*

Taminy shook her head. "Trust is hard given in matters of faith. Saefren is loyal to you and to his House. For now, that's enough."

"Aye, well." Iobert Claeg settled another disgruntled glance on his nephew, then turned his attention to Catahn. "We'd best see to the arms I brought up and ride herd on that young Osraed you put in charge of the pilgrims. I've family among 'em. Wanted to come up and study under the Lady." He dipped his head to Taminy. "I dare say there're some of us could use instruction in humility."

Saefren hid a grin as he watched his uncle bow himself over Taminy's hand before taking his leave. Catahn made the same obeisance, then trailed the Claeg Chieftain from the room, turning at the door to fix the still stationary Saefren with a wolfish stare.

That was a disappointment. He had hoped for a moment alone with her, though he was uncertain why. Perhaps he thought she might perform some pretty petty miracle to ensnare him. But under the Hillwild's regard, his body moved involuntarily toward the door. The Ren grunted and passed from view.

"Saefren Claeg."

He turned back to look at her. She was an unlikely visitation of the Divine in her breeches and leathers. She took several steps toward him, stirring dust motes into the pattern of light from the northern windows. They shimmered around her head, seeming to radiate from the pale gold of her hair.

She stopped just before him, hands clasped demurely. "The 'Golden Wicke' will perform no Weaves to snare your soul, nor miracles to capture your approval. I meant what I said about your doubts; you may keep them as long as you need them."

He marveled at that, covering himself with a chuckle. "Am I such an open book to you, mistress?"

She smiled. "Deliver my girls safely, please, Saefren Claeg," she said, and moved past him out the door.

CHAPTER 4

Don't look at beginnings. Raise your eyes to the ends.
This time is like the Spring sowing; it seems the earth is barren
and the weeds mighty and the stones hard, but the end-time
holds harvests and gatherings-in. Then, you'll see the issue;
then you'll reap the bounty.

—Utterances of Taminy-Osmaer,
Book of the Covenant, #14

✧   ✧   ✧

He stood on the banks of the Halig-tyne and looked east
toward Nairne. Behind him, the Sun set into the Western Sea
and color drained from the sky in runnels of red and purple.
He waited for the Rose. It would appear in the sky over Halig-
liath and his invisible wings would take him almost there to
watch it shed its radiance over sleeping Nairne.

But the night sky grew dark and stars glinted and above
distant Halig-liath was nothing but a swathe of dewy black
velvet. Anxiety tugged at him. Where was she? Had something happened to her? He fidgeted. He heard himself
moan.

"You look for me in the wrong place, Leal."

He shivered, eyes darting. Had he heard those words
or imagined them? In their feverish dance, his eyes caught
a gleam of light to the south, high over the Gyldan-baenn.
He fixed on it, and before he had taken two breaths, the
light blossomed into a thing that was both crystal and rose
and yet neither. Golden, the spreading, translucent petals dripped glory onto the tops of the mountains, strew-
ing the snowy peaks with Eibhilin wealth.

Leal puzzled. Where was this? He tried to distinguish the mountains, number them, name them, but they remained huge, dark and anonymous beneath the spreading splendor. He remembered Catahn Hillwild and tried to recall where his capitol lay among those titanic shapes, but could not.

Fhada! Fhada would know. If he could only wake. Wake! He willed his eyes to open. *Wake!* Tried to conjure a bright sunrise, a splash of cold water. WAKE!

He sat up abruptly, brain reeling from the sudden charge of warm energy that flushed him. The room was not dark, for someone stood beside his bed with a lamp. He blinked. No. There was someone by his bed, but there was no lamp. The light he saw radiated *from* the figure.

He choked, suddenly unable to breathe. "Taminy! Mistress!"

She raised a radiant hand. "Peace, Lealbhallain."

And he felt peace. Like warm water, like soft sunlight, it poured over him. He smiled.

"I'm sending you someone," she said, and in that moment, he saw Aine-mac-Lorimer as clearly as if she stood before him. A wash of indecipherable sensation came with the vision. "Listen to her. Learn what she has to teach. Teach her what she must learn. . . . Be patient with her. She comes with the Claeg."

"Wha—?" Leal's eyes stared into complete darkness. He was surprised to find himself still lying flat on his back on his low pallet in his room at Care House. Windowless, the chamber admitted daylight only through a narrow aperture high on the western wall. In a flutter of stunned blinks, that feature appeared as a grey, poorly defined rectangle. In the meager light, Leal could see the solid shapes of his sparse furnishings.

He suspected it was near dawn, but it hardly mattered. Regardless of the time, Fhada must be told of the aislinn. Leal scrambled to find his boots and coat and hurried to the elder Osraed's room. It took several moments of tapping before a groggy Fhada let him in.

"Taminy-Osmaer has left Halig-liath," he blurted, before he'd even cleared the door.

"She—what? How—how do you know this?"

"I had a dream. An aislinn. She's gone to the Gyldans."

"Hush!" Fhada pulled Leal completely into the chamber and shut the door firmly behind him. "Are you certain?"

Leal nodded emphatically, flopping unruly red hair into his eyes, and rubbed his coated arms against a frenetic chill. The aislinn still held him, rattling his teeth and quivering his innards. "I saw the Crystal Rose high over the mountains. Then Taminy, herself, appeared to me and told me she was sending Aine-mac-Lorimer to Creiddylad to teach us."

"To teach us what?" asked Fhada.

Leal scraped the suddenly empty insides of his mind. "I . . . I'm not sure. . . . No, wait. Yes! So we might speak with her as clearly as we speak to each other now."

The older Osraed peered at him in the mellow light of his single light-bowl, then threw back his head and laughed. "My dear Leal, I hope it's somewhat clearer than that!"

Leal came down to breakfast to find an unusually somber Osraed Fhada sitting in the small refectory, staring from the window. His tea mug, clutched in both hands, was quickly losing the heat of its contents to the chilly room.

"Your tea's getting cold," Leal told him when he sat down with his breakfast some minutes later.

Fhada's eyes dropped to the cup; Leal wasn't sure he actually saw it. "Daimhin Feich paid a visit to Ochanshrine yesterday," he said.

Leal set down his spoon. "And?"

"According to Osraed Eadmund, he entered the Shrine and displayed some interest in the Stone."

"Interest?" Leal shrugged. "He's an unbeliever. What interest could he possibly have in it, other than as a means of coronation?"

"He didn't mention a coronation, at least not in Eadmund's hearing. He did express concern that the Crystal seemed . . . lifeless, dark. He evidently regards it as a powerful talisman, regardless of his disbelief in its spiritual significance."

"But that . . . " Leal shook his head. "That's *good* . . . isn't it?"

Fhada made a wry face. "I'm not sure. Whether he believes in the Stone may not be so critical as that he knows *we* believe in it. Eadmund said the Abbod seemed distressed over Feich's interest in the Stone. Perhaps he also sees the possibilities inherent in the situation."

"You mean, that Feich might contrive to use our belief against us—the way he did with Cyne Colfre. The Stone could . . . could become his hostage." Lealbhallain found it suddenly difficult to breathe. "Eadmund said Osraed Ladhar seemed distressed. . . . Surely he can be counted on to protect the Stone."

"Can he? Can we be sure of that?" Fhada left his stool and moved to dispose of his cold tea. He poured himself another cup from the eternally steaming pot on the stove. "Ladhar went with Feich to Halig-liath in pursuit of Taminy. He's a politically astute man. He knows what his presence at Feich's side implies: That the Osraed are acknowledging Feich's right to be where he is—ensconced in Mertuile. Leading what's left of the Cyne's forces. Placing the Chalice on his battle standard."

Leal glanced down at his cooling porridge. It no longer seemed appetizing. "I must believe that what binds Ladhar to Feich is a shared hatred of Taminy. A—a desire for order. If Ladhar is not acting out of loyalty to the Covenant—as he perceives it—" If. That hardly bore thinking about. "Might Osraed Eadmund be able to determine where the Abbod's loyalties lie?"

Fhada shook his head. "I can't ask the Taminist brethren at Ochanshrine to place their lives in jeopardy. Their very presence there puts them in enough danger. Ladhar already views Eadmund as a weak brother. If he hadn't been a member of the Osraed Council, and if the Osraed at Ochanshrine weren't suddenly so loathe to look each other in the eye, he wouldn't have lasted this long. The others are too junior to draw any interest. In pressing for such information, they could very likely reveal their loyalties."

Leal nodded. "And leave us with no contacts inside the Abbis. We must get to Ladhar, Fhada. There must be some way to get to him."

Fhada smiled wryly. "I'm too well known there. You might walk up to the gates in your ritual robes and hope to pass without comment, except for that Kiss." He glanced pointedly at the bright golden star on Lealbhallain's brow. "Even drabbed, the color would give you away."

"Still, Siusan's theatrical cosmetics do a good enough job at most times. As long as no one challenged me . . . "

"Good enough to go about in the street, perhaps. But to enter Ochanshrine? Eadmund says they're checking visitors very carefully at the gate. However . . . if we were to, say, bump into the Abbod while he was about in Creiddylad . . . "

Leal sat up straight. "That's it, then. Eadmund can let us know when he leaves—"

"We won't see Eadmund for three days."

"Then we must call to him in some way."

Fhada raised his brows. "Infiltrate his dreams?"

"Why not?"

Fhada came back to the table and sat down next to Leal, eyes intent on the boy's face. "Do you think you could?"

"*Together*, I know we could. We were able to Weave a connection to Osraed Bevol."

Fhada shook his head. "Bevol was a giant among Osraed. His Gift was as bright and strong as the day it was given. He had knowledge neither we nor Eadmund possess."

"Have you looked at yourself in the mirror lately, Osraed? Your Kiss is as bright as a moon. And Eadmund is also a believer." Fhada made a wry face, causing Leal to wriggle forward on his stool. "Look, Fhada, if we didn't have the capacity to Speakweave, Taminy wouldn't be sending us someone to help us discipline ourselves to do it. No amount of discipline can make up for a nonexistent Gift. We may be weak, but we're not impotent."

"All right, all right. Supposing we could reach Eadmund and either summon him here, or indicate what we want him to do. How does he tell us what we need to know— when Ladhar leaves, where he plans to go?"

Leal was fairly hopping up and down on his stool. "He can come here, he can Weave a reply, he can . . . run up a flag or send pigeons. It doesn't matter how he gets us the information; that's up to him. He's a *believer*, Fhada, in the Meri—in Taminy. I think—no, I *know*—that bestows real power."

Fhada's brow furrowed.

"Have you forgotten how it was in the Great Hall that day? Have you forgotten the—the blazing light, the sheer power of *these*?" He opened his left hand, and the *gytha* in his palm gleamed.

"But that was all *her* doing, Leal. We had no part in that."

Leal clutched his friend's sleeve, leaf-green eyes gleaming no less brightly than his *gytha*. "No, you're wrong, Fhada. We *did* have a part in it. We were channels. Imperfect, but usable. *That's* what she's trying to teach us, don't you see? That we really do have the Gift, and that there's more to it than we dared dream. We may need training to use it fully but, Fhada, it's there to use."

Fhada looked down at the hand on his sleeve. After a moment, he met Leal's eyes. "Well," he said, "I don't suppose it would hurt to try."

It was dark yet, and a chill, damp wind twisted the Claeg banner around and around its standard, making the standard-bearer curse and his horse dance nervously over the flagstones of Hrofceaster's main courtyard. It was going to be a grey day—colorless—and that suited Aine-mac-Lorimer just fine. A bright flower or a ray of sunlight would have thrown her into a fury; she wanted the weather to agree with her mood. Only that agreement kept the fury under control.

Damn Wyth Arundel, anyway! Not even offering a word of regret or argument at her leaving. Not that he should be expected to argue with Taminy, but he might have uttered a gasp of protest, a moan of disappointment. But no. "You'll want them to leave with the Claeg, then." Like she was a piece of mail, a bit of baggage, a—a *nothing*!

And she'd been stupid enough to think he looked wistful when Taminy first made the announcement—no, the request. A request she had no choice but to honor. Taminy's requests were like that.

Catching the rebellious tenor of her thoughts, Aine blanched. Not that she begrudged Taminy *anything*. She'd go to the ends of the earth for her. Die for her, if necessary. It was just so humiliating to think that Wyth thought so little of her. . . .

She was going to go to futile tears in a moment and prayed for something to save her from that. "Something" turned out to be the strong sensation that someone was watching her. She raised her eyes. Standing not ten feet away was a young man in Claeg colors holding a large, fractious horse by its bridle. He was regarding her with the most brazen, bald, humiliating directness. Though he was obviously eight or ten years her senior, she returned the look with equal brass, her face flaming.

He smiled. It was a harsh smile, not at all friendly or welcoming. "That's quite a shade of red, cailin," he said. "You'll be hard put to hide in Creiddylad."

He meant her hair, of course, although her face was by now a near match for it. Furious, Aine strode right up to him and peered into his eyes. They were peculiar eyes—as colorless as the morning, if not quite as chill. Camouflage. He thought he could hide behind them. *Odd thought.* She tossed it aside and said, "I'll thank you to keep your opinions to yourself, sir. And I'll have you know I'll do no hiding in Creiddylad."

"Oooh, brave words, little one. I'll remind you of them when you're quaking beneath your bed some night."

"I don't quake," Aine said, which was a lie, because she was quaking now, albeit with indignation. "And I don't hide. And I wouldn't have you within twenty miles of my bed!"

It took Aine only a second to realize how that must have sounded to her adversary. Though the realization came only because she could suddenly read the trickle of wry humor that oozed from him. Her face felt absolutely scalded.

The young man made an odd clicking sound with his tongue. It put her in mind of a fox smacking its chops over a fat young hen. "My, my!" he murmured. "An outraged virgin. My first. No need to worry, firepot, I value experience above sport."

"Sport!" Aine clenched her fists hard enough to drive her nails into her palms. "You're beyond luck I don't know an inyx for making a man's tongue drop out of his head. But I do know who to give tell to of your cheek. I'll tell The Claeg."

"Oh? And what will you tell him?"

"That one of his men was rude, insulting, mocking—"

"Cavalier? Insolent?" He was chuckling openly now.

"You won't laugh when he bastes you for it."

"Ouch! That sounds rough. I've never been basted."

"Well, then, it'll be a new experience for you. I hear you value experience." She turned on her heel (and gracefully too, she thought) and marched to where Iobert Claeg was preparing to mount his horse.

She hadn't a chance to reach him before the whole column mounted and began to swing into line. She was ushered to her own horse, where Taminy and Iseabal and a knot of well-wishers waited to exchange good-byes. Then she was whisked into tearful embraces, loaded with small gifts to put in her pack, patted on the back, kissed on the cheek. Eventually, she fetched up before Taminy, who took her hands and met her eyes and made the rest of the universe disappear entirely.

"This is not good-bye, Aine," she said. "Don't ever believe it is. And when you're in Creiddylad, don't ever believe there's a thing you can't do. Promise me, Aine. Promise me never to say, 'I can't.'"

Of all the things she could have asked. . . . "I . . . of course, I promise."

Taminy smiled and all of Aine's anguish and anger at leaving evaporated like dew in the sun. "I love you," Taminy said and Aine poured herself into her Mistress's arms.

"I love you," she murmured close to her ear, "Take care of Wyth."

Taminy chuckled. "Wyth thinks he's supposed to take care of *me*."

In mere moments Aine was mounted and riding next to Iseabal behind Iobert Claeg. They'd just cleared the gates and begun the short descent into Airdnasheen when she remembered that there were words she must have with the Claeg Chieftain. She gave her horse the heel and came level with him.

"Pardon, sir, but may I speak to you for a moment?"

The cloud-belly eyes moved to assess her. She seemed to please them, for the great man smiled at her and nodded for her to continue.

"As we prepared to leave, one of your men offered the direst insult."

The Claeg's glower was like the sudden assault of a gale force wind. "What insult?"

"Well sir he—" Now that she'd gotten this far, she was suddenly at a loss. What exactly had he said? "First, he ridiculed the color of my hair which, as you can see, is a rather . . . forceful shade of red."

The glower lightened and he eyed that feature respectfully; long streamers of it had escaped Aine's cowl and jigged about her head. "Oh, aye," he agreed. "That it is."

"Then, he accused me of cowardice—implying that I was going to Creiddylad to hide. Sir, I am no coward."

The Claeg nodded, his face smoothing further. "No. Apparently not."

"And finally, he— I hardly know how to put it into words, sir. He impugned my—my maidenhood and made ribald comments about—about experience and . . . and sport."

The storm was back. "Sport? Who spoke to you like this? Point him out to me! By the Meri's Kiss, if we have to go through every man in this column—"

Aine turned in her saddle, peering over her left shoulder at the double rows of horsemen. It hadn't occurred to her that she'd have to sort through every man here. She met Iseabal's startled eyes for a moment.

What are you doing? The thought was as clear as if the other girl had spoken it.

Aine turned back round and swung her gaze over to

the right. Seated on the horse flanking hers was the man with the colorless eyes. The wry grin that passed for a smile was still smugly in place. "Why it's him!" said Aine and pointed as dramatically as she could.

When she looked back at Iobert Claeg, his face was a-flicker with warring emotions: fury, exasperation, resignation.

"Cailin, what you say about this fellow doesn't surprise me. He is rude, unpleasant, stubborn, impudent, vulgar and mouthy. But since he is also my nephew, I suppose I must forgive him those things. I only hope you can find it in your heart to do the same."

Aine whirled on the elder Claeg. "Your nephew?"

"Aye. That's Saefren Claeg, my field Marschal."

"But he—he called me a *firepot!*"

Saefren Claeg's grin dug further in to Aine's ego. "Well, Uncle did say I was mouthy. When you know me better, you'll appreciate that that's one of my better qualities."

Aine's anger turned cold in her breast. "I've no doubt I would, *if* I was to get to know you better—which I won't." She turned her horse back and made her way to several mounted pairs deep in the column, her face burning so hot even the icy wind couldn't cool it. Iseabal joined her a moment later, eyes enormous.

"What was that all about? Did Saefren Claeg really say those terrible things to you?"

"Of course he did, Isha." She raised her hand, baring the *gytha* on the palm. "Do you imagine I'd lie? Only I can't believe The Claeg, defending him like that!"

"Now, Aine, he didn't actually *defend* him. He merely asked you to forgive him. Besides, look—" She nodded toward the head of the column where Iobert and Saefren Claeg rode side by side.

The Chieftain's face looked like the dark side of hell and he was apparently giving his kinsman a severe tongue lashing. Although the younger man's mouth popped open once or twice, it formed no words and finally he spurred his horse and trotted ahead.

Aine smiled. *Well, Saefren Claeg. Now you do know what it feels like to be basted.*

✧   ✧   ✧

The tiny, lightless world reeled and jigged and creaked like a boat with a drunken helmsman. Within, in a cocoon of wool and fur, Airleas rattled back and forth, up and down; rolled this way and that. Fleece tickled his nose; the tiny burrs in it itched. A late clipping, indeed. The entire fabric of early autumn was imbedded in it.

At least he was warm—too warm. The only part of him that was not over-heated by now was his sense of adventure. That had been replaced by fatigue from the constant swaying and bouncing and trying to lie still in a world that refused to *be* still. How long, he wondered, must he lie here beneath this freight of pathetic Hillwild produce before it would be safe to emerge? How far must they go before turning back became impossible? He had no way of knowing how long he'd already been here; he'd certainly have to count in something other than conventional time: five thousand bumps, four hundred jostles and fifty-seven full-on bounces. Oh, at *least* that long.

Of course it would be best to wait until nightfall before he took a chance on showing himself. He imagined slipping from the narrow covered wagon into scattered firelight, his soft-shod feet silent as a catamount's on the chill rock of Baenn-an-ratha, his eyes scanning the huddled groups of men hard at their eating and drinking and storytelling. He'd smell the food cooking, and hungry, would sneak along the line of horses—closer, closer to one of the firelit groups. The group that would contain Aine and Iseabal would be the smallest, the easiest to draw close to. Few of Iobert Claeg's men would want to be near them. Those who were believers in the Osmaer would be too respectful of them to intrude, unbelievers would want to avoid close contact. Either way, who'd want to have his brains picked over by those two? They would be practically alone with Saefren and The Claeg, himself.

He pictured the place; how Aine would sit huddled and pouting and Iseabal would be gandering all about trying to see the mountains in the dark. Iobert and Saefren would be rapt in warrior's conversation. And he'd sneak up to their fire and snag himself some supper.

His stomach uttered a pathetic whimper at that, then, when he mentally shushed it, gave forth with a solid growl of discontent. He froze for a moment, wondering if the driver could hear it, then laughed at himself. Whatever else he was, he was also well-insulated . . . and hungry . . . and bored. Stiff. And sleepy. Very sleepy.

He tried to take a deep breath of the musky, stifling air, but found it a chore. His breathing would be shallower if he slept. Perhaps he should indulge his growing drowsiness.

He'd all but given in to the idea when it occurred to him to wonder exactly how shallow his breathing would become in this increasingly rancid little tomb. Tomb. Oh, he didn't like the sound of that at all. Was it possible he was too well insulated? Was he in danger of running out of air? Suffocating?

Adrenaline careened through his veins making them icy as a sled run. He gasped, pushed against the weight of the hides and pelts and bundles of fleece that lay over and around him. Hands and feet, arms and legs, all thrashed in discordant harmony, achieving little but to wind him.

Stop it, Airleas, he told himself fiercely. *You're only making things worse. Don't panic. Breathe calmly. Here, the Peaceful Duan. That's what's needed. Sing.*

He called the duan to mind, letting the music float through his head—tranquil enough to soothe, spritely enough not to induce sleep. A walking rhythm, Taminy had said. A rhythm that would set pace for the blood and the spirit.

His heart picked up the rhythm of the duan, his breath filed in and out in an orderly march. Calmer now, he pushed upward against the hemming pelts with both hands. He was curled half on his side, making his efforts awkward, and something seemed to have fallen across the top of his sheltering crate. No matter how he tried, he could not lift the cargo from his body.

Damn and damn. He chided himself for being so stupid

as to stow away in an enclosed space. He hardly deserved
to be Cyne of Caraid-land if he couldn't think more sharply
than that. Now he was stuck and there would be no sneaking
around campfires to cadge supper from the unawares.
There would be no victorious moment of revelation when
the caravan reached the point of no return.

Airleas tried to calculate how long it would take to reach
Nairne, where they might be expected to unload the cargo.
The journey up Baenn-an-ratha took the better part of a
week; surely they'd move faster on the way down. But how
fast? And once in the foothills, how long to reach Nairne?
He'd starve to death or die of thirst before then.

It occurred to him, belatedly, that this entire adventure
was lame-brained. He was still a boy—a child. And he was
only Airleas, not Bearach Spearman. Unlike his distant fore-
bear, he'd been raised gently. His father's domain hadn't
been torn by insurrection and unease. He hadn't been
trained for battle or schooled in wiliness. He knew of those
things only what he'd read in the histories. If he'd stayed
put, he might've been taught how to fight, lead an army,
regain his throne. Catahn could have taught him those
things—turned him into a Cyne worthy of the title.

And worst of all—*worst*—he'd disobeyed Taminy.
Shrugged out from under her tutelage as if it were a burden he could do without. Well, he couldn't do without it.
More than the use of a sword, he needed to learn the use
of his mind, the use of his *aidan*.

All that would be academic if he couldn't get out of
here.

He thought for a moment about his predicament. Perhaps there were ways other than the physical to lift the
weight above him. He conjured to mind the image of a
pair of fiery hands—No, not fiery! God's grace! He'd burn
himself alive! Iron hands, strong, mighty. They took hold
of the fleeces and furs and whatever lay above them and
lifted . . . lifted . . . *lifted*.

The load lightened measurably. Airleas concentrated
harder. *Lift and throw. Lift and throw.* Lighter, still, grew
the suffocating heap and in a corner of Airleas's mind a

small boy jumped up and down with glee. Wait till he told Taminy what he'd done—how he'd saved himself from—

The pile collapsed, stunning the breath from his lungs. For a moment, he was poised to begin another physical struggle, but regained control of himself before he did something so stupid. He silently hummed the Peace Duan again, slowing his rebellious heart and steadying his breathing.

If only he could signal someone that he was here, make a noise, make—a *Speakweave*. He chewed his lip, considering that. His imagination supplied him with the humiliation he would suffer to be found huddled—no, trapped—beneath this pile of burr-infested stuff, looking supremely un-Cyne-like. Well, and who would he call? He was surrounded by giftless Claeg; his only chance was to reach Isha or Aine.

He sneezed just then, his nose tickled by a wad of fleece, and found the regaining of his breath difficult. Spurred by fear, he formed a cry of distress. Pride modified it. The finished Speakweave was much more dignified than his reflexive yelp for assistance, but urgent, nonetheless.

Inside his increasingly muzzy head, a time-piece marked the seconds—five bumps, now seven, and uncounted jostles. Dear God, would no one sense him? Were Aine and Iseabal as dense as these ungifted ones?

He was at the point of giving up when the wagon stopped its mad jostling. He all but held his breath in anticipation, celebrated wildly when he felt the thing rock gently, when he sensed the presence of another person. Only when the weight above him began to lift, did he school himself to calm. By the time the last layer of hides came off, he was, he thought, suitably unruffled-looking.

A stranger's face peered down into his. "God-the-Spirit! It's a boy!"

Hands reached in to pull him up into the cold air—air that smelled strongly of moist wood and dust and tanning herbs. Behind the Claeg kinsman's cowled head, a halo of grey light marked the entry of the small, hide covered drey. In a moment he was being hauled toward that opening, stunned by the realization that this oaf didn't know who he was.

"Let go of me, you clod! Where's Aine and Iseabal? Where's The Claeg?"

"At the head of the column, if it's any business of yours, scrap," the clod replied and lifted Airleas clear of the wagon to dump him unceremoniously overboard.

He landed on all fours on the damp earth, but was quick to regain his feet. A circle of Claeg faces peered at him from beneath cowls and caps, the wind that sucked Airleas's breath away in misty streamers, nipping at any untucked edges of cloth. The man who'd evicted him from his hiding place crunched to the ground behind him.

"By the Cleft Rock, Brunan," exclaimed one of the onlookers, "what've you got here? A stowaway?"

"What you've got," said Airleas, "is the Cyneric of Caraidland."

"A stowaway, indeed," said Brunan. "Oddest thing, you know. I just got this sudden feeling that there was something amiss. It was like—like a voice whispered in my ear that if I looked, I'd find a stowaway in my wagon."

"I'm not a stowaway," Airleas insisted. "I'm Airleas Malcuim."

"Oh, aye," said his rescuer, "and I'm the Ren Catahn in disguise." He winked.

Furiously reining in his temper, Airleas pulled the glove from his left hand and raised his palm to them. Their reactions to the *gytha* were mixed, but gratifying; one man simply walked away, another retreated a step while his neighbor came forward, face screwed up in awe. There were gasps of amazement, finger signs made to ward off any possible evil. Behind him Brunan leaned about to see what had his comrades so addled and swore under his breath.

Airleas glanced up at him. "Well, Ren Catahn," he said. "Do you believe me now?"

The man stammered. "I—I—"

"Happens you should believe him," said a voice from just beyond the circle of onlookers and Iobert Claeg strode through his men with Aine and Iseabal in his tracks.

"Airleas!" Iseabal reached him first, taking him in a fervent embrace, while Aine stood back, scowling her disapproval. "Airleas, whatever are you doing here? You're supposed to be back in Hrofceaster with Taminy."

Airleas sighed. She would state the obvious. "I was trying to get to Creiddylad to—"

"To avenge your father." The new voice, immediately recognizable to the young Malcuim, came from the back trail.

Everyone turned. Astride a red roan horse, the slight figure swaddled in green seemed impervious to the wind. She rode forward, the folds of her cowled cape stirring only slightly.

"Osmaer!" Iobert Claeg dropped to one knee before her, while Aine and Iseabal sprouted smiles that cut the grey day like spears of light.

The Claeg men reacted as they had to the sight of Airleas's *gytha*; repulsed or drawn, awe-struck or fearful. One young warrior moved surreptitiously to place a tentative hand on the roan's steaming flank as if by so doing he could receive a benediction from its rider. As if she sensed the gesture, Taminy looked down at him and smiled. Airleas was sure the young man must've nearly swooned. He remembered what he'd felt the first time those green eyes had caught him unawares.

Foul luck. No, not luck, he realized as Taminy continued to regard him. He came forward to stand before her, head bent, hands busy with a loose close on his coat. "You knew all along, didn't you? You knew I meant to leave Hrofceaster."

"Aye. So did Gwynet. You put her in a terrible dilemma, you know. She wasn't sure whether to tell Catahn on you or not. But then, of course she realized I must know too."

Airleas looked up at her, puzzled. "But you let me come. Why?"

Taminy tilted her head and the Kiss on her brow gleamed in the semi-dark beneath her cowl. "Tell me, Cyneric Airleas, what was your opinion of your adventure when you embarked on it?"

"I thought it was . . . necessary." He squared his shoulders and lifted his head. "I thought I must do it. That it was the brave thing to do. The—the thing any Malcuim would do. *Should* do."

Taminy nodded. "You thought to prove yourself. To be a true Malcuim, worthy of the throne of Caraid-land."

"Aye," Airleas mumbled, melting beneath her eyes. The murmurs of approval from the warriors around him meant nothing now. Only hours ago they would have been musical—magical.

"And what do you think now?"

Airleas sighed deeply. Galling, this was, to admit this before men who, in his daydreams, marched behind him into battle. "I committed an error in judgment, Mistress. I proved nothing but my own lack of forethought and wisdom."

"And what do you think of your adventure?"

"It wasn't adventure; it was folly." He dared to raise his eyes again. "I have much to learn about being Cyneric Airleas Malcuim."

"That is why I let you come."

Airleas's world became suddenly very still. His breath stuck in his throat, hope and humiliation struggled in his heart, and on some barely palpable level, he felt his hushed soul expand. A smile twitched the corner of his mouth; despair tugged it down again. He found he had nothing to say except, "I'm sorry, Mistress."

"I know," she answered him and turned her beautiful face away from him to Iobert Claeg. "We'll be going now, Chieftain. I don't want to slow your progress. Meri's grace to you, sir." She raised her hand. The *gytha* showed clearly in her palm. Claeg's men murmured, eyes wide.

Taminy crooked a finger then, and the circling watchers made way for a second, riderless horse to pass among them. It was Airleas's own mare, Shena. He mounted in silence and, pushing back through the assembled warriors, clattered up the trail toward Airdnasheen. Behind him, he vaguely heard Taminy give her blessings and good-byes to The Claeg and her two other *waljan*.

He was on the verge of kicking his horse into a dangerous gallop when she caught hold of his mind, bidding him wait for her. He hesitated, then obeyed, knowing that anything short of obedience would be fruitless and stupid.

He felt her close regard of him all the way back to the holt. Was this what it was to be a Malcuim? he wondered. Was this what his father had been as a boy—a stew of angers and vanities and false bravery? Was the essence of the Malcuim a rebellious soul? A soul only humiliation could impress for good or ill? A soul that could be led about by its own pride?

"I don't want to be like my father," he said to the silence of the trail.

Taminy's hand lit on his shoulder, fanning a strange Eibhilin warmth through his body. "Many people will be eager to tell you that you are your father's son. But don't mistake that to mean you are your father's *likeness*. You are not."

Airleas flipped the reins against his horse's neck. "I look just like him. *Just* like him. Even mother says so."

"Appearances are deceiving. Colfre Malcuim may have shaped your body and your face, but Toireasa has done more to mold your heart and mind. And your soul has a shape of its own that no man or woman in this world can mold."

"Except you, right, Taminy? You can mold it, can't you?" He was desperate to believe that.

She shook her head. "Only you, Airleas. Only you can mold the contours of your own soul."

Well, now there was an unsettling thought. Airleas let himself back into the rhythm of his mare's stride and rode to Hrofceaster in silence.

Saefren Claeg stretched out on his bedroll, his eyes on the leather satchel his uncle had settled gently on the ground-cover of their tent. "The Lady's talismans?"

Iobert nodded. "Aye."

"What are they?"

In answer, the elder Claeg pushed the satchel toward

his nephew. "Open it," he said, and lowered himself to his own bedroll.

Saefren tried not to appear over-eager as he picked up the satchel and flipped back the flap. Inside were a number of soft, dunnish leather scrolls tied at both ends with twine. Curious, he removed one and turned it in his hand. Painted on or pressed into the outer surface of the scroll, roughly at its center was the Gilleas crest—a white star on an irregular field of purple. Inside was a small, hard lump.

He raised questioning eyes to his uncle's impassive face. "What are they?"

"The scrolls are messages. As to what's inside . . . " He shrugged.

"You didn't ask?"

"Why should I? I'm not among those who need to see such talismans."

And damn proud of it. "May I look?"

Iobert seemed poised for a sharp retort, then merely shrugged again. "Aye, if you must."

Saefren untied the twine at one end of the scroll and parted the soft folds. Light from the tent's single lamp glittered on something within. "It's a shard of crystal!" When Iobert said nothing, he opened the scroll further. "There's nothing on it. This scroll is empty." He shook his head, incredulous. "You said they were letters."

"I said they were messages."

"That say nothing."

"To you, perhaps."

Saefren laughed, letting a bit of his scorn escape. "And for these you'd have us travel miles out of our way—to put an empty skin and a chip of rock into the hands of the Gilleas?"

"We'll not go out of our way."

"Uncle, the Gilleas holdings are well away to the northeast—"

"I know where the Gilleas holdings are, nephew. We shall not be troubled to go there. The Gilleas will meet us in Nairne."

Saefren was dumbfounded. "How can you know that?"

"Taminy said he would be there. He and his elders."

Saefren held up the scroll. "To receive a blank message."

His uncle rolled onto his side. "Put that away carefully," he said, and closed his eyes.

Exasperated, Saefren could only stare at him. A moment later, one frosty grey eye opened. "And put out the lamp. Makes it hard for a body to sleep."

Saefren did as ordered, hoping he'd be around to see the Gilleas Chieftain's face when he opened his talisman.

CHAPTER 5

The World of Form and Shadow is set about by the direst of afflictions and the sorest of trials. It wastes away of its disease while those who hold power in their hands seek to treat its ills by their own devices. Yet, they are unable to fathom the cause of the disease and can only guess at its remedy. Only the Divine Healer can cure this patient, but these jealous doctors have imagined that Friend to be an Enemy.

—From the Testament of Osraed Bevol

✧   ✧   ✧

"A distant ally is better than no ally at all."

Ruadh Feich raised his finger from the map and looked his cousin Daimhin in the eye. "You think so, do you? It will take weeks for the Teallach to assemble even a token force and get them here."

"Then we can march on Halig-liath in four days with Malcuim regulars, our own men and the Dearg's. The Teallach can meet us there in two weeks—one and a half if the weather holds and the rivers aren't too high."

"Ah." The younger Feich traced the march between the Teallach lands northeast of the port of Eada and the foothill village of Nairne. "That's always supposing they don't have to take the long way around through the midlands."

"Now, why on earth should they have to do something like that? Surely it's more expedient to cut directly through the hills."

Ruadh's finger lit solidly on a green-tinted cluster of mounds just south of the lands held by the House Teallach.

It sat squarely in the line of march he'd traced the moment before. "You forget the Cuillean. Intelligence suggests they've shown support of the Taminists. They're unlikely to let a large force of our allies cross their lands unremarked."

Daimhin sat back in his chair and tried to look more relaxed than he felt. He was damned tired of this sitting around, waiting for the Houses he had been romancing to come into the fold—the Malcuim fold, he told them, hoping they would believe him. Some did. Some didn't. The Chieftain of the House Gilleas had told him flat out that he thought Daimhin Feich's demonstrative love of his dead Cyne was a sham and that Airleas Malcuim in any Feich's hands was as good as dead. He'd been uncertain if he wanted to return a Malcuim to the Throne of Caraid-land; he'd been damn certain he'd not help to put a Feich there.

Anarchy. A return to the days when the Houses fought, each for its own piece of the land. That was what Daimhin Feich faced if he could not get Airleas Malcuim back to Mertuile—and soon.

"What do you suggest, then, Ruadh?" he asked.

The younger man drew himself up, looking every inch the young Marschal, every inch a Feich. Daimhin was as proud of him as he might be of his own son, had he a legitimate one.

"I propose," said Ruadh, "that we meet the Teallach forces just south of Cuinn Holding, between the Ead-Tyne and the Bebhinn. That'll take them two weeks the long way round—southwest and up the Ead. And this I believe they should do to avoid confronting the Cuillean and the Gilleas. We'll march our own forces up the Tuine side of the Halig-Tyne and cut a wide sweep around Nairne so as not to arouse any notice from that quarter. When we've amassed our army, we split it in two; one half seals off Nairne, the other half lays siege to Halig-liath."

"Siege."

"Aye."

"And how long do you think that'll last?"

"As long as it takes to force capitulation."

"How, force capitulation?"

Ruadh shrugged. "How long can they last sealed off from the town? When they run out of food, water—"

Daimhin smiled. "Cousin, you underestimate our persuasive power. With an entire town of innocent hostages at our disposal, the siege will last only until the first cailin screams. But . . . " Daimhin Feich held up his hand. "That will be only our contingency plan. I've my reasons for wanting to take Halig-liath in honest combat." He came forward in his chair, breath quickening. "There is a great symbology in breaching that sacred wall, Ruadh. Don't underestimate it. Halig-liath as an institution is legendary. The man who takes it . . . " His sword hand clenched and he paused to savor the sensations tightening his jaw and burning in his breast. "The man who takes it and subjugates it, subjugates the religion it represents."

Ruadh faded back from the table, an odd expression in his eyes. "*Our* religion, too, cousin. It is not the sole property of the Osraed you so detest."

"Well, of course! That's exactly it, don't you see? I want to take the Faith of the Meri out of Osraed hands and put it into the hands of the people. And for that reason, I believe we must be able to take Halig-liath by force. We'll lay siege only until we can penetrate its defenses."

Ruadh snorted. "Tell me, when we were at Halig-liath last, did you notice the blackened areas on either side of the main gates?"

"Aye, I did that."

"Do you know how they came to be there?"

Daimhin was wary of his young cousin when he was in one of his professorial moods. Ruadh often forced him to reveal that his own knowledge of military history was lacking. "Not precisely. But I suppose you're going to tell me somebody tried to take them out with explosives or some such."

"Diomasach Claeg, to be precise. He trailed Cwen Goscelyn there after she absconded with little Thearl, and attempted, vainly, to blow up the front gates of Halig-liath . . . " He glanced at Daimhin significantly. " . . . after the dear Cwen dropped the portcullis on 'im. The wood is oak, reinforced with straps and rods of steel. Impenetrable."

Daimhin sucked the inside of his cheek. Bugger the brat for reminding him how cleanly and unintentionally he'd repeated history with his own unsuccessful doings at Haligliath. "That was nearly two hundred years ago, cousin. Weapons technology has improved a great deal since then. Even I know that." He leaned across table and map, pale eyes glinting with zeal. "I propose to use a new type of cannon with *exploding ordnance*."

Again Ruadh snorted derisively. "And where do you propose to come by such a weapon?"

"The Deasach."

"The Deasach?" Ruadh repeated. "You've continued Colfre's negotiations with them?"

"I have."

"Trusting of you to tell me."

"Trust had nothing to do with it. Expediency was all. You have your work; I have mine. No reason for you to become distracted from yours. Anyway, I'm telling you now. There has been a Deasach commission in Creiddylad since spring. You may have noticed them at Colfre's funeral." Ruadh nodded and his cousin continued. "My intentions toward them are somewhat different than our dear departed Cyne, however. He was looking for weaknesses in them, something he could exploit with an eye to conquest."

Ruadh's eyes nearly popped out of his head. "Colfre? Colfre Malcuim, Peacemaker? The Dove of Mertuile? You scandalize me. I'd suspect you of such manipulations, but not Colfre."

Daimhin inclined his head. "Thank you, so much, for your vote of confidence. As it happens, I disagreed violently with Colfre's intentions toward the Deasach. I find their strengths much more interesting than their weaknesses. They have, as I mentioned, some very progressive military resources. They also have mineral resources and agricultural products we don't. On the other side of the coin, they would like expanded access to our fishing waters and our markets."

"Ah, a bargaining chip."

Daimhin smiled and let himself be distracted by a luxurious heat that tickled his bowels. "Oh, there's more. The Deasach are a perverse lot. They have no Cyne. All my meetings, indeed, all of Colfre's meetings were with a gentleman known as a Mediator. He is the representative of a sovereign *female* ruler."

Ruadh gaped. "A sovereign Cwen?"

"They call her a Banarigh—literally, 'a woman ruler.'"

Ruadh's brows drew together. "'Bana,' that's a Hillwild word, isn't it?"

"Indeed. Makes you wonder, doesn't it? At any rate. I'm of the thought that my face-to-face meeting with this important lady must be accomplished in the near future."

"You'd go there? To the Suderlands? Cousin, that's taking an awful chance."

"Of what? Do you imagine that there are monsters behind their rocks and bushes that are not also behind ours?"

Ruadh flushed as if that was exactly what he imagined. "Of course not. It's just that, well, we know so little about them."

"I know that the Banarigh is a woman. Her Mediator describes her as a 'mature' woman. I reckon that puts her between the ages of thirty and sixty. He says she's a beauty, although what that means to a Deasach may be something incomprehensible to us. Frankly, I don't care whether she's a beauty or as ugly as the backside of a pig. She's female, and that means she will ultimately succumb to flattery and charm."

Ruadh puckered his lips. "Oh. The way the Wicke Cwen succumbed?"

Anger, swift and black, rose from Daimhin Feich's belly and threatened to overwhelm him. He forced his hands around the arms of his chair so they would not fasten upon Ruadh's young neck or shake as they so desperately wanted to do. "Taminy-a-Cuinn is not a woman," he murmured. "She is a demon, spawned in chill hell. She has a stone for a heart and ice in her belly."

Ruadh whistled. "Dear cousin, such passion! Was it her you dreamed of the night you nearly set your rooms on fire?"

Daimhin twitched. He'd nearly forgotten. Oh, not the dream—he'd never forget that, for he'd written it down on waking—but the overturned lamp . . . "What do you know about it?"

"I'm the one who heard you screaming your lungs out, remember? What *were* you dreaming about? Or won't you tell?"

"It was a simple nightmare. I . . . I dreamed I fell from my horse during a hunt."

Ruadh shrugged. "Yes, well, if I were you, cousin, I'd remove anything breakable, flammable or sharp from the vicinity of my bed."

"I'll do that. Now, are we agreed on a course of action?"

Ruadh eyed him. "You want me to gather our forces for the march?"

"Aye. And I want the Teallach summoned. I'll let you draft the message to them. Please be diplomatic. Have their liaison send it out immediately. And tell him to use his fleetest pigeon."

"What about your Deasach cannon?"

"I'll speak to the Mediator about it today. If it must come to us later, that's fine. Halig-liath will fall. One way or another."

He meant to go to the Deasach Mediator straight away, but with Ruadh gone, Daimhin Feich found himself lethargic. The nightmare still haunted him with its fire and fury. The face in the crystal mocked him. He found himself recalling his visit to the Shrine of Ochan, recalling the way the Crystal's heart had leapt with flame when he drew near.

He suspected it was his presence the Stone reacted to for the old Abbod had clearly been astonished and dismayed at the display. The implications were startling. It suggested his gift for reading people, for moving them, directing their actions, was more than the intuition of a bright mind, more than the homely, utilitarian thing he'd

once believed it to be. Though he'd never even held a
Weaving crystal in his hands, he now felt the flicker of
power within him. The Crystal felt it too. Did the Wicke?

He rose from the long, polished table and wandered
the edge of the carpet it sat upon, tracing the pattern of
braided gold at the perimeter. Was the Osmaer woman
connected to the Osmaer Crystal? Did the little flame he'd
called from the Stone of Ochan, locked within its holy of
holies, find an echo in the heart of the woman barricaded
behind the walls of Halig-liath?

The thought amused him. *The two connected.* And if
he'd summoned that much fire from the Osmaer without
conscious effort, what could he do if he half-tried? A curious
thought, and one worth pursuing. His siege of the sacred
might then take place on two fronts at once.

He met the Deasach Mediator in an elegant private parlor
in Creiddylad's finest Inn. He had invited the man to
Mertuile several times, but had never been able to get
him to do more than pay a brief visit. He supposed it was
the constant threat of mischief at the hands of a displeased
citizenry that kept Loc Llywd from accepting his hospitality. That or the fear that to appear cozy with a Feich
might prove injurious to a relationship with any future
Malcuim Cynes. Those were valid concerns and Daimhin
no longer pressed the issue. He was beginning to feel claus-
trophobic within Mertuile's confines, anyway; any excuse
to leave them was to be anticipated.

Loc Llywd welcomed him cordially, but with a diplomatic reserve that Daimhin found vaguely irritating. He
hated formality; it precluded satisfactory knowledge of the
opposing individual, allowed them to hide behind proto-
col. Only when someone ceased to be that which they represented and became an individual could he really get his
hands on them. Loc Llywd the Taciturn was not likely to
allow that.

They sat at opposite sides of a table made of glowing
cherrywood and laden with little cakes on fine porcelain
and an urn of some hot aromatic beverage Daimhin Feich
had never before tasted.

"We call it *karfa*," Llywd told him in lightly accented Caraidin. "We find it . . . braces the body and sharpens the mind."

Daimhin smiled, lifting his cup. "Always a good idea before negotiations."

"There are really no negotiations to undertake," said Llywd. "I am ready to sign a preliminary trade agreement. I was ready before your Cyne met his unfortunate end. All that stands between El-Deasach and Caraid-land enjoying commerce is the agreement of our respective rulers." He paused and laid upon Daimhin the full weight of his dark gaze. "The rumors about the state of Caraid-land's leadership are disconcerting, to say little. One tale has it that the Malcuim's young heir is dead, another that he turned heretic to your religion and ran to the hills, yet another that he is hiding from someone at court who means to do him the same violence that took his father's life. There are any number of people who believe Caraid-land is now leaderless."

Feich relaxed back into his chair with an effort. "Nothing could be further from the truth."

"And what is the truth, Durweard Feich? Who leads this country?"

"Presently, sir, I do."

"And indefinitely?"

"That is something I am working on. Even as we speak, steps are being undertaken to return a Malcuim Cyne to the Throne of Caraid-land."

"Then—"

"Then the first of the tales is a vicious lie. Airleas Malcuim is not dead. He lives. The second is also untrue. He did not turn heretic. But unfortunately . . . " Daimhin sighed deeply and rose, cup in hand. He moved to the hearth, feeling the heat of flame on his face, the eyes of the Deasach on his back. "Unfortunately his mother did." He turned back to face the Mediator, wearing an expression of great concern. "Cwen Toireasa was seduced from the path of true faith by a dazzling Wicke who convinced her to kidnap her own son and place him in the hands of his enemies."

"A Wicke? A magical being, is this?"

Daimhin nodded. "Magical, yes. A woman. A young woman, beautiful of face and form, hideous in spirit. A woman who Weaves potent magic, confounding even our most learned Osraed. She mesmerized our Cwen. And, Mediator Llywd, I must be honest with you—this creature even laid her infernal hands upon the spirit of the Cyne. He was a broken man when he died—by his own hand, more's the shame. And I, dear God—!" He broke off to draw a tremulous breath and blink suddenly teary eyes at the ceiling where firelight danced with shadow and muted sun-dapples. "I nearly followed him, so great was my own entanglement."

Llywd watched his performance silently, eyes cryptic, sheeny as jets. Only a tightening around the corners of his mouth betrayed any emotion—but there was no such thing as a trivial betrayal. "You say you were embroiled with this—this sorceress?"

Yes, this had been the right gambit, after all. This talk of sorcery and Wicke, this baring of the presumably embarrassing secrets of a younger man's soul—this might drag Loc Llywd from his diplomatic distance. Daimhin raised his head, straightened his back. "I was. I fancied myself in love with her. Mediator, you can have no idea—!" He put the keen of frustrated passion into his voice. "She was so young-looking, so—so fragile and innocent-seeming. I had no idea until it was too late that beneath that facade was an ancient monster. I, who had set out to seduce her— yes, I admit that; believing her to be an innocent seventeen year old girl, I tried to beguile her. But in the end, the seducer was himself seduced. I chose not to follow my Cyne into oblivion, Mediator Llywd. But I understand all too well what drove him there."

Llywd's dark face was unreadable. "You admit much to a stranger, Durweard Feich."

Daimhin returned to his chair and leaned forward in it, every line in his body speaking of urgency. "I admit it in the hope that the stranger will become an ally. Understand me, Loc Llywd. I am a man with a cause. This talk of trade agreements and commerce is—pardon me—but it is irrelevant. Before he died, Colfre Malcuim made me Regent to his absent son." He uttered a bark of mirthless laughter. "He so believed I would bring the child back to him while he lived. But I failed him. I didn't bring Airleas back. The Wicke had so torn the fabric of loyalty in Caraidland that I was unable to raise more than a token force. And at that, I didn't raise it in time. Colfre died bereft. I am sworn to keep my promise to him, Mediator. I have but one duty at this moment: to bring Airleas Malcuim back to Creiddylad and set him before the Stone of Ochan. To place the Circlet upon his head. If I can avenge the death of his father, so much the better, but even that is of less importance than tearing Caraid-land's rightful Cyne out of the grasp of this insidious monster."

"What you are telling me, if I understand you, is that any treaties between our two lands must await the successful return of your . . . Cyneric—that is the correct term?"

Daimhin nodded. "What I am telling you is that any treaties between our two lands is *dependent* upon his return."

Llywd scratched his clean-shaven jaw. "There was a rumor about that you had declared yourself to be Cyneric of Caraid-land."

Daimhin made certain his expression suffered not so much as a facial tic. "There is a provision in the testament of Cyne Colfre to the effect that if, for some compelling reason, Airleas is unable to take up his place on the Throne, I will be next in succession. I did not suggest this provision to the Cyne. It was the recommendation of the Osraed Ladhar, Abbod of Ochanshrine."

"Ah, yes. The rather large *mullih* with the prodigious scowl."

"Pardon?"

Llywd smiled. "No, pardon me. Occasionally, my mind becomes lazy and neglects to reach far enough for the Caraidin term. A 'holy man,' I suspect you would call him."

Daimhin Feich would not call Ladhar that, but there

was no reason Loc Llywd should know it. He merely nodded.

"He is your religious leader, then?"

"Yes, he is. And that is testimony to his spiritual strength, I can tell you. The Wicke struck at the very heart of our religious order, seducing even the most learned, the most devout, then casting them aside when they no longer pleased her."

"She sounds to be extraordinarily powerful, your Wicke. How do you imagine you can defeat her and win back the Cyneric?"

"By making allies of those who can aid me in my cause. The Abbod Ladhar, as I mention, is a man of extreme spiritual power. And there are others who were able to withstand the Wicke's evil." He paused and looked into his half-empty cup. "Then too, we must field superior physical forces. I have among my allies the Houses Dearg and Teallach. I expect that the Skarf and the Madaidh will soon join us."

"And where is the sorceress now?"

"Barricaded in a fortress in the foothills of the Gyldanbaenn."

"Halig-liath," said Llywd and drew a tilt of surprise from Daimhin's brows.

"Yes. You've heard of it?"

"The Holy Fortress? Of course I have heard of it. The place is legendary even on the other side of the mountains. It is said to be impregnable."

Daimhin nodded, letting his mouth droop at the corners—but only the tiniest bit. "Aye. It has proven to be so. And that, Mediator, is one area where an agreement between our respective countries does seem relevant."

Now it was Llywd's turn to display surprise. "You seek a military alliance?"

Feich raised his hands. "Please. I would not be so precipitous or so bold. All I ask—*all*—is that you might lend us one of your great cannon. I am told they fire exploding ordnance. Mediator, such a machine is the only thing I can imagine to be capable of breaching the walls of Halig-liath."

Loc Llywd rose and began a slow circuit of their chairs. "This is important to you, obviously, or you would not admit your own lack of such a weapon."

"We are a peaceful nation, Mediator."

"Yes, well, I once had cause to doubt that. But" —he waved the comment aside— "that is neither up nor down. What is important to us is commerce. Specifically, the opening of Caraidin markets to Deasach goods and the permitting of our ships in your fishing waters. What is our cannon worth in that regard, Regent Feich?"

What indeed? Now that he was faced with the decision, Daimhin Feich was at a loss to know how to respond. It seemed so simple: Yes, he could say, whatever you want, only let me have the cannon. I will blow away the gates of Halig-liath, breach the walls, take the prize. The cannon must be had.

Yet, when he opened his mouth at last, a saner voice came out of it. "We have nothing like this *karfa* of yours, nothing like that red fruit my Cyne was so fond of. I am willing to agree that such foodstuffs as are not grown in Caraid-land may be imported from El-Deasach."

"And the fishing grounds?"

"I will agree that once my cause is complete, I and my . . . The government of Caraid-land will consider your proposals in all earnest. And Mediator, to show that I have no ulterior motives, I also agree to return the cannon to you upon the successful completion, or abject failure, of my mission to return Airleas to the throne."

Llywd favored him once more with that dark, unreadable stare. Daimhin Feich smiled within. The man was not nearly so opaque as he studiously tried to be. That facade was only a detriment to those whose senses ended with the physical.

"We are in agreement, Regent," said Llywd at last. "I shall make arrangement for the immediate importation of the foodstuffs . . . and the weapon."

"And I will make arrangements for a document to be drawn up stating terms. It will be signed by all the appropriate parties, rest assured. I trust that you can work out the details with our Minister of Commerce." Llywd inclined his dark head and

Daimhin rose. "I wish to send some gifts to Banarigh Lilias. Is there anything in particular the lady favors?"

Lòc smiled, for the first time revealing some real emotion. "The Lady Lilias favors anything that displays the craftsman's expertise; a handsome adornment, a splendid piece of clothing, a fine sword. Oh, and horses. The Banarigh is inordinately fond of riding and hunting."

Feich returned the smile. "A woman after my own heart. It sounds as if I can't do wrong by sending her the very things I'd wish for myself."

"Well, Regent, doesn't the Holy Book say that one is not truly faithful to God unless he desires for his brother or sister what he desires for himself?"

Daimhin Feich was once again genuinely surprised. "It does indeed." Odd, too, considering that the Deasach did not even worship the same God. He could only imagine the remark was part of Lòc Llywd's polite diplomacy.

Once safely in his Mertuile-bound carriage, Daimhin could not restrain a chuckle. Here was a man much like himself, then, willing to mock his own faith by pretending to comprehend another's. He began to like Lòc Llywd.

Of the three minds caught in the sudden web of Lealbhallain's Speakweave, he would be hard pressed to decide which was the most surprised by the event. With a jolt like lightning Leal and Fhada made contact with Osraed Eadmund and that poor soul, on his knees in prayer, fell over onto his nose.

It was difficult, but Leal and Fhada were able to create the aislinn images and Eadmund was able to perceive them and comprehend. A miracle, Leal thought. The good Osraed's amazement washed over them again and again with his increased comprehension and he astonished them, as well, by conjuring the image of the Abbod Ladhar at Cyne's Cirke. After some trial and error, Eadmund, by focusing on a simple calendar, was able to make known the critical information: The Abbod Ladhar planned to be at Cyne's Cirke that very day.

❖   ❖   ❖

The sanctuary was silent as the sunlight that fell from its high windows in almost solid beams; pigeons mimed shadow plays behind the leaded panes, voiceless. No noise from the plaza penetrated this far. Even the gears of the old water clock, hidden behind the wall of the nave, were silenced.

It made Leal want to sneeze.

He did not sneeze, however, or cough or make any other inappropriate noise. He could not chance being heard, not chance being seen until he wanted to be. He had been waiting here for hours, easing his impatience by pretending to be back in school taking a test, asking himself questions for which he had to formulate complex answers. It wasn't unbearable, the waiting. He wasn't completely alone, after all; Fhada was at the back of the sanctuary somewhere, also hidden from sight, Weaving his own means of combating boredom.

It was during his fiftieth drill on the course of the Battle of the Crystal that Leal at last sensed movement in the outer corridor. A frisson of anticipation and dread coursed up his spine. In a moment, he knew, he would hear voices, for Abbod Ladhar was not alone. Before he could question his own certainty of that fact, he heard them, seemingly engaged in an argument; Ladhar and another man—a man whose presence generated an odd, prickly heat like . . . like fear.

"He must be either a friend or an enemy, Abbod, he cannot possibly be both." The stranger's voice came from the doorway. Leal would see them only if they progressed down the aisle to the Altar.

Ladhar spoke then—that voice he knew intimately. "Of that I am aware, Caime. He simply will not allow me to divine which. He speaks to me as if I were a partner, a friend, and yet . . . I feel him laughing, mocking. He is the most confusing individual I have ever known."

"He was intensely loyal to Cyne Colfre. I don't doubt returning his heir to the throne is the most important thing in Feich's life. Men so driven can seem . . . confused in their other loyalties."

There was a long, pregnant pause during which Leal could hear only the sharp click of town shoes and the swishing of fabric. In a moment he would see them.

"You set store by his loyalty to his Cyne, do you?" asked Ladhar at last. "You might not if you saw how he manipulated the provision in Colfre's last writ that he be made Cyneric if Airleas should prove irrevocably delinquent. I can't help but wonder if the same wiles went into securing the Regency."

Just within Leal's sight the two stepped up to the Altar and stopped. Recognition of the spare man at the Abbod's side nearly cost Leal his concealment. It was the cleirach who had flown at Taminy with a spear in the Assembly Hall. Leal found a name for him—Minister Cadder. A horrid black heat arose in his breast and his face felt scorched. He would have to do a year's contrite praying to shed the guilt of the thoughts he was having. If there was ever a person Lealbhallain-mac-Mercer wanted to do violence to, it was Minister Caime Cadder.

Those poisonous lips were moving again and the young Osraed in his quiet rage could barely force himself to listen.

"You say he manipulated the Cyne's writ of Regency? Have you proof of this?"

"Proof? Caime, I was there. Feich brought me over from Ochanshrine himself, saying the Cyne was dying. When we arrived at Mertuile, he told me I was needed to witness a writ of Regency. Enroute to the Cyne's salon, Daimhin Feich voiced his fear that Airleas was lost—that even if he could be returned, he might still be under the sway of the Wicke, might never be free of her."

Cadder's already gaunt face somehow managed to look even more sunken. "I pray the child is not yet completely lost, Abbod. He's only a boy. Surely if we get to him in time—"

"Oh, yes, *if*."

"Daimhin Feich was Cyne Colfre's Durweard, more than that, he was a lifetime companion. And given the power of the Wicke, his fears are surely understandable. By God, I know I share them. How do you imagine you were manipulated?"

Abbod Ladhar's porcine face reddened. "I did not *imagine*, Minister Cadder. I was manipulated. Daimhin Feich planted in my mind the idea that another Cyneric should be appointed in case of Airleas's default. One moment I was discussing the Regency with Feich and the next, I was pressing Colfre to make that godless wretch his son's surrogate."

"Dear God! Do you—? You're not suggesting he *Wove*?"

"Hell's ice, Caime! Of all the appalling . . . I would never suggest . . . " Ladhar's face quivered like jelly and fear stood out in his pale eyes. He turned away from the cleirach and moved his bulk to the Altar. "Absurd," Leal thought he said, but knew beyond doubt that his fear was real.

At the Altar, the Abbod turned back to his companion, smiling. "Your imagination is amazing, Caime. How in the name of all holy can you even think an unbeliever might possess the Gift?"

The cleirach admitted, blushing, that it was a ludicrous thought and the two men set to discussing the Cirke-dag worship. Leal found himself beyond belief as they calmly planned a series of small counterfeit miracles to awe the worshipers. Smoke balls and little Fireweaves to amaze; the chiming of the wind bells at an auspicious moment; and, if those things were not bad enough, an Osraed would fall to his knees and fabricate an aislinn vision which, Ladhar implied, would be no more than some whirling lights appearing around the Crystal.

When Leal was woozy from what he'd overheard and despairing that he would ever have a chance at Ladhar, the cleirach left to fulfill some errand, leaving the old Abbod on his own. Leal didn't wait, but came to his feet, stepped from behind the rows of benches and approached the other, shedding his timidity as one sloughs sleep.

"Abbod."

The Osraed Ladhar turned, his expression going from blandly benign to utter disbelief. "You! How do you dare speak to me? How do you dare show yourself—here, of all places!" He glanced up the broad aisle, made an indecisive move in that direction and halted as Osraed Fhada appeared, wraith-like, from of a row of benches between Ladhar and the open doorway.

Face purpling horribly in the ruddy-gold glow from the stained windows, the Abbod wavered. "What is it you want? Have you come to kill me? Be quick about it then, but know that you will not go unpunished. The Meri will scourge you through all eternity for such an act."

Fhada, advancing slowly up the aisle, shook his head. "We've neither the desire nor the means to harm you, Abbod. We came only to talk. To speak to you about the things that have befallen Caraid-land and to express our concern about what is yet to come."

"I'll tell you what is to come," barked the old Osraed and his jowls shook like the wattles of a hen. "Airleas Malcuim shall be liberated from your Taminist comrades and placed upon the throne. Then, I swear, you will all be hunted down and destroyed like the disease-carrying vermin you are."

"And at whose command shall this be done?" asked Fhada. "Surely you don't expect young Airleas to order it?"

"His Regent will order it."

"Ah, yes. Daimhin Feich, the man you just accused of manipulating you into voting him surrogate Cyneric."

The Abbod's face paled. "You heard—?"

"Everything," said Lealbhallain.

Ladhar's head swiveled, tracking him. "I don't know what you imagine you overheard—"

"That you suspected yourself to have been the victim of Feich's manipulations, just as Cyne Colfre was. Abbod, if you believe that, surely you must see that Feich didn't perform those manipulations without reason. He seeks to take the throne."

"And what is that to me?" asked Ladhar. "Do you imagine I have some great loyalty to the House Malcuim? I have not. My loyalty is to the Meri. I care very little whose buttocks grace the throne of Caraid-land as long as their owner does not seek to undermine everything I hold dear. Only the Meri's grace saved us from having that Wicke holding court at Mertuile. If Airleas Malcuim cannot be brought out of her influence permanently, then I will support Daimhin Feich. Whether it's him or some distant Malcuim cousin at Mertuile, it makes no difference to me. Either is far better than having a little Taminist parked there."

"Are you sure?" asked Fhada. He moved to stand below the Altar just far enough from Lealbhallain that Ladhar still had to twitch back and forth to watch them both.

"What do you mean, am I sure? Taminy would have Airleas destroy the Osraed."

Fhada shook his head. "Taminy wanted only to renew the Osraed, to make us pure and whole and strong again. Yes, I know you'd argue that. Let me ask you this: What would Daimhin Feich do to the Osraed? What does he intend for the religion of the Meri?"

"He intends that it be left alone, in our hands. He's an unbeliever, an atheist. He doesn't care about our doings for any spiritual reason, I know. But he does care that the Osraed institution is his best chance of controlling the hearts of the people—"

"When Taminy has won so many of those hearts to herself?" asked Leal.

"Taminy is no longer here. People will soon forget the supposed miracles she performed. We will win those hearts back through miracles of our own."

"Ah, yes." Fhada nodded his mop of curls. "With Fireweaves and little smoke balls and colorful lights. Do you imagine that can compare with making a broken body sound or bringing real Eibhilin light into a soul?"

The Abbod reddened. "We will win those hearts back."

"And what will Daimhin Feich do with them once you have done that?" asked Fhada. "Do you think he will let you keep them?"

"Where are your loyalties, Abbod Ladhar?" asked Leal, taking a step forward. "You say they are with the Meri. If that is so, they cannot be also with Daimhin Feich, for his loyalty is to himself alone."

"I am Osraed," Ladhar answered. "My loyalty is always to the Meri—*alone*. I also believe in Her power. If Daimhin

Feich threatens to undermine Her religion, She will thwart him, just as She thwarted your Wicke Cwen. She will raise up Her forces—"

"She already has," Leal observed, "and you fight us."

"I will never believe that. I am at the Apex of the Osraed now. I will appoint my Triumvirate and as the tools of the Meri's will, we will destroy the forces of the Wicke. We will restore Her religion and renew it, purge the unworthy from our ranks, recover the prestige of our institutions. And if Daimhin Feich stands in the way of that, we will see him destroyed as well."

Leal and Fhada's eyes met in a silent exchange, then, with one accord, they began to withdraw toward a side entrance. The Abbod Ladhar, still bristling, watched them depart, mute. Only when they had gone did it occur to him to raise an alarm, and by then it was too late.

Safely away from Cyne's Cirke, Leal reflected on what he had learned. Of one thing he was absolutely certain; Abbod Ladhar was no sycophant to Daimhin Feich. Not knowing Taminy, he might despise her, but he was not an enemy of the Meri's, merely a misinformed defender. And perhaps, if he could be convinced that Feich was not to be trusted . . .

Leal pulled himself out of his reverie enough to note his surroundings. He had separated from Fhada lest Ladhar send someone after them, and now stood on the edge of the marketplace. He tugged at his forelock, making sure it covered his forehead and aimed a small obscuring Weave at the heavily camouflaged Kiss on his forehead. When he'd left Carehouse that morning it had been a muddy green-gold stellate smudge. He prayed it still appeared so, then dove into the crowds.

It seemed to him that people were a little less on edge today than they had seemed the last time he'd been out. A week ago, now. He lingered by knots of gossip, to glean any news from Mertuile. Regent Feich had been seen about in the late Cyne's carriage. Some thought that an outrage, some thought it was his due—all had seen the bans proclaiming his Regency.

Leal wended his way through flocks of market-goers, side-stepped strolling merchants and performers, passed by bright tents and stalls, eyes peering, looking for a certain little flower cart. At last he spied it and made his way over to where another of Tammy's followers, Haesel Sweep, now pursued a new and flourishing business. Around the cart was a knot of well-dressed gentlemen engaged in animated discussion of the muddy affairs of state.

"Still," opined one stout fellow, "to be a Regent without a Cyneric is a pretty meaningless station. It'll be of extreme interest to see how all this turns out."

"And who's to say there's no Cyneric?" asked an older gentleman with a long grey beard. "I reckon that whole story of Airleas Malcuim's kidnap to be just so much piffle. Good God, all that about Eibhilin fires and Hillwild hordes. Pah! A bunch of hysterical old women must've come up with it."

"Do I look like an hysterical old woman?" asked a third man. "I was there. Granted I was at the back of the public gallery, but I saw what I saw. That young woman whipped fire and lightning all over the place. It was a thing of awe. And there were Hillwild all over as well. But it was Iobert Claeg who helped the girl escape. I saw him myself leading the way from the Hall."

"And speaking of the Hall," said the first man, "have any of you heard aught of their meeting?"

"I heard the last attempt ended in a riotous roil," said the greybeard. "The noble Houses are not falling in line behind our Regent, the Osraed are fractured and fractious—"

"Give me a tell I've *not* heard!"

"Aye, well. I heard from the Regent's own scribe that other than a few Chieftains, only the Eiric and Ministers put in their appearance, and even they were fewer than ought to be. Looks as if our government has ground to a halt."

"Near tax time, too," mewed the stout one. "Tsk! Such a shame. Come, let's find us some hot cider—spend before Feich wakes up and duns us double."

Off the three of them went, chuckling.

Leal sidled up to Haesel and pretended to be looking over her flowers. "They seem happy enough," he commented.

"Oh, aye." The woman patted a lock of brown hair into place and surveyed the crowd. "Government may have ground down, as that one says, but commerce sure han't. Things've settled a bit here, too. Looting's down since the merchants got together and formed a vigilance group. Funny, though, how long it took 'em to come to the knowing that our Regent Feich is keepin' all his guards to himself. Some of the old Malcuim regulars still patrol here, but not enough to keep these poor merchants from losing their goods. Well, they says, we'll just defend ourselves. See, there's one of the market guards now." She dipped her head in the direction of a young man with restless eyes and a heavily knotted club at his side. "Thieves can't tell them from any other body here. Makes 'em real careful, I wager."

She glanced at Leal's face. "What's the word from Cyne's Cirke?"

"Word is," said Leal, "the Abbod is not Feich's man, no more than he's Taminy's."

"And whose will does he bend to, then?" Haesel asked.

"The Meri's, he thinks. I only pray She will find a way to prove to him that he's wrong."

Daimhin Feich sipped his wine and reflected that it tasted much better when things were going well. The whole dinner had seemed a feast from the Eibhilin realm and he congratulated himself that he had only his own pretty diplomacy to thank for it. It was a dance, he thought. Show the right face to the Mediator, make the right requests; the cannon was secure. Dispatch worthy gifts to the Banarigh of El-Deasach and . . . ? Who knew what might be accomplished? Perhaps the illustrious Lilias, herself, would see fit to let him keep the cannon, or perhaps she would dispatch a gift to him in return—some fighting men wouldn't come amiss.

He'd lied a bit to Loc Llywd in saying he expected the Skarf and the Madaidh to fall in behind him. He was working on that, certainly, had gone straight to meet with the

Chieftains of those Houses from his conference with the Deasach Mediator, had told them about the marvelous cannon and the alliance forming between the Feich and the Teallach and the Dearg. He'd hoped it would decide them, but both men hemmed and hawed and prattled about needing to convene a council of House elders. Fools. In their desire to stay on the sidelines as long as possible, they let destiny slip from their hands.

Daimhin swirled the wine in his goblet. Through the golden liquid in its cut crystal he could see the dancing flame of one of the myriad candles that graced the dinner table. It reminded him of the Osmaer Crystal sitting aloof on its pedestal, sealed within its shrine. He recalled that little spark of luminance he'd called from it and felt for a moment as if hot honey flowed through his belly. The spark of desire. Then it was her face he saw in his golden wine—green-eyed, flax-haired Taminy. The Wicke who called herself Osmaer.

He smiled. Woman and Stone were connected. The two were One.

"All right, cousin." Ruadh's voice was tinged with irritation. "You've been sitting there all through dinner with that cat-eat-cream grin on your face. I'm damn tired of waiting to find out what it's pertinent to. So's the Abbod, I reckon, eh, Abbod?"

The old Osraed, lost just then in his own thoughts, looked up from his half-empty plate and nodded. "Yes, of course, em—it's good to see you looking so happy."

Daimhin took another sip of the sweet, thick wine. "I am happy. And I'll tell you why. The cannon is ours."

Ruadh raised his glass to his cousin in silent applause, but the Abbod could only stare vacantly and murmur, "Cannon? What cannon?"

"The one that's going to blow the doors of Halig-liath to the skies."

"What?"

Now the old boar was clearly dumbfounded. Daimhin was both amused and irritated. "I've convinced the Deasach to lend us a marvelous new machine of war. A cannon—

three horses in length—that fires explosive ordnance. With it, I intend to go up to Nairne and, by fear or force, bring back Cyneric Airleas."

"Destroy Halig-liath?" gasped Ladhar. "No. I won't have it. Attacking an Osraed institution—"

"At this juncture, Abbod, Halig-liath is no longer a *legitimate* Osraed institution. It is taken over by the Wicke and her disciples. I intend to give it back into your hands. Consider it a gift expressive of my . . . regard."

Ladhar's full lips puckered mutinously. "And Taminy-a-Cuinn?"

"I intend to bring her back to Creiddylad and drown her. She should never have escaped the Sea in the first place; she will not do it again."

The large Osraed took a deep, noisy breath. "I'd rather see her burned. It's more certain."

"Abbod, there is, in the depths of Mertuile, a chamber which admits the Sea. There is always at least one hand's width of water covering the floor and, as the tide rises, so does the depth of the water in the cell. When the tide is high, sea water fills the chamber to a depth of four feet."

"Four feet of water," said the Abbod, "will not drown a woman who is over five feet tall."

Feich smiled. "Everyone must sleep, Abbod. Even the wicked."

Ah, the implications had sunk in; the Abbod's chubby face was gratifyingly pale. Daimhin almost thought he'd beg mercy for the poor girl, but in a moment, he'd squared his massive shoulders and fixed his face with stern determination.

"That could take forever."

"Why do you care how long it takes? The longer it takes, the more time you'll have to visit her and listen to her screams and pitiable cries for help."

"God's mercy, Daimhin!" Across the table from the Abbod, Ruadh shook himself. "I had no idea you were such a bloodthirsty monster. Surely you can think of a quicker, saner way of putting the girl away."

"Not one I would enjoy so. I would like very much to hear her beg me for mercy. I look forward to it."

Ruadh threw back some wine and grimaced. "Well, don't expect me to enjoy it with you. I think it's above cruel. I also think it's a dreadful waste. If the late Cyne's portrait of her has any truth in it, your Wicke is an astonishing beauty."

Daimhin snorted. "That portrait only hints at the truth, Ruadh. But you see, that's part of her guile. Her face seduces a man's eyes; her voice, his ears; her craft, his soul. Ah, see how our friend, the Abbod, shivers? He knows it's true, don't you, Abbod?"

"I do. I've seen it happen to many, yourself included. Which is why I maintain, more strongly than ever, that her death should be quick. Terrible, terrifying, but quick. A lingering death gives her too much opportunity to Weave her wiles on you all over again."

"Oh, very well," said Daimhin easily. Easily, because he had no intention of placing Taminy anywhere near that wretched sea-pit. That would be, as Ruadh so aptly put it, a dreadful waste. "There are iron rings set into the floor. I shall simply shackle her to those. The first high tide will set your mind at ease." *And what will it do to your soul, old man*, he wondered. *You speak so glibly of quick deaths. I wonder if you've ever witnessed one.*

The Abbod seemed somewhat mollified, and so Daimhin proceeded down an intersecting path of conversation. He drew his brow into a careful frown. "But your reminder of her cunning disturbs me, Osraed. I've tried to put out of my mind how strongly she . . . affected me. She's powerful, and I'm probably a fool to think I can simply trot up to Halig-liath and bring her back by mere physical force. Have you no means of protecting us spiritually?"

"Spiritually? I didn't think you even believed in anything so intangible as spirit. See, you've even boggled your young kinsman."

Ruadh, insolent lip curled, said nothing, but merely poured himself another goblet of wine. Daimhin carefully considered his next words. "Abbod, I would be a fool to deny that she wields some power I do not understand. Some . . . force beyond my ken. I saw her blaze of glory. I witnessed her miraculous escape. I saw the very mouth of hell when I raised that crossbow, thinking I could simply shoot her where she stood. But then, I also saw a spark in the heart of that great Crystal your Osraed lives revolve around. I begin to understand that it, and the Art you Osraed practice, are the only things that can protect us from Taminy's venom." He stared moodily down the table, his frown slipping toward a twisted grimace. "She visits me in my dreams, Abbod. She haunts me, teases me, allows me no rest. And though, in those dreams, I take up a bow or a sword or a dagger—weapons I understand—I cannot touch her, for she holds the reins of a power I cannot fathom."

"We Osraed will do what we can," the Abbod assured him. "When you travel to Halig-liath rest assured the full force of every loyal Osraed in Creiddylad and beyond will be with you. I myself will be with your host. I will Weave what protection I can."

"And for that I thank you," said Daimhin, bowing his head. "But for myself, for the nightmares that plague me and the fears that beset me—breathe no word of this outside this chamber, either of you—for those I would ask one thing more."

"Ask."

"A crystal. A crystal with which I may learn to Weave a ward to protect myself from the Wicke's haunting."

The Abbod's face was whiter than the breast of the gamebird that sat, half-eaten, on his plate. "A . . . a crystal? You wish to learn how to Weave inyx?"

"Small Wardweaves only. For my personal protection. I now realize that physical weapons are useless against a spiritual enemy."

"But you have no training in the Art, no Gift. Good God, you have no *belief*! The purest Weaving stone in the world would do you no more good than a hunk of plain rock."

"I think I may have some small . . . talent, Abbod. And as for training, you or one of your cohorts could provide that. The Osmaer Crystal winked at me, Osraed Ladhar. You saw it. I think that might have been a benediction, a blessing. Leastwise, let me have a crystal. If I've no Gift, then I'll do no harm. But if I do, I'll be able to protect myself."

The old fool was already shaking his head, jowls flopping like the dewlap of an aging mastiff. "I cannot allow it, Regent Feich. All the rune crystals in Creiddylad are registered at Ochanshrine. They go to none but Osraed. Even the Aelder Prentices there are not allowed them. So it has always been. So it must remain."

"*She* has a crystal. Every one of her minions probably has one by now—pilfered from the reliquary at Halig-liath. And she is no doubt teaching their use. Abbod, please, consider what you're saying. You are, in effect, condemning me to enter a battle weaponless while my adversaries are fully armed. I go to Halig-liath to return your Cyne to his rightful place. Would you deny a man a knife after he had pledged to march into a den of armed thieves to return your stolen goods?"

"A good analogy, Regent, but not apt. Yes, you will march into that den of thieves, but neither weaponless nor alone. A spiritual army will surround you. Further, I will perform a Wardweave this very night to shield your dreams from the Wicke's intrusion."

Frustrated, Daimhin shook his head. "No, Abbod. I am no coward. I will find my own way of safeguarding my dreams. But as to the other—you certainly shall accompany me to Halig-liath. I expect you and your fellow Osraed may be as effective a weapon as the Suderlander cannon."

The Abbod looked quite pleased at that. "I assure you, Regent Feich, we can be very effective indeed. I think you will find us the greatest of allies in assuring the future of Caraid-land."

Daimhin raised his glass. "I'm sure I will."

"The greatest of allies," he snarled some time later when the Abbod had removed himself to Ochanshrine. He and Ruadh had withdrawn to the warmth of his favorite salon and sat before the fire drinking hot *karfa* and trying to stay warm. "I find them the greatest of irritants. A shame they've woven themselves so inextricably into the fabric of this society. God, what I wouldn't give to rip them out."

"I'm afraid that would be impossible," said Ruadh. "And, as the Abbod said, they can be helpful. . . . Did you mean what you said about believing yourself at risk from the Wicke's devices?"

Daimhin chuckled. "What would you say if I said 'yes'?"

"I'd say you'd suffered a life-changing experience."

"Eh, well, as it happens I did. I didn't think, didn't really believe, she had the powers everyone ascribed to her. I didn't see the healings in the street. I didn't witness her handling of the Stone. Until the night she stood in the Assembly Hall and confounded everyone there, I saw only one supposed miracle. I saw her cause a rose to bloom from a desiccated bud. But I was far away, it might've been faked—for a long while I believed it was. But I've changed my mind. I believe she really did it. Just as I believe she once picked up a crossbow bolt and read from it that the man who'd fired it at her was a mercenary. I had him killed, Ruadh, because at that moment and *from* that moment I knew that if she but saw his face, she'd know *I* had paid his fee."

He rose and moved to stand nearer the fire. "But as to believing her able to harm me . . . " He shook his head. "She won't harm me."

"So certain?"

"Let me share a secret with you, Ruadh. The Lady Taminy is many things; she is manipulative, powerful, seductive. And she is dangerous to the Osraed and to my own aspirations. But she is not evil. She honestly believes it is her duty to reform and renew and recreate the religion of Caraid-land and change its fortunes. But she wants to put a Malcuim Cyne on the throne and she wants to stand, alone, beside him. There is no room for Daimhin Feich in her government. And for that reason, she is the Enemy."

"Not evil?" repeated Ruadh, and for a moment, in the amber light of the fire, he looked like the boy Daimhin had taught to hunt not that many years ago.

"Not evil. That Taminy is evil is a game we play so that this pathetically divided country might not suffer any further dissolution. And that a Feich may always stay near the throne."

"Or in it?" asked Ruadh.

Daimhin smiled. "If that is our destiny, Ruadh. If that is our destiny."

"The man is a blasphemer! If I could I would call down a blast of fire out of the sky and cook him where he stands. I can't fathom why the Meri hasn't dealt with him already."

Caime Cadder stood by silently, watching his Abbod pace his chambers and steam as if he were freshly cooked. He understood the great man's perturbation—no, anguish—for the Regent of Caraid-land was a lawless man, a self-absorbed man, in a word: amoral.

"Perhaps," Cadder offered, struck by sudden inspiration, "it is because She sees in him a tool—a means to an end."

"And what end might that be?"

"The return of Airleas Malcuim to Mertuile. Feich is set on it and he will accomplish it, I've no doubt, though his motives be . . . questionable."

Ladhar looked at him with interest, now, a rare thing that always made him feel as if he'd been blessed.

"An interesting idea, Caime. It is like Her to manipulate the wicked."

"Yes."

"To make them feel it is their will they serve."

"Yes," Caime repeated, then jumped when the Osraed poked a chubby finger at his nose.

"Do you know what that arrogant Feich asked of me today?"

"No, master, I do not."

"He asked me for a crystal. A Weaving stone. Can you believe it? Can you take it in? The damned idiot thinks he can Weave—thinks just *anybody* can Weave. You, of all people, know how wrong *that* is."

Cadder winced, stung by the cavalier way in which the

Abbod referred to his Great Failing. Damn, but the man could be cruel. *But no*, argued an inner voice. *You did fail. You reached the Meri's Shore only to become so afrighted by dreams of Her coming that you ran. Ran! Such cowardice warrants occasional cruelty.*

"Why," Cadder asked carefully, "why would he wish . . . that is to say, what reason did he give for wanting a Weaving stone?"

"Protection," spat Ladhar. "He's taken it into his head that the Wicke is reaching into his dreams."

Cadder blanched. "Has he reason to believe this?"

"He's had some nightmares, that's all. Rich food and late nights will do that to a man. Not to mention the stress of sitting inside that castle knowing that half the populace of Caraid-land would like to pry him out."

"As the Wicke would like to pry him out," Cadder said. "Could she?"

Ladhar fixed him with a look that would have perforated the walls of Mertuile. "I refuse to believe she is capable of that. No, she can't be capable of that, otherwise she'd be reaching into *our* dreams as well—or trying to."

"And she hasn't . . . reached into your dreams, has she Abbod?"

"Don't be ridiculous. None but the Meri touches my dreams, Caime. I permit no other access."

"Daimhin Feich," Cadder reminded him, "is not an Osraed. And you said yourself, she does manipulate the wicked to her will."

The Abbod had nothing to say to that except that, of course, Mertuile was surrounded by Osraed and the Wicke Taminy was far away at Halig-liath and had shown no ability to reach them from there. He seemed content to let it go at that, but Caime Cadder could not help but recall that Mertuile had always been surrounded by Osraed and it had not helped poor, weak Cyne Colfre at all.

CHAPTER 6

We are what we think, having become our thought—like the cart that follows the horse that pulls it, grief follows evil thought.

And delight follows pure thought, like a man's faithful shadow. We are what we think, having become our thought.
—*The Corah, Proverbs of Ochan vs. 20*

It had been nearly a week since his humiliating escape attempt. Airleas Malcuim had rededicated himself to his lessons and his worship and his learning of the Art. It was on the fourth day after that, during an exercise in Mapweave that he began to wonder, seriously, if he would ever be worthy of the Meri.

"Will I," he asked Taminy one evening at supper, "ever take Pilgrimage to the Meri's Shore?"

She looked at him and then away from him, and her eyes became misted, focusing on somewhere that was not part of the warm, noisy refectory. "You will make a Pilgrimage."

He started to be elated, then checked himself. "You didn't answer directly. You didn't say I would go to the Meri's Shore. Won't I?"

"Everyone's Pilgrimage is unique. This is a new age," was all she would say.

Before he could frame another question, she said, "You've set yourself a difficult path, Airleas. Your Pilgrimage has as many facets as a Weaving stone. You are *waljan*. You are Cyneric. You are a youth, growing to manhood. I see three Pilgrimages in your future."

"Then I'll become Osraed?"

"Airleas, have you ever stood at the top of the Airdnasheen wall and looked off down the pass?"

"You know I have."

"And did you see the path to the bottom of the mountain?"

"Aye."

"And did you see Creiddylad at the other end of it?"

He frowned. "Of course not. It bends and winds and vanishes. And it splits into branches long before it reaches Creiddylad."

"So Creiddylad is not the only place it goes?"

"No, it . . . " He saw the point of her questions then and did not like it. "You're saying our future has branches that we mayn't see."

"Yes."

"But *you* can see them. Surely, you can."

"I see possibilities. And I see only those possibilities that the Meri and Spirit will me to see. Think of our lives as bits of a Tapestry. I am a thread and you are a thread, as is everyone here. Some threads are longer or stronger or more colorful or shiny as gold. Some threads are holy and pure and some are sullied. We are all weaving away at the tapestry, Airleas."

Her eyes lifted, unfocused, and he thought she must be envisioning the Tapestry. "Every soul has been called to the weaving," she said. "Some have heard a Voice, others an inarticulate cry, others only an annoying whisper. They have been called to a forking of paths, a Cusp, a choosing. Some souls understand that, but may fail to see the nature of the choice, or that it must be made. I can't make this choice for Caraid-land, nor can you, nor can even the Meri. The choice is not Daimhin Feich's. The Abbod Ladhar cannot make it, nor any other single human being. It lies not with the Council, nor the Body, nor the Hall. For the Tapestry is choices upon choices, woven through and into and over each other until a pattern emerges and a new fabric is created. The Spirit is the Weaver and all these souls provide the thread. The Meri adds Her own

Thread to the weaving and the Spirit guides the shuttle, ever mindful of the patterns.

"The destiny of Caraid-land lies in a handful of threads. I will Weave Mine, also. *We* will Weave it, ever mindful of the Pattern."

Strange, Airleas felt as if the entire room held its breath as she spoke. As if the entire fortress listened. He stared at her, suddenly mindful himself that he was part of the Pattern.

"I might've ruined it," he murmured. "By running off like that, I mean. I wasn't thinking of the Pattern then. I was thinking of myself."

Taminy only looked at him and smiled. He was about to ask her what he should do about the weaving of his own thread when the Ren Catahn came and sat next to her and speared Airleas with his strange amber eyes. "Boy, you've some desire to learn swordsmanship?"

"I . . . I did, sir. I'm not so sure now."

"Aren't you?" Catahn glanced aside at Taminy.

"No, sir, at least . . . I'm of the mind that there are more important things. Like learning the Art and—and statesmanship."

"Oh, aye, that." Beneath the Hillwild's thick beard, the corner of his mouth curled upward. "I'd likely not know anything about that."

Airleas's face flamed and he tried to remember if he'd ever said aloud the thoughts he'd had about Catahn's ability to lead civilized men. He decided he hadn't, which gave him a new appreciation of the Ren's *aidan*. "I imagine, sir," he said carefully, "that you do. I believe I could learn volumes from you."

Catahn grinned at him. "Aye, well. I've things I can teach you, I reckon, when you're sincere in that belief. For now, I'm asking about the sword, not the throne. Have you any interest in learning that?"

Airleas looked to Taminy, trying to read her, to gauge her reaction to this. Was this a test of some sort? If he admitted he still harbored a yen to learn swordplay, would he fail the test? "What do you think, Mistress?" he asked her.

"I think Catahn is asking you, not me. I've no interest in learning the sword. I doubt I'll ever have need of one."

"Will I?"

"You may."

"Then, I suppose the answer is: It might be a handy skill for a Cyne to have. After all, I may have to lead men into battle someday."

Taminy lowered her eyes and Airleas felt his heart take a long sickening slide toward his stomach. Had that been the wrong answer? "I—I—I mean . . . " Flustered, he stopped the garbled flow of words. "Is it wrong to fight, Taminy? The Ren Catahn is a fine swordsman; so is The Claeg."

The Ren made a humming noise in the back of this throat. "So, I imagine, is Daimhin Feich. Every man in every Noble House is trained to the sword. Every man, woman and child in the Gyldans learns to handle one— the bow and the dagger as well."

Daimhin Feich. Airleas's hackles rose. "Well, if Feich is learned at swordplay, shouldn't I be? Won't I someday have to face him? Fight him?"

"And do you imagine this will take place in the Great Hall with lights blazing and citizens watching and the rules of proper swordplay being observed by all?"

There was a tang of irony to Taminy's words and Airleas blinked at her in surprise. That was exactly the way the scene always played out in his mind. His ears burned and the sounds in the large stone hall seemed suddenly amplified out of all proportion to the number of people dining there. It wouldn't be that way, he realized. Daimhin Feich would play by no one's rules but his own, and the chances of his attack being open . . .

Taminy sighed. "Airleas, there is nothing wrong with you knowing how to defend yourself against attack . . . both physically and through the use of your *aidan*. This is not a perfect world. This is not a sane or safe time. Catahn has brought to my attention that your use of the sword has been just what you called it—swordplay. That, I think, will do you more harm than good. Your *aidan* is strong, but it is yet undisciplined. I think Catahn can teach you something about discipline. I think you should learn from him."

Airleas lowered his eyes, trying not to show how much the thought excited him. He *would* learn to be a warrior after all. Maybe he would even mark the Crask-an-duine before he left Hrofceaster. He stabbed a chunk of stew meat and stuffed it into his mouth, barely aware of the flavor.

Catahn nodded. "In the morning then—fourteenth hour. Meet me and Broran in that little courtyard beyond the kitchen."

Airleas nearly choked on the plug of meat. Gasping, he grabbed for his mug of water and gulped down a mouthful. While he was indisposed, the Ren gave him a stone-faced stare, got up and headed for the kitchen. Taminy, meanwhile, watched him painfully regain his composure.

"What's wrong, Airleas?" she asked quietly, when he'd stopped coughing.

"Broran?" He hated that he sounded whiny, but there didn't seem to be anything he could do about it.

"Why not Broran? Catahn says he's an excellent swordsman. Probably the best to teach you the basics and serve as a sparring partner."

"But he's . . . "

"He's what?"

"He's just a—a *boy*."

"He's about a year older than you are. He's marked his Crask-an-duine. By Hillwild reckoning that makes him a man."

"But he's not—I mean, at home my weapons tutor was a man of the House Madaidh. One of the young Elders."

"Yes, so?"

"Well, Broran *isn't*."

Taminy looked at her half-empty plate. "Broran isn't a nobleman, you mean."

"I . . . yes. That's what I mean. I've always been taught by nobles, cleirachs. . . . "

"I see. Never a commoner."

He shook his head.

"And what am I?"

Airleas's eyes fairly bugged out of his head. "You're Osmaer!"

"I'm also a commoner."

"Your father was an Osraed."

"I see. And what about Catahn? You'd learn from him."

"He's the Ren of all this holt. He's the Hageswode."

"And that's why you'd learn from him, Airleas? Or from me? Because we have titles: Osmaer, Ren?"

Airleas sincerely wished he had never opened his mouth. He was wrong. He knew that intellectually, but it didn't alter the fact that he was a Malcuim at heart. By God, he was *The* Malcuim. And a Malcuim never took lessons from commoners.

Her eyes were all over him; he was surrounded, out-flanked. "Tell me about Ochan-a-Coille," she said.

He opened his mouth on the legend, ready to parrot it; it was ingrained in every Caraidin mind. "In his fifteenth year, Ochan, son of—" His voice died in his throat. Son of the Cyne's Woodweard. He stared at the fork in his hand, another piece of meat already impaled there. "Ochan, a commoner, went to the Malcuim, who was Cyne by might. Ochan-a-Coille, a commoner, was chosen by the Meri to be Her first Osraed. Osraed Ochan taught the Malcuim how to be Cyne by right." Airleas raised his eyes to her face again, praying to see the light of approval there.

"You have been taught," she told him, as the Hillwild Ren reseated himself at her side with a plate overladen with food, "that there are classes of men and women. That how you are born or how you marry determines how you will live. Unlearn this, Airleas. It is a lie. Broran is a Hageswode and your kinsman, but even that is irrelevant. Whether he be a Hageswode or a Madaidh or a Mercer or a Smythe, Broran has something he can teach you. *That* is what matters."

"Yes, Mistress," he murmured and comforted himself that at least she was not angry with him. He'd never seen her angry and didn't think he wanted to.

"So what is she like, this Wicke of Catahn's?"

Eyslk, laying out the lovely, thick violet cloth that would

make the dress for her Crask-an-bana, glanced up in confusion. "Wicke? Whoever can you mean?"

"Don't be dense, girl. I mean your mistress. The woman he has you serving day and night."

Flustered by her mother's apparent hostility, Eyslk wallowed among possible replies. *She's not Wicke, Mama* or *I serve her because I want to* or . . . "She's lovely."

Deardru-an-Caerluel rolled dark eyes and chuckled. "I can see that, child. I meant what sort of woman is she—or should I say 'girl'—I hear she's no older than Desary."

"And I meant she's lovely," said Eyslk. "She's . . . brave and full of compassion and love. And she's . . . sad."

"Sad? Why ever sad? She's got Catahn and you all wrapped about her. Not to mention having a handful of lowland Chieftains and the Cwen and Cyneric of Caraidland among her baggage."

"You've heard the tell, Mama. How can you ask?"

"Oh, aye—the poor little orphan girl, everyone she knows dead an age, whole world on her shoulders, and all the Cyne's men against her. Sort of a fish out of water, isn't she?"

Deardru smiled at her own play on words and Eyslk cringed, finding the close kitchen suddenly over-warm. "Please, Mama, don't say such things."

Deardru tipped her head back, smile twisting wryly. "Why, because your magical Mistress might hear me? Strike at me?" She leaned forward then, her hand stopping Eyslk's anxious tugs on the unresisting material. "Remember, daughter, before you pity the woman too much, that she can Weave her every want. More than you or I can do."

Eyslk lowered her eyes to the fabric she'd been stroking and smoothing for the last several minutes.

Her mother chuckled. "Ah, but she's teaching you, isn't she, the beautiful Wicke? Someday you, too, will reek of magic."

"She's not a Wicke, Mama. She's Osmaer."

"But she *is* beautiful, isn't she?"

"You've seen her."

"Only from a distance. . . . I suppose our mighty Ren is smitten with her."

Eyslk caught the venom in her mother's voice and was repulsed by it. "You'd have to ask Uncle his opinion of her, Mama. I only know what *I* think." She gathered up her fabric then, folding it hastily against her chest. "I'll take this to Gram Long for sewing. There's cakes for Da's supper in the pantry." She bolted from the kitchen then, ignoring her mother's amused glance.

"Eyslk."

Halfway into their small parlor, she paused, clutching her fabric.

"Don't forget your jacket. It's chill out."

"No, Mama," she said and made good her escape.

Airleas lunged, arm thrusting upward, swinging inward. He grunted, throwing himself into the thrust, allowing himself an instant of satisfaction that he had performed the move exactly as Broran had shown him.

Satisfaction was short-lived. The blade caught Broran's parry and spun out of his hand—for the fifth time that morning. He scrambled after it, pride and face in flames, eyes averted from Broran's smug grin and Gwynet's ever-watchful eyes.

"Not bad, Cyneric. The move looks good enough, but you've got to keep a better grip on the hilt."

"Before, you told me I was holding it too tightly," Airleas complained.

"You were. And I didn't say you should hold it tighter. I said 'get a better grip.' Don't try to block my blade, try to gate it. Grip tight; wrist flexible."

Trying not to look at Gwynet, who watched from the bottom of the kitchen steps, Airleas retrieved his sword and held it out, wrist wobbling. "Flexible? How's that supposed to work?"

Broran scowled. "I said *flexible* not limp. Hell's wind, but you're stubborn, midge. If you'd rather not learn what I have to teach you—"

Smoke curled in Airleas's heart. "Don't call me that. I'm not a midge."

"No, you're the Cyneric Malcuim. And I'm just a lowly

mountain boy. I know what you think of me, *Cyneric* Airleas. And you'd best believe I'm no happier teaching than you are learning. But Catahn's lady wants me to tutor Your Loftiness, and that means Catahn wants me to. I obey my Ren, but I can always tell him you just aren't learning."

The embers in Airleas's heart burst into flame. "You wouldn't!"

Broran's wide mouth pulled into a tight smile. "I surely would. You've a head as hard as iron, Your Worthiness. You know the difference between a limp wrist and a flexible one, you're just pretending to mistake me. I don't want to teach you any more what you want to learn." He turned and started to walk away, moving past the gawping Gwynet as if she weren't there.

"I *can* learn, damn you! And I'm *not* pretending!" Knowledge of his own lie added more heat to Airleas's fire. *Damn* Broran for seeing through him! *Damn him!* He spat the thought in full fury, feeling it as a rush of physical heat that flowed from the crown of his head and radiated from his eyes.

Broran stopped and snapped around to face him as if jerked on the end of a chain. His face, drained of its normal ruddy color, was cloud pale below his tawny hair.

Beside him, Gwynet gasped in open-mouthed amazement. "Airleas! *Don't!*"

Airleas, face flaming, dashed his hot gaze to the ground.

Broran shook himself and took a backward step away. "You're an evil boy, Airleas Malcuim," he said and fled to the kitchen.

Airleas might have sneered and called the older boy a coward, but he was caught in the talons of a cold so complete he thought his soul had frozen. Gwynet came to him, bombarding him with concern and distress. He could only blink at her and whisper, "What did I do?"

She stopped toe to toe with him, looking into him through his eyes.

"What did I do?" he asked again.

"You Wove, Airleas. But . . . it wasn't a good thing."

"I didn't mean to. I *didn't*. Don't tell Taminy," he pleaded.

"Oh, Airleas, she already knows."

Eyslk-an-Caerluel rose from sleep in a bubble of happiness. Yesterday she had seen Gram Long's pattern for her Crask-an-bana dress, had seen the wonderful material cut and pinned. Today she knew the sewing would begin. She was glad to contemplate a day of service up at the fortress, for otherwise she would surely be in Gram's hair all day, watching every stitch.

Now she kept her mind on the trivial—heating water for her ablutions, picking out warm clothing, braiding up her hair. She was in the kitchen putting on water for tea when her step-father came in, broad, handsome face worried and tense.

"Eyslk, it's your mama. She's taken ill."

Eyslk let the teapot down onto its hearth-hook too quickly, spilling water into the flames below. They spat and hissed like disgruntled cats. "Ill? How ill?" She was already following him from the room, heading for their bedchamber beneath the loft stair.

"She's in a cold fever. Got a wretched cough. Can't seem to keep warm."

She heard the cough as she entered her parents' room; it was a terrible, dry, hacking cough that wracked the bundled form on the bed. "Mama?"

Deardru gazed up at her through glazed eyes, seeming not to recognize her own daughter. She shuddered, gasped breath into her lungs and began coughing again. Eyslk put a hand to her forehead. It was, as her step-da had said, a cold fever, and Eyslk hadn't a clue as to what might cause it. She'd never seen the like. She wiped her palm on her woolen breeches, chewing her lip and trying to make sense of the picture—cold sweats, ruddy face, cough, chills. She sought one of her mother's hands to see if they might be swollen and found them both clenched fiercely beneath the covers, knuckles white.

"You've some healing, Eyslk," said her step-da. "What do you think it is?"

She shook her head. "I don't know, Da. I've never seen

it." She chewed another tiny strip from her lower lip. "I'll get Roe Kettletoft. She'll know."

But Roe Kettletoft was just as boggled by Deardru's sudden illness as her daughter was. While Garradh-an-Caerluel occupied himself and his two sons with caring for their small flock of sheep, Eyslk and the village healer practiced their skills on his ailing wife with no result. She continued to cough, to shiver, to bathe herself in sweat. It seemed, in fact, as if their ministrations threw her into even deeper agony. Her face screwed into a horrible grimace, her eyes all but rolled back in her head, Deardru finally brought the young healer to a rueful admission of defeat.

"I can do nothing for her, Eyslk," Roe said. "This is no ordinary sickness. I sense magic in it. Can someone have cast inyx on your mama?"

The very thought was terrifying. "Who'd do such a thing?"

"I'm sure I don't know. My *aidan* is for healing, Eyslk. It goes no further than that, so I can't tell you. I'm desperate to believe no Hillwild would do such a thing to one of their own. I can only think it must be one of the strangers among us."

"But why? Why would any of them want to hurt my mama?"

Roe shook her head. "I've not the skills to tell, Eyslk. Perhaps Mistress Taminy can."

Eyslk chewed yet another strip from her lip. She hated to pester Taminy with her family's problems, but if what Roe Kettletoft said was true, if her mother's illness was caused by a purposeful inyx. . . .

Her step-father came in then, to see how his wife was faring. He was beside himself when Roe told him she could be no help. He ranted at her at first, blaming her, denigrating her skills. But he drifted, at last, into a terrible, dark calm, and Eyslk was afraid he'd given Deardru up for lost. When she had seen Roe Kettletoft from their house and returned to her mother's room, he looked up at her from the sickbed, clutching his wife's knotted hands and said, "You must ask your Mistress to help us, Eyslk."

She chilled. "But, da, she's so much more important things to do than—"

"Save the life of an innocent woman? I heard a bit of what Roe had to say about inyx. If someone's Weaving against your ma, it's sure that none of us is able to stop it. But Taminy could."

"I'd be afraid to ask."

"Afraid? Of what? If she's so dear and kind and loving as you keep telling us, how could she not help?"

Deardru groaned then—a horrid, thick, painful sound that rocked Eyslk to the soles of her boots. Her step-da continued to gaze up at her, his dark eyes hot and demanding. "Get up to Hrofceaster, girl. Beg if you have to. If that doesn't work, *I'll* beg."

Still, she hesitated.

Garradh-an-Caerluel's face twisted with anguish. "For God's sake, child, it's your mama's life!"

She ran—coatless, hoodless, ignoring the cold—all the way up the steep path to Hrofceaster. To beg.

"Please, mistress, do forgive me." Airleas delivered his impassioned plea to Taminy's back. She would not turn her face to him, gazing instead from the window of her audience chamber into the courtyard below.

"What did you do, Airleas?"

He held his breath, quivering. "Don't you know?"

"Yes. I wondered if you did."

He breathed again. "I Wove something bad. Without meaning too, though. I didn't realize I was Weaving at all. I . . . I was just angry."

"At whom?"

"At . . . at Broran. For mocking me. He—he calls me 'midge' and insults me every chance he gets, and—"

"So he insulted you and you hurled inyx at him."

"Well . . . no. Not exactly." Airleas shuffled his feet beneath his chair. "He walked away from me. He said he was going to tell Catahn I wasn't learning anything."

"And were you—learning anything?"

"Yes, but . . . "

She turned to face him suddenly, her face caught half in shadow, half in light, making her expression difficult to read. Tentatively, he tried to touch her with his *aidan*. Blocked.

"But?" she prompted him.

He looked at his mud-stained knees. "I was . . . I was being stubborn, I guess."

"You guess."

Humor tickled him. He kept his mouth straight. "I know I was being stubborn."

"So you don't really think Broran was off the trail in walking off on you."

"I suppose not."

"Then why were you angry at him?"

"He just makes me feel bad."

"And how does he do that?"

"He . . . he knew how I felt about taking lessons from him. He said I thought I was the great Malcuim and he was just a lowly mountain boy."

"And is that what you were thinking?"

Airleas could feel tears pressing behind his eyes. He nodded.

Taminy moved toward his chair then, steps measured and soft on the woven rugs. "He makes you feel bad because he can see through you. He sees some ugly things, doesn't he, Airleas? Stubbornness, prejudice, arrogance, pride."

He nodded again, eyes blurring.

"And that's not what you want him to see, is it? You want him to see courage and honor and trustworthiness— the sorts of things that inspire loyalty." She stopped less than an arm's reach away. "So, is it really Broran you're angry with?"

The tears slipped their bonds and fled down his cheeks. He shook his head.

"And are you angry with me?"

He shivered convulsively, realizing that he *had* been angry with Taminy. Angry that she had insisted he keep company with the likes of Broran; angry that she, too, saw through him; angry that she counseled him to caution and made his dreams of revenge seem like childish fantasy; angry that because of her, his father was dead and he and his mother were in exile. But it was a child's anger and he saw it for what it was—shallow, ugly, unreasoning. *She* made him see it and that, too, made him angry.

"I'll take that as a 'yes,'" she said. "Is there anyone else you're angry with, Airleas? Your mother, perhaps, or Catahn or . . . ?"

The tears were a flood now and, in them, his voice nearly drowned. "*Me!*" The word came out in a trembling wail, making Airleas Malcuim despise himself even further for sounding so infantile. "I'm angry at *me*! I can't *learn* anything! I can't *change* anything! I can't *do* anything! Just—just sit up here in this heap of stone and—and hide!"

She merely stood and watched him for a while then, while he soaked himself in abject misery. Then she moved past him toward the hearth. He couldn't have stopped the tears if he'd tried, so he didn't try. He let them fall, listening to the sounds of his own labored breathing in concert with outside wind and inside fire.

When at last he was gutted and empty and feeling incredibly alone, he dared turn to see where Taminy had gone. She was sitting on the floor before the hearth, but her eyes were on the flames, not on him. He rose and went to her and, standing beside her said, "I'm sorry, Taminy."

She neither spoke, nor looked at him.

He sat down next to her on the hearth rug. "Who will be Cyne of Caraid-land? Will Daimhin Feich be Cyne or the Ren Catahn?"

The corners of her mouth twitched. "No, Airleas, neither. One way or another, you will be Cyne of Caraid-land."

One way or another? What did that mean? "But surely, I'm not worthy to be Cyne. I'm . . . I'm terrible."

"Airleas, have you ever seen a fledgling bird?"

"Yes."

"Was it beautiful?"

"No. It was ugly. All eyes and beak and talon."

"Can it fly?"

"No."

"And when it tries it falls out of its nest and lies, flailing, on the earth. You might look at it lying there and say that it had failed. But that is the natural course for a bird, and if it survives its trials and tests, it *does* learn to fly. It learns, too, how to use its beak and talons properly. It becomes a songbird or a courier pigeon or a royal falcon."

"But, I'm not a bird. I'm a person."

Now she did look at him. "You're a boy. A boy who is endowed with a fierce, strong Gift—a Gift you must learn to control. A bird can't decide not to fly. But you can decide not to learn what you need to know to become Cyne of Caraid-land. What you did to Broran this morning was not evil. But it *was* irresponsible. Now you know you have a very strong *aidan*. What do you choose to do with it?"

He looked down at his hands, folded meekly now in his lap. And he realized something else. *Those* were the hands that controlled his fate, not Taminy's. As much as he wanted to deed his destiny into her hands or the Ren Catahn's or his mother's, he knew he could not. The choice Taminy held out to him now was his alone to make.

"I choose to learn how to be a Cyne. A good Cyne, pleasing to the Meri."

"Then learn from those who have things to teach you. Learn swordsmanship from Broran; statesmanship from Catahn; discipline from me; love from your mother. Learn from anyone who offers you knowledge, Airleas. No matter how lowly you esteem them to be."

He mulled all that over as he slept away his emptiness, his head cradled in Taminy's lap. He dreamed pleasantly of galloping his horse across a great meadow of rippling grass, hands firm on the reins, the animal solid between his knees. The grass rose up in waves and became an ocean and the horse became a fantastic boat, whose tiller he leaned upon. Wind filled its sails and pulled it toward a great, gleaming moonrise.

But the journey was interrupted by a terrible pounding, and Airleas feared he had run his magical barque hard aground. The deck shifted beneath him and he was falling and a voice was calling, "Come!"

He woke with a start, blinking groggily as he made out Eyslk coming through the chamber door, twisting the hem of her sweater in her hands. "Mistress," she said, and he realized that her voice trembled no more than the rest of her did. Her distress washed over him in a great tide, waking him completely. He sat up; just as swiftly, Taminy came to her feet.

"Eyslk! We missed you this morning, whatever is wrong?"

The girl paled. "It's my mother, Mistress, she—"

"She's ill." Taminy went to the girl, took her hands. "What's wrong with her?"

"I don't know. There's this terrible cough and she seems to be in such pain. She sweats buckets, but she's cold as ice and shivering herself all apart. I called the village healer first thing, but she says she can't do aught. She says she thinks it's an inyx. That someone's put magic on her."

Taminy's brow furrowed. "Who'd want to do anything like that?"

"I can't think, Mistress. My mama's a good woman. Fierce sometimes, but good. I can't think anybody we know'd want to harm her. But . . . but she's awful sick and I'm afraid, and step-da's afraid—"

"I'll come at once, of course."

Eyslk wobbled with relief. "If it's no trouble, Mistress."

Taminy fixed the younger girl with a penetrating gaze. "You were afraid to ask me." She put a hand on Eyslk's shoulder. "Don't *ever* be afraid to ask me anything, Eyslk. Ever again. And Eyslk, why ever did you run all the way from Airdnasheen? You could have Woven a message and I'd've gotten it just as clearly."

Even in her anxiety, the girl nearly giggled. "I . . . I didn't even think of it."

"Next time you need me, or any of the other *waljan*, *do* think of it, please. It could mean all the difference in the world."

They left together, hurrying out into the afternoon chill, while Airleas went in search of his Hillwild swordmaster.

Taminy stepped across the threshold into Deardru-an-Caerluel's small bed chamber and knew that Roe Kettletoft was right; the place quivered with the tension of a tightly directed *aidan*. A strong will worked here. Her gaze traveled from the two sad-eyed little boys huddled by the door to the handsome, stocky man who had leapt up from the bedside to face her. They came to rest at last on the woman shivering on the bed. From the man and the boys she sensed only fear and distress mixed, now, with a modicum of hope. From the woman . . .

Puzzled, she turned to the husband. "May I be left alone with her, sir?"

He raised dark eyebrows. "Whatever is best, Mistress. Thank you for coming here. For helping us."

"I'm more than happy to help, sir. And Eyslk, might I have you boil these herbs for a tea?" She laid a fragrant pouch in the girl's outstretched hands, then saw the others from the room. Only then did she turn her eyes and senses back to the woman in the bed.

What Roe Kettletoft had called magic was strong here. Oddly, Taminy found it had a different quality and texture than the workings of the Divine Art practiced by the Osraed. Like a basket held together with pitch and twine, or a patchwork garment, it was rough to the touch and straining at its joints.

Taminy sat on the edge of the bed and looked into Deardru-an-Caerluel's half-closed eyes. "Now, mam, will you tell me why you've inyxed yourself into a sickbed?"

The *aidan*-thick atmosphere quivered momentarily, further straining its crude seams. On the heavy quilt covering her chest, Deardru's knotted fists relaxed, loosing their hold on the inyx. She breathed deeply, closing her eyes. When she opened them again, gone was the glaze of concentration. In its place was a bright, voracious curiosity and a small, grudging respect.

"Well, Mistress Taminy, you *do* have a mighty touch of the *aidan*. Even Roe Kettletoft couldn't tell the inyx I was suffering was my own." She opened her left hand, causing the small amulet she held there to fall and bob at the end of its leather thong. The jet catamount caught light from the chamber's single deep window and glittered.

A family icon, Taminy realized, and knew it to be the Hageswode's totem. "But why, mam?" she asked. "Why put yourself in a sickbed?"

"I only wanted to meet you, Taminy-Osmaer."

"You could have come to Hrofceaster with Eyslk."

"I avoid Hrofceaster. I wanted you to come here."

Into your territory. Taminy smiled. "You might have simply invited me."

The woman's eyes glinted. "And you'd've come, would you?"

"Yes."

"To break bread with the likes of us? You, who count Cynes and Cwens and Osraed in your circle? Who break bread each day with the Hageswode, himself? You'd sit at table with your own serving maid?"

Taminy shook her head. "Eyslk is not my serving maid, mam. She's my student and my friend. She has a fine Gift."

Deardru's chin lifted. "She's a Hageswode."

Taminy tilted her head toward the jet catamount now lying atop the quilt. "I recognize the totem. Is that your family?"

"My first husband's. He was killed when we were quite young. Eyslk never knew him."

There was bitterness in that, and anger. Taminy felt immediate sympathy. "How did he die?"

"A border skirmish with the Deasach Kartas. He was pledged to the clan forces under Ren Morgant. When I became pregnant, he pled release to his family obligations and was granted the request. But before he could come home to me he was killed. His family was less family than I thought them. After Eyslk was born it was as if neither of us existed. She was twelve years old before Hrofceaster paid her any notice, and then it was Desary who spoke for her. You've noticed they look a great deal alike. They should. They're cousins."

Frowning, Taminy sifted through the other woman's splintered thoughts and feelings. "And you brought me here to tell me this? Why?"

"So you understand what sort of man Catahn Hageswode

is. A man who would pledge his only brother, newly married, to a dangerous posting far from home while he basked in the glory of his station and the adoration of his own wife and child. A man who then treated his kin as if they were clanless strangers. If Desary hadn't possessed her mother's good heart, Eyslk would have never met you or placed her Gift in your hands."

Stunned, Taminy could only think to ask, "And why would Catahn do such a thing to his own brother—to his brother's family?"

Deardru's smile was grim. "Pride. What else would make a man like Catahn Hillwild behave so?"

Taminy turned the words in her mind as if they contained poison; she could feel the blood draining from her face. She had never known Catahn to be a pride-driven man. Had he been that different as a youth?

Deardru's eyes acknowledged that they hadn't missed her discomfiture. "I neglect to mention that Raenulf was Catahn's older brother. It was he who should have been Village Elder, Catahn who should have been bound by *his* pledges. For his own reasons, Raenulf rejected the status Catahn craved. Old biddies like Gram Long and Eldress Levene will tell you that it was strength of character that brought Catahn Hageswode early power. It was not. It was Raenulf's yielding nature. Because of that, Catahn stood to be Ren and Raenulf willingly served him. But both knew the truth, and it ate at Catahn, so he put Raenulf away from him into Morgant's hands. And when Raenulf was killed, guilt drove Catahn to ignore his second family. I married Garradh, because Catahn could not be bothered to care for us."

Taminy shook herself. *I shouldn't listen to this. Only Catahn's words should tell me tales of his life.* "And why should I hear this?"

"He takes you into his home. He calls you 'Mistress' and 'Lady.' Should you not be aware of the flaws of those who serve you?"

"Catahn is no more my servant than Eyslk is, mam."

"Oh, no, of course. He's your friend. Your bosom

companion. But he would be more if you bid him. So, I warn you what sort of man you've Woven to your side."

"You mistake me, mam. I Weave no inyx to ensure Catahn's loyalty. He is where he desires to be."

The other woman laughed aloud at that. "I think not. But be wary, or he will be."

Eyslk all but fell through the door then, spilling tea and cakes onto the floor in her haste. "Mama! Mama! You're—you're! I heard you *laugh*! Oh, Taminy, you've healed her! Oh, let me tell step-da!" And she was gone again, leaving the upset tea things on the floor.

Taminy rose. "You don't need my help, mam, so I'd best leave. If you ever *do* need me, call and I'll come."

"What will you tell my family?"

"That you've healed. The rest is up to you." She turned to leave just as Garradh-an-Caerluel and his sons rushed in. They beamed at her, then gave their full attention to Deardru. Taminy slipped quietly into the hallway and was surprised to find Eyslk waiting for her in the parlor.

The girl's face was an agony of indecision and anxiety matched and amplified by her unabashed chaos of spirit.

"Mistress Taminy," she whispered. "I—I heard—oh, more than I ought!" Her eyes went to tears. "Oh, please, I can't imagine why Mama'd do such a thing as this, or say such things about Uncle. I've always known they—they didn't get on, but— Oh, Taminy, I'm so sorry!"

She put a hand on the girl's shoulder, blocking her own distress from flowing between them. "You've nothing to be sorry for, Eyslk. You couldn't have known what your mother meant to do."

"Couldn't I? She's my mother. And I'm supposed to have the *aidan*. How could I *not* know?"

"Having the *aidan* and learning to use it are two different things, Eyslk. One of the most important things you must learn is that strong emotions like fear and worry and anger can make the *aidan* capricious and harder to discipline."

"So we must avoid strong emotion?"

Taminy smiled, taking a tighter hold on her own inner

processes. "No, we must learn to control both the emotion and the *aidan* so that they become a help to each other and not a hindrance. Now, then, will I see you tomorrow up at Hrofceaster?"

Eyslk managed a weak smile and nodded. "If you'll have me, Mistress."

Taminy shook her gently. "Of course I'll have you, Eyslk. Tomorrow. I'll teach you how to start the fire without your precious flints."

The smile was genuine this time. Taminy carried it with her on the walk back up to Hrofceaster, as if with that warm amulet she might ward off the unsettling effects of Deardru-an-Caerluel's accusations.

CHAPTER 7

You truly cannot guide whom you desire; but the Spirit guides whom It will and It, alone, knows who will yield to guidance.

—from the Testament of Osraed Bevol

✦　　　✦　　　✦

The place was dark, and fog clung to him like a shroud of damp gauze, choking every pore. He was walking, but realized he had no idea where he was going or why. He wallowed for a moment in weightless, placeless confusion. Was he moving toward a goal or fleeing an enemy? Was he awake or dreaming?

In the instant the question was asked, it was answered, and now, consciously dreaming, Caime Cadder struggled for awareness of his surroundings. He was not often visited by dreams; when they came, he took them as welcome affirmations of his worthiness to serve the Osraed—or as chastisement from his divine Mistress. He didn't know which this would be, and so waited—anticipating, dreading—for the aislinn world to reveal itself.

A point of light pricked the darkness and, before his straining eyes, the fog lightened, struggling from black to grey. He glanced quickly around; on all other sides, the clinging veil of darkness pressed against him. He edged forward—the light his goal. Ages or moments later, he attained its precincts, entering a circle of gleaming mist that seemed to lock behind him, closing in the light and its source. He saw that source now, at the center of the circle— the Osmaer Crystal on its burnished pedestal.

He was not surprised, but awed. He fell to his knees, worshipful. A bounty, this was. Only in his dream was he allowed to face the Osmaer without Ladhar or some other Osraed as intermediary and guardian. He resented that and despised the resentment. It only served to remind him that it was through his own poverty of spirit that he was not, himself, Osraed.

But now the resentment was quelled. Neither Ladhar nor his lieutenants were in sight. Caime Cadder was alone with Ochan's fabulous and holy Relic. Without their censuring presence, he dared approach it. And he could feel— yes, *feel*, with every fiber—its warm, life-giving emanations. But no, it did not emanate, it channeled. It was the Meri who fed Her healing rays through the earthy substance, who brought light to its cold facets.

Staring into those facets, longing, adoring, Caime Cadder became only gradually aware of another presence in the chamber of mist. He glanced up past the Crystal, his eyes drawn to an amorphous cloud of luminance behind it. Cadder licked dreamer's lips, aislinn eyes bright. For a moment he let himself hope that this night he would be granted his heart's desire—that what he had denied himself on his Pilgrimage, the Meri would grant him in this corridor to the Eibhilin world. A *glance*, he prayed. A *glance, only*.

The paeri form resolved itself gracefully, taking on a female shape. Cadder shivered, uncertain. Perhaps he should avert his eyes; perhaps he should genuflect. He only knew that this time he would not turn and run. He *would* not.

But as the image struggled to clarity, it seemed to the bemused cleirach that it was too human. He could now make out features. He could now—

His entire being froze, hopes unraveling into chaos. In less than a heartbeat, he fell from bliss to terror and stood face to face with his nemesis. The aislinn Taminy smiled at him—he quivered with dread and disgust. She held out her gleaming arms to him—he flinched away. But he would not run. He *must* not. This scene played on an aislinn stage and his Mistress' eyes watched his spirit's every move.

Evil. Oh, evil!

But between him and that, the Stone. Yes, the Stone would protect him. He smiled into the Golden Wicke's face and stepped closer, bringing the Osmaer within arm's reach.

As if to mock his certitude, the Wicke reached out her white hands and laid them upon the Crystal. In response, the facets exploded with light. If he had been corporeal, Cadder would have shrieked aloud. But he was mute and the shrill sound of his cries reverberated only in his mind. Fool, he was, to believe the Stone could Weave its own protection. He'd seen the Wicke lay hands on it in the Shrine, to his personal pain and humiliation. Now, he recognized this nightmare as the Eibhilin shadow of that waking one. He had failed then. He could only view this dream as a second chance to succeed.

He could see now what he had been meant to see before—that this Wicke was indeed an Evil Being of such great power that she could manipulate even the Stone of Ochan. It was no wonder that Daimhin Feich trembled in fear of her. How was Ladhar so dense that he did *not*?

Why am I receiving this vision?

It came to Caime Cadder forcefully as he stared into the Wicke's green eyes that he must be in a position to protect the Stone. Protect it he must. His aislinn self reached out to pry the Evil's hands from the Great Crystal. Her flesh was warm, soft. The surprise of that hit him with the same force as the blinding wash of radiance that blew him back into the realm of form and shadow.

Waking, quaking, Caime Cadder lay and considered his dream. He had been shown two things: Feich was right about the immensity of Evil's power and Ladhar was a fool.

It seemed as if they had been on the road for weeks when at last the ramparts of Halig-liath came into view through the forest canopy. One moment they were riding in the chill, fragrant gloom of the deep pines, the next the boughs thinned to let through a cascade of sunlight and a view of Halig-liath gleaming atop its palisade.

Aine was inordinately thrilled to see it. Somehow she had expected it to have been washed away in the great tide of war she had once dreamed, or reduced to a ruin by Daimhin Feich and his allies. But no, Taminy had been right; Feich had not yet budged from Creiddylad and Halig-liath still stood guard over Nairne's beautiful river bend.

"Happy to be home?"

Aine jerked her head around, startled. Where Iseabal had been not a moment ago rode Saefren Claeg. She swept him with her eyes and her *aidan*, but found his thoughts as hard to read as his colorless eyes. She shrugged, too tired just now to be prickly. "I'll only be here as long as your uncle is willing to stay. Besides, it doesn't much feel like home anymore."

Saefren returned the shrug, his eyes now on the sun-washed fortress. "You don't have to go on to Creiddylad, surely. At least not right away. Why not visit awhile, then take the river packet down?"

Aine glared at him. "You'd like that, wouldn't you?" she retorted, then grasped tight hold of her temper and shook it. "I'm sorry, but you'll just have to suffer my bad company all the way to Creiddylad."

"It's been months since you've seen your family, girl. Don't you want to stay?"

"Taminy wants me to go to Creiddylad—with you. Now."

"And so, you'll obey. Without question or thought. Have you no sense of *family*, Aine-mac-Lorimer?"

Fire blazed in her head, making her face hot and prickly. "I have every sense of family, Saefren Claeg. Only my family's gotten much bigger, suddenly. My family in Nairne is safe and happy. My family in Creiddylad needs me more."

Saefren shook his head. "You lot boggle me."

"Us lot?"

"Taminists. Do you know, my uncle firmly expects to find the Chieftain of the Gilleas awaiting us in Nairne with his chief Elders?"

"I know. Taminy said he'd be here." She glanced back up through the trees at Halig-liath, framed now by the golds and reds of autumn. "He's up there." She was both surprised and pleased by that freshly caught knowledge, annoyed when Saefren's chuckle of derision snuffed her pleasure.

"Like I said, you lot boggle me. Pretend all you like, Lady Red. But you'll soon find that all the make-believe in the world won't make it so. Your Lady's talismans are empty and so's Halig-liath, I'll wager."

Aine looked at him sharply. "What do you mean?"

He leaned toward her, making her wish she dared reach out and yank him out of his saddle. "I've glimpsed the 'messages' Taminy-Osmaer's dispatched for the noble Houses. There's nothing in them."

Face flushing hot and cold, Aine faced front. What could he mean—nothing in them? In a moment, indignity had settled on her and she prayed time would speed so Saefren-the-Smug could sooner learn how wrong he was.

They entered Nairne along the up-river road from Linliath, banners snapping. It seemed the whole town had come out to meet them. The redhead's parents appeared and literally dragged her from her mount in their exuberance. *Wasted on her*, Saefren thought, though she returned tear for tear and smile for smile.

The dark-haired beauty, Iseabal, was already shedding tears of her own and begging to know if her own parents were at home. Finally, she got word from some scrub-faced boy that her da was up at Halig-liath and turned her horse cross-river. Iobert bid his men accompany her, and so they left the Lorimer tribe by the wayside, still making much over their big, fire-breathing daughter.

Once across the river, they caught a cross road that ran east up the flank of the holy hill and west past the village Cirke. Above the autumnal glory of its surrounding grove of trees, the Cirke spire showed its stellate crown. The Cirkemaster's girl laid her pretty eyes longingly on the place, on the woman who had appeared behind a gate in the low wall. The girl raised her hand and waved, reining her horse toward the Cirke grove. The woman turned away and disappeared beneath the trees.

His eyes on the girl's pale, tragic face, Iobert Claeg turned the column eastward and led up the long ridge to Halig-liath.

The gates were wide open—a thing Saefren thought peculiar and foolhardy under the circumstances. In the huge central courtyard, a bevy of Osraed and Prentices met them. Foremost among these was the Cirkemaster, Saxan, and the rotund, bird-eyed Tynedale. Iobert Claeg had no sooner delivered the Cirkemaster's tearful daughter into his arms than he asked the man where he might find The Gilleas.

Saefren felt his face burn warm with embarrassment. He glanced away, making a point of ordering the horses fed and watered. When he looked after his uncle again, the Claeg Chieftain was already halfway to the main rotunda of the Osraed academy in the company of Tynedale, Saxan and Iseabal. He trailed them to the Academy's small sanctuary where they were met by a handful of men in the purple and white of the House Gilleas.

Saefren didn't know The Gilleas on sight, but his uncle obviously did. He greeted the white-hair in the group and fell to conversing with him in quiet tones. Bemused, Saefren approached the group. The damn Wicke had been right. Well, of course, she'd gotten The Gilleas here, but that didn't mean the summons had come by supernatural means. There were always pigeons.

Uncle had the satchel out now, and withdrew the Gilleas scroll, placing it in the House Chieftain's hands. "From Taminy-Osmaer," he said, and stood back to watch The Gilleas open the scroll.

Saefren folded his arms across his chest, eyes on the old man's face. The twine loosened and fell away, the scroll opened and the shard of crystal rolled out into The Gilleas's palm. The white brows furrowed as he scanned the scroll. Saefren was vaguely aware of hurried footsteps behind him in the aisle, but did not pull his eyes from the Gilleas Chieftain's face.

Dark eyes glittered in the light of scattered globes as the old man raised them to Iobert Claeg. "What is this?" he asked, holding the talisman in outstretched hands. The surface of the scroll was as blank as it had been when Saefren had seen it last.

There was a soft intake of breath at his shoulder and a moment later, someone slid past him. It was flame-haired Aine. In a twinkling, she stood face to face with the Gilleas Chieftain and lifted the little shard of stone from his hand.

The moment she touched it, the shard's entire nature changed. Before it had been stone, now it was fire. Before it had been lifeless, now it blazed with kinetic light. The village cailin held the living flame in her hand and passed it back and forth over the empty scroll and the scroll was no longer empty. Words appeared there in characters of light. Saefren Claeg could not see what they said, for they seemed to say nothing, but he knew his eyes were as wide as everyone else's.

Now, Morcar Gilleas's face bore an expression of complete amazement. His eyes scanned the scroll again, this time filling themselves with the bright words. And when they had read, those eyes glittered with dew. Clutching the scroll to his breast, the old man fell to one knee and kissed Aine Lorimer's hand.

The girl withdrew it immediately, the little crystal she held leaking glory through her fingers. "Oh, no sir!" she cried. "You mustn't bow to *me*. I'm only Taminy's student."

Morcar remained on his knee. "If you are but a student, then your Mistress must be great, indeed. These are her words? This is her fire?"

"Yes, sir."

The Chieftain rose, his gaze going to the faces of his Elders. The fire of the little shard had leapt to his eyes, and his teeth shown in a fierce grin. "It is just as I remember—just as I told you. She is Osmaer—living link to the Meri. Her voice, Her face. And we, the Gilleas— Disciples of the Meri—are now *her* disciples."

Caime Cadder did not tremble as he made his way to Mertuile the next morning. He did not quake as he followed his Dearg escort to the throneroom. Only there, in the presence of Daimhin Feich and his smirking, irreligious minions, did he realize the import of what he intended to do. At the point of quailing, he reminded himself that *he* had been given the dream. Only he could act on it.

"And what may I do for you today, Minister Cadder?" asked Daimhin Feich, his mouth drawn into that irritating half-grin.

He believes himself superior, Cadder thought. *Well, he is superior—a superior idiot.* But he lifted his head and said, softly so as not to be overheard by every gaping toady, "Actually, Regent Feich, I have come to discuss what I might do for you."

Feich's brows ascended. "Really? And what might *you* do for me?"

The emphasis in that sentence was enough to make Cadder bristle, but he hid his hackles and leaned closer to the throne in which the usurper sat. "You intimated to Abbod Ladhar that you desire a Weaving stone. . . . "

Feich's expression altered satisfactorily and Cadder leaned away again to watch.

"Let us move our conversation to a more private place," Feich said, and rose. The courtiers were left behind; even the ubiquitous young cousin remained outside the confines of the small but sumptuous salon he led his visitor to. Once there, he turned to the cleirach, his pale eyes alight with curiosity.

"You have brought me a rune crystal?"

Cadder nearly laughed. Was the man so daft as to think a mere cleirach might lay hands on a Weaving crystal? "That would not be possible, sir. Only the Chosen have Weaving stones and every one is registered. To possess one, I would have to steal it, and I am no thief."

Feich frowned. "Then how can you help me?"

Caime Cadder's resolve almost buckled, then, for he knew he was about to cross over a sacred line. "Perhaps you have wondered where rune crystals are found?"

"I hadn't really thought about it."

"There is a cave below Ochanshrine," said Cadder. "The cave in which Ochan originally saw the Meri. He took the

Osmaer Crystal from that cave. Every crystal bestowed upon a Pilgrim since that day was cut from the same chamber."

Daimhin Feich's eyes lit once again. "The Cave of Ochan! I had thought it merely a legend. There is some truth to the tale, then."

Cadder bit back a caustic reply. "The legend is entirely true. Ochan's Crystal exists; his cave exists. And it is the only source of Weaving stones."

"Then you will get me one."

"I? No, Regent, I cannot. To do so would be to . . . to violate my oath of service to the Osraed. However, I can tell you how to get into the cave without being observed."

"And in doing this, you will *not* be violating your oath of service?"

Feich's evident amusement nearly cost Cadder his poise. But Caime Cadder bit down hard on his wretched pride, on his revulsion at giving a Weaving stone into such hands as Daimhin Feich's. "I have no Gift, sir. No . . . talent for the Divine Art. It is clear that you do. At the very least, you have sensed the danger posed by the Wicke of Haligliath. You recognize her as the source of an immense and palpable Evil—a dark Power. I, personally, believe such a thing is hinted at in our Scripture, yet the wise among us seem not to recognize those references. Therefore they do not recognize the threat."

"The wise among us . . . You mean Osraed Ladhar, I suppose."

Cadder put a hand to his breast. Within, his heart clenched with sorrow. "My master regards Taminy-a-Cuinn as a heretical trickster. He refuses to grant her more power."

Daimhin Feich's expression darkened. "Perhaps she does not invade his dreams, Minister. She does mine."

"And mine," Cadder told him. "That is why I am willing to act so . . . dangerously. I understand—that is, it was given to me to understand—what forces she is capable of marshalling if she is allowed to get her hands on the Crystal she has so blasphemously made her namesake."

The bright Feich eyes pinioned him where he sat. "And

do you believe that is her intention? To wrest the Stone of Ochan from its Shrine?"

"Isn't it obvious? She has named herself for it. She has laid hands on it, to my personal humiliation and injury. And in my vision—last night, it was—I saw her hovering over it like a bird of prey. Most horribly of all, she has the Malcuim heir in her clutches. Caraid-land cannot be whole as long as Airleas Malcuim and the Osmaer Crystal are separated. He must be set before it to be Cyne. She knows this. She knows they must be reunited. And she must believe that when they are, *she* will be the ultimate victor, for she will have the Stone and the Cyne in her embrace."

Daimhin Feich's eyes did not waver from Cadder's face. "Is it that important, do you think, that a Malcuim be set before the Stone or, indeed, that anyone be set before it?"

"How can you ask that? The coronation of a Cyne is no mere symbolic rite, Regent. The power that unifies Caraid-land flows through the Crystal. It has always been, and must always be, bound to the Malcuim line. So it was ordained when the Meri sent Ochan-a-Coille to the first Malcuim. He did not go to the Claeg or to the Feich or to the Madaidh or to any other House. The Stone will seek a Malcuim to guard it and the Malcuim is in the hands of Evil." His eyes fell to the clenched fist he had raised between himself and Feich. He lowered it. "The Evil must be stopped."

Feich nodded, eyes narrowed. "Indeed, Minister, she must. You fear you may have erred in coming to me. Fear no longer. Your vision is true. Your instinct has served you well. As you perceive, I too am visited by aislinn visions. And, as you so perceptively note, I have a small Gift for the Art. I can only believe that it has been bestowed upon me for the protection of Caraid-land. But if I am to fight this Evil we both recognize, I must be armed. Tell me, Minister, how I am to obtain my crystal."

Saefren Claeg settled himself into a low sling chair next to his uncle. After so many nights spent on the hard, freezing ground of the trail—a trail made dangerous by the fall of early snow—to be bathed and curried and taking a soft seat next to a roaring fire was a luxury to be savored. His enjoyment of their comfortable room in Halig-liath's visitors' quarters was dampened a bit by the cool pressure of Uncle Iobert's eyes.

They hadn't spoken since their lengthy consultation with the Gilleas. The upshot of that consultation had been that the Gilleas elders would accompany The Claeg to Creiddylad, there to petition Daimhin Feich to willingly return Airleas Malcuim to the Throne—on Taminy-Osmaer's terms. First though, there were other stops to make to deliver the Osmaer's messages and gather House support.

"So," Saefren said, finally breaking the silence. "Tomorrow we make for the Jura holdings. . . . Do you think Mortain Jura will also be won?"

"The Jura are mystics. What do you think?"

"That perhaps Lady Red will not even have to inyx up so much as a spark. The talisman itself may be enough."

Now he felt the full force of his Uncle's gaze. "Do you still not understand? The scroll is no more than a fleshed skin, naked until written to by Art. The shard of crystal is just that—a piece of rock—lifeless unless touched by the *aidan*. Aine-mac-Lorimer is the talisman, nephew. Without her, the other things are so much hide and stone."

Saefren found himself with nothing to say to that. Unlike the House Jura, the Claeg was not a House of mystics. Claeg had been farmers, warriors, landlords, and occasionally courtiers. They had never produced an Osraed, and few, if any, Prentices or cleirachs. They were practical people—strong of bone and will—pragmatic, above all things. Now here was The Claeg, himself, speaking mildly of the touch of the *aidan* and of a flesh-and-blood girl who was also a magical talisman for an even greater magic— also incarnate in a young, self-possessed cailin.

Saefren had seen the magic—the Weaving, as the initiates preferred to call it. He could not deny its existence, nor, strictly speaking, could he doubt its source. That Airleas Malcuim on the throne of Caraid-land with Taminy-Osmaer at his side was preferable to being lorded over by a Feich was obvious. That Taminy, though possessed of great power, was a good, gentle girl was also obvious. But was she Osmaer? Was she allied with the Meri? Or was she literally self-possessed—seduced by her own abilities into believing herself more than she was?

Uncle Iobert would say such a strong Gift could only be wielded by one aligned with the Spirit of the Universe, but Saefren had heard scripture quoted to support the idea that there was another force in the world—a force as evil as the Meri and the Spirit were good. Saefren would never call himself a scholar, but it seemed to him that the very fact the Corah sometimes referred to this world as the World of Light and Shadow surely alluded to its dual nature.

So then, if the Meri was the Light, what was the Shadow?

It was cold in the cave, and wet and dark. Daimhin Feich found all those things exceptionally depressing. Especially so in the middle of a cloudy night; there would be no walking out into the warmth and light of the sun. Soaked to the knees, Feich, his cousin Ruadh and two kinsmen waded through the surf into a narrow slit in the cliff face, and negotiated a close, dark passage where their torches and lamps smudged the hemming ceiling with soot and stained their eyes with glare.

Without warning, the walls and ceiling flew away and what had seemed like blinding light was all but swallowed in a chamber so large it dwarfed the throneroom of Mertuile. Blinking, shivering, Daimhin Feich tried to take it in—tried to see what the chamber contained. When his eyes had adjusted to the balance of light and shadow, they began to register the peculiar shapes that surrounded them, the tiny points of light scattered throughout the gloom like stars in the night sky. In a moment, the shapes began to resolve and Feich found himself in the midst of an eternally frozen congregation in an underground Cirke. He swung his lamp to dispel the impression; the forms were mere stone. But they were covered with jewels.

Heart tripping over itself, Feich splashed through a shallow pool onto a gravelly shore. It took him a long moment of groping toward the nearest misshapen pillar before he realized that even the sands beneath his feet glittered. Stunned, he stooped to scoop up a handful of jeweled grains. Though the largest were only the size of pebbles, the sight of them amazed him beyond words. Not so, his young cousin.

"I thought you were here for something a bit larger than that," he said sharply. His voice shattered on the crystalline walls and fell to fragments in the rush of surf.

Daimhin let the gem-sand slide through his fingers like a rain of solid rainbows. "Nervous, Ruadh?"

"This is a holy place."

How matter-of-fact he sounds. How anxious. Daimhin looked around at the glittering chamber. Legends were strong here—ancestral fears hard to set aside . . . for some. "You think so?"

Ruadh didn't answer, but his feet made uneasy sounds in the crystal gravel.

Daimhin raised his eyes and lamp to the pillar before him. Even this close, his eyes tried to tell him this lump of rock was a cowled and cloaked penitent, frozen in the act of bending the knee to . . . He turned his head, following the direction of the stone worshiper's devotion, and saw the largest structure of all—the gleaming altar of this stygian sanctuary. Seeming at once liquid and solid, it appeared to have been caught in the act of pouring from a long crevice in the wall. And it, like every other structure in this place, wore a mantle of pure crystal.

He moved across the jeweled strand until he was within arm's length of the great mass. That other prospectors had been here before him was obvious from the gaps and holes in the altar drape. Still, it was awe inspiring, the individual stones ranging in color from dark blues and violets to bright gold.

Color. He hadn't even imagined the colors. He had figured to march in, chip out the first stone that came to hand (or two, perhaps, to be safe), and leave this dank hole as quickly as possible. But now he realized that color was critical. The color had meaning. He wanted the color of power. The color of passion. His eyes scanned the altar mass until, in shadow beneath a fluted ledge, his lamp light fell upon what he sought.

Summoning his silent cousin to hold the lamp, he took from his belt pouch a silver chisel and a small silver hammer brought him by the superstitious Cadder, and set to chipping. The lamp quivered in Ruadh's hand, scattering quaking brilliance over the glittering form. Still, Daimhin Feich chipped at the root of his crystal until at last it succumbed and tumbled into his open hand—big, heavily faceted and the color of fresh blood.

CHAPTER 8

Beg forgiveness and pardon from the Spirit alone. Confession of your transgressions before men is unworthy; it has no relation to Divine forgiveness. Confession before others results only in humiliation, and the Spirit—beloved is She—does not desire the humiliation of Her lovers.

—*Utterances of Taminy-Osmaer, Book of the Covenant*

The chamber was dark except for the four points of flame that danced atop candles set at the corners of an invisible square. The place reeked of incense; sweet, pungent, musky, its smoke lay in loose coils about the candlesticks. In the midst of it all, Daimhin Feich sat crosslegged, the blood-red crystal cupped in his hands. His eyes watered and stung. That was the sole result of his efforts so far.

Cadder had spoken of "communing with the stone." He'd tried that; he'd only given himself a headache. He knew Taminy was rumored to have conjured in the old tongue, but Cadder assured him no Osraed had ever used it. Just as well; he knew not one word. He knew singing was part of the ritual of Weaving. Knowing no duans, he put his plea for the stone's acknowledgment into clumsy words, then constructed a simple melody. Mellifluous as his voice was, the stone remained unimpressed.

He opened his eyes now, sniffling and hacking a little, and glanced around. Was the room wrong? He had assumed darkness was beneficial, if not necessary. If nothing else, it helped him concentrate. Should he not sit on a carpet? Were special words needed—what the Osraed called inyx?

144

If so, was there somewhere at Ochanshrine a book of such incantations?

Frustration roiled in him like a wind-bedeviled cloud. Damn Cadder! He clearly knew more than he was telling. Offers of reward had not helped, perhaps a subtle threat would pry some artful information from those zealot lips.

That in mind, Feich rose stiffly, moved the candlesticks back to the fireplace mantle, doused the wretched incense and opened a window, letting in cold night air. Then he gathered up two of his personal guards (one was a Dearg, now, so as to send a strong political message), and went over to Ochanshrine.

Caime Cadder, he knew, was wont to worship at night when the holy Osraed were tucked away in their private chambers or dining in the Abbis refectory. Accordingly, he went to the Shrine proper and was not disappointed; Cadder was there in the bottom-most tier of seats, eyes rolled back into his head, lips moving soundlessly, hands folded obsequiously in his lap.

Feich's lip curled. Perhaps that had been his failing with the smoky red stone—he had not made himself look ridiculous enough. Leaving his guards to hover nearby, he moved to sit next to the cleirach, pinning him with a gaze as chill as the water in the belly of Ochan's sea cave.

As if he felt that chill, Caime Cadder shivered and opened his eyes. He all but leapt from his seat when he saw who sat beside him. "Regent Feich! What—whatever are you—?"

"I have it," Feich said, patting a velvet pouch at his waist. "But I can't use it. *You* must show me how."

"I have something to show you," Catahn had said. The air around him shimmered and danced with anticipation and Taminy, looking up at him from Wyth's manuscript, smiled.

"Show me?" she said. "Show me what?"

"If you'd come with me . . . ?" Diffidently, he'd held out his hand. Taminy took it and allowed him to lead her from the room.

They had passed through the heart of Hrofceaster and out again into a courtyard snug in the windless lee of the crags. It had been showered with sunshine the moment they stepped from the shelter of the fortress and she had been delighted with the play of light on the water of a spring-fed fountain—water cascading from the mountain face that rose steeply to form the rearward wall of the court. Twisted pines sat here and there in huge wooden pots amid hand-hewn benches; wild vine roses twined up walls that glittered with mica and quartz. A few brave blooms even dared the wintry day.

"It looks poor now, I know," Catahn had said. "But in spring—"

She hadn't let him finish the apology, but leapt to throw her arms around his neck and kiss his bearded cheek. "It's beautiful," she told him. "The most beautiful gift I've ever known. Thank you, Catahn." A second kiss deepened the stain of red that hid beneath his beard. He had barely spoken to her as they sat together watching the Sun shift the shadows across the little court.

She sat now, blanketed, on one of the wooden benches in a small pool of sunshine—soon to disappear as the Sun traveled over the ramparts of Catahn's fortress. The roses were bloomless and nearly leafless, the conifers shivered in a chill breeze, but the Sun yet gave warmth and strewed diamonds in the spring's icy flow. The Ren's gift was beautiful and dear.

She had been in commune with Iseabal, ensconced now at Halig-liath, and mulled over what the girl's aislinn messages told her. The Gilleas had come to Nairne at her summons, had met with the Claeg and had been delivered his talisman. None had been more astonished than Aine-mac-Lorimer to discover that she was, in spirit, the key to that talisman. Taminy afforded a smile for that. Her message had been well-received; The Gilleas had enlisted himself in her Cause and would travel with The Claeg to Creiddylad, but not before they visited the Jura, the Graegam, the Madaidh and the Skarf. With the strength of those Houses they would press Airleas's Regent to return Colfre's heir to the throne of Caraid-land.

She prayed for them every success, but knew that, ultimately, the Chieftains themselves must decide the fate of their Houses. She could only speak to their spirits, seek access to their souls. If they barred those doors in her face . . .

She looked up, sensing approach long before the heavy pinewood door in Hrofceaster's flank creaked to announce her visitor. She frowned. Odd, this visit, and unexpected.

"Such a marvel!" Deardru-an-Caerluel stopped in the middle of Taminy's courtyard before the fountain pool, her eyes on the cascade of water from the riven rock of Baenn-an-ratha. "A garden in the heart of Catahn's fortress. Eyslk told me of it, but I could not believe. I had to see it with my own eyes before that." Those eyes moved to Taminy's face. "A gift from the Ren, she said."

Taminy nodded, smiling now, but still attempting to probe gentle fingers of sense into the older woman's mood. "He wanted me to have a bit of home. I'm looking forward to seeing the roses bloom again."

"He wants you . . . to make this your home, Lady. Those roses will not bloom until late spring."

Unease fluttered in Taminy's heart. Deardru was overfull of something that clearly distressed her. "Speak plainly, mam. Why have you come?"

The full lips twisted upward. "Your magic doesn't inform you? You're not the Wicke Eyslk believes you, then."

"I'm not a Wicke, nor does Eyslk believe me to be one. She knows what I am."

The Mistress-an-Caerluel turned to face her full on. "And you know what Catahn is. Yet you let him stay close to you."

"And this distresses you? Why?"

"I have told you why. Catahn is not what he seems to be. Perhaps your Gift has bewicked him, confused him, made him seem gentle and meek. He is neither. Catahn is a man of strong will and stronger desires. He sees what he wants and takes it and what he doesn't want, he puts aside—forever."

Taminy tried to fan warmth into her suddenly chill core. "You speak of your husband—Catahn's brother."

"I do. Catahn wanted . . . " Her lips thinned, tightened. " . . . what he knew was his brother's by right. And he did not care whose suffering he caused in having it."

Taminy looked over at the fountain, its water bubbling clean and cleansing from the ageless rock face. There was a message in that wonder of nature, but she was unable to fathom it. What had she said to Airleas—that strong emotion and the *aidan* combined with difficulty? "I have not spoken of this to Catahn," she said. "I felt no need—"

Deardru laughed. "Liar."

Taminy glanced at her sharply. "I felt no need to confront him with accusations or humiliate him by insisting that he resolve my—"

The older woman's dark brows flung upward. "Your what, child? Your fears? Your distress?"

"My unease. I can't believe Catahn guilty of what you suggest."

"That he caused his brother's death."

Taminy nodded. "That he deliberately put his brother in death's way. I can believe that *you* believe it. *That*, mam, is what distresses me."

"And it distresses me to see you—a young, innocent cailin—fast in the clutches of this man. A man I *know* to be guilty. Speak to Catahn—"

"Perhaps *you* should speak to him, mam."

She shook her head, dark hair a cloud on the peaked folds of her woolen cloak. "I have spoken to him, child. Years ago. But you see, I have a child to think of. A family. To speak further would be unwise."

"You can't believe yourself in danger from Catahn." A statement of fact. Deardru-an-Caerluel did *not* believe herself in danger from him.

Still, she pretended, lowering her head and quivering as if near tears. "If he were to find me here, talking to you . . . "

Taminy rose. "Please, mam, let us stop this dance. You aren't afraid of Catahn. But you do hate him—that much is clear. I understand that you believe he has taken your dead husband's birth-right—"

Deardru's head jerked up, her eyes flashing. "He took more than that, Lady Taminy. Yes, let us now stop the dance. I'll tell you what Catahn Hageswode took from his brother—*his* place in my bed. It was *me* Catahn wanted, as he now wants you. And he had me, and fathered a child on me. Eyslk isn't Catahn's niece, she's his daughter."

It took all of her strength not to thrust her hands over her ears, not to cry the words that shouted in her head: *Stop! Oh, stop! Take back these things! Unsay them!* But they could not be taken back nor could what lay beneath them in Deardru-an-Caerluel's heart and mind—the memory of Catahn's overwhelming presence, the galling hatred at his later betrayal. And so Taminy forced different words to her lips: "Why do you tell me this? What is it you imagine I should do?"

Deardru moved to stand before her, to take her hands in a motherly grasp. "Osmaer you may be, Lady, but you are yet a child. I cannot help but look at you and see my own daughter, Catahn's own child, not so much younger than you. And again, I look at you and see myself all those years ago. I cannot stand by and see your life played as mine was. You think he is a convert to your Cause." She shook her head. "He is a convert only to his own cause. As to what you should do—I think you must free yourself from his grasp. Escape this place."

"But I'm not a prisoner here, mam. And Catahn befriends me in all sincerity."

"You forget who you deal with, child. A Hillwild. A Hageswode. The *aidan* is strong in these mountains, but nowhere is it stronger than in the men of that family. They could confound the Meri, Herself, with that guile."

Through their clasped hands, messages flowed. This is true, proclaimed one; that is not, whispered another. And which was which? Taminy, for all her attention to those messages, could not tell. Not now. Not here. Not under the barrage of Deardru-an-Caerluel's regard. She would need to put on Truth to determine the truth. But first, she must speak to Catahn.

She composed herself carefully, looked the older woman in the eye and said, "Thank you, mam, for your concern.

I will speak to Catahn of this, if nothing else, for Eyslk's sake. Does she know . . . ?"

"That she's Catahn's child? No. I never told her. For her own sake, it's best she believes her 'uncle' is a great man."

"I see." Taminy disengaged herself from Deardru's touch. "Please, I must excuse myself. Catahn is looking for me."

Deardru's face blanched, betraying real fear. "Then I must go. He must not find me here." She reached back momentarily to grasp Taminy's hand again. "Please, don't tell him of this visit. With your *aidan*, you might have gleaned this knowledge elsewhere. Please, Lady."

"I won't betray you," Taminy said and watched as the other woman bolted from the courtyard. She looked back at the bench where she had sat. The spot of sunlight was gone. Reaching to the Meri for warmth, marshalling her composure, Taminy went to meet Catahn.

In the aislinn world of Catahn's *aidan*, Taminy's distress had sounded as loud as the fortress's alarm bell. He had no way to interpret its meaning or determine its source, he knew only that it was. And before he even knew where it had arisen, it was lidded. He feared a physical attack on her, but couldn't imagine who might perpetrate such an attack. Then he thought that she must have received some disturbing news from Iseabal or Aine.

He searched the fortress from bottom to top, checking her favorite haunts, asking every *waljan* he encountered where their Mistress might be. It was Wyth Arundel, as always slaving over his manuscript, who said he thought Taminy might have gone up to her garden to meditate, Catahn was headed there when he saw her coming down the stairs from the upper reaches.

She hesitated when she saw him and there was no welcoming smile on her lips when their eyes met. Instead, she searched him inside-out while he, astounded, let his guard fall open and waited, daring to think nothing.

At last, he dared speak. "My Lady, what's happened? I felt . . . " He wasn't sure what he had felt, so the flow of words stopped.

She beckoned him to accompany her and he did, moving in silence beside her to her private rooms. He did not come here often, had never stayed more than a second or two. It seemed inappropriate for him to see the place where she slept and bathed, where she walked clothed for sleeping . . . or unclothed. He set a guard on his thoughts, afraid what they might betray.

Once inside, he stood uncertainly by the door while she moved to rouse the embers sleeping in her hearth. She seemed preoccupied, her movements stiff and tentative. The empty time gave him a chance to study himself as he stood there, waiting. He could almost laugh at what he saw; Ren Catahn Hageswode, Chieftain of the most powerful of the Hillwild clans reduced to a large, uncertain puddle by this lowland woman. The smile that tugged at his lips ossified. No, not a woman, a girl. And not merely a girl, but Osmaer. The Meri's Essence, Firstborn of the Spirit, had resided in that pure form. She was a walking beam of light, compared to which he was a clot of filthy clay.

She turned to look at him, her green eyes filled with what he could only take as great sorrow. Impulsively, he started forward. "Lady! Taminy! Please speak. You wither me with such looks."

She did speak, then, and the words that came out of her mouth struck him all but dead. "Desary is not your only child."

Somehow his dead husk produced a voice. "No."

Taminy nodded. "Eyslk is also your daughter. Out of your brother's widow, Deardru."

He closed his eyes. Dear God, surely he would be permitted to die now, but he doubted even that would provide escape from this. What must she think of him? "Yes."

"Catahn, answer me plainly. Did you keep your brother up at Moidart in the hope that he would die?"

Eyes open now, Catahn, felt a roil of anger surge beneath his shame. There was only one place she could have heard that tell. His fists clenched hard on his growing rage.

"Deardru. Only she would have laid that blame at my feet. No, Taminy. I did not deal my brother into death's hands. I loved Raenulf, and were I not the village Father, I would have happily gone up to Moidart myself. I even offered— and I say this with shame—that I would ask one of our cousins to go in his stead. He refused. With him it was a matter of family honor, of duty to our southern kin. Only when he found his wife pregnant did he ask to return, and I agreed, gladly. I can only believe—and I've never understood this—that it was the will of God that he die before he could return home. Days, Lady. Mere days and he would have been home. Safe again with his wife and unborn child."

"With *his* child? You said Eyslk was *your* daughter."

Catahn's face reddened. "Eyslk is my daughter. I admit that. But the child Deardru carried then was Raenulf's, not mine. God take my soul if I would lie with my brother's wife while he lived." The anger turned another time, trying to unseat shame. "Deardru led you to think I coveted her and made her an adulteress. I did not. She was not. She was true to my brother's love as I was true to my wife's, until Raenulf died."

Taminy sat down on a couch near the hearth. He sensed that, heard it rather than saw it, for he could not bear to look at her. He listened to the fire whispering in the hearth, the wind prodding the windows. In a moment, he began to fill the silence with words. They were difficult words, each a sliver of shame, extracted with pain.

"When news came to us that Raenulf had been killed, Deardru fell ill with grief. She lost the child she carried— their first child. It all but killed her. Desary was above a year old then, and Geatan was pregnant a second time. I think it was more than Deardru could stand to see our happiness. She came to me one day and begged me to father a child on her. She'd been deprived of bearing a child to the Hageswodes; she made it no secret that she thought I bore some fault for it. It seemed right to her that I should replace what she had lost. I was stunned mute."

His face burned now as it had burned then. Then, he had felt as if the Baenn-an-ratha had heaved beneath his feet—now it seemed to shudder like a sick dog. "I could only believe she was grief-kissed. I bid her think what she was asking. When she pressed me, I told her what she wanted was unthinkable. I was husband to Geatan; it was Geatan I loved. I had no desire for Deardru—none. I tried to stay aloof from her—hard, as she lived at Hrofceaster— and, for her part, she reminded me constantly of her plight.

"Some months after, Geatan sickened. She lost our child and grief stole away her health. I lived in fear that I would lose her as well. For a while, it seemed she lingered between life and death. Deardru began to nurse her then, and was a great help—a great solace to us both. I thought she had forgotten her desire for a Hageswode child until one day Geatan . . . " Possessed by a sudden nervous energy, he tugged at his heavy wool tunic, at his belt. He moved restively to the window.

"Geatan?" Taminy prompted him, her voice gentle.

He closed his eyes momentarily. Such was his shame, even that gentleness was brutal. "Deardru laid her case before my wife. My wife who, in her weakness, could not fulfill my desires. Spirit! My only true desire was for her health! But Geatan saw that Deardru was bereft, while she had a husband and a daughter and her own life, now mending. And she saw a family obligation to be met. And she . . . saw that, in my own weakness, I now found Deardru appealing. She added her voice to Deardru's and begged me to give her a child."

He shook his head, making the silver bells woven into his hair sing. "Such a twisted dance the mind does when it seeks to convince the heart a foul path is fair. Who was to be harmed? My own wife had given me leave, my daughter need never know. I was not unfaithful. Deardru needed what I had to give—a seed, nothing more. Pretty speeches, all, but what it came to was my own desire. Need, I called it, as Geatan had. I went to Deardru, burning beforehand, cold as ice, after. I was glad when she conceived. I didn't touch her after that.

"Soon, Geatan's health returned and I thought it was over. But Geatan's sickness had ended her childbearing days. She grieved a bit for it, but we were happy. We had Desary. We were a family. Not long after Eyslk's birth, Deardru came to me again and, again, asked me for a child. For my sake, she said. She knew Geatan could have no more babies; she offered for the sake of the Hageswodes. I refused. Again, she asked, and again I refused. She began to hound me, to speak to me of love and desire. I believed she saw my brother in me and that her grief had overpowered her. I felt pity for her, but when she tried to get to me once again through Geatan, I sent her from the fortress to live in the village."

"And she has never forgiven you."

"She has never forgiven me."

"And this is your horrible, shameful secret?"

"There is more. When Desary was twelve, Geatan died." Dear God, he could still feel the shaft of bereavement. "It was a stupid thing—a fall from her horse. The village Healer was away at Lac-an-Ghlo. On the night we buried her, Deardru came to me to offer comfort . . . and more. Perhaps I thought that in the dark I could pretend that Deardru was Geatan. Whatever the dance my mind did, I took Deardru into my bed. Once. Once was all. In the morning, she put to me the idea that I should marry her and acknowledge Eyslk as my own. She was already married to Garradh-an-Caerluel—had two sons by him—but for me, she would let them go. I put her out of Hrofceaster and have not spoken to her from that day to this."

"But you brought Eyslk here to be educated."

"Eyslk is my daughter. She shouldn't be punished for the manner of her birth; for her mother's willfulness and her father's weakness. I sometimes fear that there is a poison in Deardru. If I can keep that poison from infecting Eyslk . . ."

"Eyslk is a good child, sweet and bright and true. She doesn't carry her mother's poison. Nor do you."

"I carry my own."

"Poison? Weakness, you called it. Is it so evil to be weak? No one is entirely without weakness."

"You are."

"Not even me."

He looked at her then, saw the pensive look on her face, and knew she contemplated a weak moment of her own. From something Desary had told him of her time at Mertuile as Taminy's companion, he suspected one such moment had come at the hands of Daimhin Feich. The thought of it made his brain burn with anger—with hatred. When Taminy raised her eyes to his, they quickly extinguished the flame, leaving ashes.

He crossed to the hearth, throwing himself down before her on the thick rug. "Forgive me, Lady. Forgive me for throwing my shame open to you. Forgive me my weakness."

Head in her lap he felt the soft caress of her hand upon his hair. "It is Eyslk who must forgive you these sins, Catahn. As she must forgive her mother. A woman should not bear a child for honor, but for love. She should not bear it to a family name, but to a man."

She raised his head with her hands then, framing his face with them, gazing down at him with eyes as deep and limitless as the Sea whose color they wore. "There is one other whose forgiveness you must have. Yourself. Forgive yourself these things, Catahn. Then take up your life and move forward. Move upward."

The touch of her eyes, of her hands, opened in his soul a great river canyon of hope and joy—a canyon only her Sea could fill. But as glorious as that was, it seemed to Catahn Hillwild that he stood at the bottom of that chasm, forever staring up, unable to climb out. Forward? Upward? How could he move in either direction when the very Touch that warmed his soul, also heated his blood?

Cadder's eyes leapt anxiously about the circular room. "*Please*, Regent Feich!" he whispered. "Please! I can't possibly—"

"You can. And you will. Indeed, you must." Feich lowered his voice a notch. "You're holding out on me, Minister. You know more of this . . . aislinn business than you're telling. I've stared at this damned crystal, I've burned incense to it, I've sung to it. It *does nothing*."

"I don't know what to tell you."

"*Tell* me what *they* do." Feich jerked his head toward the Abbis.

"They . . . they use duans, the—the Gift. Regent, Feich, I *can't*—"

"Use that word one more time, Cadder, and I'll start shouting my demands. Is it the chamber? Must I use a circular room?"

Cadder scanned the room, mouth working. "It—it could be the chamber. The aislinn chambers of the Osraed are circular."

"Fine, then I will build such a room. What else?"

"Of—of course, they don't always *use* their aislinn chambers," babbled the cleirach, "but then they're trained Osraed and you're—" He broke off and swallowed several times in rapid succession. "It—it could be the duans—there are different duans for different purposes."

"Is there a book of them somewhere? Surely, they're recorded."

"I—I—I've seen—Yes, there are books."

"In the library here."

"Yes."

"Fine. Get one for me."

"Regent, I—"

"And I warned you what I'd do if you uttered that word again. *Think carefully* before you speak."

Cadder squirmed and sweated. "I—I shall attempt to procure it."

"Good. What else?"

"What else? Regent Feich, I don't *know* what else. Either one has the Gift or one has not."

"What about the crystal itself? Might I have gotten a flawed one?"

"I suppose that could be—"

"Here. Here is the crystal." Before Cadder could protest, Feich had opened the velvet bag and revealed his prize.

Cadder's mouth clamped shut and his sweating increased.

"What? What is it?"

"An Osraed would not use that crystal. It is stained."

"I'm not an Osraed. Can I use it?"

"I don't know."

"I'm warning you; that is beginning to annoy me as much as 'I can't.'"

"It's a blooded crystal, Regent Feich. No Osraed has ever used one with that stain."

"Does that mean it can't be used to conjure?"

Cadder's gaze flew, once again, around the room. "Please, Regent! The Osraed do not *conjure*. They Weave. There is a great difference."

"They are words."

"They are the difference between the Art and Wicke Craft. I'm sorry, Regent, I cannot help you with either."

Impatient, angry, Feich rose. "Damn you, Cadder. I should reveal you to Ladhar this very night."

The cleirach paled, but did not protest. "If you must."

"Worm. Haven't you even the courage to defend yourself? You're pathetic. It's no wonder the Meri rejected you."

Cadder's eyes, fixed now on the Osmaer crystal, misted. "Yes, Regent. I'm sure that's true."

To be confronted with such complete self-abnegation, such unabashed cowering, drove Daimhin Feich to rage. "Damn you, man! Have you no spine? Have you no dignity?" He moved closer to the quivering cleirach, turning his back on the Osmaer, and lowered his voice to a growl. "You are everything I despise about the religious. Instead of giving you strength, your faith makes you weak and useless. It must give Ladhar great personal pleasure to have you about—someone who will be kicked and cuffed and murmur only *thank yous* for the abuse. You are a poor excuse for a Caraidin, Cadder, and a poorer excuse for a man. You make a god of me."

Cadder's only reaction to this tirade was a sudden widening of his eyes. His lips, open now, moved without sound. It took Feich an angry moment to realize that the miserable little creature was reacting to something other than his cruelty.

He turned, and was struck with quaking; deep within

its translucent facets, the Osmaer Crystal's heart glowed a deep, ruddy gold.

She was nearly asleep when she felt it—a glacial wind that caught her tethered loosely to her body, and slapped her back to wakefulness. Shuddering, she sat up—would have flown from the bed had she wings. It was like nothing she had felt before, that chill-hot kiss of terror. Its touch was unclean, horrific, a finger of pure malice that trailed along her spine and dug at her heart. It told her, wordlessly, what she did not want to know; a connection had been made between Daimhin Feich and the Osmaer Crystal. And in contact with that, he was somehow, hideously, connected with her.

The contact was brief; ambient anger faded swiftly as it was swallowed by surprise. Still, it left Taminy shaking, holding her breath. When it was gone, she dared breathe. Then she reached out shaking hands and called silently for aid. It came in the form of Skeet, who scratched softly at her bedroom door and came to sit upon the foot of her bed. As she looked at him, it seemed an Eibhilin radiance rose from him to embrace her.

"Feich," she murmured. "Feich has touched the Osmaer Crystal with his *aidan*. I felt it. It . . . it connected us for a moment. He has the Gift."

Skeet nodded, shedding boyhood as if it were a costume he wore. "It's a capricious Gift. Unsettled, disloyal, as treacherous as its master."

"And just as dangerous."

"In every age," said Skeet softly, "there is an Adversary. One who, out of desire for what he does not understand, makes himself an enemy of desire's Object."

"I once thought Osraed Ealad-hach was the enemy," Taminy whispered.

"He was once. That changed. He changed. In the twinkling of an eye, you changed him. Now, there is a new Enemy, dangerous because he knows no Law above his own."

Taminy studied the young-old face. "Does that grant him power?"

"It grants him license. He may not accomplish what you *can't*, but he can assuredly accomplish what you *won't*."

"And mine is to thwart him. The Stone. He mustn't get his hands on it."

Skeet's brows rippled—a peculiar expression reminiscent of the Osraed Bevol. Such tiny things had given birth to the rumor around Nairne that Skeet was not a boy at all, but a golem created by Bevol to take the place of a lost child. "Then," he said, tilting his head so that she must see Bevol in him again, "it must be got into other hands." In an instant the boy was back, grinning at her. "Sleep well for the rest of the night. It seems the enemy is gone, for now."

"For now," Taminy echoed. "But not for long."

CHAPTER 9

Anything, no matter how wonderful, no matter how good, can be misdirected and abused. A lamp in the hands of the blind will more likely burn its bearer than light his way. To the sighted and wise, the lamp is a guide, to the blind and ignorant it is a danger.

—*Utterances of the Osraed Ochan #19*

The Jura were a House of poets and musicians, scholars and storytellers. They'd produced a good many Prentices and Osraed over the centuries, but few great warriors. The bright-eyed Osraed Tynedale was a Jura—historian and philosopher, Osraed and Taminist. Mystics, all of them, and therefore incomprehensible to Saefren Claeg. That they accepted Taminy's "talisman" did not surprise him, though he was a bit taken aback by the amount of celebrating it engendered. The fiery scroll was immediately affixed to a standard and paraded through the Jura holt, collecting a parade of curious and jubilant folk who followed the new icon from village to manse. There, in a great walled court, a bonfire was set and the Jura Chieftain, Mortain, his young heir at his side, recited the story of Taminy's escape from Mertuile and how the Eibhilin scroll and sacred Shard (which he now wore in a small bag dangling from a cord about his neck) had come to be among them.

The Jura were impressed with their Chieftain's Tell. He was, Saefren had to admit, an impressive figure—a young man with gleaming red-gold hair and large, pale green eyes that made the recipients of their gaze feel as if they had

160

just been read, mind, heart and soul. Many of his people came forth after his Tell, both men and women, young and not-so-young, and pledged themselves to travel with him to Creiddylad to impress their petition upon the Feich Regent. The celebration of their journey, intermixed with preparation for it, lasted the night.

After a night of feasting and festing, Saefren felt barely able to drag himself out of the fine bed The Jura had put him in for his meager hours of sleep. Yet, not long after sunrise, he found himself on the road, headed for the Graegam holdings by way of Claeg, where Uncle Iobert expected to take on more men.

That the Jura contingent was made up of both men and women was a source of bemusement to the Claeg kinsmen, but put the annoyingly clear-eyed Aine in a high mood. She spent the traveling day chattering with the Jura cailin and flirting outrageously with the Jura youth.

Saefren was tired, hungry and in a foul mood when they stopped to make their evening camp. He fully intended to retire early to the tent he shared with his uncle, but the Jura Elders, seemingly none the worse for the wear of the previous night, set up a great, roaring fire in the midst of their colorful tents and settled down for a round of tales.

As Aine-mac-Lorimer was the guest of honor at these proceedings (the Jura even called her Alraed Aine, according her a station on a par with the Osraed), Mortain Jura asked her to settle on a Tell. She diplomatically chose the story of Bearach Malcuim and the Jura ancestor, Osraed Gartain. Obviously pleased, The Jura launched into the Tell while Saefren sullenly chewed at his stew.

It was during the reign of Kieran the Dark (said the Storyteller), son of Niall Cleirach, grandson of Bitan-ig, called the Preserver. Kieran was a much weaker Cyne than his father and owed much to the solid framework his grandfather had built and his father built upon. Alas, his weakness did not go unnoticed by those who watched for such things. These bided their time and, upon the death of Bitanig's old advisor, the Osraed Abhainn, the ever-rebellious House Claeg arose to establish control over the Throne.

(Looks were passed here between Claeg and Jura, and Saefren thought his uncle's face darkened, though he said nothing. There was nothing to be said to the truth.)

In a handful of years (continued The Jura) the Claeg had reduced Kieran to a mere puppet, through the agency of a soothsayer named Suardalin-a-Troddan. Now, Kieran was a superstitious man, easily led when it came to protecting his timid self. In those days, it was the custom for the Cyne to be married at Halig-liath. But Suardalin prophesied that if Kieran was wed in the Holy Fortress, the roof of the Sanctuary would fall in upon the guests. Kieran consulted the Osraed, who protested that they'd been given no such aislinn message, but so fearful was he of Suardalin, that he rejected the Osraed counsel and had a chapel hastily built at Creiddylad in which he and his betrothed, Ailis Graegam, were married.

In this way, the Claeg began to drive the wedge of distrust between the Throne and the Osraed. A further prophecy that Kieran would fall from the battlements of the Holy Fortress when he next ventured there, kept him from ever again entering its sacred precincts. Thereafter, he presided over Farewellings from Nairne's village green.

The Claeg Chieftain, Buchan by name, saw to it that the Cyne was surrounded at court by Claeg advisors and, using the soothsayer, Buchan had himself put in a position to defend the Cyne's gates against all others. Kieran Malcuim was quick to make Buchan his Durweard at Suardalin-a-Troddan's say-so.

Yet even timid Kieran had his limits. Realizing how he'd been led, galled by his own cowardice, he at last sought counsel from the Osraed at Ochanshrine. With their strength, he was able to stand up for himself. He sent his family away into hiding, then attempted to throw off the yoke of Claeg domination by ejecting Buchan Claeg from his position as Durweard and barring all Claeg kinsman from Mertuile.

But alas, his efforts ended in failure and humiliation. While Kieran worshipped in his little chapel among loyal subjects, Buchan Claeg rode up to the altar on a fully armored war horse and snatched the royal Circlet from the Cyne's head. He then dragged Kieran from the chapel by the hair and staged a mock coronation in which he had the Circlet placed upon his own brow. In further retaliation for his resistance, The Claeg appropriated the Graegam family estates and laid waste to the village of Ailis Graegam's birth, slaughtering hundreds of innocent men, women and children and leaving their bodies lying out for all to see.

(Saefren laid aside his stew, finding it suddenly difficult to chew.)

Other Chiefs and Eiric whom The Claeg considered possible adversaries, Buchan had brought to the village by force so they might view the carnage. He then imprisoned the Cyne beneath his own castle and ruled openly from Creiddylad as Regent, proclaiming the Cyne mentally unfit to mount the throne.

Kieran's son, Bearach Malcuim, was now seventeen years old. Outraged by the actions of The Claeg, the young Riagan left his hiding place in the village of Storm and moved about the countryside in disguise, rallying the lesser Houses, nobles and commoners who were now chafing to be rid of the brutal Claeg.

(*I should leave*, Saefren thought. *I should get up and go to my tent*. But he didn't leave; he stayed and listened further to the Storyteller.)

Most of all did the Osraed want the Claeg usurper gone, for in his rage at their support of Bearach, he had placed Halig-liath under virtual siege. But Bearach infiltrated the Holy Fortress and found the Osraed willing allies. They had already been using the Divine Art on his behalf, and were cheered when he turned to them for aid. His foremost champion among the Osraed was Gartain Jura, whom he made his Durweard. The two became as brothers—never separate, always together, always of one mind and heart. Together they brought the people of Caraid-land to revolt and challenged the Claeg at every pass.

Buchan Claeg had grown tired of keeping Cyne Kieran as pet and now, enraged by the bold actions of Bearach and Gartain, he let it be known that he had every intention of setting himself before the Stone of Ochan in a real coronation.

This was the rallying point Bearach and Gartain had been waiting for. Moving swiftly, they visited Ochanshrine just long enough to remove the Osmaer crystal. When The Claeg rushed in, seeking to lay hands on it, it was gone. Buchan Claeg demanded it be handed over to him so he might be set before it, but Bearach, now called Spearman for this bold thrust at his enemy, rejected Buchan's demand, knowing that once the Stone was in The Claeg's hands, his father's life would be forfeit. Alas, it was lost anyway, for the treacherous Claeg, in retaliation for Bearach's effrontery, tortured and killed the Cyne.

Bearach was mad with grief. At once, he launched an attack on the Claeg forces. Passion driving him, bolstered by the Art of the Osraed, he routed the enemy from Creiddylad, but in the battle to take Mertuile, Osraed Gartain was captured and carried away to the Claeg capital.

Hoping to save his beloved friend's life, Bearach Malcuim went into the Cave of Ochan and brought out a crystal all but identical in size and color to the Osmaer. He offered this false Stone to The Claeg in exchange for Gartain's life.

The counterfeit nearly fooled The Claeg, but even as the hostage Gartain was on his way to Creiddylad to be released, the cautious Chieftain took the stone and presented it to a Hillwild woman of his household. The woman tested the crystal and found it to be false.

Furious, The Claeg raced to Creiddylad, reaching the release point in the court of Kieran's Chapel as Gartain began his walk to freedom and reunion. In full sight of Bearach Malcuim and the people of Creiddylad, Buchan Claeg took up a crossbow and shot the young Osraed in the back. The heroic Gartain fell dead into the arms of his young Cyneric.

Grief doubled and driven by vengeance, Bearach entered into a pact with the Chief of the House Feich, knowing that with the forces of this mighty family, he might hope to trample the Claeg once and for all. They might have done this if The Feich had not played traitor and run straight to Buchan Claeg with the news that Bearach Spearman was planning a massed attack on the Claeg estates.

Learning of his ally's treachery, Bearach confronted the Feich Chief in the Cirke at Storm. There he reviled him for his disloyalty and then, when The Feich drew sword, he slew him, saying, "I, Bearach Spearman, make certain." Ah, but the murder lay heavy on his conscience, so he hastened to Ochanshrine to beg forgiveness of the Osraed, bringing with him the Osmaer crystal. The Osraed rejoiced in the return of the sacred relic. The Osraed assured Bearach that his forgiveness was in the hands of God. They bid him take the Great Crystal up to Halig-liath where he might safely be set before it.

At Halig-liath, one week before Solstice, Cyneric Bearach Malcuim was set before the Stone by the Osraed at Apex, Affric. The Malcuim Circlet, however, was still in the hands of The Claeg.

Bearach remained at Halig-liath only long enough to preside over the Farewelling within its walls. While he did this, Buchan Claeg dallied outside, trying to get in. It was his opinion that the right to oversee the leave-taking belonged to him and he presented the false Osmaer as proof. The Osraed, who now possessed the true Stone, challenged him and cleverly kept him at bay. When Farewelling was over and the Pilgrims at last departed the fortress before the eyes of Claeg's men, Bearach Malcuim was among them.

Now, while Bearach hid in and about Caraid-land, aided by loyal commoners and lesser nobles and Chiefs, his family dispersed to the four winds. But it was to no avail. The Claeg got his hands on them and treated them all shamefully, humiliating and imprisoning them all—men, women and children.

Bearach, meanwhile, fled into the Gyldan-baenn and threw himself on the mercy of Garmorgan, Renic of the Hillwild clan of Mor. She kept him safe in her stronghold at Moidart, while his countrymen rallied to his aid. He was close to losing faith during this time, when one night he was visited by a vision of his beloved Gartain. In the aislinn, the Osraed showed Bearach a spider patiently weaving its web in the lee of a window embrasure and bid him perceive how the tiny creature persevered regardless of how many times the strong winds about Moidart blew its silken home away. Bearach was cheered by this lesson and began to plan his return to Mertuile.

As for Garmorgan, she became Bearach's fast friend and when, in the dead of winter of the Year of Pilgrimage 168, Bearach led his troops down out of the Gyldans, she rode beside him.

By now, The Claeg had set up court at Mertuile, openly flying the banner of his House over its ramparts. Bearach Malcuim, accordingly, seized the Claeg estates and stronghold and raised his own standard there. He allowed the "escape" of the House Steward who carried the tale of Claeg's capture to his master in Creiddylad.

The Claeg at once assembled his troops for battle, but on the eve of their departure for Claeg, Buchan fell ill. In a matter of days, he was dead of the mysterious malady, but not before he extracted a harrowing promise from his heir— that he would retake the Claeg lands, boil the dead Chief's flesh from his bones and bury those relics in the retaken soil.

The son, Gery, made the grisly pact, then violated it as soon as his father's spirit fled its body. He carried his father's corpse to Ochanshrine, where it was prayed over by the Osraed and buried in the wood overlooking that sacred place. The new Claeg Chieftain then went straight to Bearach, relinquished Mertuile in return for his own lands, and made a pledge of fealty to the House Malcuim.

The Claeg kinsmen were furious with their young leader and attempted to continue the struggle against the Throne, but Bearach had the will of the people, the forces of Garmorgan, and the spiritual strength of the Osraed. With those he could only be victorious. He brought his family out of captivity, restored the Osmaer crystal to Ochanshrine and began a long and glorious reign. The Malcuim were back in Mertuile to stay.

After a moment of silence, the Storyteller bowed his head to indicate he had finished his Tell. The others about the fire nodded and hummed in approval.

"Until now," murmured Saefren.

Heads turned.

"What do you mean?" asked a Jura kinswoman.

He hadn't meant to say it aloud; it had just slipped out. Saefren reddened, but stood his ground. "You say the Malcuim were back to stay, Mortain Jura, but there is no Malcuim at Mertuile now."

Protests came from Jura and Claeg alike, while the Nairnian girl sat back and watched all with eyes the size of silver sorchas. The Jura Chieftain stopped the outcry with a raise of his hand. He spoke, but Saefren barely heard him. His eyes were riveted on the palm of that hand. The star-shaped mark there gleamed brightly enough to rival the light of the fire. He had never seen a *gytha* before, though he knew from talk that it was the Sign that accompanied initiation into the ranks of the *waljan*—the Osmaer's elect.

The sight of the thing stunned him. Before, he had thought of the *gytha* only in connection with those close to Taminy-Osmaer—Aine, Iseabal, Osraed Wyth. It had never occurred to him until this moment that the circle of chosen might expand, might embrace people like Mortain Jura, who had only seen the woman once. He found his eyes drawn to his Uncle Iobert. Was there also such a mark in his palm? Saefren had never seen it, but he realized now that it was likely there.

He glanced around now, noticing only that The Jura had stopped speaking and was watching him. "I'm sorry," he murmured. "I meant no disrespect. Only perhaps . . . that it is the lot and duty of the Claeg to return to Mertuile what we once attempted to remove from it—a Malcuim Cyne." He had acquitted himself well and would have begged leave to go to his tent, but The Jura turned immediately to Aine-mac-Lorimer and respectfully requested her to give a tell of the Lady Osmaer. Aine complied, timidly at first, regaling them with a tale that kept Saefren sitting right where he was.

She spoke of an evening in summer past when Taminy had told her what she had not wanted to hear—that she, Aine, had the *aidan* and a Gift for prophecy. She had fled, rushing on horseback into Nairne where, hard by the Cirke, her horse had shied and thrown her into a stone wall.

"My neck was broken," she said, "and I died." Just that, so calmly—I *died*. "The Osraed Torridon Wove over me and tried to save me. But he couldn't. When he'd turned his back and given up, Taminy came and laid her hands on me. She healed my broken body and gave my spirit back into it."

The group by the fire sat in awful silence, listening to the whispers of the flames. That they believed the tell, Saefren could see in their firelit eyes. He could only suppose that Aine believed it too. He shook his head. A glowing mark in the palm, words of fire written on hide by a flaming crystal—these things were difficult to accept, though having seen them, he had no choice but to do so. But this—a resurrection of sorts . . .

He rose, weary and overwhelmed, and went to his tent.

The Graegam put up little more fight than The Jura had done and, two days after adding representation from that House to their contingent, they were trekking southwest again, angling toward the seaside holdings of the Madaidh. They would lay by there to await the arrival of some Gilleas kin. If nothing else, Saefren reasoned, they would impress Daimhin Feich with their sheer numbers. At worst, they would scare him into a fight which he might lose, even ensconced in Mertuile . . . unless, of course, he had managed to win some allies in his time there. Saefren considered recommending the construction of a few siege engines while they were at Madaidh, but hearing the religious tone of the Chieftains' conversations, thought better of it.

Instead he sought to spar with Aine. "That story you told our first night out of Jura . . . was it true?"

His opening gambit caused a gratifying reddening of

the girl's face. He'd expected that, and sat back to watch the fireworks. There were none. Aine fought her obvious outrage to a draw, returned her red face to a mere pink and said, "It was true."

Disappointed and curious, he pursued the subject. "But such an incredible tale! Can you honestly believe you were dead?"

"Yes."

"And Taminy resurrected you."

"It's called an Infusion Weave," she said as if that label made it any less miraculous.

"Whatever. But you believe she did it?"

Aine turned to look at him, eyes kindling. "There were enough witnesses, including Osraed Torridon, who first tried to save me."

"Ah, but they're all in Nairne."

"Ask Osraed Wyth the next time you're at Hrofceaster. Or wouldn't the word of an Osraed be enough for you?"

"Well, he might be rather partial to his Lady."

"You're a Claeg, all right," Aine told him. "Stubborn as that sword-poked lump on your standard."

"It's a rock."

She'd nettled him a bit and her eyes said she knew it. "A lump of clay, more like—your House namesake. But a hard lump. *Very* hard. You could never *really* get a sword through it."

"As it happens," Saefren informed her, "that rock forms the altar of the Claeg chapel. It's been an altar stone since our ancestors worshiped in the fields. And you're right— it's damned hard."

She laughed at him. Actually *laughed* at him, the ignorant creature. He bit back his annoyance that she couldn't have more respect for an elder, for a House kinsman. But then, what was she, after all—a lorimer's daughter? A maker of saddles and harnesses? What sort of manners could he expect of that? He could even see how she might believe in these supposed miracles . . . but what excuse had Uncle Iobert?

Unable to muzzle his annoyance, he pressed on. "So

you were dead. Your neck was broken and your head rattled.
Now, *that* much I believe."

She might've set his clothes afire with that look. "Does
it make you feel quite great and powerful to cross words
with a mere lorimer's daughter, Saefren Claeg?"

Foolish was how he felt. He made a point of noticing a
pack horse with a loose cinch and rode ahead to set it
straight. He'd let her get the better of him and she knew
it. He gritted his teeth. If not for Uncle Iobert, he'd turn
his horse about now and head straight back to Claeg.

His anxiety grew when, half a day out from the Madaidh
estates, a rider caught them up with news from Creiddylad.
Daimhin Feich had officially declared Taminy-Osmaer an
enemy of the Throne.

"Regent Feich? If you've a moment to spare, sir?" His
Dearg guard, for all his imposing size, seemed uncertain.

Daimhin enjoyed his diffidence, awarding it with a scowl.
"What is it? I'm in a hurry." He turned back to watch a
stable groom work about his horse.

"I recognize that, Regent, but thought you might find
this of interest."

Daimhin Feich shrugged. "You've my ear till my horse
is saddled. Best hurry."

"It's about the other night at Ochanshrine . . . I couldn't
help but hear, when you spoke to the Minister . . . "

Daimhin sent his brows gliding up his forehead.

The guard hesitated, then said, "It's like this, Regent. I
know a woman. A Hillwild who married into our House."

"And why should this be of interest to me?"

"Well, I'd style her a Wicke, though she'd likely deny
it. Fact is, she's been known to Weave a few inyx in her
time. Got her own crystal too, though I can't say how she
come by it."

Daimhin Feich forgot for a moment that the Deasach
Mediator awaited him in Creiddylad and speared the Dearg
with an avid gaze. "What is her name? How can I meet her?"

"Name's Coinich. She's a Mor before she came to Dearg.
Married my uncle Blair."

"I care very little who she married. How might I contact her? I suppose she's at Dearg."

"As it happens, she's here. My uncle's an Elder, advisor to Eadrig Dearg—"

Daimhin's heart leapt in his breast. "She's here? At Mertuile?"

"Aye."

Daimhin put his hand on the man's shoulder. "I can't avoid this meeting I'm to attend, or I'd see her this minute. Speak to her for me. Tell her I'd be pleased to meet her when I return from the city."

The guard blinked. "But Regent, should I not go with you? My duty—"

"Is to follow my orders. I can find another bodyguard. It is far more important to me that *you* make certain this Wicke doesn't leave Mertuile this afternoon. I'll wish to speak with her directly I return."

The man nodded. "Aye, then. I'll see to it she's awaiting you."

On his return trip to Mertuile, Daimhin Feich wished his mount might have flown. The great Deasach cannon was en route, would be here in mere days, the Banarigh would no doubt be pleased with his gifts, and a Dearg Wicke awaited his return. Fate rolled with him now, he could feel it. Things moved in the direction he sent them, guided like sheep by a shepherd's staff.

His pleased reverie was interrupted at a streetcorner near Mertuile when a lump of rotting fruit flew out of nowhere to collide with his horse's head. The animal started violently, and before Daimhin could regain control of her, a second piece of refuse struck him in the neck, exploding in a soggy spray of fetid perfume.

Fighting his mare under control, he glanced around, trying to see where the attack arose. He was appalled when, out of the crossroads, two small mobs appeared, wielding their foul projectiles and more dangerous weapons. Bystanders and passers-by fled like startled chickens into storefronts and parked carriages. In mere seconds, the street was deserted but for the approaching mobs, Daimhin Feich and his two guards.

He pulled his sword, his guards echoing the movement. Another piece of fruit struck him, then a lump of coal. He was not a man for flight, and so spurred his horse toward one of the converging groups, shouting at them to desist. The guards followed, pushing their nervous horses toward the teeming threat.

Above the scarves that obscured their faces, Daimhin Feich could see eyes aglint with anger. He tried to make himself heard above their noise, but the shouts of rebellion drowned him out. "The Malcuim! The Malcuim!"

He was struck again, this time from behind. Then something whistled past his cheek followed by a blossoming pain. He put his hand up to his face and felt blood. Turning, he realized the folly of confrontation. The group behind had drawn nearer; in a few seconds more he and his guards would be cut off, surrounded. Swearing, he pivoted his horse and sent it into a careening gallop, forcing it between the closing jaws and up the naked street toward Mertuile. He only vaguely heard the sounds of other horses behind him.

Only when he had reached safety behind the inner curtain of the castle, did he turn to see if his kinsmen had escaped. They had, but not without injury. Both were bloodied, as he knew he was. Furious, Daimhin Feich threw himself from his horse and raged into Mertuile. Now, more than ever, did he feel the hunger for control of the *aidan* he knew reposed within him. Now, more than ever, did he long to take that red crystal in his hands and strike out through it at all who opposed him—from that rabble of worthless dirtbags to the so-called Osmaer.

He would learn the use of that crystal, God smite him if he didn't.

The Madaidh received his talisman without comment. Only a slight widening of his eyes betrayed any response to the glowing words. When he had read them, he looked up at Iobert Claeg with a complete lack of expression on his broad face. "Where is the Lady now?"

"With the Ren Catahn at Hrofceaster."

The Madaidh nodded. "Daimhin Feich doesn't know this." When Iobert's brows knit, he said, "Seeking allies, he trumpets his grand designs; we know much of what goes on. He has spoken to me of a siege of Halig-liath and of a mighty Deasach weapon which the Regent has appropriated for his use. And he has allies, Iobert—the Teallach, the Dearg, perhaps the Skarf . . ."

"And the Madaidh?" Iobert's eyes were wary.

"The Madaidh are the Madaidh. We don't toady to the Feich. Nor to the Malcuim."

Saefren was not surprised by these words. The Madaidh had always considered themselves a breed apart. They traced their lineage to nomads who had wandered from El-Deasach over the southern chain of the Gyldan-baenn hundreds of years ago. Among the fair coastal hills they established a permanent capital. Their dark eyes and dark skin spoke of their southern heritage, as did their customs and traditions. Even after centuries in Caraid-land, their customs were markedly different than their neighbors'. The Madaidh elected their Chieftains, much as the Hillwild did. Their current leader, Rodri, had followed in the footsteps of a woman named Vaida, renowned, in Cyne Ciarda's time, for the strong opinions she voiced in the Hall. Though they practiced the religion of the Meri, they kept their own holy men and women to advise them.

"Will you join with us in petitioning for Airleas Malcuim's return to Mertuile?" asked Iobert. "Will you join us in negotiating Taminy-Osmaer's safety?"

The Madaidh glanced around the light-washed room, his eyes going for a moment to the odd eddies of luminescence cast on walls and ceiling by the sea below his stronghold. He seemed, almost, to be listening to the rhythmic drumming of its waves on the rocky roots of his home. "Daimhin Feich has just declared your Lady of the Crystal Rose an enemy of the Throne. His Abbod has called her Wicke and demon and has suggested in recent gatherings that she is the representative of some supremely evil being. There are those who believe these things."

Iobert moved restively in his chair. "You are surely not

among them. You saw her in the Hall. Her actions were not evil."

"Her actions spoke of a power I have seen wielded by no other." Madaidh held up the scroll, still dripping light. "I hold a piece of this power in my hand."

"That doesn't make her evil," said Aine-mac-Lorimer.

Damn the girl! Saefren glared at her and signaled her to be quiet. Couldn't she keep her mouth shut even in an assemblage of Chieftains?

She had caught the Madaidh's attention. "This is so," he said reasonably. "But Daimhin Feich represents opposition to her. Powerful opposition. To ride into Creiddylad and ally yourselves to her by word or deed may be dangerous—to yourselves, to those of her followers who must exist within the city, even to those who possess no strong opinions. If Taminy-Osmaer is an enemy of the Throne, what does that make those who identify themselves with her?"

"She *isn't* an enemy of the Throne!" Aine protested. "She's protecting Airleas Malcuim. Teaching him, preparing him to be Cyne."

"You will never convince Daimhin Feich of that. He believes she perverts him, bends him to her will."

Aine leapt from her chair, face flaming with anger. "You're a coward, Madaidh! Afraid for your own skin, looking to your own interests—"

Saefren roared. "Damn you, Aine! *Sit down!* Have you no sense in your head at all?"

The Madaidh silenced him, his dark eyes still on the angry girl. "I am not a coward, child," he said quietly. "But I am wondering where the power is tipped at this moment. I am wondering what life will be like for those in Creiddylad if it is tipped to the side of Daimhin Feich."

"He can have no power compared to the Meri's," argued Aine. "Compared to Taminy's."

"You speak of spiritual power. I speak of temporal power. I do not think Daimhin Feich knows the difference. At *this* moment, that may give him an advantage."

"And so," said Iobert Claeg, "you'll side with him?"

"I side with no one, Iobert. The Meri's will out. Neutrality has its own advantage."

Iobert stood, the other Chieftains and Elders mirroring the movement. "So, you will sit on the border?"

The Madaidh chuckled softly. "We have always sat on the border. From here we can watch both friend and enemy come and go."

"Perhaps the young *waljan* is right," Iobert observed. "Perhaps you are a coward, after all."

The Madaidh bowed his shaggy head. "If it pleases you to think that."

"No, Rodri. It does not please me. I doubt it pleases any of us."

When they were out of earshot of the Madaidh Elders, Iobert Claeg gathered his allies to a council. "Before we enter the city," he said, "we need to get the Lady Aine to safety. She mustn't be seen with us by Feich's people."

You mean, Saefren thought, *that we mustn't be seen with her.* With the open enmity between her Mistress and Feich, Aine-mac-Lorimer was an exceedingly dangerous person to be around.

"Our Mistress intends that she go to the Osraed Fhada and Lealbhallain at Carehouse," Iobert continued. "I will take her there."

Before Saefren could protest, The Jura spoke up. "I'll go with you."

"Nonsense." Both Chieftains turned to look at the younger Claeg.

"Rodri Madaidh is right about at least one thing," Saefren told them. "To be identified with Taminy-Osmaer right now could be fatal. I don't believe it would do for any of the Houses to lose their heads to Feich's purges."

"There are no purges—" began Iobert but Saefren interrupted him.

"There soon will be. Think, Uncle. It's the next logical step. Declaring the Mistress enemy is but a heartbeat away from purging Creiddylad and beyond of her servants."

"What are you suggesting, then?"

"I am suggesting that *I* take Aine to Carehouse—if,

indeed, there's anyone there to greet her. Either of you will be easily recognizable in Creiddylad; I won't be. I don't think it wise that you be connected with Taminy-Osmaer at this moment."

Iobert's face grew deeply red. "It is far too late for you to worry about me being connected, nephew. I would sooner die than disavow—"

"Iobert, Iobert!" The Jura patted his volatile companion on the shoulder. "Saefren is right. We may go farther with Daimhin Feich if our allegiance appears uncertain. If we declare ourselves too openly we may undermine our Lady's Cause rather than help it. Let your nephew take the Alraed Aine to her companions in Creiddylad; let *us* sit down with the others and decide what our strategy must be with Daimhin Feich."

Aine could not claim to be pleased that Saefren Claeg was to be her escort to Carehouse. His open disdain of her, of Taminy, produced in her the most dreadful, sinking feeling. It also inspired her to flashes of equally dreadful anger. But, as they rode beneath the port city's open main archway and negotiated the evening streets, Saefren did not speak to her, disdainfully or otherwise. Finally, she could take no more of the taciturn silence and asked, "Do you know where you're going?"

He swept her with his colorless glance. "My uncle wouldn't have sent me if I didn't."

"Then you've been to Carehouse before?"

"Aye. Once or twice. And been past it often enough. There're some haunts in the neighborhood I've been fond of."

"Oh? What sort of haunts?"

His gaze came back to her, bearing a touch of derision. "I doubt my uncle'd be pleased with me if I discussed them with you. They're not the sort of places a cailin would find . . . agreeable."

She knew what he meant, of course; she wasn't completely naive. Even a town the size of Tuine had "haunts," as he called them. She suspected her brothers knew those quite well judging from after-dark conversations she'd overheard. She was pleased not to have blushed or paled or done something else to give Saefren Claeg more ammunition against her. "So what's it like, this Carehouse?" she asked.

"It's a big, old stone place with miles of dusty, dark and damp corridors, tiny, cheerless rooms and rat-infested attics. It's like a little fortress . . . or a prison. Walled courtyard, parapets. Looks like it might have been an asylum once upon a time."

"An asylum?" she echoed.

"Where they keep crazy people. If that's the case, I can't think all that much has changed."

"They're not crazy," she said, her voice deliberately soft. "No more than your uncle is. They just . . . know something you don't."

He pursed his lips. "My uncle . . . I'll tell you what I think of my uncle. I think he may be under some sort of enchantment."

Aine couldn't help but stare at him, nor could she keep the laughter from bubbling out of her mouth. "Enchantment! What—by Taminy-Osmaer?"

Saefren jerked his head around. "Hush, you! Keep your voice down! All that's holy, you crazy girl! Yelling that name in these streets could cost you your life!"

"Well, then you'd be rid of me. Though I wouldn't like to be you facing your Uncle Iobert if that happened." She could feel his discomfiture clearly—the rankling annoyance, his anxiety over his uncle, his suspicion, something else, nervous and twitchy. She was pleased with that insight—as pleased as she'd been when she'd caught his disparaging assessment of her as a mere saddlemaker's daughter. And though, this time, there were no words or thoughts attached, the roil of emotion was as vivid as one of her worrisome dreams.

"With my luck," he was saying, "I'd probably be killed right along with you."

They took a circuitous route to Carehouse, wending their way through narrow back streets and dimly lit alleys, beneath little footbridges that crossed from building to ancient building. She saw what she fancied were some of Saefren's haunts; inns that were little more than a hole in some sooty wall beckoned the passerby with a wash of light and music that tumbled from the front door and rolled across the street to tug on ears and eyes. Sometimes the smell of cooking food tumbled out along with the rest of the overflow, making Aine realize how hungry she was. Often patrons fought their way in against the tide of light and noise, alone or with one of the many women who offered their own enticements from patio and walkway.

Occasionally, Saefren would turn his head to gaze at a doorway or the form within it, and Aine suspected that after he dropped her off, he might find his way back to his haunts. But when he spoke, he disabused her of that suspicion.

"Funny," he said. "When I was younger, I thought this place was full of intrigue and adventure and mystery. Now it only seems . . . dark and poor and sad."

They spoke no more after that and soon arrived at their destination. Aine pulled up her horse just outside Carehouse's huge, thick gates and stared up at the stone walls. Saefren was right; it did seem a fortress. She shivered at the unbidden thought that someday it might have to be just that.

She turned to the man beside her. "You can leave me here."

He shook his head, his thick chestnut hair frosted gold by the lamps above the gate. "I promised Uncle I'd see you safe inside and that I'll do. Besides, I'd like to meet these Osraed of yours. See if they're all so blindingly virtuous as that last bunch." He reached up and pulled the bell rope.

A young face popped out to peer at them from a slit above the gate. "Who goes?" asked an equally young voice.

In answer, Aine merely raised her left hand so that the youthful guard could see the palm. She heard the muffled gasp of recognition just before the face disappeared. In a moment, the gate swung open just far enough to admit them in single file. Inside, Aine slid from her horse and found herself enveloped in a strong embrace.

"Oh, Aine! How good to see you! Are you tired? Are you hungry? Come inside and sit! Who's this?"

The embrace loosed a bit and Aine found herself staring eye on into the face of Lealbhallain-mac-Mercer. *Now, this is all wrong*, she thought, because the last time she'd stood face to face with Leal, she had been looking down at him. "You've grown," she told him, as if he mightn't have noticed.

He grinned at her, freckles dancing in the glow of the lightglobes that bobbed along the front of the huge stone building they stood before. "I know. Probably never be as tall as Fhada, though. He's waiting to meet you, with the others. I felt you coming. I was waiting. I didn't even need to hear Ferret shout but that I knew you were here." His eyes moved to Saefren, then. "And you are?"

"Saefren Claeg. My Uncle Iobert and a troop of Claeg, Gilleas, Graegam and Jura are camped outside the city this moment, preparing to meet with Daimhin Feich."

Leal blinked startled green eyes. "Meet? You don't mean—?"

"I don't mean a battle, no. The Chieftains plan to petition the Regent to return Airleas to Mertuile and set him before the Stone."

"Good luck to them."

"They'll need more than luck, I fancy." Saefren seemed unable to keep his eyes from Leal's Kiss. The golden star shown from his forehead with enough force to cast shadow. "The others were green," he said. "Yours is gold like Osraed Wyth's."

"I'm Osraed by the Golden Meri, after the Cusp."

"And *waljan*, like the others?"

Leal raised his hand. The *gytha* also cast shadows.

"How does it happen?" Saefren asked.

Leal shrugged, smiling. "She touches you and you begin to burn." He glanced down at his palm. "They can be inconvenient when you're trying to stay hidden."

"Oh, but you can cloak them," said Aine. "That's part

of what I've come to teach you. You won't have to use green paint anymore."

Leal laughed, taking the girl's elbow and guiding her toward the house. "And how did you know about that?"

"Taminy told me. She was worried about you, Leal. About all of you here in Creiddylad."

The boy's face darkened. "Well, she'd have reason to be. It's not been easy. No way to tell who's friend and who's foe." As the door to the huge stone barrack opened before him, Leal turned back to face Saefren. "Come in, friend, and welcome. We've laid on a feast for this lady, and you're more than welcome to our hospitality."

Saefren started to protest, but Leal cut him off. "I'll hear no argument, Saefren Claeg. We owe you much for getting Aine to us safely."

With a guarded glance at Aine, Saefren inclined his head in acquiescence and followed them into the house.

The Dearg's Hillwild was legend's own Wicke. Fey yellow-amber eyes gazed cat-like from under a thick mane of unruly black hair, full lips pouted arrogance beneath a long, aquiline nose. Her skin was the color of foothill clay and her body echoed the contours of the hills; she was voluptuous as the earth itself. Feich had no doubt she'd borne her Dearg husband many fine, strong sons and earthy daughters. She was neither young nor old, neither homely nor fair, but there was about her the quivering energy that exists in fire. Her entire being was wary; he could almost hear the aislinn growl. But there was more—a haughtiness that lay behind the eyes like laughter behind a closed door.

It was the Hillwild in her, Feich thought, and was not altogether surprised when she did not bow to him. It didn't anger him. He admired it. "I'm Regent Feich, Moireach. And you are . . . ?"

The woman's mouth pulled up at the corners. "Moireach, I'm not. I'm Coinich Mor of Dearg. My husband's a shepherd as well as an Elder and what land we've got's owned by the House, not by us. Call me Coinich. That'll be fine."

"Well, Coinich Mor of Dearg, do you know why I asked to see you?"

The smile deepened. "You need my help."

"Is that what your nephew told you?"

She chuckled. "My nephew barely knows his own name. Blessedly, he's not hard to look at. No, my *aidan* told me."

"Really? What else did your *aidan* tell you?"

"You have a crystal."

Her nephew might've told her that, too, but it hardly mattered. Let her show off if she wanted, he'd soon see if she could inspire his stone. He drew it from its belt pouch and held it out. It caught light from the chamber window and fired with a ruddy gleam.

The Dearg woman's cat-eyes widened and he half expected her to hiss at the thing. "Red," she said. "The color of passion . . . and of blood." She held out her hand and Feich let the crystal fall into it. Her eyes followed the fall. "You know, don't you, that 'red' in the Old Tongue is 'dearg'?"

In the moment he opened his mouth to answer, the red stone came to sullen life in the Hillwild Wicke's hands. It was a reluctant light—not so much a spark as an ember. But it was enough. Feich's heart leapt up in his chest and bolted. It took effort to hold his excitement in check. "Impressive, Coinich Mor. But can you teach *me* to light the stone? To Weave with it?"

She looked up at him, golden eyes almost saucy in their regard. "Oh, more than that, Regent Feich. More than that."

CHAPTER 10

The faithful lover hunts only the object of his Pilgrimage, and has no passion but union with the Beloved. He shall not attain this object until he sacrifices all. That is, what he sees and hears and knows—all must be given up, so that he might enter the abode of the Spirit, which is the City of Light. This Pilgrimage demands labor and ardor; and if we taste of this glorious reunion, we shall gladly cast away the world.

—*Book of Pilgrimages, Osraed Gartain*

They rode beneath the great arch when the light of morning was still slanting across the low hills. Shadows lay deep among the buildings of Creiddylad, yet already there were people on the street. And the people looked up in amazement as the assembled ranks of the Four Allies rode through.

Saefren could not help but feel a swell of pride and exhilaration. He rode between his uncle and the Jura Chieftain at the fore of the long column. The other Chieftains rode one rank back, their standard-bearers just behind them, carrying aloft the pride of the Houses.

They drew people to them as they moved through the city. By the time they made the final climb up the long slope to Mertuile, they had a long train of citizens spread out in their wake. And when they halted in the great square that held the Cyne's Market, those citizens eddied and pooled behind them, murmuring among themselves.

Iobert sent Saefren to ask admittance for the Chieftains. He could see the unease and perplexity in the gatekeeper's eyes as he spoke with him—the way they darted again and again to the mounted multitude. But Saefren's words were mild; the Chieftains wanted only an audience with the Cyneric's Regent. The man hurried away to deliver his message, leaving Saefren to study the sun-warmed stone of the castle's outer curtain and become mesmerized by the snap of banners in the sea breeze and the rhythmic drumming of surf against the base of Mertuile's rocky scarp.

The gatekeeper's return was swift. The gates of Mertuile swung open and the four Chieftains entered with their respective aides-de-camp. As was custom, their standards were carried to the top of the southeast wall above the city gate and flown beside the three already there—the Malcuim, the Feich and the Dearg. Saefren thought it ironic to see the Malcuim banner still flying over Mertuile when there was no Malcuim in residence.

Feich did not keep his guests waiting long, but that he kept them waiting at all was significant to Saefren. Feich was still playing the politics of the game, still assuming that his was a position of power or at least of control. But while Saefren chafed at the delaying tactic, his uncle and the others seemed almost too relaxed.

Feich appeared at last, placing himself brazenly in the Malcuim throne. Saefren gritted his teeth, glad he would not be called upon to speak; he doubted he could be civil. It was The Jura who presented the petition, and The Jura was ever the diplomat.

"We bring you greetings," he said, his elegant voice filling the large room, "from the Houses Claeg, Gilleas, Graegam and Jura."

Feich gave his head a token nod. "Your greetings are accepted, Mortain Jura. To what do I owe the honor of your overwhelming presence?"

The Jura smiled, teeth white and even in his fair face. "As you can see, many of our people wished to travel with us to Creiddylad to show their support of our petition."

Feich's brows rose. "Petition?"

"Regent, we have come to enjoin you to return Airleas Malcuim to the throne of Caraid-land."

Feich spread his hands. "What would you have me do, gentlemen? What powers have I in the matter?"

"You can guarantee the Cyneric's safety and his independence of coercion."

"And how can I do that?"

"We propose," said The Jura, his voice taking on a subtle edge, "that Airleas be brought to Mertuile under an escort made up from among these Houses." His hand swept the group arrayed about him. "Once here, he will be set 'fore the Stone at Ochanshrine and given his rightful place on the throne."

Feich smiled. "Airleas is a boy. I would yet have to serve as Regent."

"We have no argument with that, save to propose that his Regents shall be three—yourself, as you were appointed by Colfre and approved by the Abbod Ladhar, Iobert Claeg and myself."

Feich was clearly amused. "You realize, of course, that the last time a Claeg and a Feich shared Regency the results were disastrous."

"Surely, Regent, we are capable of learning from history." The Jura's smile did not reach his eyes.

Daimhin Feich's gaze moved to the Claeg Chieftain. "Are we, Iobert Claeg, capable of learning from history? Or shall we only repeat it?"

"I can only speak for myself, Regent," replied Iobert, laying a slight and condescending stress on the title. "I want what is best for my people—by that, I mean *all* Caraidin. It is not best that the throne of Caraid-land remain empty."

Saefren swore Daimhin Feich actually flinched. But he did not rise from the throne he occupied. Instead, he leaned back in it with studied calm and folded his hands upon his stomach. "And for this you bring your assembled forces to Creiddylad—to make this benign proposal?"

The Jura shrugged, smiling. "Forces? Regent Feich, the people outside your gates are merely well-wishers of Cyneric Airleas. They are here voluntarily to show support for the young Malcuim's return and call for his continued success.

I assure you, Daimhin Feich, that any fighting force we sought to assemble would be much more formidable."

Feich's jaw tightened. He rose from the throne at last, straightening his tunic with sharp, jerky motions. "A triune Regency? Why should I accept this proposal? I *am* Airleas Malcuim's Regent by royal decree."

"To show good will. To satisfy the people of Caraidland."

"You are not a popular man," added Iobert Claeg. "By demonstrating a willingness to work with other Houses . . . "

"I work with the Dearg and the Teallach—"

"Such as the Jura and the Claeg," Iobert persisted.

"Surely, you can see the advantage of that," added Mortain Jura. "As you say, you are Regent. It behooves you to choose your allies carefully."

Feich's pale eyes flickered between the two Chieftains' faces. "You are undoubtedly right. It behooves all of us to choose our allies well."

Fencing. That's what they were doing—fencing. And so the subject of Taminy was broached without her name ever being mentioned. Saefren's hand worked the leather-wrapped hilt of his sword. *You know each other's thoughts. Why won't you speak them?*

"What of Cwen Toireasa?" Feich asked. "You've not mentioned her."

"The boy needs his mother," The Jura observed.

"The woman is a Taminist."

"She is also a Malcuim. Mother of the House Chieftain. Respect is due her, regardless of how little real influence she has at court."

"She'll have neither if she comes here," Feich promised. "She is a traitor to her husband's House and his memory. A heretic. Perhaps even a Wicke. Yet you wish me to install her at Mertuile?"

"Airleas needs his family about him."

"Airleas needs discipline. If he needs family, we will import cousins from Creiddylad or Storm."

Mortain's eyes flicked to Iobert and back. "Will you agree to the triune Regency?"

"Perhaps. But Toireasa Malcuim shall not reside in Mertuile, unless it be in her dungeons."

"That one concession we are willing to make," said Mortain mildly, casting another glance at The Claeg. "Toireasa may return to the Selbyr estates to live with her family. That is as lenient as I am prepared to be." He waited for some response from Feich, and when there was none said, "Shall we send to Ochanshrine for a cleirach and have an agreement drawn up?"

Feich raised his hand, remounting the dais to the throne. "Too hasty, brother. There is another name that's gone unmentioned here." He seated himself and gazed out at them, eyes cold. "What of Taminy, who dares call herself Osmaer?"

Saefren's blood iced over in his veins and he felt, suddenly and to the bone, the rashness of this undertaking. The Madaidh was right; all they would get for espousing Taminy's Cause was Daimhin Feich's enmity and with it the enmity of his allies. Before Saefren's inner eye was the specter of war—horrible, mad war between Houses that had been at peace for a century or more. He could hear the clashing of swords and the cries of a torn land. The sudden vision rattled him, making his knees quiver. He was not a coward, but he had no illusions that there was glory in battle. Perhaps he was less a Claeg for that.

He shook himself. The Jura was speaking, his face still composed and smiling. "What of her?"

Feich's eyes narrowed to icy slivers. "Do you not serve her?"

Mortain Jura looked down at his hands. Gloved, they rested on the eagle's head cap of his staff. An affectation, Saefren had once thought, till he discovered that the ornately carved thing housed a thin sword. "We serve none but the Golden Meri, Regent. We worship none but the Spirit of All. We venerate Its Chosen Ones and we obey Its precepts."

"Then Taminy-Osmaer is nothing to you?"

"She is as the air, Regent Feich. One looks, and sees nothing."

Saefren expelled the draft of air he'd been holding and hastily sucked up another lungful, this time vowing he'd remember to exhale it. There was a warning in his uncle's eyes and a spark of something sterner. He said nothing.

"Then you are not one of her followers?"

"How does one follow the wind?"

"Your words are elusive, Mortain. Speak plainly: Are you or are you not a Taminist?"

"I am not a 'Taminist.'"

This seemed to mollify Feich. He looked to the other Chieftains. "And what of the rest of you?"

"I worship the Spirit of All," said The Gilleas. "I serve the Golden Meri; I venerate Her Chosen Ones and obey Her commandments."

"The Gilleas speaks for me, as well," said Karr Graegam.

"I am no Taminist," said Iobert Claeg and his nephew remembered to breathe.

Daimhin Feich smiled. "I'm not certain I believe you. I seem to recall you arising to proclaim the truth of her mission not so long ago."

"The Dearg also proclaimed it," Mortain reminded him. "And the Teallach. Yet . . . " He shrugged. "Taminy has great powers, Daimhin. Can you doubt them capable of bewicking the Hall? We are not Osraed to be able to withstand such Weaving."

"And the inyx has worn off?"

"So it would seem. We are not now bewicked."

Feich's eyes were wary, if hopeful. Saefren wished he could read minds as the *waljan* were said to do. He could only read the Regent's sharp features and try to wring meaning from his words. "Are you then saying you are my allies?"

This time it was Iobert Claeg who spoke, and his voice carried steel. "We are the subjects of the Cyne of Caraidland and the allies of his House. Our cause is his cause. His success and safety is our mission."

"You would have a Malcuim Cyne?"

"We *have* a Malcuim Cyne. We would have him set upon his throne." Iobert Claeg's eyes would have flayed a lesser man than Daimhin Feich—or perhaps a man more aware of his moods. But Feich continued to sit in his pirated throne and smile as if the Universe had arisen to call him "beloved."

"Then you are neutral?"

"We are committed to Airleas Malcuim."

Feich inclined his head. "As I am. Very well, gentlemen. Let us have an agreement. Airleas Malcuim will be returned to Mertuile and be set before the Stone. He will have three Regents: myself, and the Chieftains Jura and Claeg. Do you gentlemen intend to reside at Mertuile?"

The Jura glanced at his Claeg peer. "We do."

This seemed to surprise Feich. "But your holdings—"

"Will be in the hands of my brother," said Mortain.

"And you, Iobert? Will you, too, hand your powers of estate into the hands of a kinsman?"

"I intend that my powers be vested in my eldest daughter."

Saefren was all but felled by amazement. Apparently, Feich was similarly afflicted. Fortunately, he was seated— Saefren merely *wanted* to sit. Damn, Uncle Iobert and his Claeg gall!

Feich quickly regained his composure. "A Taminist idea that, isn't it?"

"An Osraed idea, Regent. The Meri decreed that a woman may now became Osraed. If that is so, surely she may also be a House Elder, or even a Chieftain."

Feich let that pass and, apparently satisfied that the four Houses had drifted from Taminy's influence, sent to Ochanshrine for a cleirach to draw up an agreement and an Osraed to witness it. It was the Osraed Ladhar, himself, who appeared, the Minister Cadder in tow. Saefren was much impressed—Feich seemed to hold some sway with the illustrious Abbod.

He was impressed with something else, as well—the Abbod's Meri Kiss. Where the Taminist Osraed wore stars of the brightest emerald or gold, Osraed Ladhar's glimmered a reluctant peridot. He wasn't sure what that meant, precisely, but suspected it spoke of Taminy's power and the Covenanter Osraed's lack.

Before the Abbod, the Chieftains once more stated their loyalty to the House Malcuim and disavowed their Taminist leanings. The Abbod was clearly unconvinced. Further, he raised objections Feich had not. "The boy is a Taminist. How can you contemplate putting him in a position of power?"

"He is a boy, Abbod," The Jura told him mildly. "His education is far from complete."

"The Jura is right," Feich assured him. "Airleas is not lost. And frankly, I doubt the child gave willing consent to his abduction."

Ladhar glanced at him sharply. "Abduction?"

"Surely you don't believe a twelve year old boy is to be held responsible for decisions made under duress. He did not ally himself with Taminy, but with his own mother. What else could be expected of a child?"

Ladhar's expression was sour. "He will turn thirteen before long. Malcuims that age have *ruled* this country."

"If Airleas has grown in maturity, he may be quite ready to be reunited with his heritage."

"And if he's not ready?"

Feich looked to the Chieftains. "These gentlemen will assist me in readying him."

The agreement was haggled over and, some hours later, signed by all present either as party or witness. Feich agreed to dispatch a message to Halig-liath, disclosing the nature of the agreement to Airleas and offering him safe passage to Mertuile. A last minute stipulation had it that, except for a small contingent from each House, which would accompany Daimhin Feich to retrieve Colfre's heir, their forces would disperse to House-held lands. Saefren didn't like that stipulation. He liked little about this agreement.

"You changed your petition," he observed as he and his uncle rode side by side through Creiddylad to their hillside camp.

Iobert nodded. "Aye. Madaidh is a fool to eschew Taminy, but he is no fool when it comes to reading Feich. Nor are you. You were both right—now is not the time to antagonize."

"Do you trust him?"

"Does rain fall up? He will serve his own interests, not the Malcuim's. I trust him to do that."

"So, you let him believe the Cyneric is still at Haligliath."

"Even so."

"Even so . . . you lied."

Iobert scowled. "I did not."

Saefren laughed. "Come, Uncle. 'Taminy is as the air—she is as nothing.' I heard The Jura."

"Aye, but did not understand him. How long, Saefren, would any of us survive without air? How precious is that invisible substance?"

Saefren had to smile at that. "Clever. A riddle."

"Aye. And is it not true we worship the Spirit, serve the Meri, revere Her Chosen and obey Her commandments?"

"As you perceive them."

"Of course."

"But you denied being a Taminist."

"I'm not a Taminist, nephew, nor do I know what that is. I am *waljan*." He lifted his left hand from its resting place on the pommel of his saddle and turned the palm to Saefren's gaze. He only offered a glimpse, but a glimpse was enough.

Saefren's heart stuttered in his breast. There was no doubt—Iobert Claeg belonged completely to Taminy-Osmaer.

"We will post troops here, here and here." Ruadh's finger found the ridge-back road up the Holy Hill, the river below Nairne, the quay beneath the Halig-liath's massive flank. "The main force will follow your mighty cannon to the gates of the Fortress."

Daimhin Feich had scarcely heard his cousin's words. In his mind a variety of battles played out. The battle for Halig-liath was the least of them; with the combined forces of the four Houses arrayed behind Iobert Claeg, he'd have the little Malcuim back in no time. It was the matter of a triune Regency that disturbed him. It couldn't happen, of course. It was out of the question. Airleas would be in his power alone or Airleas would be dead—it was that simple.

The key to that was Taminy. Despite the Chieftain's protestations to the contrary, he knew where their allegiance really lay—his Gift told him that much. He would never confront them with it, of course—not as long as he could string them along, manipulate them to his own ends. Besides that, the last thing he wanted or needed was an all-out war. It was clear to Daimhin Feich that, in addition to Airleas Malcuim, Taminy controlled at least four Chieftains. Therefore, he must control Taminy.

He realized, suddenly, that his cousin had stopped speaking and was staring at him.

"Did you hear me, Daimhin?"

"Yes. Yes, I heard you. A good plan, Ruadh."

"With one flaw. Your wonderful cannon is nowhere in sight. Will we wait for it, or will we simply have our men clamber over Halig-liath's walls?"

"The cannon will be here in a matter of days. It will take that long to assemble our forces and brief the House Marschals on the plan."

"Aren't you forgetting something?"

"And what might that be, dear cousin?"

"That Halig-liath is protected by magic as well as stone."

Feich smiled. "No cousin, I have not forgotten. That, too, is being taken care of."

"This is the place!" Gwynet clambered down over the rocks to the pool, evidently mindless of the chill. Airleas followed, reluctantly at first then, realizing the rocks cut the buffeting wind, with more enthusiasm. By the time they reached the pool, he was warm with exertion. The sun penetrated this little grotto, the wind did not.

Once at the bottom, Airleas gazed about, fascinated. Jumbled blocks of stone formed uneven walls on both sides of the steep rill, looking as if a giant had thrown them there in displeasure. Downstream, the water tumbled away toward Airdnasheen; he could see the sharp peaks of roofs

and the tops of ancient pines. Upstream, was the fall—a
cascade of liquid crystal that plummeted twenty feet into
its pool, raising a froth of silver-white.

Airleas moved to the edge of the water, peering into it.
It was dark, even in sunlight, blue-violet like a twilight
sky. His eyes couldn't penetrate to the bottom. "Is that
where she lives, d'you think?" he asked.

Gwynet squatted, following his gaze. "I don't think she
lives in the water at all. Not really. I don't think she lives
any place. Taminy says she just *is*."

"Well, then, a person would be able to see her anywhere
at all, wouldn't you think?"

"I think some folks can. But here, it's just easier."

Airleas glanced at the veil of water cascading from above.
He could feel the spray, icy and wet on his face. He licked
his lips. "Do you think she'll come with both of us here?"

"I don't know. I don't think so. She comes to each heart,
the Hillwild say . . . " She caught his look and grinned.
"Anyway, I got studies."

With Gwynet gone, Airleas sat crosslegged on a large
flat rock whose hollowed surface looked as if it had held
the huddled forms of a thousand-thousand aspirants to
the Gwyr's favor. He breathed deeply, cleared his mind,
tried to open his heart and free his spirit. His mind was a
bird—an iolair—climbing, climbing, soaring toward the
Sun, reaching for the supernal. The chill of the day fell
away, and the icy spray, and the Sun, itself. Even the pool
and the falls disappeared. He wondered, at once detached
and curious, if this was what the pilgrim Prentices experienced at the end of their journeys. This, too, was a Pilgrimage of sorts. He felt he'd been tested—just being here
was a test. And between Feich's treachery and the lessons
he'd had to learn at Taminy's hands—and Broran's—he
certainly had been tried.

He peeked at the pool. Nothing.

Patience. Taminy was right; he needed to develop
patience. He wondered if he might ask the Gwyr for that.
He also needed maturity. A Cyne must be mature, whatever his age. He must be a man, not a boy. And justice—

he must be replete with justice. And honor, trustworthiness, devotion to the Meri . . . to Taminy.

His meditation became a litany—a catalogue of the qualities he must have—*must* have—to be a fitting Cyne. How could he possibly acquire them? His life at court had not prepared him to be a man—to be Cyne. His father had not been prepared to give up what Feich had snatched from him. At Mertuile, Airleas had learned only self-indulgence and pride. Except for his mother's loving influence he might not have been capable of recognizing Taminy at all.

Airleas's eyes, half open, caught movement below him in the pool. His heart fluttered. Draped across the deep violet mirror was a veil of tatted mist. As he watched, the mist circled, drawing into a lacy spiral. At its center there appeared a peak and, in a moment's time, a translucent mountain rose from the cycling mist like a miniature ghost of snow-capped Baenn-iolair. Heart racing, expectant, Airleas could hardly contain himself. It was happening. The Gwyr was forming before his eyes. He wanted to leap up and dance; he wanted to cry with relief. He had learned something here, after all.

The form was no longer a mountain, no longer amorphous. In a moment more he would gaze on the face of the White Wave—mystic Gwyr-Gwenwyvar, believed by the Hillwild to be an aspect of the Meri. He would receive her benediction. He shivered in delight. Taminy would be so proud of him, and his mother, and even Catahn. He'd be given his own Weaving Stone instead of the little schooling crystals he now used. He'd be eligible for the Crask-an-duine; he'd be a man in the eyes of all. Broran would respect him then, by God, for surely, *he'd* never seen the Gwyr.

The misty shape quivered over its dark pool, tenuous and uncertain. In a breath it was gone and all of Airleas's daydreams with it.

He sat long by the pool, trying to call the Gwyr back. Chill permeated his clothes as the Sun slid away from the grotto, leaving a deep pocket of shadow. At last realizing the futility of his efforts, he gave up and left, trekking forlornly back up the trail to Hrofceaster. He reached his room without drawing notice and curled up before the fire to contemplate his failure. He had trouble accepting it as that. After all, the Gwyr had been there, had formed almost completely. Most people probably never even saw the mist. But what had made her vanish again? Was it something he'd done or thought? Had someone been watching and impinged on his aislinn?

He knew he should seek out Taminy and ask her what it meant. Had he failed, or had he nearly succeeded? Only she could tell him which. He wanted to go to her this minute; he dreaded going to her at all.

"Airleas?"

He started guiltily and looked up to see his mother standing in the doorway of his room.

"Airleas, are you all right?"

"Oh, just cold, Mam."

The Cwen moved further into the room and perched on a fur-covered chair. "Gwynet told me you'd gone down to the stream—to the Gwyr's pool."

Drat Gwynet! Couldn't keep a thing to herself. All anybody had to do was ask a direct question . . . Well, the damage was done and his mother was sitting here, looking at him with searching blue eyes and he, too, was powerless to dissemble. "I wanted to see her," he said simply. "I wanted to . . . to see if I was ready for Pilgrimage."

"Don't you think Taminy must be the one to tell you that?"

"I guess I was hoping . . . "

"To prove yourself?"

He nodded, bleak.

"What happened?"

"She *came*, Mam! I saw the mist rise and form, and then, just before it was finished, she disappeared—as if the wind had blown her away."

"Why do you think that happened?"

"I don't know, really. Gwynet says the Gwyr usually appears to only one soul at a time. Perhaps someone was watching me."

Toireasa tilted her head, sending a cascade of honey-gold hair over one eye, and Airleas realized how different she looked now, wearing simple clothes, her once carefully styled hair left to its own devices. He wanted to ask her how she felt about that—about the loss of their home, their way of life.

"Do you think that's what happened?" she asked him. "That someone was watching?"

He blushed. "No. No, I don't. I think I did something . . . wrong."

"But you don't know what."

"No . . ." He looked up at her. "I should tell Taminy, shouldn't I?"

"Well, I think if it had happened to me, I would tell her."

Of course she was right. And of course he'd known already what he should do. Now, finally, he did it, pulling together his pride and taking himself off to Taminy's parlor. She was not alone, but seeing him, she bid him sit beside her until she had dealt with a roomful of supplicants. There was a mother whose baby had been born with a withered arm, a pair of inveterate enemies—once friends—who begged the Osmaer to settle their decade-long dispute, a woman torn because of a wrong she felt she had done an old friend, now deceased.

Airleas sat and watched and listened while Taminy carefully handled each situation. She called Blue Healing down to make the child's arm well and whole; she uncovered the common bond between the two adversaries, bringing to light their long-buried friendship; she gently and reasonably relieved the guilt-ridden woman of her anguish.

When they had all gone and Eyslk-an-Caerluel, acting as gatekeeper, had closed the thick door to the corridor, Taminy turned her eyes to him. He knew she expected him to speak—to tell her he had gone to find the Gwyr and failed to draw her out. He cleared his throat, searching for the words.

"Airleas," she said before he could find them, "what does it mean to be Cyne?"

He blinked up at her, startled. "What—what does it mean?"

"Your father thought it a position of power, of leadership. He believed a Cyne lived to be obeyed and to be served by the obedient. What do you think?"

"Well, I . . . " *Well, what, Airleas Dimwit? You've dreamed of being set before the Stone every day since your father's death. What is it you dream of?* "It *is* leadership, surely. A Cyne must lead his people to prosperity and strength."

"And how must he lead? By force? By guile?"

"By . . . by force of example." There, that sounded good. And he also felt it to be true. "A Cyne must not be treacherous or greedy or hard-hearted. He must be honorable and trustworthy and compassionate. And just—of course, he must be just."

Taminy rose and walked slowly to her window where the mullioned glass refracted the waning violet light of day. "And why must he be these things?"

"Well . . . because it would please the Spirit. For the Spirit says, 'The most beloved of all things in My eyes is justice; turn your eyes toward it if you love Me.' And it would be a blessing to the people. If a Cyne isn't just and honorable and compassionate, his people will not be content, nor his country healthy."

"Then the Cyne is governed by and dependent on the good-pleasure of others?"

"Of course. He must obey the Spirit and the Meri; he must respect the Assembly and the Houses and the advice of the Privy Council . . . and the people, naturally, who speak to him through these means."

"So, he is guided by those who look to him for guidance. Yet, is he not their master?"

Airleas knew a trick question when he heard one. He knew Taminy was leading him toward some end and cursed his feeble wits for not divining what that end was. He called to mind the Cynes of Caraid-land who had been lauded for their spiritual greatness: Malcuim the Uniter, of course; his son Paeccs, Peace-Lover; Bitan-ig, called the Preserver;

Bearach Spearman; Siolta the Lawgiver; more recently, his grandfather, Ciarda, Friend of All.

Tales of Ciarda's exploits had always thrilled him—especially those that related how the young Cyneric had courageously weathered his own father's distrust and treachery to take the throne at a young age; how he had braved the censure of the Assembly and Privy Council in permitting his sister, Fioned, to marry a Hillwild Ren; how he had judiciously handled the trespass of Deasach fishing fleets into Caraidin waters; how he had gone about the country in disguise to see how he might better serve his people.

Airleas met Taminy's eyes. That was it! And in the life of a great Cyne like Ciarda it was so plain to see. "The Cyne is not the master of the people, but their servant."

Taminy didn't even leave him a moment to feel proud of himself. "And what," she asked him, "is servitude?"

Airleas sighed and pondered the question. It was not something he'd thought about much—at least, not in connection with being Cyne. He suspected he was about to have that error pointed out to him. "Well, it's . . . ah . . . serving the people, I suppose. Doing what's best for them."

"And how does a Cyne serve his people? How does he determine what's best for them?"

Though Ciarda Malcuim had toured the country seeking the answer to that question, Airleas suspected that would not work for every Cyne. *Well, I can keep blathering and make a real fool of myself and I can just admit—* "I—I don't know, Mistress. I suppose that's what I'm trying to learn."

"Servitude," said Taminy, "is the station of preferring another to oneself. It is embodied in the act of putting another's welfare or interests before one's own. It is the continual bowing of one's will to the will of another."

"The Meri," he said. "I must bow to the Meri's will. That's what you're telling me, isn't it? And that I must put the interests of my people before my own desires. . . . But I do that already, don't I? The Meri's will is my will and my people's interests are my own."

"Your people. They belong to you, do they?" There was

a glint of humor in those green eyes, but Airleas saw nothing even remotely humorous in the situation.

He was frustrated, and let his frustration answer. "They belong . . . Yes, of course they do. They certainly don't belong to Daimhin Feich. A Malcuim has *always* been Cyne."

Taminy smiled, but behind that smile, Airleas sensed something darker, more urgent. "The people you saw here this afternoon—do they belong to me?"

"Oh, yes! They adore you! They love you!"

"Why?"

"Be—because you heal them and—and soothe their anger and mend their broken hearts."

"Odd. It seems to me that I belong to them."

Airleas paused to consider that, and in the pause, light dawned. "You *serve* them. That's what you mean. That's what a Cyne must do for his people. He must heal and soothe and mend . . . and guide—the way you guide me, with love and respect."

"Why, Airleas? *Why* must a Cyne do these things for his people?"

"Because they're the right things to do. The Spirit blesses a Cyne who does these things with happiness and prosperity, and blesses his people likewise. And the people adore and obey such a Cyne."

"And what lies at the heart of a Cyne's justice and compassion? The hope of happiness and prosperity? The promise of obedience and adoration?"

Airleas chewed his lip. He wanted those things, all of them, but knew without doubt that they were *not* what a just Cyne—a Cyne like Ciarda—would base his Cyneship upon.

"Find the answer to that question, Airleas, and you will know why the Gwyr would not be seen by you today."

A chill trembled up his spine and his lips went numb. "Did Gwynet—?"

"Gwynet said nothing. Nor did she need to."

"Will you tell me, please?" he begged. "Will you tell me why the Gwyr slipped away from me? It would be so much quicker than me guessing."

She laughed. "Airleas, the only real answers are the ones we find ourselves. The ones we must buy with our tears and longing and desire. I will tell you this: The seat of a Cyne's power isn't the Throne, nor even the Stone of Ochan. And his strongest fortress is not Mertuile, nor even Halig-liath. The seat of a Cyne's power and his fortress is the Covenant between God, Man and Meri. The more you understand the Covenant, the more firm will your rule be, and the more true your servitude."

Away he went, feeling as he imagined a Prentice must feel on his first day of Pilgrimage when the Weard has at last set a riddle to be solved and a quest to be undertaken: inspired, inadequate and a little confused.

CHAPTER 11

Alas, for when the weapon is in the hand of the ignorant and cowardly, no one's life and belongings are safe; thieves grow in strength. Likewise, when a flawed priesthood acquires control of a system, it becomes as a wall between their people and the light of faith.
— *Osraed Tynedale, A Brief History of the Cusps*

It filled the eyes terribly and ten horses drew it. Even lashed down to its sledge, its muzzle lay level with the shoulders of its mounted escort. Children followed its progress through the streets of Creiddylad. Their elders stopped and stared as it passed by, squinting against the glare of sun on the burnished black barrel. It gleamed golden, too, with radiating curls of some yellow metal that trailed from muzzle to flank as if spewed from a small Sun trapped within the gaping maw. Up the Cyne's Way it rolled, ponderous, making its way to the gates of Mertuile.

Ruadh Feich's heart cowered in his breast as he watched its approach. He'd never seen anything like it—or even imagined that such a weapon existed. His eyes turned to the half-dozen dreys behind it and tried to picture what its ordnance must be like. Below him, the gates of Mertuile swung open to admit the colossus. Sweating cold with awe, Ruadh hurried down from the parapet to join his cousin in welcoming the Deasach party.

In the confines of Mertuile's outer ward, the great cannon was even more soul-chilling. Ruadh gazed up at the gleaming muzzle and realized that it was designed to look like a sea snake—a fire-breathing sea snake. The barrel he had thought was black had a sheen of emerald to it, and great, glittering orbs of red agate were set in brass behind the mouth, forming gold-lidded eyes.

His own eyes full of the marvelous weapon, Ruadh barely noticed the Deasach contingent, scarcely heard the first murmurs of diplomacy. Finally, he noticed them—tall, slender men, all, dark-skinned and dark-eyed, dressed uniformly in flowing black robes over conspicuously non-uniform garments in vivid hues.

From among these dignified figures stepped the Mediator, Loc Llywd, in his hands an ornately carved box, inlaid with sea shells and stones Ruadh didn't recognize. Approaching a smiling Daimhin Feich, he proffered the box. "Noble Regent, the Banarigh Lilias of El-Deasach, called the Raven, gratefully accepts your most delightful gifts and is pleased to offer you these tokens in return."

Ruadh suspected his cousin was interested in nothing but that stupendous cannon, but his sense of politesse prevailed. Daimhin graciously accepted the box, even making a pretty speech of his own as he slipped the clasp and opened the lid. But that action stopped the flow of words and Daimhin's eyes fixed on something within the box.

Ruadh moved closer to peer over his cousin's shoulder. There was jewelry in the box and a letter on gilt-edged linen rolled and tied with a cord of braided satin. There was also a dagger with a gem-encrusted hilt and scabbard. But none of those things were what had arrested Daimhin Feich's eye and now held Ruadh's as well. Rather, it was the portrait of a woman fitted into the satin-lined lid. Eyes the color of wine, large as a doe's, were set aslant in a heart-shaped face that spoke at once of delicacy and strength. The full, smiling lips were the color of Daimhin's red stone, and so great was the artist's skill, that they seemed about to speak. Her hair was the color of the raven's wing, and so complemented the milky-bronze flesh that Ruadh could not tear his eyes from the perfection of the image.

That Daimhin was also stunned was obvious. "This is Lilias?" he asked, forgetting his acceptance speech.

The Mediator nodded, smiling. "Indeed."

"And this portrait—?"

"Hardly does her justice, Regent." The smile deepened. "And you know I am not a man to exaggerate."

"Understatement, Mediator," Daimhin returned. "You make a habit of it. You claimed your cannon was merely monstrous. It is a good deal more than that. I can only imagine the virtues of your sovereign. Come now, gentlemen, I have a campaign to plan." With a last look at the inyx-weaving portrait, he at last forced himself to close the box and lead the Deasach delegation to the castle.

Ruadh gave the great Deasach cannon a parting glance as he followed his cousin across the ward. Monstrous. Aye, it was that at very least.

The hillside grove where the Four Allies camped was purposefully chaotic. People hurried here and there, carrying saddles, packs, provisions. In a matter of hours the camp was divided; at the crown of the slope, gathered a large contingent that would remain camped in the hills just out of sight of Creiddylad on Madaidh land, so as not to violate their agreement with Feich. At the foot, a smaller force prepared to travel with Daimhin Feich to Nairne.

Saefren was no military strategist, but it seemed to him that accompanying an enemy's siege force to Halig-liath was a peculiar way for the *waljan* Chieftains to protect their Lady's interests. He didn't quite understand the ploy. What he did understand, with increasing unease, was that since falling under the influence of the Nairnian, his uncle was a different man—harder to read.

Saefren shivered and blinked at the hard steel sky. Likely, it would rain tonight. He didn't relish the thought of bedding down beneath a dripping sky when Creiddylad beckoned. Smoke tickled his nose, drawing his eyes to where a campfire's plume curled through the trees. He moved toward it automatically, finding himself among the Chieftains. Attended by their aides-de-camp (which Saefren noted included The Graegam's eldest daughter), they huddled in discussion of tomorrow's events.

"Ah, Saefren!" his uncle said. "Come, your opinion is wanted."

He dropped to the couch-roll beside his uncle, shrugging within his thick cloak in hope of generating some warmth. "Really?" he said. "I thought your course was already set. You send forces to Nairne."

Iobert's iron brows rippled with bemusement. "This troubles you." It was not a question.

"It seems odd."

Mortain Jura, sitting opposite them on the other side of the fire pit, chuckled. "What better way to keep an eye on our noble Regent?"

"But to what end? Do you hope to assassinate him?"

"While he's surrounded by his kin?" asked Graegam's girl.

Her father laid a cautionary hand on her knee. "This is no place to speak of murder. You both forget why we are here. We show support for The Malcuim, and try to impress Daimhin Feich with our unity."

Saefren nodded. "While those who remain behind keep an eye on things here."

"The *waljan* in Creiddylad may be in danger," said Mortain. "Even in Feich's absence."

"Or perhaps especially then," observed Iobert Claeg.

Mortain conceded that with a nod of his head. "Then, too, we have yet to hear from the Skarf and the Glinne."

Saefren frowned. "The Floinn have gone to Feich, then?"

The Gilleas, nearly invisible huddled in his thick fleece-lined coat, snorted. "The Floinn have gone to the Floinn. I think they've always awaited an excuse to move for autonomy. They all but own the river south of Norder, which is as good as owning Norder itself. They've no great love of the Feich."

"Chill hell, Morcar!" chuckled The Graegam. "They've no great love of anyone!"

"Aye. Isolation does that. Appears that Rodri Madaidh plans to take his House down the same road."

"And the Cuillean," observed Mortain Jura, "are split. They agree only that they hate the Teallach and will likely fall to Taminy merely because their near neighbors have gone to her enemy."

"So the Skarf and the Glinne must be approached," observed Iobert. "And the *waljan* of Creiddylad must be protected and informed."

"I would go to the Skarf," said the Graegam woman and her father nodded approval. "Perhaps Feich has not yet gotten to them."

In short order, it was decided that Mortain Jura and Iobert Claeg would lead the Allies within Feich's force, taking Elders from the Houses Gilleas and Graegam to complete their number; The Gilleas and his son would coordinate the troop left at Creiddylad through the most senior House kinsman; Mortain Jura's young brother, Hethe, would lead spies to scour Creiddylad; The Graegam would accompany his daughter to the Skarf and the Glinne, if time allowed.

There was that feeling, Saefren thought, listening with half an ear to the arrangements being made, as if time was rushing by in an invisible current, cascading headlong to some *point*, some crux. *Not much time left*, he thought, but had no idea for what. He realized that the discussion had ended without a decision as to his own disposition. He felt his uncle's eyes on him.

"I would stay in Creiddylad," he said, glancing up and about at the firelit faces. He smiled wryly. "It's a damn sight more hospitable than this soggy wood."

There were appreciative chuckles from the others and his uncle slapped him on the shoulder. "Stay wakeful," he admonished. "Perhaps you should leave tonight since your tent will be departing at dawn with me."

He did not have to be coerced. Light had bled from the sky and already a fine, cold mist was settling among the trees. Saefren and his Jura companions hurried to saddle their horses, collect their belongings and get on their way. They ate together at a tavern near the landward gate, then decided it would be advantageous to separate. Hethe elected to ply the water front; Saefren headed for the cluttered environs below Mertuile. He had an inn picked out for his evening's pleasure and, riding there, justified the move as a good way to hear the local gossip. He knew the place well from some years earlier when a cousin had taken him there. He recalled that the girls there were young and willing and occasionally even pretty, and that the drink was strong and hot and made even the homeliest girl a goddess.

Reluctantly, he remembered that it was not a place where either the eyes or the ears worked well, but where the mouth was likely to function altogether *too* well.

He rode past the inn and reined his horse in beneath the gates of Carehouse.

For two nights, the Dearg Wicke had tried the red stone and spoken of history and of Weaving. She had quoted Scripture and Tradition at him until he wanted to rage at her. But one thing he had learned was that the woman could not be bullied. To snarl at her provoked nothing more than a patient, stony gaze. To snap only brought forth the arrogant smile. "Find someone else to school you, then," she'd say and begin to walk away. And he would stop her and promise to be more patient.

Now, on the eve of his departure for Halig-liath, she at last said the words he had been waiting to hear, "Tonight, you'll take up the stone and Weave."

They were seated on the floor within his makeshift aislinn chamber—a series of carved wooden screens he had gathered from around the castle and arrayed in a circle on his hearth rug. The place was dark, lighted only by candles and a dim flood of luminance from the fireplace. Outside, wind moaned in the dark and rain rattled the windows. It was a fitting atmosphere for what Daimhin Feich hoped to accomplish.

"What must I do?" he asked.

Coinich Mor smiled. "What did you before?"

"Does it matter? It didn't work."

"Hm. What d'you think *they* do—your Holy Ones? What d'you think *she* does—your beloved Wicke?"

"She's not—" He dammed the words. "I've seen her Weave only once. It seemed she . . . pulled the power down from . . . " He shook his head. " . . . somewhere. She draws it. The Osraed, too, speak of drawing Blue Healing or drawing Red Power."

The Wicke nodded. "Aye. They draw on the Source."

"The crystals."

"No, Regent. The stones're mere channels—talismans. Did you not even learn that much from your Osraed? The Spirit of All's the Source of their Weaving. The Meri's the Mother of their duans."

"And how do I tap that Source? How do you?"

She laughed at him, candlelight glinting from her fox eyes. Oddly, she reminded him of his dead Cyne, Colfre. "The Spirit don't suffer Its power to be drawn upon by the likes of us, Regent Feich. The Spirit commits Its energies only to those who serve It, who pleasure Its eyes."

Feich sat forward, quivering, intent. "Ladhar's mewling cleirach speaks of a great Source of Evil let loose upon the world by this Cusp. He believes Taminy is its minion. Are you telling me that Evil exists? Is that what I must draw upon?" The thought thrilled and chilled him at once, made him quiver with a dread so delicious it terrified him, excited him.

But the Dearg Wicke was shaking her dark head, smiling at him as any indulgent teacher might smile at a naive pupil. "There's no such source of evil, Regent. I know this cleirach you speak of. I've known men like him. Men who must believe in such a power because to do else'd be too terrible a burden."

"I don't understand," murmured Feich.

The Dearg tapped her breast. "*We*, Regent Feich, we are the source of our own dark Weaving. To work what the Spirit abhors, we draw upon our own forces and on the forces of others."

Captivated, Feich leaned closer still. Close enough to smell the scent of her—spicy, smoky. "Others?"

"The weak. The foolish. The strong, but unaware. You understand." She nodded, smiling.

By God, he *did* understand. It was what he had always done—used the weakness and foolishness and naivete of others to his own advantage. He manipulated and, behind each manipulation, put the full force of his will. But . . . "You speak of a real drawing of power. How may I—?"

She picked up the red crystal from where it rested between them on the floor and put it in his hands. "Begin within. Draw from your own self. Bring to mind that night at Ochanshrine—how the weakness of the cleirach maddened you. It was your *rage* that forced a spark from Ochan's Stone."

He did as she said, recalling vividly the scene; Cadder cringing on his bench, peering about, no doubt praying none would see him quivering before a Feich. Scorn poured forth. The blithering, pious fool! He'd wanted to strike Cadder physically, knock him from his perch—but Daimhin Feich was no bully. And so his scorn had turned to rage in the face of Cadder's obstinate cowering and, released, had touched the Great Crystal, sparking it.

"Ye-es," breathed the Wicke, and Feich could feel her rising excitement. "Good."

He glanced at the crystal in his hands, saw the light pulsing within it. No sudden flare, this, no tremulous flame, but a deep, ruddy glow, constant as the hot emotions that burned in his heart. He thought of that other Wicke then—of Taminy—and his rage blossomed beyond reason. In his hands, the red crystal blazed, showering the screened chamber with flaming glory, catching Coinich Mor in its brilliance and transfiguring her.

"Yes!" she said again, moaning the word as if in some pagan ecstasy. Her parted lips were blood red in the fey light and her Hillwild eyes glittered like the sands of Ochan's Cave. Her scent washed over him again—hotter than before, spicier. Shifting the stone to one hand, Feich tangled the other in the Wicke's dark hair, drawing those red, red lips to his for a taste of that spice.

She did not pull away, nor did she demurely yield as the women of his experience usually did. Instead, she swarmed him, flooded him with awareness of her. Her hand joined his around the stone and they met at the center of the aislinn circle, pressing body to body, straining into embrace. She devoured him, and he, her. They were wildness upon wildness, bodies tangled impossibly in the brilliance of Feich's red crystal, their voices wrenched from their throats in coarse harmony again . . . again. . . . He heard laughter more than once, deep-throated, frenzied, feral. It amused him to realize it was his own.

When exhaustion at last claimed him, he turned his eyes to the crystal. Clutched still in their joined hands, its radiance was fading. His thoughts turned, unbidden, to Taminy. Drained by the wantonness of his coupling with Coinich Mor, he could still hate the Nairnian Wicke, still wish—yes, and imagine—that it was her body that lay, docile beneath his, legs locked around him. The thought filled him and, gazing down at the Hillwild woman, he could almost see wheat-pale hair, not black—sea-green eyes, not fox-amber.

The Wicke laughed, her legs releasing him. "You are a troubled man, Regent Feich."

He laid his head down upon her shoulder and slept, too spent to decipher her meaning.

Rain fell in a sullen veil, washing Airdnasheen in moist shades of grey. Even the pines had surrendered the pretense of color to the fall of mist. But Eyslk-an-Caerluel could not be sullen, for today she was moving to Hrofceaster. It was not raining in Eyslk's world; she looked from her window and imagined that Airdnasheen existed inside a cloud—a cloud of glorious silver.

She sang a little as she packed her belongings into a single large duffel and small, painted trunk. Happy melodies they were, though that happiness was tinged with surprise and a little bemusement. She had dreaded asking her mother for permission to move up to Catahn's fortress—dreaded it because she had expected to win Deardru-an-Caerluel's resentment, not the instant approval she got.

Eyslk had ever been aware of the coolness and alienation between her mother and Catahn. It had been difficult to gain her permission to be educated at Hrofceaster. Only a letter from Catahn and the reasonable arguments of her stepfather had given Eyslk access to learning beyond that of hearth, home and village. Deardru had seemed to take an instant dislike to Taminy, though she had only seen her from afar. And, though she pleaded sympathy for the Osmaer's plight, she seemed to take perverse pleasure in mocking her, making vulgar comments about the nature of her relationship with Osraed Wyth and the other male *waljan*. Which was, in part, why Eyslk had beseeched Taminy to grant her asylum at Hrofceaster. Her mother's antipathy—the way it was vented—left her feeling uneasy and depressed.

She laid a pretty purple blanket into the chest and, on top of it, some books Catahn had given her. She read well now, and loved the stories of magic and heroism, the little book of duans and scriptures.

"Before you close that," said Deardru from the doorway of her daughter's little room, "I've some clothing in my trunk you may have. Come, take it, if you wish."

Eyslk followed her mother to her bedchamber, as much surprised at the smile on her face as she was at the gesture. The clothing in question turned out to be an array of items from finely sewn undergarments to a soft velvet cloak, lined with fur. There were dresses, too, of beautifully woven wool. And there were leggings and fine hose and shoes.

Eyslk glanced up at her mother from where she sat before the large chest of keepsakes. "Mam, are you sure you wish me to have these things? They're so beautiful. So elegant."

"Aye. Too much so to be kept in a trunk. I haven't worn these things since I lived up at Hrofceaster myself. They're not quite suitable for village life."

Eyslk ran her hand over a velvet hoodlet. "You wore these when father was alive."

Deardru didn't answer. "You may have whatever you wish," she said. "There's even a small box of jewelry there. That, too, you may consider yours. I've surely no use for it."

She was gone then, leaving her daughter to wonder over the treasures she'd been awarded. There were three fine

dresses, two embroidered skirts and a number of delicate
sous-shirts. There was a pair of vivid scarlet breeches and
a long, loose, split coat that matched. She wondered if
her mother had ever worn the outfit to ride with her beloved
Raenulf. Eyslk pictured them together, her mother young
and happy, her father tall and handsome and laughing.
She imagined he must have looked much like Catahn,
though her mother had said Raenulf Hageswode's eyes were
dark and his hair a gleaming, lightless, blue-black. She had
seen only one portrait of her father, painted when he had
completed the Crask-an-duine at the age of thirteen.

She had sometimes been tempted to envy Desary her
father, but reasoned that she, at least, had both a mother
and step-father while Desary had only Catahn. But now,
of course, there was Taminy . . . for both of them.

That thought shook her from her reverie and set her
to folding her new clothing. It was a tall stack she carried
back to her own room, the small, intricately inlaid box of
jewelry balanced on top. She had just gotten through her
curtained doorway when the tower of cloth collapsed, spilling the top layers and the jewel box. The little casket hit
the floor and broke open, scattering its contents all over
the rough planks.

Eyslk felt immediate, sharp remorse for her careless-
ness. Dropping the rest of the clothes atop her duffel, she
fell to her knees and scrambled after the spilt jewels. *How
stupid!* She should never have tried to carry it all at once.
She should have gone back for the box. She tilted it upright, noting with relief that none of the seashell inlay had
been damaged. Her father, Raenulf, had given her mother
that box at their betrothal. It would break her heart to
damage it. She picked up a necklace, a brooch, a pair of
silver earrings set with tiny red stones, a hairclip, a ring,
and started to put them back into the box.

She paused. Oh, but it *was* damaged, after all. The side
of the largest of three compartments had broken and stuck
up at an odd angle. She tried to push it back into place,
but could not; it was solidly wedged. Maybe if she could
remove it and try reseating it level . . . She laid the jewels

in her lap and grasped the little piece of wood between her fingers, wiggling it until it worked loose. She tugged and it shifted slightly. Encouraged, she tugged again. This time, it came free, bringing the bottom of the compartment with it. Something fell out to plop into her skirts atop the little pile of jewelry.

It was a packet about the size of her open hand—a packet of soft, woven paper. She picked it up, surprised at the weight of it, and turned it in her hands. The paper was yellow with age, though still pliant beneath her fingers. She toyed with the careful folds, wondering if she might open it and see what was written. She felt immediate guilt. This was surely some treasured keepsake of her mother. She ought to take it to her at once. But, again, the contents of the jewelry box had been given to her. Surely, that included the mysterious packet. Perhaps it was another brooch or some other piece of jewelry.

After a moment of hesitation, she opened it. A lock of dark hair fell into the palm of her hand; a folded piece of paper fluttered to her lap. She ignored both, her eyes on the thing that had given the packet its weight and stiffness. It was a portrait of a young man, and Eyslk could only believe it was Raenulf Hageswode whose painted eyes gazed at her from the small, linen-covered slab of wood.

A wave of tenderness engulfed her. *Poor mother*, she thought, and tried to fathom the devotion that had caused the pragmatic Deardru-an-Caerluel to save and treasure these mementos of her young husband—to pass them on to her daughter.

Eyslk opened her hand on the lock of hair. It lay across her *gytha*, its black-cherry strands catching more light from that than from the weak fire in her room's tiny grate. She frowned, rubbing the silken threads between her fingers, and glanced again at the portrait. The young man's hair was the same ruddy black as the lock she held. And his eyes . . .

Putting down the portrait, Eyslk scrabbled amongst the jewelry for the fallen scrap of paper. She unfolded it and read the faint writing there, scrawled in ash ink: *My Chieftain. You think me a woman of duty? You believe I am*

*blinded by my desire for another Hageswode child? That
might once have been true. But it is love that blinds me,
now. It is desire for you that drives me to seek you out.
What drives you, my Chieftain? Pity? Responsibility? I
care not. I accept any feeling you may have for me. If, as
you say, there is none, leave this letter where it lies. But
if you would have me again, take it, and I will meet you
tonight in the chamber below the stair.* There was no signature, only a single initial: D.

Her mother had written this—to "my Chieftain." As
much as Eyslk wanted to believe that might be an affec-
tionate reference to the man who *should* have been Ren
in Deardru's eyes, she could not believe it. The object of
the letter's passion was the man who gazed at her from a
painted bit of cloth and wood, and a lock of whose hair
curled, silkily, across her palm. Not Raenulf Hageswode,
but his younger brother, Catahn.

Eyslk wallowed in confusion. Had there been no love,
then, between her parents? Had her mother been that faith-
less, that wretchedly fickle? Shaking her head, she scanned
the letter a second time. *Another Hageswode child.* That
could only mean she had already been born; Raenulf
Hageswode was dead and her mother, widowed. Still . . .
still . . . She put a hand to her head. But her uncle had
obviously not taken this missive from whatever place
Deardru had left it. Catahn had refused her advances, had
remained faithful to Desary's mother, and Deardru, disappointed, had kept this reminder of his rejection. But,
again the letter said—if you would have me *again*.

Eyslk turned the paper over; the back was blank. She
glanced at the back of the portrait; only the artist's signature appeared there. She looked down at the linen paper
that had wrapped it all; there was writing there—a handful of words in an unfamiliar hand: *It is agreed. I shall
give you what you ask, but there is nothing more I can
give.* The signature was a blur of ink, but Eyslk could make
out the letters "C" and "n" at either end.

Confusion spun her thoughts away. Surely, this was not
a response to her mother's note. Might it have preceded

it? That seemed just as unlikely. She gave up trying to piece the story together. One thing she understood quite well: In the very act of keeping these things, Deardru-an-Caerluel had betrayed herself. She did not hate Catahn Hageswode as Eyslk had suspected; she loved him and had once wanted to bear his child. That the Ren had not given in to that request was obvious; there was no other Hageswode child born to Deardru. Garradh's sons were clearly his own, for both bore his bluff, ruddy features. There was only Eyslk. Yet, Catahn's note . . .

Hearing movement without her room, Eyslk leapt to gather up the contents of the little box and thrust them hastily inside. The portrait she stuffed into her duffel, covering it with clothing.

The curtain swung back from the bedroom doorway and her eldest half-brother regarded her, red-faced, from the threshold. "Are you ready to go, then?" he asked, his voice belligerent. "Da bid me help you carry your things up to the fortress."

She smiled at him, her eyes watering, her heart still banging out a wild rhythm in her breast. "Aye, Con, thank you." She rose and put on her cloak before taking up the duffel. Con hefted her little chest of books and linens and winter things.

"You know," she told him, as he turned back through the door, "you'll see me often enough. I won't be a stranger, I promise."

He glowered at her. "You're a Hageswode again, Eyslk. You're a stranger already."

The words wounded, more so because, lately, she had begun to think of herself as a Hageswode—more Desary's cousin than Con and Gery's sister. "That's not true, Con. I'll be in the village all the time."

"Not if he gets *his* way," Con said, and jerked his head toward Hrofceaster. "And mam says he always does get his way. You're good as gone, Eyslk." He grunted, tossing the chest to his shoulder and led from the room. He didn't speak to her again, even to say good-bye.

CHAPTER 12

Whoever makes an effort on the Spirit's Path shall find their steps guided. The Meri is with those who travel this Way.

—*Utterances of the Osraed Gartain #45*

Ruadh Feich found himself riding in column next to Sorn Saba, brother of the Deasach Banarigh. The young Suderlander, who had accompanied the Deasach party (he said) out of curiosity, was remarkably like his sister. He had the same creamy bronze skin, dark hair, and dark, liquid eyes. He was almost surreally beautiful—again, like his sister; Ruadh had no doubt he blazed quite a trail among the young women in his sister's court.

Sorn was a last minute addition to their number—a late volunteer cousin Daimhin was only too happy to accept. He welcomed Deasach interest in his doings—after all, he hoped to make fast allies of them for the realm he fully expected would one day be his.

Ruadh watched his elder cousin's machinations with a peculiar detachment. He had no personal attachment to the idea that Daimhin should be Cyne, but that the House Feich be elevated above all others—the Claeg, the Malcuim, all—*that* he was committed to. Whether that meant pulling the strings of a Malcuim puppet or setting a Feich before Ochan's Stone mattered little. Either would be a victory. Indeed, there were ways in which the former scenario was preferable. Daimhin Feich was greedy and self-centered. What he did, he did for his own good, not for

214

the House. That rankled at times. More so when Ruadh considered that without Daimhin's self-seeking tenacity the Feich would not be standing so close to the all-but-empty throne of Caraid-land.

His Uncle Leod, Daimhin's father, was a weak Chieftain. A man who, though only just reaching his middle age, was content to hide behind his petty infirmities like an old man. He neither censured his aggressive only son, nor gave him any more than tacit support. Leod Feich was at home with his senior Elders. Only the young bucks were here, but they had brought nearly every able-bodied Feich kinsman with them.

That was enough to impress Sorn Saba. He ogled at the congregation of Chieftains and Elders (more so at the kinswomen brought along by the Jura and the Graegam). "I stand amazed," he commented, his wide-eyed expression making him look younger, even, than his nineteen or so years, "that such a force should be mounted to capture a single sorceress."

"We go to Nairne to free our Cyne," Ruadh told him. "Still, if the Wicke be captured, so much the better, I suppose."

The Deasach's raven brows quirked in query. "Your cousin spoke with much passion about this sorceress. He blames her for the defection of your little Cyne. He seems all intent on her capture. When I spoke to him last eve, he said not a word of the Malcuim boy. He spoke only of this Taminy."

Intent. Yes, that described cousin Daimhin well enough. "I don't doubt he speaks of her—and with reason. He tells me she invades his dreams. But I assure you, *Shak* Saba," —he hoped he'd gotten the alien title right— "Daimhin is as aware as I that our first duty is to the safe return of Airleas Malcuim to his capital."

"Please, let's not do the form. We are really youths still, and you, the elder. Call me Sorn, and I shall call you Ruadh. Your dear cousin has already made me call him Daimhin."

Ruadh smiled, unwillingly charmed by the not-quite-perfection of the Deasach's pleasantly accented Caraidin and warm voice. "Sorn, then."

"Now, tell me: Why doesn't your cousin simply declare himself Cyne of all this Land Between Streams? He seems to have his hands all over the Throne."

Ruadh, to his credit, did not show his amazement at the young man's brazenness. "There is a long tradition in Caraid-land of Malcuim Cynes. The Meri has always upheld them."

Sorn nodded. "Ah, yes. Through the succession of Osraed. We have something like your Osraed. We call them *Imrigh*—spiritual rulers. They do not dabble in politics, however." His eyes wandered to the group ahead of them—composed largely of Chieftains and Elders. "So tell me, Ruadh, what will you do with this sorceress when you get her?"

Ruadh grimaced, recalling a certain dinner conversation not that long ago. "I'm sure only my cousin knows the answer to that."

"You've no prescribed way of dealing with them?"

"We're rarely called on to deal with them. The last Wicke trials in Caraid-land were during the reign of Cyne Liusadhe the Purifier. That was two centuries ago."

Sorn turned sideways in his saddle, all interest. "And what did this Cyne Purifier do with his Wicke?"

"Exiled them." Ruadh smiled wryly. "Along with some other folk he'd no love for." He neglected to mention that those other folk were members of the House Feich.

"In El-Deasach, we put our sorceresses to the torch. But that is only the end of their humiliations. By the time they reach that pass, they bless the flames that devour them." His voice was still warm and sweet; he might have been describing a lover's caress. "Would you like to know what comes before?"

Ruadh glanced at him and saw the same warmth reflected in the dark eyes. The pit of his stomach shrugged. For all that he had never seen battle, Ruadh Feich thought of himself as a plain and simple soldier—a defender of Feich lands and honor. Men like Sorn, who seemed to find pleasure in the spilling of blood, he did not understand. "No," he said, "but you may find my cousin Daimhin a willing listener. You two are much of a mind when it comes to

Wicke. I believe he would take Taminy-Osmaer and drown her."

Sorn's brow wrinkled. "What—throw her from a boat or a cliff? Lower her into a well?"

Ruadh was finding this whole conversation distasteful. Courtesy would not allow him to let it show. "There is a chamber beneath the castle Mertuile where the sea flows freely. At certain times it has been used to . . . discipline the enemies of Mertuile's lords."

Sorn laughed. "How polite you are! You mean that, there, people were tortured and died. Superb! Then you can watch the death throes of the enemy as well as hear them. Perhaps an improvement over fire, yes?" He nodded, as if in answer to his own question. "Yes, and the body is spared mutilation. An unfortunate thing about fire—it destroys so utterly." He smiled at Ruadh—a bashful, boy's smile. "Your cousin showed me a painting of this Taminy done by your poor, dead Cyne Colfre. She is an exotic beauty, is she not?"

Ruadh flipped his reins, casting about for a way to extricate himself from this increasingly morbid dialogue. "I've never seen her, but in that portrait. I concede that Colfre must have thought her beautiful. But then, he was enamored of her."

"As is your cousin, I think."

A startling thought. "Daimhin? No. You misunderstand him. He was once enchanted by the Wicke, but no longer. He is driven only by hatred, believe me. She laid hands on his soul not that long ago—or tried to. Tried to manipulate him as she had our Cyne. My sense of it is that she humiliated him. Daimhin doesn't tolerate humiliation. It's revenge he seeks."

"Ah, revenge." Sorn nodded knowingly. The little-boy smile was back. "A powerful aphrodisiac."

Ruadh shook his head. "I don't understand . . . what's an a—"

Sorn reached over and patted his arm. "A powerful inyx, friend. A potent Weaving that causes the vengeful to burn with desire for the object of vengeance."

"You mean she Weaves lust upon him so he will spare her?" He hadn't thought of that.

Sorn let loose a cascade of ebullient laughter. "Not at all! Passion needs no Weaver, friend Feich. It Weaves its own enchantment."

Sorn, a loquacious companion, continued to chatter his philosophy regarding sorceresses (he seemed much less interested in sorcerers, though he claimed El-Deasach had known plagues of them from time to time). Ruadh declined to listen, turning his attention instead to the group ahead of them—Chieftains and Elders all. The only exceptions were the inclusion of the Abbod Ladhar and Blair Dearg's wife, Coinich Mor. She was Hillwild and a seeress, according to Daimhin. A novel resource, he said. She would be able to tell if they were being Woven against.

Her presence in the party bothered Ruadh, and he had protested it. More so than he had protested the inclusion of the twenty or so females from the Taminist Houses (and he could think of them in no other way, regardless of the professions of their Chieftains). It seemed odd to him that they should carry one Wicke to deal with another. Couldn't that damned Abbod tell if they were being Woven against? If not, what good was he?

Ruadh allowed himself a mean-spirited smile. If the presence of a Dearg "seeress" unsettled him, what effect must it have on the corpulent Abbod?

Ladhar was exhausted by the time they made camp the first night on the banks of the Halig-Tyne. The damned cannon slowed them to a crawl and the oversized wheels of its heavy undercarriage kept up the most horrendous racket—a cacophony that sounded like the screechings and wailings of every lost soul since Creation's distant beginning. It was torment to listen to it, but a worse torment was having to ride in such close company with the Wicke, Coinich Mor. Oh, she didn't call herself a Wicke—neither did her husband or any other relation—but Wicke she clearly was. A "sensitive soul," Feich called her, and her grinning husband spoke of how marriage to her had improved his fortunes. He was bewicked by her, no question. Must be to have brought her on this march.

Ladhar had asked after it of course, joining his protest to the young Feich Marschal's, but they were roundly ignored. She was here, he was told, to enhance his own powers. If the Wicke of Nairne were to try a Weave on them, two watchdogs were better than one.

Effrontery! Daimhin Feich was full of it. The Dearg Wicke had some motive of her own for being here, a motive Ladhar could not fathom, but which he was determined to know before they reached Nairne. He didn't like the way she looked at Daimhim Feich—as if she marked his every move. He didn't like the way she wielded her ample body—as if aware how well her own movements were marked by the men around her. He despised the way she made him feel—as if tiny, invisible vermin crawled ceaselessly over his body. He had felt like that before—when Taminy-a-Cuinn was near. It was the prelude to a storm of the spirit, the kind of storm Taminy had precipitated when she stood in the Assembly Hall and spun lightning out of the air.

Exhausted, he was. Road-weary. Bone-tired. But not so worn that he couldn't keep an eye and ear on the goings on about camp. He made it his business to watch Coinich Mor—or rather to have Caime Cadder watch her. It was a special talent of Cadder's that in any group of people he was virtually invisible. Ladhar doubted Daimhin Feich even noticed his presence at Ladhar's side, though he'd spoken over the man's head a number of times on the ride. It was a pathetic distinction, that invisibility, but it served Cadder's master well.

Well after sunset, when the rheum of the river had permeated every pore of Ladhar's tent, Caime Cadder scratched on the door post and made a shivering entrance. "The Dearg woman," he said, teeth chattering, face pinched with distaste, "has gone to the Regent's tent."

Ah! His suspicions confirmed, Ladhar squeezed out of his shelter into the sodden night. The Wicke was surely after something. Perhaps now, she was making some move.

Perhaps she was even a secret cohort of the Nairnian Wicke. Well, if she was, by God . . . He felt his belt pouch for the comforting bulk of his crystal, Scirwyn.

The Regent's tent was closest to the river, shielded from the rest of the camp by a circle of low shrubby trees. It was three times the size of anyone else's, dwarfing even the tasseled black tent of the visiting Deasach Marschal. This was a festival tent, hardly suitable for a battle camp. Ladhar pursed full lips. As annoying as was Feich's ostentatious taste, his penchant for isolation would work against him this time; the shadowy hedge was perfect cover for a spy Ladhar's size. The old Abbod pretended to make for the downstream wash pool, then squeezed behind the screen of greenery. The sounds of his discomfort covered by the whispered roar of the Halig-tyne, he stationed himself at a corner of the tent where inconstant light leaked from a long narrow gap in a corner joining.

Ladhar put his eye to the gap. The Dearg woman was there, just as Caime had said. She sat opposite Feich beside a small brazier, conversing in low tones. So soft was their discourse that the voice of the river obscured it. Ladhar could only tell that the Wicke was reporting something to Feich, her hands weaving illustrations in the air between them. For his part, Feich merely nodded, uttered a word or two here and there or laughed. His eyes were bright— too bright, Ladhar thought—and his body twitched as if in unbidden reaction to his companion's words.

When the Wicke's hands at last fell still, Feich brought a box into view. It was a small box, and covered with beaten gold. *Ah, now!* Ladhar thought. *He pays for her report.* Desperately, he wished to know what intelligence she had brought her lord. Had she some knowledge of treachery within the House Dearg?

Feich lifted the lid of the box, and the brazier glow picked flashes of sequined light from its contents.

Jewels! Jewels for a damned Wicke! Is there no end to the man's outrageous—? Ladhar's innards were at once as chill as his corpulent body. Breath froze in his lungs. No. It was clear, there *was* no end—no depth to which

Daimhin Feich would not go. For the gilt box contained only a single jewel—a large, bloody red crystal that Daimhin Feich now removed from its velvet bed and held before him in cupped hands.

How—? *How* had he gotten the stone? Dear God, did he intend to give it to this creature? Or had she brought it to him herself? Ladhar all but gasped when the woman, a taunting smile on her broad face, took a second, smaller stone from a pouch that hung between her ample breasts. She held the little yellow crystal up before Daimhin Feich's eyes, smile deepening, and spoke. Ladhar made out only the word "warm." Feich laughed and shook his head and the two of them began to Weave.

Afterward, Ladhar would wonder how he had stayed still through what followed—how he had not cried out with each new outrage. For the couple practiced Weaving an array of inyx: they caused the fire to dwindle to an ember then flare blindingly in its bowl; they made the brazier itself to rise from the carpeted ground cover, then descend as if winged; they riled the winds outside the tent so that they beat at Ladhar and whispered to him in turns; they woke day birds from their slumber and coaxed them to light upon the center pole of their garish tent.

Last of all, and more unsettling than their Weaving of the wind, they caused a sleep-befuddled Ruadh Feich to stumble from his own small tent to the Regent's grand shelter. Bewicked, he asked why he had been summoned and inquired after his lord's pleasure. His lord's pleasure was to send him away again, back to his tent, but not before bidding him remove his nightrobe and dance naked upon it in the brazier-lit doorway.

Gales of laughter followed Ruadh Feich, still unclad, back to his tent. The entire storm was from his elder cousin's throat; the Dearg monster only sat and smiled that secret, know-all smile with her cat's eyes as bright and hot as the flames leaping in the brazier at her side.

When Feich turned to her from his cousin's humiliation, he was jubilant, his face alive with mirth, with exultation. Dear Meri, he was drunk with power, intoxicated beyond reason. Ladhar quaked like the breeze-blown trees overhead, horrified.

His horror would only grow. For now the Dearg Wicke laid her yellow stone aside on the medallioned carpet Feich had carried from Mertuile and wordlessly removed her clothing, eyes gleaming with feral light. Daimhin Feich watched her, his own crystal clutched in his hands, his eyes mirroring Coinich Mor's heat and brightness. Ladhar watched, too, as the woman began to weave and dance, sporting her abundant, rounded body before the rapt gaze of Caraid-land's Regent and would-be Cyne. Her movements grew in wantonness, her gestures gracefully obscene, until at last she lay beside the brazier, writhing in the wash of kinetic light, there giving her companion mute intimation of her desire. Feich complied, laying his glowing stone beside Coinich Mor's, stripping his own garments in fevered haste, lowering himself to her undulating body.

Their joining was violent, Feich assaulting the woman as he must dream of assaulting Halig-liath. She was silent; only Feich seemed capable of sound. Ladhar barely heard him—barely saw the pair as they writhed in the crawl of firelight. His eyes were on those two crystals, covered now by the lewdly shifting shadows, but blazing-bright nonetheless. They pulsed with their own comingled fire—the red and the yellow-gold—power upon power, feeding on itself, growing fat on its own heat and light. Brighter than the brazier light the crystal glory grew, until the tent blazed with it.

Near blinded, Ladhar at last tore his eyes away and sank back on his fat haunches, chilled to the soul, numb to the core of his being. He managed only barely to haul himself to his feet, not caring that he made loud scuffling noises. They would be covered by the river's murmurs and Daimhin Feich's fierce cries. But he must get away, because the light had blinded him and the sights he had witnessed were now burnt into the darkness behind his eyes, and Feich—*damn him!*—was plundering the woman with increasing ferocity. She had begun to whimper and moan and the old Abbod could not bear the sound. A moment more and the rhythmic keening would become shrill enough for others to hear and he could not be caught here, cowering in a frozen heap.

So, he willed his rebellious legs to obey him and dragged himself from tree to tree, from bush to bush, away into the darkness to a place where the sound of the Holy River might wash over him and soothe the tumult of his soul. He had been there for some time when he realized that he could still hear the sobs of the Dearg Wicke. The sound tore at his ears. Holy of Holies, how could he yet be hearing that terrible sound? Shuddering, he forced his hands over his ears . . . and knew that the pitiable cries were his own.

Ladhar was alone in the Inner Chamber of Ochanshrine. Alone, but for the seemingly sentient Stone.

But no, he was in a tent on the banks of the Halig-tyne, the uneven ground wreaking havoc with his back, exhaustion putting sand beneath eyelids too heavy with fatigue to open.

A dream. He was dreaming. Dear God-Spirit, Precious Meri, he did not want to dream. Perhaps, if he whimpered he might wake himself, or Cadder might hear and wake him. But he could make no sound, so the dream claimed him.

Alone in the Shrine, his eyes on the Great Crystal, he sensed danger all around him. He could hear deceit whispering in the halls above and behind, and perfidy scuttling in the eaves. Profanity quivered in every dark nook; blasphemy shivered invisibly in the air. As he stood guard here, the shadowy forces coalesced and took on a loathsome form. Ladhar could not see it, but he knew its aspect; it was writhing darkness and flame; it smelled of incense, oils and lust-born sweat; it sang lewd duans and whispered obscenities. It fed on power—the sort of power that could be channeled and amplified through the Crystal on which he now fixed his eyes. It was approaching from behind him. Coming to steal the Stone. And he was alone.

Not alone.

A voice. A thought. "Mistress!"

But no. A pair of eyes gazed at him from the dark beyond the Stone, seeming to float in its gentle aurora. Icy, blue eyes. Familiar? He was unsure.

Never alone, the Voice insisted.

Behind him, Ladhar heard the obscene darkness laugh. Reflexively, he reached out to the Stone. He would perform a Wardweave. Quivering, he drew upon the Crystal, but the Weave was weak with panic. He cried out to the Spirit—to the Meri—begging more strength. Why did They not give it?

The cord is frayed, brother. The bond is weak. You have only your own resources to draw on, as you have done for many, many years.

My own . . . ? No. He rejected the idea. If that were true, then he really was alone.

There is help. The eyes vanished.

Help? From where? He could feel the foul, hot breath of the Darkness, sense its desire for the Stone. It was then that he saw the two shadowy figures—one on each side of the Stone's pedestal. Like silvery phantoms they shimmered in mid-air, seeming not even to touch the earth. Yet, they had hands, and those hands reached toward him (in supplication?) or toward the Osmaer Crystal—he could not tell which.

Was *this* his help? The Darkness breathed and shuffled. The silvery figures gestured at him to do something—to . . . to give them the Stone? The Darkness pressed at his back.

No, he *couldn't*. He would let no one touch the Stone. Not the grotesque Darkness, not the unknown shades. No one. *No one!*

Something seized him and shook him, prying him from his vision. Darkness was everywhere, formless, void. Blessedly void.

"Abbod!" The frantic voice was Cadder's. His, too, were the hands that shook Ladhar to grateful waking. "Abbod, are you . . . ?"

Ladhar forced his eyes open, certain they would spill sand onto his cheeks, and croaked, "I'm . . . all . . . right."

Later, as he sipped hot tea, he told Cadder of the dream,

for the second time this night, sincerely glad of the man's presence. For it was Cadder who had found him quaking and muttering by the river and unquestioningly brought him to his bed. For all his faults, the man was a good listener. He listened now, and when Ladhar had finished, he asked, "And what do you take the two phantoms to be, Abbod?"

"I don't know. Though the Voice that spoke to me seemed to indicate they were allies."

"And the Darkness?"

Ladhar shivered, reliving those hideous moments when he had cowered outside Daimhin Feich's tent. His mind's eye could see her, the Dearg Wicke, her broad, homely face alive with pleasure as she witnessed Ruadh Feich's humiliation, as she enjoyed his cousin's carnal worship. "Perhaps," he said, "it is that Dark Force you spoke to me of. Perhaps I am finally coming to believe in it." He hesitated, wondering how much he could confide in the cleirach. "Daimhin Feich . . . has a rune crystal and he has learned how to Weave."

Caime Cadder's face was as grey as the coming dawn. "He has . . . But how . . . ?"

"Apparently, this Dearg seeress he's brought along gave it to him and . . . is schooling him in its use."

The color came slowly back into Cadder's narrow face. "Then he has a Gift?"

"So it would seem."

"Then perhaps all is not lost."

Ladhar glanced sharply at his companion. "What ever can you mean?"

"Only that armed with the ability to Weave, he may be able to defend against this Evil Force."

"Not if he is co-opted by it."

Cadder's small eyes flashed fear. "Regent Feich is a man of strong will, Abbod. If his Gift is equally strong . . . "

Ladhar shivered despite his many layers of clothing, the stoked brazier and the cup of steaming liquid between his trembling hands. "Pray that it is, Caime. No. Pray it is stronger."

✦   ✦   ✦

"Then there is still a force outside Creiddylad?" The Osraed Fhada digested this intelligence with a furrowing of his Meri-Kissed brow.

"This displeases you?" Saefren asked.

Fhada smiled and shook his leonine head. In the spot of late morning sunlight that pooled about his desk, he looked less a man and more a creature of legend—an aingeal, a paeri. "I was merely concerned that your uncle felt the *need* to leave a force behind, especially since, as you say, our Regent specifically asked him not to."

Saefren answered the smile. "I believe Uncle Iobert may have left a force behind chiefly *because* 'our Regent' asked him not to. But they are deployed on House lands as the contract stipulated—Madaidh lands, to be exact."

Fhada laughed at that, but the girl Aine—*Alraed* Aine, Saefren reminded himself wryly—sat in her own puddle of comparative gloom looking taciturn and even disapproving.

"I don't understand any of this," she said sharply. "And less than I understand why the Chieftains *left* men here, do I understand why they took men with them on Feich's march to Halig-liath. The man means to harm Taminy."

"Who is no longer *at* Halig-liath," said Saefren reasonably. "But as long as Feich believes she is, he'll be unable to cause her any real harm."

"Moreover," Fhada added, "he may reveal his deeper intentions and plans to his supposed allies."

Saefren shook his head. "Doubtful, Osraed. Feich is a sly man, to all accounts. Sly men rarely confide their deeper intentions to anyone."

"And what happens when this sly man realizes Taminy is not at Halig-liath, but at Hrofceaster?" Aine asked. "What's to stop him from taking his forces there?"

"The winter snows, for one thing; the trail all but closed behind us as we descended. My uncle and the combined forces of the Claeg, the Graegam, the Gilleas and the Jura, for another."

"All well and good, unless Feich can call up an equal force. In which case . . ."

"Civil war," murmured Fhada. "Unless some other Force prevails."

Aine shifted in her seat. "I must let Taminy know what's going on."

"And how do you propose—?" Saefren halted. She wasn't listening. Her eyes were closed and her lips moved silently. He glanced at Fhada. *What?* he mouthed. But, the Osraed merely raised a finger to his lips. Saefren turned his attention back to Aine.

Head back, eyes open again, she stared fixedly at a point on the ceiling. Saefren watched, unsure whether to be amazed or amused as a cascade of expressions flowed across the girl's face—concentration, pleasure, concern, outright glee, concern again.

For several minutes this went on, then Aine lowered her eyes and turned them to Saefren. "How long before they reach Nairne?"

"Five days—six, perhaps. Uncle reckoned the cannon would slow them down more than a little."

Aine nodded and closed her eyes again briefly. A moment later, she seemed to have concluded her communication and stood to move closer to the fire that roared in the large hearth.

"You've . . . told her about Feich's march, then?" Saefren asked. "Just now?"

A malicious glint entered the redhead's hazel eyes. "Do you doubt that? Do you think perhaps I only pretended the Speakweave?"

"I'm sure you believe you . . . communicated with her. But then, how can you be certain?"

Aine ignored the question. "Saefren Claeg," she told him, frank annoyance souring her already less-than-sweet features. "You are the most hard-headed, cold-hearted—" She broke off, her body and face suddenly stiff with tension.

Glancing at Fhada, Saefren saw that he too had frozen in mid-chuckle, responding to something the young Claeg could neither see nor hear nor sense. Moments passed without movement, the only sound, that of flames crawling up the flue. Impatient, Saefren longed to demand to know what was going on. But he did not. Instead, he waited until Aine came back from wherever she had gone. Only then did he open his mouth to ask his question, and was roundly ignored.

Aine launched herself toward Fhada's desk, behind which, the Osraed now stood, eyes fastened on her flushed face. "It was Eadmund!"

"I caught that much—and his distress—but what was the message?"

"The Abbod Ladhar's deputy, Tarsuinn, has been given an edict to post. Drafted by Regent Feich and countersigned by the Abbod himself. We are to be denounced as heretics and enemies of the Throne, Osraed. And there will be a bounty on our heads—a hundred ambre for every *waljan* brought to Mertuile."

Fhada paled. "But surely the Privy Council—?"

"Eadmund says that a quorum of the Council witnessed the edict only this morning. It's to be posted in a week's time. Can he *do* that? Can he bypass the Assembly?"

"What Assembly? The Assembly is effectively disbanded, and I doubt Regent Feich has any intention of seeing it re-elected. As to the Privy Council—it appears a significant number of its members are in agreement with our Regent."

"Aye," muttered Saefren. "And it appears he made certain those who were not were safely out of the way." He felt the others' eyes on him. "You see what he's done, don't you? He drew up this edict—perhaps even at the last moment, when he knew the *waljan* Chieftains would be on their way to Halig-liath in his company. With only partisan Eiric, Osraed and Ministers left to convince . . ."

Fhada nodded grimly. "He pressed his advantage and had the edict passed and witnessed in the absence of strong dissent."

"And posted to coincide with his arrival in Nairne," Saefren concluded.

"So we are now heretics," murmured Aine, her ruddy complexion for once devoid of color.

Saefren grimaced. "Or will be in a week's time."

The girl shot him a sharp glance and he realized that he had crossed over an intangible line between skepticism and acceptance. Once again, she surprised him and did not gloat.

CHAPTER 13

Worship the Spirit in this way: If your faith lead you to death, alter it not. If your faith lead you to heaven, likewise, alter it not. This is the quality of faith that befits the Spirit of the Universe.

—*From the Testament of Osraed Bevol*

Ruadh Feich sat uneasily astride his horse this morning—uneasily and wearily. He had slept poorly after that bizarre dream and had hardly been prepared for the shock of waking to find himself naked within his bedroll with his nightrobe lying in a heap just inside his tent flap. Daimhin had only laughed at him when he worried that he might have been sleep-walking, and teased him that he must surely have been enchanted into a tryst with a wood paerie—or perhaps with the elusive Gwenwyvar.

All joking aside, Ruadh was afraid someone might have seen him dancing naked in the light of his tent brazier. At least he hoped that was all he had done. He *did* recall dancing, and the transient light of fire. But, somewhere in the confusion of compulsions and memories were fragmentary images of wandering across chill open ground, of approaching a large, lighted tent—Daimhin's tent, he thought—and of being watched by shadowy figures.

His skin crawled and he wondered if it were possible that the Nairnian Wicke was responsible for this. Perhaps she knew they came to confront her. Perhaps she had laid aislinn snares for them, hoping to inspire fear. Fierce Feich pride rose in Ruadh's breast. Well, if *that* were the case, she'd have to do much better than a simple nightmare to turn back the Feich.

Today again, as he rode at the head of his troop of kinsmen, Sorn Saba was beside him. Today the journey was more pleasant. There was no talk of Wicke-burnings or drownings or other tortures. Instead, the Deasach spoke of life in the court of his sister, the Banarigh Raven, of hunting and riding and sailing. He bragged a bit about being the youngest Marschal in the history of El-Deasach and, while Ruadh suspected the position was the result of nepotism, Sorn was quick to disabuse him of the idea. He had led a number of guerrilla attacks against the Southern Hillwild, he claimed—two in the last year alone. He had a talent for it. Or so he said.

The day passed uneventfully enough, though Ruadh could not shake the idea that he was being watched. He imagined with irritation some old dogs chuckling at what they had witnessed the young Feich Marschal doing in his sleep. The thought made his face and stomach burn.

Sunset found the company camped, once again, on the banks of the Holy River, and it was to the river that Ruadh went, as the Sun dipped below the Western horizon, to wash the grime of the road from his body. Sorn, seemingly unwilling to be separated from him, went along, and even joined in the chilly ablutions. That didn't bother Ruadh, though it seemed an intrusion into his privacy. He attributed it to differences in the Deasach concept of courtesy. Sorn had been a pleasant enough companion during the ride and Ruadh was inclined to merely ignore his presence, answering the younger man's grumbles about the abominable climate with grunts and monosyllables.

He'd just put on a clean pair of leggings and was unfolding a fresh shirt when the sensation of being watched assailed him more strongly than ever. Sorn, still shivering and complaining vociferously about these hardships, seemed to sense nothing. Skin crawling, Ruadh reached reflexively for his sword.

"I mean you no harm, young Marschal."

Startled, Ruadh whirled, sword clutched in one hand, shirt in the other.

Coinich Mor stood not five feet away, laughing at him as silently as she had appeared. "How like a young buck you are," she told him, and stepped nearer. "Ready to leap up and run. Not very warrior-like. Perhaps manhood sits lightly on you."

Face burning, Ruadh forced himself to ignore the jibe. He put down his sword with deliberate motion and prepared to pull the thick shirt over his head. "You startled me, mistress. I'm not used to having people sneak up on me in my own camp."

"You needn't hurry so in covering yourself, Marschal. You please the eyes greatly."

Ruadh was vaguely aware that Sorn had ceased his chattering. Only the river spoke. He pulled on the shirt, nearly tearing it in his haste; his arm caught halfway up one sleeve. Cursing, he pulled it free and tried again, this time succeeding in covering himself.

The Dearg woman moved closer still, her strange yellow eyes never leaving him. "I was watching you today."

"I felt you," he admitted, then wished he hadn't when the woman smiled at him.

"I wanted you to feel me."

She stopped no more than an arm's length away and Ruadh realized with a mixture of shame and anger that he had been retreating from her. He stopped his backward progress with a will. "Why have you come here, mistress?" He reached for his cloak and brought it around his shoulders.

"To ask how you slept last night."

Ruadh was certain every drop of blood had fled his face and extremities.

The Dearg woman tilted her head—a gesture that would have been charming and pert in a prettier, more delicate woman. Coming from Coinich Mor it held predatory undertones. "And if you found your nightrobe this morning," she added.

Ruadh finally forced words from his open mouth. "I don't know what you mean." He moved to take up his sword again and strapped it on, aware of Sorn's silent watchfulness.

"You were not wearing it when last I saw you. I thought you might've lost it."

Anger brought the blood back to Ruadh's face. "I am not a game-player, mistress. Kindly come to your point."

She laughed softly. "You're not like your cousin, the Regent. He likes games. He likes my . . . company."

He boggled at the implications of that—that Daimhin was dallying with the wife of a Dearg ally right beneath the man's nose. "And so, I'm sure, does your husband, Mistress Dearg."

"Is that what stops you? That I've a husband? Your cousin has no such worries."

"If you have my cousin to play with, why should you want me?"

"Shall I come to your tent tonight and *show* you why I want you?"

"No, mistress. You shall not." Flushing with outrage, Ruadh scooped up his dirty clothing and thrust through the screen of shore-hugging bushes. Behind him, Sorn Saba's voice said, "You may come to *my* tent tonight, Mistress Dearg. Unlike Ruadh, I am not afraid of you," and the Dearg Wicke laughed. The sound would haunt Ruadh Feich's dreams.

When Daimhin Feich had first marked Coinich Mor's interest in Sorn Saba (among others), his reaction was anger. The very thought that she should spread her favors among other men while he was her sponsor filled him with an overwhelming desire to strike at her with his new-found powers or, at the very least, to leave her behind him on the trail to Nairne.

The anger hadn't lasted. He quickly realized how ridiculous it was that *he* should be jealous of her time and talents when it was her husband who was being cuckolded several times over. She was teaching no one else to Weave, so there was no threat from that quarter. His anger was ill spent.

From then on, his attitude was one of knowing amusement. She was, after all, doing only what she had taught him to do; she was drawing energies from her trysts with the Deasach boy and her other paramours. Perhaps she even sucked forces from her doltish husband.

Daimhin found the thought amusing: Coinich Mor gathered potencies from other men and brought them to him so he could feed upon the pilfered energy. A twisted sort of mother bird, that made her, and he wondered if she realized that he also fed on her own forces, weak as they were.

It had surprised him, when first they Wove, that she taught so well who could martial so little real power. She had barely been able to call even a fitful glow from his red crystal—Bloodheart, he called it. Yet, with her guidance, he had made it scream glory. She could do little with her own stone besides make it pulse and flare. Only when they coupled did the yellow crystal catch fire. There was a soul-deep satisfaction in that that went worlds beyond the physical act. His powers grew with every encounter and this last time . . .

He paused to savor the memory, his loins quivering with anticipation of the night to come. Last night, in his tent, after she had been with the Deasach boy, the power he drew was such that, for a measure of moments, Coinich Mor had ceased to be Coinich Mor. She had been Taminy, the chaste, the pure, burning like a golden flame in his arms. No mere imagination, this, it was an aislinn vision of such strength that it had taken his breath away. He had stilled and stared, unable to believe what he had done, what he had Woven. The pale hair, the sea green eyes, the silken skin. He had savored every moment of the vision, knowing he embraced prophecy.

A thought had occurred to him then: If such power could be drawn from a minor Wicke like Coinich Mor, if such power (to direct the winds and even the minds of others!) could be channeled through an imperfect red crystal, what could be possible with Taminy under his control and the Osmaer Crystal in his hands?

He glanced back at the Dearg Wicke and caught her watching him, her face devoid of expression. When their eyes met, she smiled briefly, passion—or something like it—leaping in her yellow eyes. He turned front again, breathing deeply of the autumn air and feeling fit and fine and powerful. His eyes encountered another pair in their travels; the Abbod also watched him, gaze burning.

Someday, old man, Feich thought, and nodded to the Osraed with a smile. Ladhar turned away, leaving him with a sudden realization. *He fears me. Years of Osraed schooling in the Divine Art, the Osmaer Crystal at the heart of his domain, and yet he fears me.* The thought was electrifying.

Daimhin Feich set about anticipating his future, impatient to reach Nairne where he would lay hands on it.

Dreams, dark and chaotic, once again denied Taminy sleep. She woke and prayed, communing with Comfort in its pure form. Comfort came, but with it comprehension; a predator circled, growing in strength, cleverness and acquisitiveness. He didn't know where she was; still, he reached for her. Tonight she'd felt his breath on her again—hot, insistent—making her skin creep and her heart pound. She threw out a Wardweave, concentrating on the person of Daimhin Feich. She knew where he was, knew where to direct the Weave, but its web fell without effect; his Touch still lay upon her soul, fading only gradually.

She continued her prayers until the oppressive presence was gone, then calmed, if weary, she rose to take up her pen and write, pouring words onto the pages stacked upon her little writing table. In a few hours Wyth would arrive to collect them, add them to the volume he painstakingly compiled against the future.

Uncertain future, Taminy thought. She leaned back in her chair and rubbed weary fingers, Weaving warmth into them. She glanced at the window. The Sun wove too, applying a pale wash to the panes—blushing silver gleamed on a coat of crystalline frost.

Pages stacked where Wyth would find them, Taminy dressed in warm, sturdy breeches, boots and sweater, pulled on a quilted jacket—product of Gram Long's loving skill—

and left the fortress. The lookout marked her passage with
a bow. Perched high above her on the gate-top, he
reminded her of a morning bird bobbing in silent song.

Once she had cleared the shadow of Hrofceaster's walls,
and headed down the trail to Airdnasheen, the silence was
broken by the calls of jays and daws, crows and ravens.
Taminy wondered why winter's birds had such grating
voices. She had never thought to ponder that during her
time in the Meri's Realm. That sojourn had taught her
why men thought women beings apart, and why the
Deasach had darker skin and different ways than their
northern kin. She knew that beyond these lands were others
Deasach and Caraidin alike would find strange, exotic,
dangerous, even repellent. She understood that beyond
this world were others, peopled with men and women that
the citizens of this world would not be ready to meet for
a thousand thousand years. But the voice of a crow was a
mystery she had never plumbed.

She took a narrow, snow-brushed turn-off just outside
the village and made her way to the grotto of Airleas's latest
defeat. There was solace here and solitude and hours before
anyone would seek her out.

Ah, but not so. Even as she slid into the aislinn state
wherein the Gwyr-Meri, and even dear Bevol, were more
real to her than the rocks she sheltered against, she felt
eyes on her. She ignored them and slipped completely into
the Realm of Light.

The deep pool wore diamonds in this Realm and the
air was warm and sweet and laced with pine perfume. The
leaden gleam of dawn on frosted stone was transmuted
into Eibhilin gold. Coin was never as dear nor flame as
bright as this Light. Taminy basked in it, fed upon it, took
instruction from it. There was not, in all the world at that
moment, as glorious a place as the Gwyr's grotto.

Time had no place in this placeless realm and so Taminy
had no way of knowing how long she had visited there
when the sounds of approach tugged at her physical senses.
She read astonishment there, and a little fear mingled with
a stronger imperative—she was the thing sought. Folded

behind the Eibhilin veil, she waited. Would fear be overcome? She rose—a matter less of motion than of will—and moved to the center of the jeweled pool.

Above, on the slippery, rock-strewn descent, fear trembled more mightily. Yet . . . The visitor came on again, ignoring fear. At the edge of the water, movement ceased.

Taminy turned her attention to the figure wavering on the rocky shore, his breath issuing in a cloud from his open mouth. *Come, Airleas,* she told him.

Head up, eyes wide, he dropped to his knees and began to pray.

COME, Airleas, she repeated, and lifted a hand to him, knowing that in his eyes it appeared as if it might singe him.

He stood and took a hesitant step to the very edge of the water. There, he lowered his eyes to regard it with dismay.

Come, Airleas.

He hesitated. Could she mean for him to swim to her in the icy pool? He considered that. Accepted it. Began to step into the water. Hesitating, he raised his eyes to her again.

She read the bemusement in them, the sudden comprehension and excitement. He eyed the glittering wavelets speculatively. She beckoned. Excitement rippled through the golden atmosphere of the vale, uncertainty close on its heels. Surely, he could not—yet, she *did* beckon . . .

Wielding determination, Airleas stepped from the shore and walked the liquid trail to Taminy's side. Wonder poured from him as she took his hand and continued the walk, leading him to a jut of rock just beyond the fall's bright veil of perpetual mist. They sat upon the rock in a blanket of soft, radiant and silent warmth, Airleas gazing open-mouthed around the pocket of enchantment.

Finally, Taminy spoke, though not aloud: *You came to find me?*

"I . . ." Airleas's voice was swallowed in the bright haze. He abandoned its use. *Osraed Wyth sent me to collect your pages this morning.*

He's busy early today.

I was to take them to him directly—he was in a great hurry to begin work.

He always is.

But—forgive me, Mistress—I disobeyed . . . a little.

A little?

I paused to read them. Just to see what you'd written.

And what had I written that brought you here?

He turned toward her, face bathed in Eibhilin radiance. *The Heart of the Covenant.*

She nodded. *And that is?*

He licked his lips, squirming in puppyish anxiety. *Worship the Spirit in this way: If your devotion ends in fire, alter it not. Even so, if your rewards are glory and peace. This alone is the devotion fitting for the people of the Covenant. This worship, alone, is worthy of the Spirit of this All. Your adoration born of fear is unseemly. Worship begotten by desire for reward makes God's creation His equal. This is the Heart of the Covenant: that you love That Essence for Its own sake, fearless of destruction, with no desire for even Eibhilin riches.*

Taminy smiled. *You memorized it perfectly.*

Is that it? Really? The Heart of the Covenant?

She nodded.

I wanted . . . want to be Cyne.

And so?

Is that wrong?

Why do you want to be Cyne?

It's my place. My duty. I'm The Malcuim.

And the riches a Cyne possesses?

They're nice, but . . . Do you know what I really want?

She did, as it happened, but let him provide his own answer.

Loyalty. And respect. Mother says people loved my grandfather. I'd like people to love me the way they loved him. I'd like to be as good a Cyne as Ciarda was.

And were you thinking that if you worshipped God and devoted yourself to me—to the Meri—you'd be made Cyne?

Shame flooded the Eibhilin place. *I did think that, Mistress, but . . .*

No longer?

No longer.

So now you've no reason for your devotion.

His eyes widened and words leapt from his mouth. "But, Mistress . . . *you're* my reason for devotion!" And . . .

And?

He hesitated. *And perhaps, if I'm devoted to God, He'll make me worthy to be Cyne.*

Perhaps. Letting go of his hand, Taminy got to her feet and moved back across the glittering liquid path. To Airleas's eyes, she knew, she seemed as a feather or a cloud or the Gwyr Herself, suspended there above the water. On the opposite shore, she turned to where he now stood on the rocks, uncertainty eddying around him. The Eibhilin world receded until the pool was only a pool—an icy one, at that—and the veil was one of mist and ice crystals, not light. The damp chill of the grotto clung to cheeks and hands and Airleas shivered.

"Don't forget, you've a sword lesson after breakfast," she reminded him, raising her voice above the riot of the falls.

"But . . . !" The boy glanced around anxiously. "But how am I to cross the stream?"

Taminy pushed cold hands into the pockets of her jacket. "I can think of several ways. The choice is yours."

She left him to puzzle that out for himself and began the long, steep ascent to the trail. She was nearing the end of the climb when the sharp regard of another watcher pricked her *aidan*. She paused, catching a flash of consternation before it was shielded. Deardru. When a moment more of hesitation failed to draw the Hillwild woman out, Taminy continued on her way back up to Hrofceaster.

Daimhin Feich brought his troops into Nairne with banners flying. He put the Malcuim standard at the forefront, making sure that his own was tactfully buried among the other Houses'. Likewise, he chose Mortain Jura and Iobert Claeg as his riding companions, placing his own allies and their House Elders just behind. As he expected, the sight of Taminy's Claeg ally had a pacific effect on the people of Nairne. They displayed curiosity, but neither fear nor hostility. Even when armed kinsmen took up positions in their streets, they seemed unperturbed, although Feich thought an old crone standing outside a Weaver's shop had sneered at him. Wicke, he thought, were everywhere.

The Teallach had joined them, as agreed, just outside the village, increasing their numbers gratifyingly. As Ruadh had suggested, he had the quay fully guarded by Teallach and Graegam men. Thinking it a sensible move, he took any female "warriors" (he could not entertain the thought without smiling) up the long tree-covered ridge to Halig-liath. The ascent seemed to take forever; the Deasach cannon, impressive as it was, reduced their speed to an aching crawl. It would be worth it, Feich thought, just to see the look of astonishment on the faces of those damned turn-coat Osraed when they saw the thing.

But Daimhin Feich was hard pressed to control his own astonishment when they took the last wooded turn in the cobbled road and the gates of Halig-liath came into view. Those gates, once barred against him, were now wide open.

They were not surprised to see Daimhin Feich and his entourage; Taminy's warning, passed through Iseabal, had given them plenty of time to prepare. Still, the sight of all those mounted and armed men and women—and that cannon . . . Even forewarning couldn't eliminate *all* surprise or sense of awe. Osraed Saxan-a-Nairnecirke could admit that awe only to himself. When he and the Osraed Tynedale and Calach faced Daimhin Feich and the other Chieftains, they kept it well hidden.

No need for fear, Saxan told himself, *Taminy and Airleas are safe*. He repeated that numerous times as he watched a furious Daimhin Feich pace and posture in the Osraed council chamber.

"What do you mean—they're not here? Where have you hidden them?" The Regent whirled on Saxan, violence in his eyes. "Are they in the village? I swear I will tear down every hovel if I have to. Interrogate every—"

"They are not," Osraed Tynedale interrupted calmly, "in the village."

Feich heard that somehow, through his own rantings, and pinned the portly Osraed to his chair with a fierce, spear-sharp gaze. "Then where are they? If you dare lie to me, so help me, I'll—"

"I wouldn't think of lying," Tynedale returned with dignity. "I am *waljan*—Chosen. They are in the Gyldan-baenn, Regent, and have been there for several months."

Saxan's attention was on the faces of the assembled Chieftains and Elders as Feich reacted to this news. Claeg and his apparent allies were mildly amused. The Dearg was dark with anger, The Teallach plainly disgusted. Reading Feich was more difficult. Oh, there was surprise and anger, to be sure, but it hardly required a Gift to read that. And beyond the obvious—or beneath it, for Feich struck Saxan as a pool of murky depth—lay currents of thought and emotion that challenged the Osraed's nascent abilities. Very disconcerting.

Doubly so when Feich reined in his temper and turned to the Osraed with sudden, calm diplomacy. "You must forgive my outburst, Osraed. I am understandably anxious about Airleas Malcuim's welfare, and eager to see him returned to Creiddylad. I should have realized that the Wicke would flee with him—that she would take advantage of her Hillwild connections. They *are* at Hrofceaster?"

Tynedale inclined his head and Saxan said, "Yes, Regent Feich. They are indeed at Hrofceaster."

"Then I suppose that is where I must go to retrieve them."

"Begging pardon, Regent," said Saxan, "but the passes up to Baenn-an-ratha are closed."

"Closed."

"Impassable. The snows are early this year and quite fierce. Several parties of travelers have been forced to turn back already."

Feich's jaw bunched. "Indeed. Well, perhaps they did not have my tenacity." He collected his party and departed.

Saxan found himself yet unable to read Feich, but before leaving the room, Iobert Claeg sent him a glance with a subtext: Daimhin Feich would be discouraged from attempting any advance into the Gyldan-baenn.

"What do you think he'll do?" the Osraed Calach asked when the huge carved doors of the council chamber had swung shut.

"What *can* he do?" Saxan returned. "Taminy and Airleas are safely out of his reach until the spring thaw. Surely by then there will be a web of such strength woven between Taminy and the people that he will be unable to break it."

Calach and Tynedale exchanged glances. "Reasonable words, Saxan," said Tynedale. "Still, I can't help but wonder, exactly how tenacious *is* our Regent Feich?"

Saxan shifted uneasily. All three of them had reason to know that Daimhin Feich was very tenacious indeed.

Feich's temper struggled to free itself from the icy control he'd imposed upon it. Would the damned innkeeper never leave? Were he not providing food and drink, Feich would have shouted him from the room. Eventually, the wine and tea were poured, the supper laid, and the innkeeper was asking if he could do any more for the Chieftains and their noble kinsman. At a glare from Feich, he bobbed nervously and quit the chamber, drawing the thick door closed behind him.

As the weight of his companions' regard fell upon him, Feich reined his temper in further, leaning back in his chair with studied calm. "Now, we may talk. Plan. Ruadh, how long would it take a force the size of this one to make Airdnasheen—given the slow going?"

Ruadh frowned. "From here or from Creiddylad?"

"From here, of course. It would be a waste of time to return to Creiddylad. We can surely provision ourselves locally."

"But you heard the Osraed, cousin Daimhin; the trail is impassable. That western approach is difficult in fine weather. In snow—"

"Are you so dim you don't see that the Osraed of Haligliath will say whatever they must to protect their Wickish mistress? The passes—"

"Are closed, Daimhin Feich. Even as Osraed Saxan said."

Feich turned the full force of his gaze on Iobert Claeg, who looked back at him with veiled . . . *amusement*! He read it as clearly as if the man had laughed aloud at him. A wave of mixed pleasure and annoyance washed through him. "And how is it you are so certain of this?"

"We came down from Hrofceaster not a month past. The trail was barely passable then. Since then it has snowed a good deal more—according to the report from Claeg."

"And why *were* you up at Hrofceaster not a month past, Iobert?"

"That, Regent, is a matter of House business. Our lands brush the hem of the Gyldan-baenn. It is in our best interest to have certain treaties and agreements with the Ren Catahn."

"Agreements that include treason against our ruling House?"

The clink of cutlery, soft as it had been, ceased altogether. Iobert Claeg leaned back in his chair and regarded Feich with sudden and frustrating opacity. "I will take it that this latest setback has left you emotionally distraught, Regent, and ignore the challenge in that question. The Claeg have not always been faithful to the House of Malcuim—"

"To say the least."

"*Neither* have the Feich," Iobert reminded him. "But I swear upon my House's honor that we are loyal to Airleas Malcuim in all things. I give my personal pledge that I will defend him *with my life*."

"Did you know Airleas was at Hrofceaster, then?"

"If I did, would I have expected to find him here?"

Feich smiled, cursing his capricious *aidan*; he could no longer read the other man at all. He scanned the stern, bearded face without success and suspected he was being intentionally blocked. "Then you will ride beside me into the Gyldan-baenn to bring him home?"

"No sir, I will not. Nor shall any man of my House. The passes are deadly. I will not sacrifice my men on a fool's errand. Airleas Malcuim is safe at Hrofceaster until spring."

"Safe? In the hands of Evil? Among apostate Osraed and Wicke and Hillwild traitors? You underestimate the danger of his situation."

"And you underestimate the danger of the trail to Airdnasheen. The Claeg withdraw from your company."

"Aye, and the Graegam," said that Elder.

"And the Jura."

"And the Gilleas."

In the silence that followed that string of pronouncements, Daimhin Feich thought he could hear his own blood boil. He turned his head so as not to touch the curious eyes of the young Deasach Marschal, and addressed his own allies. "Will you, too, join these men in their cowardice?"

The Dearg, a boulder of a man with flaming red hair, scowled so deeply his brush of brow obscured his eyes. "The Dearg join none in cowardice. We pledged to you. We stand by you. *To Hrofceaster!*" He raised his cup and drank of it, but his challenge was echoed only by his own kinsmen.

Across from him, The Teallach was shaking his head. "I find myself of a mind wi' t'Claeg. This is a foolhardy idea. More so for us, who're used to milder climes and terrain. My men are untried a'the sort of campaign you propose, Daimhin. The journey alone is near impossible, ne'er mind that you'd have 'em wage war at its end. The boy's no doubt safe up there." He jerked his chin at the Gyldan-baenn, whose oppressive presence Feich could feel through the very walls. "If they'd meant to kill him, they'd've done't. I pledge you, if you but wait till spring, the Teallach'll be with you."

Frustrated, enraged, Feich smote the table with the flat of his hand, making crockery and cutlery leap. "Spring will be too late! Do you not understand the danger of leaving the Cyneric in the hands of that Wicke? She perverts him!

Even as we sit here debating, she bends him to her evil will—as she bent his mother, as she bent his father. She aims to make a puppet of him—a tool for her own purposes. If we wait till spring to reach him, Airleas Malcuim will be fit only for the fire. More to the point, Caraid-land may be in a similar condition. If we are not to put Airleas Malcuim on the throne, then who shall we put there?"

The room went silent again save for the creak of leather and the crackle of flame. Then Iobert Claeg rose. "If you contemplate setting yourself up as Cyneric, I and mine will resist you to the last man. Be assured our allied Houses will offer similar resistance." He glanced down the table at Mortain Jura and the Elders of the Houses Graegam and Gilleas. They gave assent without hesitation. "If it is anarchy you dread, Regent Feich," The Claeg continued, "if it is disunity you fear, making yourself Cyneric without public abdication by The Malcuim would be . . . ill-advised. I return to Creiddylad tomorrow, my men with me. If you desire provisions for your . . . mission, Claeg will supply you with what it can."

He left the room, his supper all but untouched. Mortain Jura and the Elders of the Houses Graegam and Gilleas trailed him like a pack of trained dogs. Feich watched them through a hot, black swell of hatred. They had checked him while he had sat back in false confidence, anticipating anything but this.

The Teallach and Dearg Chieftains and Elders had stayed to finish their meal; it was to these allies that Feich now turned his attention. "What say you, gentlemen? Is Caraid-land to be leaderless until The Claeg and his allies see fit to aid me in returning Airleas Malcuim to the Throne?"

The Teallach finished off his wine and cleared his throat. "Again, I'm forced to agree wi' Iobert. You are Airleas's Regent, Daimhin. If you do your job well, Caraid-land should not suffer too much. We need no Cyneric. We have one, though he seems t'ave been misplaced."

He patted at his beard with a crumpled towel, then left the table, taking his own Elders with him.

At length, The Dearg spoke. "Perhaps we should make

our plans tomorrow. Surely, sleep would be the best medicine tonight."

Feich shook his head. "No, Eadrig. Thought is the medicine this situation needs—meditation upon our next course of action, upon our resources."

"You'd do well," offered Blair Dearg, pride soaking every word, "to consort with my wife on these matters. She has sharp sight, that one."

Feich growled. "And yet did not see *this*!" He smote the table again, making the Elder jump right along with the tableware. "Rest assured, I *will* consort with her, Elder. Indeed, you may go to her this moment and send her to me."

Blair Dearg glanced at his Chieftain, who answered him with a bare raising of one garish brow. The Elder left immediately on his errand.

"I, too, will give this matter some thought," The Dearg remarked and removed himself from the table as well. "In the morning we'll hold council."

"By morning, I will be in need of no man's counsel," Feich murmured as the door closed at his ally's broad back.

"What do you intend to do?" Ruadh asked. "Iobert Claeg is right about those passes. Winter is come early this year. A small party might make it along those narrow trails, but a battle company—and with that cannon . . ." He shook his head. "If we were to try to go up now, our losses would be too great to bear. It would not be a fighting force that arrived at Airdnasheen, but a funeral procession."

Feich eyed his cousin with disgust. "You too? I never thought you a coward, Ruadh."

The young man colored deeply. "I am not a coward. But my men come first in my estimation. I'll not sacrifice even one of them to your . . . ambition."

Feich became suddenly aware that this interchange was being watched on by another pair of eyes. Alien eyes. In the moment he recalled Sorn Saba's presence, the young Deasach said, "There may be an alternative to this suicide, Regent Feich." Whatever Saba had been going to say was interrupted by a knock at the chamber door. Feich scowled. Could Coinich Mor be here so soon? But the nervous energies that leaked from beyond the portal were not Coinich Mor's. They belonged to an unknown.

"Come," Feich called, and the door swung open to reveal a strapping young man—Saba's age or younger—dressed in the short robes of an Aelder Prentice.

"And who might you be?"

The youth stepped into the room, carefully bringing the door to behind him. Broad shoulders back, golden head up, he displayed a handsome face whose expression completely belied the roil of anxiety Daimhin Feich sensed beneath. "Regent Feich. I am Aelder Prentice Brys-a-Lach, Prentice to the late Osraed Ealad-hach. I have information I believe may be of help to you."

"Indeed? And why should you care to be of help to me? I thought you lot had all thrown in with Taminy-Osmaer."

The boy's face blazed with sudden anger. "She killed my master. She imprisoned him in Halig-liath and then, when he would not submit to her, she murdered him."

"Your master—this Osraed Ealad-hach you mentioned?"

"Yes, lord."

Feich nodded. "I remember him. He led the fight against her among the Osraed and accused her before the Hall. A brave man. A righteous soul."

"Yes, lord."

Feich gestured at him. "Speak, then, Brys. What information have you?"

The young man glanced anxiously at Ruadh and Sorn.

"Don't mind them. They're my closest advisors. Speak."

"You met with the Triumvirate today."

Feich nodded.

The golden cheeks flushed. "No sir. You met with three Osraed who *fancy* themselves to be the Triumvirate. Only Osraed Calach has any right to his position. Osraed Tynedale took the place of my dead master on seniority alone. Osraed Saxan was voted in by a pack of traitors. All true Osraed have either fled Halig-liath or lie low in fear, pretending loyalty to the new order. The three men you met today are Taminists."

Feich sat back, lacing long fingers over his flat mid-section. "That fact did not escape me."

The youth's blue eyes widened. "You knew? And yet did nothing?"

"Of course I knew. Those blinding Kisses they sport are ample evidence of their apostasy. But what was I to do? I was surrounded by their allies . . . which included several of the Chieftains and Elders in my own party. Is this your great news, Brys-a-Lach? If so, I am disappointed."

"Ah, no sir. I came to tell this: These false Osraed are not yet able to Speakweave directly to their Mistress. They commune with her through a girl from the village—one of her *waljan*." The last word was a sneer.

Feich sat up. "Really? This is *most* interesting. Who is this cailin and where may I find her?"

The youth smiled. "She is Iseabal-a-Nairnecirke, lord, daughter of the Osraed Saxan. And she is at Nairne Cirke this night with her mother."

She had tried to talk to her mother again about Taminy and it had ended, again, with her mother barricaded in her room and Iseabal in tears outside the door. Over the weeks that had followed her return to Nairne, Isha and her mother had slowly mended their relationship; where there was love between souls, there was a path between them as well, a path both had been eager to tread. But with the return of familiarity and intimacy, Iseabal had sought to make her mother understand what was now the center of her existence—her love and loyalty to Taminy, her belief in the New Covenant Taminy embodied. But Ardis-a-Nairnecirke did not want to understand, did not want, even, to accept or acknowledge or *hear* about Taminy-Osmaer.

So, the path of love between mother and daughter had to be cleared again and, again, trodden. This time they had gotten closer than ever, or so Isha had thought. But then she had brought up the dread Subject, and her poor mother had fled from her in fear for her own soul.

At the top of the stairs Isha sat, drying tears on the sleeve

of her sous-shirt, thinking perhaps she should tap at her
mother's door and apologize and promise never to bring
the Subject up again—never to even speak of her daily
trips up to the Holy Fortress to work with the *waljan* there.

She turned her left hand palm up in her lap and gazed,
blurry-eyed, at the bright *gytha*. The *gytha* terrified her
mother, so most of the time she kept it muted, using a
mere thread of her *aidan* to do so. It made her want to
sob all over again to think that she might never be able
to share what was now the most essential part of herself
with her own mother. If it were not for her Da . . .

Ripples. Dark ripples in the Eibhilin All that surrounded
her. She sat up.

Approach. Someone at the center of those ripples was
drawing physically near. Her heart began to pound. She
could sense him coming up the road to the Cirke, entering by the gate, skirting the manse—a living well of darkness.

She quivered, frozen at the top of the stairs. What should
she do? She was in danger, she knew it. She saw herself
in the mind of the dark one; she was the object of his search.
In that moment, she knew him—Daimhin Feich—and
knew that he must not find her here. She moved, finally,
bolting down the stairs and into her father's study.

The room was dark and smelled of dust and ashes. Her
mother had closed it off after her father had gone up to
Halig-liath. The door was locked from the outside, but
the little lock was nothing much to Iseabal. She stood in
the darkened room and sensed the ripples lapping at her
home, heard the sounds of booted feet on the verandah
and the ringing of the bell outside the front door. She made
her mind very still and open and waited.

The men outside rang and pounded, even shouting when
no one came immediately to let them in. Then Ardis-a-
Nairnecirke opened her bedroom door and came softly
down the stairs drying her tears; Isha could see her mop-
ping at swollen eyes with a bit of towel. The Cirke-mistress called to the men to hold their pounding, and hastened
to unbar the door (the door she kept shuttered against

her own husband and no one else). And then they were
there, in the hall, just outside the room where Iseabal stood
and quivered and kept her *aidan* very still.

"What do you want, gentlemen?" her mother asked, and
sniffled. "Ah, Regent Feich, isn't it? I apologize for the
delay, but . . . "

A smooth, creamy voice answered (*his* voice): "I'm very sorry
to disturb you, mistress, when you are in such obvious distress,
but we are in dire need of assistance from a member of this
household. You are the wife of the Osraed Saxan?"

"I . . . Yes, I'm Ardis-a-Nairnecirke. But if it's my husband you seek, you'll find him up at Halig-liath, not here."
There was accusation in that.

"I've met your husband, mistress. It's your daughter I
seek. Iseabal is her name, I believe."

"Yes . . . But what could you want with Isha? She's only
a young girl—"

"A talented young girl, I've been led to believe. A girl
possessed of a strong Gift."

Anger pulsed in Ardis-a-Nairnecirke's breast. "Did Saxan
tell you that? He exaggerates, I assure you. Isha is—"

"A Taminist."

Her mother gasped softly. "Oh, surely sir, you won't hold
childish meanderings against—"

"Your daughter is late of Hrofceaster, as I understand
it. She has been trained by this Taminy-a-Cuinn, this self-
styled Osmaer, to use her Gift in particular ways. Ways
which may be of help to me in finding Cyneric Airleas
Malcuim and returning him to his rightful place on the
throne of Caraid-land . . . You do *care* what happens to
Caraid-land, mistress?"

"Yes, of course I do! I—"

"Then let me speak to your daughter."

Ardis-a-Nairnecirke was uncertain; to Iseabal, her suspicion of Daimhin Feich was a palpable substance.

"Mistress," Feich said in a milder voice, "I am sorry if
my manner seems brusque. But surely you understand that
this is a matter of life and death. Airleas Malcuim is in
the hands of his enemies. I have reason to believe your

daughter can help him." He paused, and Isha could feel the dark tendrils of his *aidan* seeking, probing. "If she were to help me find the Cyneric, I'm certain her childish meanderings could be overlooked."

Relief flooded the space suspicion had lately held. "Yes sir. Thank you, sir. . . . Isha!"

Iseabal shivered, listening as her mother called up the stairs. Supposing her to have gone to her room, she led the men to the second floor and along the corridor. But, of course, her room was empty. Other rooms were checked, her mother called more loudly. Isha darted a thread of thought toward the front door. Could she escape that way? But no, Feich was no fool, he'd left men there. She might use her *aidan* against them, but the thought of using it to do violence was alien.

They were downstairs again, searching the house, her mother saying, "I can't imagine where she's gone. We had a bit of a— a disagreement. . . . You might check the Sanctuary."

They did that, and Isha moved swiftly to the window and tried to throw the catches. Her hands shook terribly and the catches were stubborn with rust and swollen wood. Dared she use her *aidan*, or would *he* sense her as she sensed him? He was in the Sanctuary now, discovering that she was not. She pushed harder at the window clasps. They rattled, but did not budge. She heard the heavy tread of bootsoles on the verandah—muffled voices moving toward the study window. They'd heard! And now *he* was coming back through the house.

Desperate, Isha tugged at the shutters with her *aidan*, an inyx on her lips, her full will behind it. In answer, the catches gave, and outside the door of her father's study a hungry voice said, "Here! What's in this locked room?"

"My husband's study," said Ardis. "I've kept it closed since—"

"Open it."

Iseabal pulled back the inner shutters and looked out. She could see the graveyard, moonlit and silent, and the vague figure of a man standing not five feet from the window.

"But no one's been in there—"

"*Open* it, mistress!"

In her mind's eye, Isha imagined a shadowy figure darting through the gravestones. *Look, you! Look! Someone escapes!* Outside the window, a male voice uttered a muted exclamation and the guard pulled his sword and leapt to follow the phantom.

"I'll get the key . . ."

Isha fumbled with the window latch.

"*Damn* you!" Something struck the door, buckling it inward.

Gasping for breath, Isha gave the window a shove and—

The door splintered behind her while her mother's voice cried, "Please, sir! Please!"

Iseabal whirled from the window casement, heart beating wildly, breath catching in her lungs. A desperate thought struck her and she grasped her *aidan* tightly and drew it about her like a cloak.

Daimhin Feich stood in the room, the wreckage of the door about him on the flagged floor. He panted like a weary dog, but his pale eyes, gleaming in the moonlight from the open shutters, were bright and searching. "Light!" he snarled. "Bring light!"

"I'll get a lamp," said someone behind him, but Feich was impatient. He pulled something from a belt pouch and held it before him. The red crystal was aglow before it even cleared the opening of the little bag. It sent bright, ruddy rays into every corner of the room as Daimhin Feich advanced.

"Empty." A younger man entered the room behind him, a lamp out-thrust in his hand. "She's escaped."

"No," breathed Feich. "Not escaped. I can feel her. Search! Search the room!"

Three men did as he ordered, even peeking behind the open shutters. The young one held his lamp close to the casement. "See here, Daimhin, she's opened the window and gone out. Probably well away from here by now."

Daimhin Feich strode across the room to the other man's side, making Iseabal, hiding behind her own fierce will, tremble at his nearness, at the nearness of that crystal. Dear God, could he possibly miss how the thing flared up when he passed by her? If she dared move . . . Only her mother stood in the doorway now, but if she twitched a muscle, the aislinn shroud might fall away. So she stayed, cloaked in tentative invisibility, while Daimhin Feich pondered her escape.

"Idiot! No one's escaped through this window. Look at the dust on the sill. Hasn't been disturbed for months. She's here." He whirled again, nearly touching Iseabal, nearly causing her to reveal herself. In his hand, the red crystal blazed with hideous brilliance. "You! Mistress-a-Nairnecirke. Where is your daughter?"

Ardis jumped. "I don't know, sir! I—I'd gone to my room. She was upstairs. I thought she'd gone to her own room. We'd been fighting, you see—"

Feich advanced on her. "You're lying. You're hiding her from me. Bring her out, woman! Bring her out now!"

"No, sir! I'd not lie to you! I—I *want* Isha to help you! She must have gone out by the Sanctuary while we were upstairs."

Daimhin Feich grasped the Cirke-mistress by the arm and shook her. "You lie! I *feel* her here. She's somewhere in this house. Bring her out or, so help me God, I'll make you the sorriest woman in this village." He let go of her momentarily and pulled a small dagger from his belt. In the light of that wicked crystal, its blade gleamed a foul red as if bloodied already. Ardis-a-Nairnecirke shrieked and twisted, catching her skirts in the ruins of the study door. He had her against the door jamb in an instant, the dagger at her throat.

Iseabal dropped her aislinn cloak. A flash of radiance washed from her, drawing all eyes. "Please let my mother go, Regent Feich," she begged. "Punish me if you like, but don't harm her. She's guilty of nothing you'd condemn her for."

A slow smile spread across the Regent's narrow, handsome face. "Iseabal-a-Nairnecirke, is it? How good of you to join us. I have no intention of punishing you, dear cailin, but rather of putting you to good use."

CHAPTER 14

The soul who refuses to let the doubts and caprices of others deflect them from the Way of God, the soul who is calm in the face of the unrest caused by the wielders of worldly authority—whether they call themselves divines or Cynes or men of truth, that soul will be respected by God as one of His own. Blessed is such a soul.

—*Book of Pilgrimages, Osraed Lin-a-Ruminea*

It was an odd imprisonment Iseabal suffered. She had been terrified when Daimhin Feich's men snatched her from her home. Her mother's cries still rang in her ears, even here in the quiet, woodland darkness of this small tent. Bound and tethered to a tent pole, she was alone but for the two guards who kept vigil outside. Feich had made no attempt to question or harm her.

Her terror calmed eventually and she began to think, began to reach out tentatively to her mother, to her father, to Taminy. Her mother was still frantic, her father distraught and angry, and Taminy . . . Taminy extended over her a silken web of calm. She, in turn, tried to extend that same calm to her parents and received, in a flash of aislinn certainty, a strange benediction; Saxan and Ardis-a-Nairnecirke were side by side again, united in their concern for their only child.

After a while, she slept, secure in the knowledge that she was not truly alone.

The girl's father visited the camp on the heels of her capture to beg her release. Since her mother was yet a prisoner in her own home, Ruadh could only suppose news of her plight had reached him through some other means . . . perhaps, supernatural ones. The thought made his skin crawl and his back creep. Almost, he could feel the brushing by him of spirits, hear their whispered conversations.

He'd suspected Daimhin had taken the girl hostage to enlist the cooperation of her father, and was astonished when Daimhin met and dismissed the man without questioning him. Instead of coercing, he threatened; the girl was a disciple of the Nairnian Wicke—she would be returned to Creiddylad for interrogation and, perhaps, trial and punishment. The Osraed begged to be taken in his daughter's stead, even admitting his own connection with the Wicke, but Daimhin Feich only accused him of a father's love and loyalty and rejected his plea. Osraed Saxan went away empty, while Ruadh wondered what his cousin could be thinking.

"Do you really intend to try this girl as a Wicke?" he asked when Saxan had left them.

Daimhin shrugged. "If it suits me."

The Osraed Ladhar who, with his toady cleirach, had been witness to the brief encounter between father and captor, was shaking so hard his jowls quivered like a pudding. "It had better suit you, sir. By the Spirit, you should try the father as well! He *admitted* his Taminist loyalties."

"That's of no importance, Abbod. In the long run, his loyalties will matter not at all."

"No importance?" Ladhar was livid. "How can you—?"

Daimhin raised his hand to forestall the impending outburst. "What is our most dire problem just now, Abbod?"

"Our most—? Our religious institutions are in tatters, our people are being assailed by spiritual storm—"

"Abbod, Abbod, look closer to earth, if you would, please! The government of Caraid-land has ceased to function— or nearly so. The Hall is a roil and the throne is empty." Daimhin smiled and leaned forward in his low camp chair. "Would you put me on the throne, dear Abbod? Declare me Cyneric in Airleas Malcuim's absence?"

"Airleas is absent, as you say, not dead. Nor has he officially abdicated. Were I to declare you Cyneric, the Houses would see to it Caraid-land was torn into tiny, autonomous bits."

"Exactly. Therefore, we have no recourse but to return Airleas to the throne, or to witness his public abdication . . . or to be assured of his death. We have lately learned we cannot get to Airleas until spring. What is our recourse?"

Ladhar glared at him uncomprehendingly.

"Abbod, we must bring Airleas to us."

"And freeing heretics will aid that?"

"No. But holding one hostage might. *This* one especially. Iseabal-a-Nairnecirke is one of Taminy's special acolytes. Do you think she will let her be lost to us?"

"You mean to draw the Wicke out?" asked Ruadh.

"I intend her to understand that if she would have her lovely young convert suffer no harm, she must forfeit her hold on Airleas."

"And how," asked Ladhar, "do you intend to make her understand that?"

"I will tell her young acolyte. I suspect she will see to it that her Mistress is informed. Simple, isn't it? Now, gentlemen, cousin . . . " He nodded at Ruadh. "I've had a most strenuous evening, which is not yet over. If you would be so good . . . " He glanced at the entry of his opulent tent.

Neither Ruadh nor his companions were slow. They returned, each, to their smaller shelters.

They didn't tarry in Nairne, but struck their tents the next morning to return to Creiddylad. The Osraed Saxan and his companions tried again to reclaim the captive girl, but Daimhin Feich turned them away. Ruadh couldn't help but feel a certain sympathy for the Cirkemaster. The girl did not seem evil. At the very worst, he could only imagine her to be misled. And, though she'd shown extraordinary powers (he still hadn't recovered from seeing her appear out of the crystal-lit gloom of her father's study), she hadn't tried to use them against the man who was surely her worst enemy. At least, she hadn't used them yet. Perhaps she was only biding her time.

Ruadh glanced at her now, as she rode beside him, bound to her saddle, her back straight with dignity. Ironic, he thought, that some of those on the side of right seemed much more unsavory than their supposedly wicked enemies. He glanced past the girl to her opposing escort, the Abbod Ladhar, happening to meet the older man's eyes. A chill rattled his spine. Ladhar was a hateful man in the truest sense of the word. Ruadh glanced away, signaled one of his kinsmen to take his place beside their prisoner and urged his horse forward to pull level with Sorn Saba.

The younger man looked over at him. "She's a rare beauty, that one."

Ruadh raised his brows and Sorn twitched a glance back over his shoulder. "The little sorceress. Such striking color! Those blue, blue eyes and that black hair. Rivals my sister, she does."

"Bored with the Lady Dearg, are you?"

Sorn's eyes widened. "Cautious of her. Have you seen her, this morning? A mass of bruises." He leaned closer, lowering his voice. "Do you think maybe her husband discovered her infidelities?"

"If he had, *you'd* be the one wearing black and blue."

Sorn's face hardened, making Ruadh believe, for a moment, his boasts of battle experience. "I assure you, friend Ruadh, I am most discreet. . . . Who else but her husband would have had cause to beat her so?"

Ruadh shook his head, suspecting it was not marital infidelity that had won Coinich Mor her bruises.

The Abbod Ladhar was as perplexed as he was furious. Twice, Feich had the apostate Saxan in his camp and twice he dismissed him as if he had not admitted to his heresies. And the girl! He had her, yet made no move to interrogate her about her Mistress's plans. Ladhar had even gone so far as to demand that she be turned over to the Osraed for trial, but Feich merely laughed at him and told him he over-reacted.

The long return trip to Creiddylad was made no shorter by the knowledge that the forces at the Regent's command

had been drastically reduced and that they were no closer
to capturing Taminy and tearing Airleas from her grasp.
Meanwhile, Feich and his Dearg Wicke still Wove and
Ladhar still slept poorly.

In the wake of Feich's decree against Taminists, crowds
once again milled outside the gates of Mertuile, one contingent protesting the bans, another protesting the protest. Fights broke out often, necessitating the intervention
of armed guards.

While it comforted Ladhar that Feich was at last *doing*
something about the Taminists and their sympathizers, he
could not believe that the Regent's decrees were any more
than a ploy aimed at eliciting some response from the Wicke
herself—a response Ladhar alternately feared and pretended not to care about. But a week passed, of riots, put-
downs and arrests, and Mertuile's gaol began to fill with
Taminists and their allies, people Daimhin Feich showed
little interest in. He gave the Abbod and his cleirachs access
to the prisoners, but they were, for the most part, ordinary citizens. Misled to be sure, mesmerized most likely,
but among them, Ladhar recognized no one from among
the Wicke's close circle of apostles.

The girl, Iseabal, was kept by herself in a chill, spartan
chamber in the lower levels of the castle proper. Neither
the Abbod nor any other Osraed was allowed to interview
her. Only Daimhin Feich was admitted to her cell.

At the end of his first week back in Creiddylad, the
Regent changed his tack with regard to the Nairnian cailin
and moved her to luxurious quarters near his own. Further, he allowed her to dine with his household, which
now included Eadrig and Blair Dearg and Coinich Mor
in addition to his cousin and the Deasach Banarigh's little
brother.

On the occasions when that household also embraced
Ladhar, he watched the girl with hawkish intensity. If that
unnerved her, so much the better. The Deasach boy also
kept close watch on her. Perhaps he expected she would
suddenly rise up and perform some bit of magic at table.
She did not.

One evening, after a fine supper, the Regent invited his guests, the young Wicke included, to his private salon. The men of Dearg, preferring more active after-supper entertainment, excused themselves and joined their kinsmen in Creiddylad. Coinich Mor stayed, but tucked herself silently into a corner near the hearth, from which vantage point she watched everyone else in the room.

They sat, drinking hot cider and listening to the harsh winds of early winter assault Mertuile, while Feich tried to engage his pretty hostage in conversation. "Your Mistress liked this room," he told her, after observing how continually awed she seemed by her surroundings. "We came here with Cyne Colfre more than once during her time here. Did she ever speak to you of that time?"

The girl blinked at him as if bemused by his sudden amiability. "She spoke of it," she said at last. "She called it a time of confusion."

Feich offered a wry smile. "For me, as well. I was . . . very fond of your Mistress."

"Yet you tried to kill her." The girl's eyes were pools of ice that made even Ladhar shiver.

"She seemed a threat to my Cyne and my country. Later events proved me right."

"No sir. They did not. Taminy had nothing to do with Colfre's death." She laid subtle stress on her Mistress's name, as if to imply that *someone* other than Colfre had had something to do with it.

Feich's eyes glittered. "She abducted the Cyneric—"

"She did not. Toireasa and Airleas came to us of their free will. She means no harm to Airleas, as you well know. She means only to strengthen him to see to it that when he does take the throne, no one will mold him to their own desires." Her voice, soft and measured, quivered a bit as she said the words, but her eyes were unwavering direct.

Feich shook his head and glanced at Ladhar. "I appreciate," he told the girl, "that you wish to believe no ill of your Mistress, but she has proven herself to be Evil incarnate."

"She has proven only to be your adversary, Regent Feich. I suppose that must make her seem evil to you."

Everyone in the room was astonished by the girl's audacity. Ladhar saw on other faces the same look he knew must be on his own.

Only Daimhin Feich took the remark blandly, his face set in a benign smile. "Unfortunately, I must regard you as evil as well, poor child. You are undeniably under her influence. If you were to disavow your Mistress, however . . ."

"I can't do that, sir."

Feich shrugged. "Then you will most likely die . . . eventually. Hanged, perhaps, or burnt, or drowned."

Her lovely face paled to the color of cream, but the girl only said, "I'm prepared to do that."

Feich shook his head. "I admire your courage, child. But what a deplorable waste. How can you love one who would so cruelly ignore your plight?"

"Taminy doesn't ignore me."

"Ah, well, if you wish to plead that she's unaware—"

"She's not unaware, Regent. She knows where I am and under what conditions. She's always with me. Always."

Feich perked up at this, his eyes lighting with interest. "You are in communication with her?"

"Yes."

"And yet, she does nothing to free you."

"Perhaps my freedom is not required."

An odd thing to say, Ladhar thought, and a part of his mind began trying to work out what it meant.

Late that night at Ochanshrine, he came to the beginning of an understanding, for Daimhin Feich arrived there, the Nairnian cailin in tow, and demanded to be admitted to the Shrine. What choice had he? He let them in, following them down into the Osmaer Crystal's sacred bowl.

The girl was clearly terrified. Wrapped in a long cloak that did not cover the soft skirts of her sleeping gown, hair in wild disarray about her shoulders, she glanced about with frantic eyes—eyes that were willing to beg even Ladhar for aid.

Meanwhile Feich, obviously excited, prattled like a

schoolboy. "I asked if she had a crystal, and of course she did—a tiny thing, barely worthy of the name, belonged to some mouldering Osraed. But she could *fire* it, Ladhar! Damn, but she could fire it! So I gave her Bloodheart and the damned thing all but ignited in her hands. Those sweet, magical hands!" He kissed them both, knotted as they were into fists, and dragged the poor girl down another three or four steps. "And I thought, if she can do that with puny, flawed rocks, then—" He broke off, staring at Ochan's Crystal.

Yes, it too had ignited, even as Feich's imperfect Bloodheart. Ladhar thought his legs would refuse to support him. He sank to the nearest bench, overcome, mesmerized as on that horrible night . . .

Feich, exultant, dragged the girl the rest of the way down the aisle, forcing her into close contact with the Stone. And the Stone burned. "Now, Wicke! Show me how you Weave with *this* Stone. Show me your Mistress! Let me see her! Does she sleep? Does she Weave? Does she feel your distress? Show her to me!"

The girl strained to pull her hands free, struggled to put some distance between herself and the Osmaer Crystal. But Feich had the advantage of physical strength and spiritual frailty. He cared little if he terrified her or caused her pain. He twisted her to face the Crystal, shrieking his commands in her ears, shaking her until the cloak slid from her shoulders.

The commotion drew an audience; Osraed and cleirachs appeared in the upper doorway. Ladhar felt their eyes on him. They hung back, seeing him there. Surely if the Abbod Ladhar, himself, was witness to this spectacle, they need not interfere.

"Show me Taminy-Osmaer!" cried Feich for perhaps the twentieth time, and the girl, sobbing, put up her hands as if in prayer.

Did she Weave? Ladhar would never be certain, but all at once he found himself engulfed in aislinn mist and he was seeing—dear God the Spirit!—he was seeing Bevol's Wicke, herself, right there in the Shrine. She appeared, suspended over the Osmaer Crystal, or superimposed upon it, her hair bound as if for sleep, dressed in a robe of blinding white. Light poured from her in waves and her lips moved soundlessly. Ladhar found his own lips were in motion, as well, releasing a flood of desperate prayer.

Feich moved to approach the aislinn image, reached his hand out as if to touch it, but it folded in on itself, disappearing into an envelope of darkness. The Regent howled. "Bring her back!" He turned to the quaking girl, who responded by collapsing into a trembling heap at his feet. Feich kicked at her. "Bring her back! I want to speak to her!"

"I can't! Please, lord, I *can't!*"

"You mean you won't. Very well, you stupid child. You've condemned yourself." Feich turned to Ladhar, who was only now getting his own trembling under control. "In the morning, I'll return, Abbod. And when I return, I will have the strength to take up that Stone of yours and Weave through it." He dragged the hapless girl from the floor, then, and all but carried her from the Shrine.

Ladhar could only stare after them in mute horror. Daimhin Feich meant to get his hands on the Osmaer Crystal and, short of hiding it, there was nothing he could do to prevent that. He turned his eyes to the Stone, silently beseeching its unseen Mistress to aid him. *If ever you have listened to me,* he told her, *I bid you listen now. Send me your two saints, your aingeals, to keep Daimhin Feich from abusing Ochan's Stone.*

"Fhada!" Leal rattled the door of the Elder Osraed's room a second time. "Fhada!" The door opened and Fhada gazed out at him, bleary-eyed, a tiny light-globe clutched in his hand.

"Leal! Meri's Breath, what is it? What's happened?"

"We must go to Ochanshrine."

"What? Now? . . . Wait . . . *How* go to Ochanshrine? We'll be caught—"

Leal waved his hands, stoppering the uneven flow of words that poured from Fhada's mouth. "I don't know how . . . yet. We'll find a way. I only know we must go."

Fhada shook his head. "But why?"

"To retrieve the Crystal. I had an aislinn—a vision. Taminy appeared to me and told me that the Osmaer Crystal is in danger. We're to try to get Abbod Ladhar to let us take it and conceal it."

"Conceal it?" murmured Fhada. "Conceal it from whom?"

"From Daimhin Feich."

Fhada blanched. "He's still a danger, then." He ran a hand through his unruly hair. "When shall we go?"

"Now. We must be there before dawn. We're to take the Osmaer and replace it with this." Leal raised his hands into the glow of Fhada's light-globe, revealing the crystal he held. Large and clear, with a slight golden cast at its heart, it looked very much like the Osmaer.

"Where did you get that?"

"From Taminy before she fled to Halig-liath. It was the Osraed Bevol's. It's smaller than the Osmaer, but not by much. And the facets are very similar."

"Similar enough to fool Daimhin Feich?"

Leal smiled, a tickle of exhilaration fanning his heart. "With a little help from Aine and the rest of us, I think it just might."

She hadn't meant to make the Stone light. She had wanted nothing so much as to appear powerless in its presence. But she could not dissemble before the Stone of Ochan. At first, she'd credited her lack of control to her fear of Feich. He seemed a cauldron of violent impulse, terrifyingly near a boil—a man of ferocious wants. But when the aislinn Taminy appeared over the Crystal as if her Eibhilin body contained it and grew from it, Iseabal understood that her lack of control was irrelevant. It was Taminy who worked through the Osmaer Crystal, Taminy who consoled her and calmed her fears with words of love that were meant for her ears alone.

And so, when Daimhin Feich railed at her and demanded that she Weave, again, the aislinn Taminy, she knew she could not.

She was afraid for her life by the time they returned to

Mertuile. Feich's rage, rather than being spent, seemed
to feed on itself and grow. He dragged her through the
castle halls, past blank-eyed guards from whom she expected
no help and got none. The noise of their passing aroused
his young cousin from slumber and, for a brief, agonizing
moment, Isha felt the young man's distress and thought
he might intervene. But he let them pass by him without
comment, his face grim.

Feich's curses ceased only when he had wrestled her
into her chambers and thrown her to the floor. She rolled
among the fine fleeces before the hearth, expecting that
any moment blows would fall, but he didn't touch her.
She pulled herself to a crouch before the dying fire and
gazed up at him where he stood, his back to the closed
door, chest heaving, face red with exertion and fury. He
did not seem quite sane.

But at the point Iseabal was certain he would lash out
at her either physically or through his *aidan*, he caught
hold of his rage, closed his glittering eyes and set trembling hands to his hips. Several deep breaths later, he spoke.
"Well, cailin, I suppose I shouldn't have expected you to
aid me willingly."

"To harm Taminy?" Isha whispered. "No, never. But in
this, I could *not* aid you if I wanted to. Taminy worked
through the Stone tonight, not I."

His eyes opened to fix her with a gaze like shadow on
snow. "But you have a great Gift. I've seen you use it . . .
to disappear as if made of smoke. That is a trick I'd like
to learn."

Isha took a deep, steadying breath. "And you'd have me
teach you?"

He chuckled. "No need, child. I have a tutor. A woman
who has taught me . . . a good many things—not the least
of which is how to harness the power of others. Or, rather,
to assimilate it, to make it my own."

Isha shifted uneasily among her fleeces. She'd learned
no such discipline and knew it was no part of the Divine
Art. "You Weave . . . without drawing on the Spirit? How
is that possible?"

He was smiling at her now, looking impossibly relaxed. It was a fiction—within him a fierce, nervous energy was building. It tingled in the air around them, making it seem to move and flicker. "I told you, pretty Iseabal. I draw on others to feed my *aidan*. I draw on Ladhar's stupid fears, on the Deasach boy's brash pride, on Blair Dearg's stupidity . . . " The smile widened. " . . . on his wife's lust. But, you see, I have learned to draw on much deeper wells. When I am one with Coinich Mor, I am one with her *aidan* and it feeds into mine, makes it grow great and deep."

He wandered a few steps toward her—to the edge of her woolly defense—his smile a warm, lazy lie. He squatted there, meeting her eye to eye, reaching out to take a lock of her hair in gentle fingers and rubbing it between them. "Coinich Mor is a second rate Wicke, a petty sorceress with barely a midge of power. You, on the other hand, are very powerful, indeed. Powerful and disciplined and in touch" —he stroked the tip of her nose— "with Taminy-Osmaer, the most powerful one of all. And you are much more desirable than Coinich Mor."

The words made no sense to her. Even so, they inspired terror. They were the last words he spoke to her that night before showing her that to be fed upon by Daimhin Feich was to be devoured by darkness.

He had been praying for hours, yet dawn seemed no closer than when he had first started. He lifted bleary eyes to the open arch of the eastern doorway of the Shrine, certain that merely wishing it would cause the Sun to rise. The corridor remained dark, but in it, obscured by the veil of incense . . .

Ladhar squinted. Vague shapes that might have been part of the smoky pall seemed to hesitate within the open arch. They coalesced even as he watched, wavering toward clarity. He made out two forms, and his heart and soul leapt. Were these the helpers promised in his vision? Were these the saints he awaited? A glance at the Osmaer Crystal assured him; there was fire deep in its heart—a warm, gentle glow that grew and steadied with the moments.

He came to his feet, heart tripping over itself as it raced to meet the visitation. "Pray enter, good spirits. I am in much need. Praise Meri, you have been sent!"

There was a moment more of hesitation, during which Ladhar thought he heard whispers from the aislinn-cloaked figures. Then they began to move down the sloping aisle toward him, step by step. Odd that spirits should exhibit such human movement. He had opened his mouth to offer another greeting when the veil they moved in was whisked aside, leaving only the very physical smoke from the censers about their too human frames.

Ladhar staggered back a step, nearly falling over the bench behind him. "Fhada. Lealbhallain. Why are you here? How did you get past the sentries?"

The two glanced at each other, then took the last several steps into the circle of the Crystal—a circle still lit by a wash of Eibhilin radiance.

"I can hardly think," Fhada replied, "that it matters how we got past the sentries. Obviously we got past them. The point is, we are here. To help."

Ladhar's face flushed with clammy heat. "To help? What are you talking about?"

Leal pressed forward, a pup's eagerness sparkling in his eyes. "Daimhin Feich means to lay hands on the Stone of Ochan—to control it as he tried to control Taminy. You know this."

"How do you know what I know?" Ladhar growled. "How do you dare suggest—"

"The knowledge has been given to us," Leal persisted. "Daimhin Feich is a danger to the Stone, to you, to all you hold dear. As loathe as you are to believe it, Abbod," the boy added, insolently, "those are the same things we love. The Meri has sent us to your aid. Give us the Stone and we'll see that Daimhin Feich never touches it."

Ladhar's body shook, evading his best attempts at control. "Ah, but your sly Mistress will, won't she? That's your plan, is it? You knew of the aislinn I have received or—dear God, worse!—you *caused* it! Was it you who put the idea into my head that I would be sent aingeals to help me?" The idea was stunning, but made a certain perverse sense. More than that . . . "Ah, *now*, Lealbhallain, *now*, I recognize the voice that spoke to me out of that vision, the cold eyes that pierced me as I prayed. It was *Bevol*, whom I thought dead! *Bevol* is the one who controls you! Admit it!"

The two exchanged a look of sheer astonishment and Ladhar flushed in triumph. "Aha! I'm right! Bevol lives! Hiding in that filthy warren of yours, no doubt. Collecting heretics and Wicke to himself, pledging them to *her* service. Tell me the truth, if you're able, Fhada. Is this not so?"

But Fhada was not able to tell the truth as Ladhar now perceived it. "Abbod, Bevol is dead—taken by stealth and force at Daimhin Feich's order, butchered and fed to the Sea."

"And his body lost forever, no doubt. Convenient. You couldn't tell me where it is or show it to me."

Fhada blinked as if a strong light had been shone in his eyes and said, "In the depths of Mertuile there is a chamber, open to the Sea by vents and sluices—"

Blood rushed from Ladhar's face and extremities as if sucked through a hole beneath his feet. "Enough! I've heard of this chamber. Believe me, I'll go there and expose your tell for the lie it is. Daimhin Feich would *never* have dared to murder an Osraed of Bevol's stature. And since he expected Bevol to be discredited—"

"How so?" asked Fhada. "Cyne Colfre had taken Taminy into his house and his heart, insofar as he was able. Bevol was Taminy's champion. A persuasive champion, if the reaction of the Hall was any indication. A threat to all Daimhin Feich held dear."

Ladhar put up his hands. "Past history. You try to confuse me. Get out of here, before I call down the guard. There are Malcuim regulars here now, you know."

Fhada nodded. "Yes. We walked past them on our way in. Listen to us, Osraed. Do not dismiss us so quickly."

"Why should I not?"

"Can you deny that Feich is a threat to the Crystal, to the Throne, to the fabric of our society?"

"I . . . I do not deny it. But he is a threat I can handle."

"He has powers," said Lealbhallain, his verdant eyes on the Stone. It turned them to topazes and his hair to flame.

"I have seen them. They are . . . limited."

"They are stronger than you think, Ladhar. Strong and capricious and uncontrollable."

"He lacks discipline. He has no real training."

"Which makes him even more dangerous," said Fhada. "Perhaps he would be less a danger if you were to teach him some discipline—or have you already tried and failed?"

"I wouldn't teach him to squat in the privy!"

"Will you let him have the Stone?"

"I . . ."

"He *will* take it."

"I won't let him take it. I will Weave a Ward for it."

"Please, let us hide it," said Lealbhallin, begging now. "Replace it with this. He need not know."

Ladhar's eyes widened at the sight of the crystal the boy clutched in his hands. It was identical to the Osmaer in every way. "Where did you get that? Whose crystal is it?"

"Bevol's."

Quivering, Ladhar sat hard upon his bench. "You mock the Osmaer."

"We try to save her." Lealbhallain moved to sit beside him, cradling Bevol's accursed Stone in open hands. "From Daimhin Feich, Abbod. Think of it. Look into your heart. Your soul. Tell me you don't see the danger here."

"Oh, I see the danger, boy. As well I see that you have given me a choice that is no choice."

"Still, you must choose."

Ladhar snorted. "The lesser of two evils? That is a choice I decline to make."

The young heretic gazed up at his elder, resignation in his eyes, the sign and symbol of his heresy bright upon his brow. Fhada, gazing back, shook his head. "You make a choice in not choosing, Abbod. You make Feich the victor by your inaction."

"If," Ladhar said, barely understanding why he said it, "if this matter is so vital, so grave, why do you not force me to part with the Stone? Why do you not take it from me unwilling?"

Lealbhallin rose. "That isn't the Meri's way, Abbod Ladhar. You know that. Violence is the way of evil." With another glance at Fhada, the boy held Bevol's crystal out to him. "If you will not let us take the Stone, at least let me give you this one."

"And what am I to do with that?"

"Replace the Osmaer with it before Daimhin Feich returns. Hide the Osmaer in some safe place."

When Ladhar made no move to take the crystal from the boy's hands, he laid it in the Abbod's broad lap. "Don't let him get his hands on the Stone, Osraed Ladhar. For love of the Meri, don't let him."

They left him then, and were wrapped in their aislinn veil before they reached the outer corridor. The weak light of dawn there rippled with their passing.

Ladhar opened his mouth to give alarm, but uttered no sound. It would do no good. The guards' eyes would not penetrate the Weave of the heretics' inyx. Besides, he no longer had the strength. Instead, he sat and stared at the thing in his lap—Bevol's crystal. Aiffe, it was named— "life-giver." Ironic, since its master was dead. He laid a hand to the facets. Beneath his fingers, the stone warmed, emitting a soft glow. Still, Ladhar shivered, wrapped in the chill of a dank, sea-fed chamber below the foundation of Mertuile.

Dawn brought storm, if only to Daimhin Feich's soul. Lightning lashed his mind and thunder shook his bones. He was beset by demons; he was in the company of aingeals and saints. They shrieked at him; they sang to him. And when he emerged from the cacophony, leaving even the quiet sobs of the Cirkemaster's daughter behind a closed door, he was certain of his invincibility.

And hungry. God-the-Spirit, but he was hungry! He returned to his own rooms long enough to bathe and change his clothing, then he ordered up a breakfast fit for two men. Ruadh came down while he was eating, but didn't stay. With a mumbled "good morning," he slunk off to the kitchen to scavenge a meal.

"Not hungry," he said.

Jealous, Daimhin thought, savoring his tea. Everything tasted glorious this morning. His senses were sharper, clearer. Sounds, sights, smells—all held a pungency he had never known. He basked in all of it, knowing without looking in any mirror, that he fairly glowed.

"So . . . you had the child."

He glanced up from his tea. Coinich Mor stood at the end of the table, smiling at him, the bruises on her face a soft pattern that contrived to look more gold than yellow. The smile annoyed him. Somehow, he had been hoping she would snarl and snap at him when she learned of his new conquest. He nodded.

She returned the nod. "And you think you no longer need Coinich Mor?"

"I suppose I could still make use of an able tutor."

"Make use of an able tutor," she parroted. "The girl satisfied you so with her virgin tears and innocent screams? I had thought you more worldly than that."

"The girl is a fountain of Eibhilin power. While it's true the fleshly satisfaction was . . . " He paused to search for the right word. " . . . meager, there was abundant compensation for its lack." He took a deep breath, stretched his muscles, feeling every ripple. "I tingle with the energies she gave up. They pulse in my blood, race through my mind. Can't you feel it, Coinich? Can't you *see* it in me?" He stood, imagining how he must look to her with Eibhilin potency leaking through every pore. He laughed and the Wicke laughed with him.

"Oh, I see, Regent Feich. I see more than you imagine." She shifted her shoulders in a manner that brought his attention to her full breasts—as it was intended to do, of course. "You can yet make use of me, lord," she murmured, and let him see the flame in her strange eyes.

He moved around the table to her side, aware, with every stride, of the power flowing through him. She watched him, smiling her cat-smile, her eyes caressing.

Her desire was a drug, a euphoric, and he savored it as he savored all else on this extraordinary morning. He stopped close enough to her that their bodies just touched, cloth kissing cloth, heat mingling with heat, her spice wrapping him pleasurably.

She gazed up into his face, telling him wordlessly that he could have her right there upon the table if he wished and to hell with whoever might find them.

But he didn't wish. Not at that moment. He was on his way to take the Stone; he was on the verge of reaching out to the Wicke of Hrofceaster in her own medium. He had no time now for Coinich Mor. She was a pleasure that would taste just as sweet later. Nor could he be certain her tainted energies wouldn't corrupt the pure power he now cradled within. But, so that she'd understand her place at Mertuile, he kissed her hard enough to punish those so recently bruised lips. He was a little surprised to lift his head and find her smile intact. He had hoped for reproach or anger.

"Don't forget about me, Daimhin Feich, because I will be with you always. To the end."

He laughed in the face of that threatening promise and strode from the room, bemused at how girlish Coinich Mor seemed in her infatuation. He was aware that she watched him all the way to the doors, but didn't look back. And so, he did not see her spit upon the place where he had stood.

He took the private way to Ochanshrine, crossing the Halig-tyne in his boat, a Malcuim regular at the oars. Abbod Ladhar seemed to be nowhere about, and so he entered the Shrine without announcing himself. Nevertheless, his presence was enough to send every Osraed, Aelder and cleirach scurrying from the sanctum. That pleased him, for he knew they sensed his power; perhaps they could even see it.

He took the steps down to the Crystal two at a time, pausing only when it was in reach. He raised his arms as if to embrace the Stone, but did not touch it. No, he would savor this. He drew in a breath, collecting the raw energies that shimmered behind his eyes, and let it all out—breath and energies alike—on a rush of exultation. The Stone flared, washing him with light.

Not enough! There must be more. Perhaps he should have practiced with Bloodheart before he came here. He gathered his resources again, reaching deep into his own urgency. He thought of his hours with the Nairnian girl, heating the power within him to a full boil. The light of the Stone grew, steadied, yet . . . where was the heady rush of power? Where the electric potency?

Damn! What was wrong? He'd channeled more force than this through the puny crystals of his Wickish consorts. Anger swelled beneath the buzz of power. Good. Coinich Mor had said that anger was good. And Iseabal had admitted that Taminy worked the Stone. Obviously, it was Taminy who kept the doors of its mastery closed to him. That enraged him further. *Yes!* He could feel the heat, feel the might building up within him. Now he was ready. Now he could grasp—

He glanced up as a disturbance near the doors drew his attention. The Osraed Ladhar, still dressed for sleep, trundled toward him down the sloping aisle of the Shrine, Caime Cadder in his broad wake. He couldn't help but smile at the look of tragic horror on the old man's face. Smiling, he laid his hands on the Stone.

He was enveloped in a veil of golden light and warmth, a veil through which he seemed to hear a voice speaking to him, and laughter. The laughter angered him and he threw his will at the Stone with every last ounce of might, thinking, at once, of Taminy. He saw her then, as in a hazy dream. She was kneeling in prayer or meditation while, around her, clustered a group of her besotted *waljan*.

He recognized some of them—the clumsy, young Osraed Wyth; the beautiful, thorny Desary—ah! Airleas Malcuim and his viperous mother; and the Ren Catahn. Hatred boiled within him at the sight of the Hillwild, at the look on that dark, bearded face, turned toward Taminy-Osmaer in carnal worship. He could well imagine the sort of relationship they shared. Had that savage yet learned to tap the well of Eibhilin power?

The thought stunned him and brought a growl of rage to his throat. The growl grew to a snarl as the image began to fade. Feich tightened his grasp on the Crystal. "No! Not yet! *I'm not finished!*"

But the Stone didn't seem to care. The vision dissolved, the light waned, the warmth died beneath his hands. No! This was all wrong! Wrong! He should have all but shattered the Crystal with the amount of power he'd consumed. He should have been able to rock the foundations of Ochanshrine and Hrofceaster alike with sheer force. He had done everything Coinich Mor had taught him—he had siphoned the energies, held them, concentrated them, expelled them . . .

Coinich Mor. He pulled his hands from the Crystal with a curse. Damn her. *She* must have done this. Or perhaps he had allowed her to do it by letting her seduce him into that one, unwitting kiss. Wherever the blame lay, she had sucked Iseabal's forces from him with that greedy mouth, or polluted them. It hardly mattered which. It meant a delay—a delay that Daimhin Feich knew he could ill afford.

He glanced up to find Abbod Ladhar watching him, those beady eyes like bits of glass in the ruddy face. Humiliation warmed Feich's cheeks. To have failed so abjectly before this swollen toad and his pack of superstitious holy men.

With an effort he calmed himself. No matter. He would simply have to return to Mertuile and visit the Nairnian girl again—always assuming her store of Eibhilin energy was renewable. But of course it was. Her dear Mistress was always with her, she'd said that herself. Just a few more hours and he could return, and this time he would see to it that neither Coinich Mor nor anything else distracted him.

He left Ochanshrine without saying a word to Ladhar or his mewling mendicants and crossed the mouth of the Halig-tyne, urgency building by the second. He was winded by the time he made the long climb from the pier to the main floor of the castle—winded, irate and far from happy to have his cousin and the Dearg accost him at the bottom of the ornate staircase that led up to the first level of private chambers.

"What is it, Ruadh? I haven't time—"

"I'm afraid you'll have to make time, cousin. There is a sizable contingent of citizens in the outer ward who insist that we produce Airleas and vacate Mertuile. They're demanding that we use our guards to clear the streets of criminals rather than having them chase down every Taminist too stupid to be in hiding."

"And how did these citizens come to be in the outer ward?"

Ruadh's mouth twitched. "I take it they bribed a gatekeep. Enterprising of them."

"Why should I care what they demand? I'm in control of Mertuile—"

"It seems, cousin, that over beyond the landward hills a considerable contingent of Claeg, Jura, Graegam and Gilleas kinsmen still sit, waiting for . . . *something*. I'd suggest that if we don't do *something* toward getting Airleas back to Mertuile, our unhappy citizens might prevail upon them to stop waiting."

Feich's jaw tightened. "I told them to disband—to return to their estates."

"They didn't listen. Does that really surprise you?"

"As I said, I don't have time—"

"Daimhin." Ruadh put a hand on his cousin's arm and steel into his voice. "I don't think you understand the situation. The people currently milling beyond the inner curtain have every intention of breaching it and speaking with you face to face. They're rather . . . upset about the demise of their representative government and are demanding its return . . . among other things."

Feich glared from his cousin to the silent Dearg, then pounded his fist on the stair banister in frustration. "Oh, very well. I'll go up to the wall and speak to them. I'll tell them we've every intention of bringing their damned Malcuim out of hiding."

"And the Hall?" Eadrig Dearg spoke for the first time.

"And the Hall . . . ?" echoed Feich sarcastically.

His sarcasm was lost on the hirsute Chieftain. "The Hall hasn't met since Colfre's death. By law, it should have sat down the next day to handle his affairs."

"Colfre's affairs are in my hands."

"Aye. And that's the trouble as far as they're concerned." He jerked his head toward the outer ward. As if in response, there was a booming report like a clap of thunder and the gates of the inner curtain shook.

Feich spared no more words for the situation, but hurled himself from the stair and across the patterned floor of the entrance hall, taking special pleasure in grinding his boot into the Malcuim crest represented there. He crossed the court at a run, climbed to the walk along the top of the inner curtain, and stood trembling, glaring down at the crowd below him. Ruadh and the Dearg moved to flank him.

"You!" he shouted. "You ungrateful swine! Is this how you treat the Regent of Airleas Malcuim?"

The rabble ceased its press toward the gate below him and jostled for a view of their Regent Feich. He recognized faces now—several prominent merchants and an Eiric or two fronted the crowd. One of them shouted back at him.

"This is how we treat a Regent who has neglected his duties to city and country alike in favor of chasing about after the members of some petty cult."

"This 'petty cult,' sir, has Cyneric Airleas in hand. Should I allow that to continue?"

"No, sir, you should not! Nor should you allow Caraidland to stand ungoverned. We want the Hall convened and we want Airleas Malcuim on the throne where he belongs!"

Around the impudent Eiric—Cearbhall-mac-Corach, his name was, and Feich noted it—began a low chant of "Malcuim! Malcuim!" It was a name Daimhin Feich was sorely sick of hearing. He raised his hands over his head. "I intend . . ." They continued to chant and he tried again . . . and again. On the third try, they let him speak. "Once my forces are rested from their *last* attempt to return Airleas Malcuim to Mertuile, we will be mounting another campaign to get him back. We had thought him to be at Halig-liath, but Taminy-a-Cuinn—who calls herself 'Osmaer'—has spirited him away from there into the Gyldan-baenn. He is now among the Hillwild in the mountain holt of Airdnasheen. I intend to go there, immediately, and bring him back."

They approved. He could see it in their sheep faces, feel it wash up from them. He drank in their approval. "Further," he continued, "an emergency meeting of the Hall will be called to consult on the replacement of its apostate members."

"*When?*" roared several of the sheep.

"As soon as I have returned with Airleas Malcuim and have set him before the Stone. Until then . . . " He raised his hands again against another outcry. "Until then, the Privy Council will handle the affairs of Creiddylad. Take your concerns to them. I expect them to give you satisfaction."

He stopped and looked down at them. They milled for a moment more, speaking among themselves, then the leaders of the group made signs of agreement. "That is satisfactory," said mac-Corach. "For now."

They began to disperse, to move back toward the outer gates. Feich heaved a sigh of exasperation. Another riot averted. He turned to retrace his steps to the castle when something whizzed by him, narrowly missing his head. Ruadh cried out and drew his sword as Feich whirled to see one of the gate guards fall under the impact of a crossbow bolt. A bolt obviously meant for him. While other men went to the aid of the fallen, Feich threw himself from the walkway and into the courtyard below.

At the bottom of the steps he doubled over, hands on his knees, to quake and tremble like a frightened child. It took him a moment to realize Ruadh was beside him, a hand on his shoulder. He straightened with an effort and pulled his clothing and thoughts into order.

"Ruadh," he said, "I will issue a new decree. As of this moment, support of Taminy-Osmaer is an offense punishable by death."

CHAPTER 15

In this Day a Door is open wide to the peoples of Caraidland. The smallest drop of faith in this Day is as an ocean; the smallest sacrifice, a holy Pilgrimage. In this Age, if a soul sow one drop of blood in the field of faith, that soul shall reap the Sea.

—*Utterances of Taminy-Osmaer, Book of the Covenant*

"Who is it? Who's at the gate?" Leal hurried across the courtyard to Osraed Fhada's side.

The older man turned to look at him, his face bloodless. "It's the Abbod Ladhar."

Leal blanched and reached fingers of sense through the opaque barrier before him. "He's alone. And . . . very afraid." He glanced up at the boy atop the gate. "Let him in, Ferret."

The bar lifted and the gate groaned inward, allowing the Abbod and his horse to enter. Covered from bald crown to booted foot in a thick, black, hooded cloak, Ladhar clearly feared recognition. When he had dismounted and set back his hood, Leal could see he'd even daubed some camouflaging color over his time-bedimmed Kiss.

"I must speak with you. In secret," he added.

Fhada merely nodded, made certain the gate was bolted and barred, and led the way into Carehouse and through its halls to his office. Aine was there, her usually ruddy face pale and drawn.

"Anything from——?" Leal began.

The girl shook her head. "Something's horribly wrong,

Leal. It was as if she was cut off. I felt her terror and then . . . nothing."

"And Taminy?"

Aine glanced at Ladhar, her suspicion of him a prickly thing in the air. "Silent. And cloaked in sorrow. What has happened to Iseabal-a-Nairnecirke, Abbod? What has Regent Feich done with her? Is she dead?"

The Abbod seemed, for once, at a loss for words. He colored and paled in turns then said, "As far as I know the girl is alive. I don't think Daimhin Feich will allow her to be killed. He believes her captivity will draw Taminy out. I suspect he also believes she has abilities he can either channel or learn. He . . . brought her late last night to Ochanshrine and tried to force her to Weave with the Osmaer Crystal. She conjured an aislinn of your Mistress, then dissolved it and refused to do more."

Aine nodded. "I saw that. Feich was furious. I sensed her fear of him. Her terror of him."

The Abbod busied himself with the closes of his cloak. "Yes, well. He . . . returned this morning, alone, and tried to Weave through the Crystal on his own. Which is why I am here." He raised his head and offered Leal a direct gaze that was somehow at once contrite and haughty.

Leal could only stammer, "Then Feich has—"

"Feich has nothing. He raised an aislinn of the Wicke at prayer with your fellow . . . disciples—God only knows what it is they pray to—but that was all he could do."

Leal was weak with relief. "Then he can do nothing with Ochan's Stone?"

"I don't know. Nor do I want to know." Ladhar reached beneath his cloak and brought out a satchel of soft, black leather. He held it out to Leal, who took it in trembling hands and pulled back the obscuring flap.

Aine, now at Leal's side, gasped. "The Osmaer!"

"I took your advice, Osraed," Ladhar admitted stiffly. "Whatever our differences may be—and they are considerable—I am certain you are less of a danger to the Crystal than Feich is. There are times I'm convinced the man is mad. Other times I think he's only completely amoral. What

I *do* know is what I have seen—he can Weave. Well enough to control the actions of others. Well enough to catch and control the wind."

Leal's brow knotted. "But Bevol's Aiffe is a crystal of great clarity and quality. Yet Feich could do nothing with it? How can that be?"

"I don't know. Perhaps your Mistress blocked him. I only know I don't want him or his Wickish mistress to lay a finger on the Osmaer. I fear they'd destroy it. I give it into your care in the hope that you can protect it better than I can. It would be much too easy for Feich to find it at Ochanshrine."

Fhada twitched. "He doesn't suspect—"

"No, Osraed, he suspects nothing . . . yet. He believes I am his ally."

"You spoke of his mistress. A Wicke, you called her. Do you mean a Taminist?"

Ladhar snorted. "Hardly. She's a woman of the House Dearg. Hillwild wife of a House Elder. But her only allegiance, I wager, is to herself. She somehow got Feich a rune stone—a hideously flawed crimson thing he calls Bloodheart—and she tutors him in all manner of . . . perversion. And there is something else you should know. Before I left Ochanshrine to come here, someone made an attempt on Daimhin Feich's life as he gave a speech from the battlements. Feich elected to blame the Taminists. Support of Taminy-a-Cuinn is now punishable by death. Or will be when the Privy Council ratifies Feich's most recent ban."

Leal's heart spasmed. "Will you vote to ratify it, Osraed?"

"I'm not stupid, young man. I have my own life to protect."

"But if we're now to be the target of Feich's purges, why bring the Osmaer to us?"

"Recent history indicates Taminy and her *waljan* are very difficult targets to hit. Now, I must go before some new crisis arises at Mertuile or Ochanshrine." He moved to open the chamber door, then paused to look back at the *waljan*. "I'm curious. What Weave are you using to create the illusion that Aiffe is the Osmaer Crystal?"

Leal blinked. "Aine modified a Cloakweave and bound it to the stone."

"A Cloakweave. Which is also what you used to get past the guards at the Shrine. I see. Bound to the stone itself, you say." He shot Aine an appraising glance. "A useful inyx. I shall probably wish I could Weave one myself before all this is over."

"How did you know, Abbod?" Leal asked. "About the Weave."

"I remember Bevol's crystal. A beautiful stone, but flawed; there was a tiny opaque smut at its base and a hairline fracture in one of the basal facets. Fortunately, Daimhin Feich could hardly be expected to know the difference." He left them holding the Osmaer Crystal with the unenviable task of determining how to protect it and a hospice full of condemned Taminists.

It was Aine who broke the silence that had settled over the group. "I'm going up to Mertuile. I'm going to find out what's happened to Isha."

"Too dangerous," Fhada objected. "With the bans—"

"I'll Weave a Cloak."

"And if you're surprised into dropping it? None of us are masters of the Art, though we may have to pretend we are."

"I'll wear a crystal to amplify it. I'll be fine."

"No, Aine, *I'll* go."

Heads swiveled to a shadowed alcove beside the hearth from which Saefren Claeg had emerged.

"It makes more sense than having you go," he told Aine before she could protest. "I can get into Mertuile *without* having to resort to inyx. I should have little trouble finding out what happened to Iseabal. No one would have any reason to lie to me or question my curiosity. After all, my Uncle Iobert was part of the party that brought her here."

"I'll go with you," said Aine.

"No, you won't. It makes no sense—am I right, Osraed Fhada?"

Fhada nodded. "I have to agree with Saefren, Aine. It makes more sense for him to go. He isn't the subject of a

Regency decree. You are. Besides, dear girl, we need you here."

Aine subsided, but Leal knew it was not out of acquiescence. There was rebellion in her hazel eyes and mutiny in the set of her jaw.

An hour after the failed attempt on his life, Daimhin Feich sat in his salon quivering between terror and rage. His mind was a roil of impulses. He wanted to strangle Coinich Mor; he wanted to seize the Osmaer Crystal and throw every smug Osraed in the dungeon; he wanted to drown the Taminists there now with his own hands. Most of all, he wanted to snatch from his young hostage every last ounce of power she had to offer.

It was difficult to restrain himself from that last action. But he had no doubt that if he went to her now, in this chaotic frame of mind, he'd leave nothing of her but a dried out husk, and he had only Coinich Mor with which to replace her.

Then, too, there was the matter of the traitorous Houses. He could do nothing about that now. They were camped just beyond Creiddylad, in position to trap his forces with their backs to the Sea if they forced a battle.

Damn, but he hated this feeling of impotence! When he could face her again without wanting to thrash her witless, he'd consult Coinich Mor about possible Weaves he might apply to this wretched situation.

Someone rattled the door and he growled permission for them to enter. It was Sorn Saba who appeared around the ornate slab of wood, bowing slightly as he entered. The momentary obeisance blended smoothly into an arrogant straightening of the Deasach's lithe body.

"Daimhin, if I might share words with you?"

Feich waved a half-empty wine cup at the seat across from him at the hearth. The youth perched himself at the edge of it and fixed his host with a gleaming, black gaze.

"You seem besieged by trouble, my friend," he observed. "Your little Cyne stolen, your arch enemy at large, and now your subjects press toward rebellion."

Brat. Feich forced his face to reflect a composure he was far from feeling. "They aren't precisely my subjects."

"They may as well be; the return of Cyneric Airleas at any time soon would seem to be impossible."

"You needn't remind me, Shak Saba. I am well aware of my problems."

"Please, friend Daimhin! Let us not return to formality. I only wonder why, in such dire circumstance, you promise your people that you will return their Cyneric to them. It seems to me you are not in a position to do this."

"Your point . . . Sorn."

The Deasach shrugged. "Only that you would appear to be in need of some help. The kind of help my dear sister, Lilias, could provide."

"Such as?"

"Men, arms. A force at your command that is well-versed in mountain combat."

Feich laughed. "For whatever good that would do. The passes are snowbound."

"Ah! The *northeastern* passes, yes. But it is much milder on the southeastern side of the range."

Feich sat forward in his chair. "You're suggesting . . . that your sister would allow us to cross Deasach land to reach Hrofceaster? She would lend me both support *and* passage?"

Sorn Saba glanced down at his hands, clasped between his knees. "If you were to offer some tribute to her and if I were to advise her that a military alliance with you would be beneficial and appropriate under the circumstances."

"The circumstances being . . . ?"

"That a powerful Enemy of the Caraidin throne holds the heir to that Throne hostage. That that Enemy is an ally of the Hillwild, who are *our* enemies. That this Enemy is strong in magic and beauty." He grinned. "A natural adversary for my very vain sister."

"And you would advise your sister to aid me?"

The boy looked up at him through dark, glittering eyes and Feich thought, *Ah, this is it. We come to the point.*

"I could be persuaded," Sorn said.

"And what could persuade you?"

"The Nairnian sorceress."

"*What*? Taminy?"

"No, no. *Iseabal*. Iseabal of the blue eyes. I want her."

"*You* want her." Feich only just kept himself from laughing. "Whatever for? Surely you would find an experienced woman like Coinich Mor more arousing than a village cailin."

The boy had the grace to blush. "I've known a score of women like Coinich Mor—experienced, as you say, and gluttonous when it comes to young men. But Iseabal is . . . innocent, exotic, beautiful, magical. I find her . . . fascinating."

"Exotic," Feich repeated. "A village cailin. A Cirke-master's daughter."

"Oh, not to you, surely. You're used to your fair women with their light eyes and snowy flesh. But what is common to you is alien to me. And frankly, I find Iseabal's very lack of experience in matters of passion as exciting, in its own way, as Coinich Mor's skill. But it's more than that, Daimhin. There is something indefinable about her, something intriguing. She seems so gentle. Yet, she has the steel to contradict even you, though you hold over her the power of life and death."

"Ah. And it would have nothing to do with the fact that magic drips from her fingertips."

The Deasach's eyes grew brighter still. "You can almost see it. Yes, there is that. She is a jewel. A jewel I intend to own."

Arrogant whelp. "Out of the question. I need her."

"As hostage? So be it. But what difference in whose tent she sleeps? Consider her your hostage and me her . . . special guardian."

"I need . . . access to her. She . . . provides me with power, you see."

The boy's brow knit. "Power? I don't understand."

"You wouldn't—not being Gifted with the *aidan*. You say she is magical. You're right. She is. But only one with the Gift, one who can Weave inyx, could possibly make use of her magic. I can channel that power. She would be useless to you."

Sorn smiled. "Oh, not useless, Daimhin. A woman needn't be dripping with the *aidan*, as you call it, to be of value. Yet, you are right in saying I have no need of her power. If you do, then of course you may use her as you wish."

"I'm sorry, Sorn. I can't let you take her."

"Then I can't give my sister a good reason to let you take your troops across Deasach land or send Deasach forces with you into the Gyldan-baenn." He began to rise.

Feich raised a detaining hand. "Wait. Perhaps we can compromise. You may visit her tonight, if you wish."

"Not enough."

"Then you may visit her at your whim until we depart for El-Deasach. You may even take her to your tent on occasion."

"Again—not enough. Look, my friend Regent, if my sister agrees to aid you, what need will you have for this girl? Surely it is Coinich Mor who aids you with your Weaving."

Feich sat up on a jolt of suspicion. "What do you know of that?"

"What I see. What little she tells me." Catching Feich's sudden scowl, he added, "You made a great impression on her. 'A man of consuming passion,' she called you. 'A man of raw power.' Surely, with such a woman at your side, you have no need to own young Iseabal. Let me have her. If you still need her on your campaign to Hrofceaster, then of course, she shall come . . . but in my custody. Tell me—what difference does it make?"

"And this is the only bribe you'll accept?"

"Ah, please—a gift."

"This is the only *gift* you'll accept from me? Is there nothing else I can give you, do for you?"

"Nothing."

"If it's village cailin you want, I can give you a dozen—each colored just like this one. Or each a different shade, if you prefer."

"But they would not be magical heretics. They would not be sorceresses. They would just be young girls. In that way, even Coinich Mor is exotic. I find I like magical women. Perhaps, when we find this Osmaer of yours . . . "

The hair rose up on the back of Feich's neck. "Precisely. Taminy-Osmaer is *mine*."

Sorn favored him with a gleaming smile. "See? Now what does any man—even a man like yourself—need with *three* sorceresses?"

Feich snorted. "What, indeed. All right, friend Sorn. You may be Iseabal's 'guardian.' Consider her your personal responsibility. I ask only that I be allowed to consort with her at will."

"Of course." The boy rose and made an exaggerated bow. "You are a most gracious host, Daimhin."

"Yes, aren't I?"

He saw the Deasach out, torn between anger at the boy's arrogance, and admiration of his sheer gall. *He might have been a Feich*, he thought and determined to visit the Nairnian immediately, before her "guardian" could lay hands on her. He would have to hurry to get another chance at the Stone of Ochan before they departed for El-Deasach. Yes, and he must give immediate orders to Ruadh about the preparation of their men.

He had not made it to the door when it rattled and opened, revealing a flushed, nervous Caime Cadder. Irritated, Feich stopped to glare at the cleirach. "It is not only impolite to enter a private room without permission, Minister, in this case it is also dangerous. You had better tell me something earth-shaking or I'll have you flung off the western battlements."

Cadder blanched, his eyes glistening. "Please, lord. I beg you—hear what I have to say before you throw me out. There is something you *must* know. The stone you tried to Weave with this morning was not the Osmaer. Osraed Ladhar has turned traitor and put another crystal in its place."

CHAPTER 16

We sent down the Scripture as a blessing for the faithful,
but it can only conduce to the downfall of the wicked—
they who hear nothing in the Scriptures but words. Consider: The Sun's blaze lights the entire sky, yet only its warmth
reaches the blind.

—*Utterances of Osraed Haefer Hageswode #36*

Ladhar's trek back through Creiddylad to Ochanshrine
was uneventful, but disturbing nonetheless. There was an
increased military presence in the streets, largely in the
form of Feich and Dearg kinsmen and Malcuim regulars.
Ladhar was puzzled by the seeming fickleness of the lat-
ter. While it was well known that a healthy contingent of
minor Malcuim kinsmen had fled after Colfre's death—
no doubt assuming the Feich would soon be at their
throats—just as many had stayed behind to lend support
in finding their Cyneric. Now they hunted down Taminist
Wicke in his name. An irony.

Curious circumstances, the Abbod thought, that had
brought a proud House to this pass. Colfre Malcuim had
been an only child; there was no brother to make a claim
to the Throne or lead the House to fight for his son's return.
The closest Malcuim relations were cousins—daughters
of Airleas's great aunts and uncles mostly, a rare son among
them—who had lives and concerns of their own, with little
interest, it seemed, in grappling the man to whom had
fallen, not unwanted, the protection of the Malcuim
Throne.

Ladhar paused momentarily to watch a couple of Dearg kinsmen drag a young girl, kicking and screaming, from a tiny Backstere's shop along a Cyne's Way back street to present her to a waiting Feich. An older woman—her mother, Ladhar assumed—followed them, protesting her daughter's virtue at the top of her ample lungs.

"She's a good girl, sirs! A *good* girl!" she cried, her broad accent marking her northern rural origins. "She never done a midge of Weaving. I swear't. She's a good girl!"

The Feich in charge—a tall, brawny man with mud-brown hair and beard—grabbed the girl's wrist and thrust her hand toward her mother's face. "A good girl, is it? Then how do you explain this?"

There was a mark on the girl's palm—a stellate smudge of rosy gold. The mother blanched. "Oh, sir! I know naught of that!"

"Or this?" A second Feich had appeared from the shop with what appeared to be a hand-bound booklet.

"I—I—I don't know what—" the woman gabbled, and the younger Feich kinsman flung the little book open and read in a loud voice. "'As a mother defends her only child from harm, let shielding thoughts for all be in your heart, and all-embracing love for the whole universe. Let your love be given without reserve, untouched by enmity, arousing no hatred.'"

"It . . . it's just *Scripture*, sir." The girl finally spoke on her own behalf. "It's a book of Scripture given me by a friend."

"A Taminist friend, I don't doubt," said the elder Feich.

"No, sir!" the Backstere wailed. "Please, sir, my daughter!"

She held her arms out for the girl, but the Dearg pulled her away. "Give me the book," said the brown-beard. His kinsman tossed the little volume to him. He turned it over in his hands. "'Book of the New Covenant,'" he read. "I never heard of such Scripture as this. And who's this Osraed Wyth who signs his name to it?"

Ladhar quivered. Books. Dear God, they were already disseminating books, making converts, winning souls.

The Feich opened the little book and squinted at the page before him. "Gibberish. You're condemned by nonsense." He read another passage in a sing-song voice calculated to show the gathering crowd how inane were the maunderings of Taminists. "'Do you not see that the Spirit causes night to follow day and day to follow night? And that this same Spirit holds the Sun and moon and seasons and all His creation to Laws which flow toward a set goal? And that this same Spirit is aware of all your doings? The promise and Covenant of the Spirit is truth, and whatever else you adore is only His creation. Let not the things you adore deceive you about the Spirit.'"

He clapped the book shut and glared at his little audience. "Taminist ravings! Of course the Spirit causes day and night. Of course He orders the seasons. Any child knows that, but you lap it up like it was news! You stand condemned by your own demon scripture, girl, for you *are* deceived about the Spirit. Deceived by Taminy-a-Cuinn. Do you deny that you are a follower of this woman?"

Whatever the girl said was completely lost in the renewed wailings of her mother, who pled her case with clasped hands and bended knees. "Oh, please, sir! You're wrong! I know you must be wrong. It's Scripture, sir! It *is*! Given us by Osraed. And my girl is a good girl! Not prone to wickedness at all, sir!"

The elder Feich, enjoying his role as inquisitor, smiled. "Well, mam, I reckon we'll learn how good your daughter is soon enough. And if she's *very* good, she might not have to die. She might only have to lose that wicked hand." He grasped the girl's wrist again and extended her arm. The book dropped, unheeded, to the cobbles as he drew his short sword.

The crowd roiled noisily. The Feich rested the sharpened edge of the gleaming blade on the girl's wrist. "Your call, mam. Let's see how well you shield your child from harm. She dies a Taminist with both hands or she lives to prove her virtue with one. And I'll be the first judge of her goodness."

Ladhar's legs tightened on the barrel of his horse,

prodding the animal to carry him forward through the knot of onlookers. Sweat beaded his brow though the air was cold enough to cloud with his breath. He broke into the inner circle of watchers and let down his hood. "Is there a problem, friend Feich?"

The elder kinsman blinked up at him, nonplused. "No, Abbod. Merely following the Regent's order to ferret out these Taminist Wicke."

"And did you intend to execute this one in the street without trial?"

"No, sir. Only trying to determine guilt or innocence."

"Ah. Surely a job for a tribunal."

"She's guilty!" cried someone in the gathering.

"She's *not!*" The Backstere now took the opportunity to throw her ample self before Ladhar's horse. "Lord Osraed, I beg you! My daughter is no Wicke!"

"Aye," snarled the Feich, "and I'm no Feich either, I suppose. We found Taminist writings."

"They're Scripture!" keened the woman.

Ladhar held out his hand. "Give me the book."

After a moment of hesitation, the younger of the Feich obeyed. Ladhar lifted the leather cover. It was a crude binding, but adequate to hold the pages. They were linen, and the first, embossed with the Sign of the Meri, was signed by Osraed Wyth, dated not a month past at Hrofceaster.

"You see, Osraed?" The Feich gloated.

Ladhar flicked a razor glance at him. "Where did you get this?" he asked the quaking girl.

"From a young Osraed. I knew him to be Osraed from the bright kiss on his brow. Like—like your own, sir, but golden."

"I see. And he told you this book was Scripture."

"Aye sir. The Book of the New Covenant. New, since the Meri has changed Aspect. It *is* Scripture, sir, isn't it?"

The Feich uttered a grating laugh. "Pretending ignorance won't save you—"

"Yes. It is Scripture."

Around Ladhar, the street and its denizens, the air and its steaming chill, stilled as if time had ground to a halt.

The Feich gaped at him. "What did you say, lord Abbod?"

"I said, it is Scripture. Compiled by our newest Osraed."

"But the girl's a Taminist! She's got the mark of the Wicke in her palm!"

"Does she, indeed? Let me see it." Ladhar's eyes fixed on the girl's hand as the men tumbled her roughly forward. The Feich brute stepped forward to pry back her fingers, exposing her palm. After a moment, Ladhar moved his eyes to that worthy's face. "I see no mark."

The girl's palm was blank, a thing which seemed to surprise even her.

The Feich gaped. "I—I don't . . . It was there moments ago, I swear it."

"Well, it's not there now. Release the child."

They hesitated. Ladhar lifted his head and roared, "*Release* her! She is no more Taminist than I am! You have made a mistake. See that you don't make the same error twice. Our Regent will be none too happy if you harass and maim his law-abiding citizens. Now, go about your business. While you loiter here, the real threat to Creiddylad escapes your notice."

Grumbling, bemused, they did as ordered. The crowd dispersed, some following the soldiers, some going about their own business, a few staying behind to comfort the still weeping mother and daughter. Eventually, the two came to Ladhar's side, their faces maps of gratitude with salt rivers marked in flour.

"How can I thank you, Osraed?" the girl mewed. She seemed unutterably fragile still, cowering at her mother's side. A fragile heretic.

What have I done? Ladhar shook himself. "I've not yet received a copy of Osraed Wyth's work. May I keep this one?"

Daughter and mother exchanged glances. "Of course, Abbod. With the Meri's blessing."

He nodded, pulled up his hood and reined his horse toward Ochanshrine. He arrived there to find that his presence was required at Mertuile. Immediately, said a dour Caime Cadder.

At Mertuile, he and Cadder were taken directly to the throneroom where Feich sat in state, surrounded by kinsmen and allies. There seemed to be an inordinate number of armed men about, but then the Regent had only this day survived an attempt on his life.

"Ah, dear Abbod! How kind of you to join us!" Feich beamed from his borrowed throne, seeming very relaxed for a man who had come that close to death. Ladhar could only suppose he must have been drinking something stronger than the summer wine he served at state suppers. "I've brought you here that I might ask of you a supreme favor. I have recently made an agreement with the Marschal, Shak Sorn Saba, to effect an alliance between ourselves and the Banarigh Lilias Saba of El-Deasach for the purpose of returning Cyneric Airleas to Creiddylad. Pursuant to that, we will be moving our forces south to El-Deasach and from there into the Gyldan-baenn east of Hrofceaster."

Ladhar was astounded. "The Banarigh has consented to this?"

"She will consent when her Marschal petitions her to do so. He travels on that mission even as we speak. And he assures me of success. This means we will be traveling on a most crucial campaign immediately upon his return. We will need all the aid the Eibhilin realm has to offer. I intend to take the Osmaer Crystal with us."

"The—! But that's unheard of!" The Abbod found he could only stand and quiver. "The Osmaer has only left Ochanshrine once in all history—for the coronation of Kieran the Dark at Cyne's Cirke."

"Ah, wrong. It also left once in the hands of Bearach Malcuim, Kieran's son. He removed it clandestinely to Halig-liath, I recall, in an attempt to keep it from the hands of Buchan Claeg."

Ladhar willed his face to remain immobile and his blood to lie still in his veins. "I had forgotten. For all that his intentions were good, it was still theft—possibly blasphemy."

"Yet it contributed to the salvation of Caraid-land, did it not?"

"I wouldn't deny it."

"And *I* . . . " Feich spread his fingers upon his breast. "I, at least, am asking permission of the Osraed charged with the Crystal's protection and care."

His thoughts fevered, Ladhar considered his response. It must depend, he supposed, on how intent Feich was on having the Crystal with him. If he was set on it, he would simply take it, just as Bearach Spearman had . . . just as Ladhar had, himself. The Abbod glanced at Feich's face and recalled being buffeted by a wind of Feich's calling. The Regent did nothing that was not driven by his full will. It would be futile to resist him. Besides, the real Stone of Ochan was several miles away in the hands of well-meaning, if misled souls whom Ladhar knew he could trust with it. Only the fraud would take the trail to El-Deasach. There was really no harm in granting Daimhin Feich his wish.

Ladhar made a display of his meditational pose, then nodded once, heavily. "Very well, Regent. Your point is well taken. I can concede that extraordinary circumstances require extraordinary remedies. Yes, of course you may take the Osmaer Crystal on your campaign."

Feich inclined his head. "Thank you, Abbod. You honor me. Now . . . where *is* the Osmaer? It is *not* in its place at Ochanshrine."

The pronouncement dropped into an oppressive silence. In the bottomless pit that opened up in his soul, Osraed Ladhar flailed for balance. Should he dissemble? Should he admit his subterfuge? Should he collapse to the floor and beg mercy? "No," he said finally. "You're quite correct. Last night, I replaced the Osmaer with a stone of similar size and appearance."

Feich seemed taken aback, affording Ladhar a tiny victory. "You *admit* your treachery?"

"Treachery, lord? Protecting the Osmaer from Taminists is hardly treachery."

"Protecting it?" Feich aimed a furrowed glance at Caime Cadder, who stared at the toes of his shoes. "How so?"

"It came to my attention that the Taminists were planning to make an attempt on the Crystal. An attempt to remove it from Ochanshrine and spirit it up to Halig-liath."

"Indeed? And how did that 'come to your attention'?"

"I was favored with an aislinn in which two people approached me and tried to lay hands on the Stone. I immediately replaced it with a crystal left to me by Osraed Bevol. Later, as my aislinn foretold, I was approached in the Shrine by . . . by the Taminist Osraed Fhada and Lealbhallain, who tried to coerce me to give up the Stone."

"And this false Osmaer . . . it was still there when I tried to Weave this morning?"

Ladhar nodded. "I thought it safest that the Osmaer remain hidden until you had dealt with the Taminist threat."

"Then, where is the Osmaer hidden, Abbod? You may speak of it here, we're among allies."

"It's hidden in a place known only to me. For safety's sake. I was unsure who I could trust."

Feich looked past Ladhar to the man eternally at his shoulder. "Is that so, Minister Cadder? Is the Osmaer's hiding place unknown to you?"

"It is, lord Regent."

Feich rose from the throne and meandered off the dais to approach Ladhar. "You possess greater foresight than I gave you credit for, Abbod. I suppose I must thank you for taking the Osmaer out of harm's way. And you know, Abbod, I *would* thank you . . . if I half believed your story. Unfortunately for you, I don't."

Ladhar was once again consigned to the bottomless pit. From its depths, all he could do was stand and tremble as Feich went on.

"You see, Abbod, your faithful lieutenant, the able Minister Cadder, observed you switching the Stone. He saw you carry it to your private chambers, which he later searched to find the exact hiding place. He found it, knowing your habits. But when he checked the hiding place again, it was gone. Naturally, he suspected, when he discovered you'd left Ochanshrine today, that you'd taken the Osmaer with you." Feich brought his face close to Ladhar's, searching him eye to eye. "Where did you go, Abbod? Did you take the Crystal to your Osraed friends at Carehouse? Or did you have another destination?"

"The Osraed at Carehouse are Taminists," said Ladhar stiffly. "I am not a Taminist, nor shall I ever be one. They are not friends, but adversaries."

"Yet it seems you may have given them the Stone of Ochan."

Ladhar was not used to lying. Except, he now saw, to himself. What had ever made him believe allegiance to Daimhin Feich was in any way allegiance to Caraid-land or, more importantly, to the Meri? His distrust and hatred of Taminy had blinded him, as it had apparently blinded Caime Cadder. "Whatever I did," he said at last, "I did for Caraid-land."

"Ah, patriotism. A noble sentiment. But hard to believe of a Taminist." Feich turned away.

"I am *not* a Taminist! I am a loyal lover of the Meri."

"Then I'll give you abundant opportunity to consort with your beloved. Take him." He flicked a glance at the hovering guards, who moved immediately to take Ladhar in hand.

The Abbod offered no resistance. He had none left in him.

"Take his cloak," Feich ordered. "He won't need it where he's going."

The Feich kinsmen did as commanded, stripping Ladhar of the warm covering. Something slipped from its folds and fell to the floor. It was the book Ladhar had taken from the little Taminist girl. Cadder plucked it from the tiles to scan the cover page. With a glance full of loathing, he offered it to Daimhin Feich who looked the pages over himself, a slow smile illumining his sharp features.

"Why Abbod, how unlike you to be so careless. Surely, you realize that carrying Taminist literature is an offense punishable by death. But thank you for so thoughtfully providing us with concrete evidence of your apostasy. You got this from Fhada, did you?"

"No, not from Fhada."

Feich shrugged. "No matter. We now have ample reason to search Carehouse. And, if necessary, burn it to the ground. I'm sure your successor will offer no resistance to the idea."

"What will you do with me?"

Feich's smile deepened. "Oh, I have a special place for treacherous Osraed. You may find it a bit lonely there. But not for long. I intend to fill it with Taminists. I think Osraed Fhada and Lealbhallain will be the first to join you there."

There. There was a place Ladhar had prayed never to see outside of his nightmares. The chamber was deeper than it was wide, darker than Ladhar's dreams, and smelled foully of brine and death. The only access was from a long flight of rheum-covered steps that tumbled from a narrow door. The only natural light that entered the dungeon floated phantom-like from mere slits of windows far up the western-facing wall. It shimmered on the seething carpet of icy sea water and glistened dully on the ever sodden walls with their covering of slime.

Up to his ankles in chill salt water, Ladhar experienced a cold of body and soul he'd never known. With the closing of the door, he suspected his life had also closed, for he could do nothing now but drown when the rising tide caught him in exhausted sleep, or perish from exposure. A thought of Bevol deepened the chill and sent his eyes skittering across the eddying carpet to search for the other Osraed's remains.

Enough! he chided himself. There would be enough time for terrible searches and self recrimination and futile analyses of what had brought him to this pass. There was something he might accomplish even here, Meri willing. They had stripped him of his rune crystal and his keystone pendant but, short of killing him outright, or rendering him unconscious, they couldn't tear from him what little Art he still possessed. His lips curled. He should probably thank God that Feich was such a sadistic bastard, else he'd be dead already. Ignoring the cold that was beyond cold, Ladhar sat in the waters beneath Mertuile and attempted what he expected to be his last Weave.

They felt it simultaneously—a crawling of the scalp, a prickling of the skin, a swift-blossoming sensation of dread.

In the midst of preparation for the evening meal, they paused in their various tasks and stared at one another, mouths open to say—what? What could be said?

Aine set down the stack of plates she had been laying out on a half-set table and met Osraed Fhada's troubled gaze. "Who?" She merely mouthed the word, afraid any sound might break the tenuous connection with the unknown. Fhada only shook his head, while behind him Leal lowered himself to a refectory bench, a large bowl of fruit in his arms. Aine could feel the gazes of others, too, who had noticed their sudden inactivity. She succeeded in blocking them out and fumbled along the aislinn thread, willing it to thicken, to strengthen. They were in danger— imminent danger. "Feich," she murmured. "He'll attack us. Tonight. Soon."

"It's Ladhar. He has Ladhar," added Leal.

Fhada's body jerked as if struck by lightning. "Ladhar knows we have the Stone."

"That's it!" breathed Aine. "That's what Feich is after."

"How soon?"

Aine looked up. Across the table from her, Saefren Claeg, dressed for travel, awaited an answer. His face was storm dark, his expression grim. "Soon," she answered him. "Within the hour."

Saefren glanced about at the roomful of people: children arriving for their meal, Prentices helping with the laying out, men and women from any number of former lives who now spent their time here for safety, for support, for community. Believers all. "Then we have to move quickly. We have to evacuate these people."

"Evacuate?" Aine echoed. "To where?"

"Outside Creiddylad. To my uncle's camp. They'd be safe there. The House Chieftains will protect them."

"Yes." Fhada was nodding. "Yes. That's exactly what we must do."

Time. That was what they needed most. Unfortunately, they had none. Though they left the refectory in a state of chaos and turned at once to packing up Carehouse's inmates for a trek out of Creiddylad, they were caught short. Warned by a cry from the gate top, they had only enough time to hide the resident children in what had once been a storage cellar before Feich's men were at their gate.

Saefren drew his sword.

"Do you really think you can defend this place with that?" Aine asked. "Put it away."

"And how would *you* defend it?"

Aine took a quick count of their assets—the handful of *waljan* gathered in the refectory by the cellar door. "Put it away," she repeated.

Daimhin Feich led the party himself. A part of him would like to have brought the Deasach cannon along and blown Carehouse's barred gates to chill hell, but he did not want to draw attention from the hills. So instead, he demanded that the gate be opened and, when that did not happen, he called Coinich Mor to his side. They used no battering rams on the barred gate, but only two crystals, a simple inyx and time. The heavy bar finally heaved itself from its place and the metal bolt slipped from its bolt hole. Guards moved forward to swing the gates open, allowing Daimhin Feich, Coinich Mor and Caime Cadder to ride through.

The large courtyard was empty. Feich had expected that. He stationed several guards in the courtyard and entered the huge stone building flanked by his Wicke, his cleirach and his kinsmen. The hall was eerily quiet. Feich swore that, above the scuffing of their shoes and the soft whisper of their breath, he could hear pigeons fluttering in the eaves, wind passing over the ridge pole, fire licking up the hearth in an adjacent room.

He glanced back over his shoulder at the men arrayed behind him. "Spread out. Search. Shout out when you find them. Gather them in the courtyard for the trip back to Mertuile."

With Coinich Mor, Cadder and two Feich cousins at his side, he moved softly through Carehouse. They had peeked into several rooms—empty, all—when he was touched by unease. It was too quiet. They had come without warning. Even if some lookout had spotted their approach, there was no way to hide all the people he knew by report lived within Carehouse's aging walls. Yet, the place seemed deserted and the refectory offered abundant proof of hasty flight. The dozen or so tables were half laid, a stack of plates had been left where someone had halted in setting them out, tableware had been abandoned in similar disarray on the end of the same table. Bowls of food sat untouched on a worn sideboard and the hearth fire blazed as if freshly stoked. In the adjoining kitchen, cookfires boiled a forsaken stew.

Touring the large chamber Daimhin Feich frowned, a creeping sensation prickling the back of his neck. He gestured vaguely at the hearth. "Fire in the hearth, but no candles or lamps. Yet, it's near sunset."

"They'd use light-globes," said Cadder. "There are none lit. They're not here."

"No, they want us to *believe* they're not here," Feich said. "This old place must be full of bolt holes and hiding places." He moved toward a small, rounded door on the rear wall of the room. "Where does this go—Cadder?" He looked to the cleirach who hurried to unlatch the door and push it open.

"If I recall, it's an access to the cellars."

Feich smiled. "Yes, of course. The cellars. What better hiding place? A dead end." He afforded a chuckle at that obvious wordplay and slipped into the dark corridor. He had Coinich Mor hold his hand, feeding her enough power to use her yellow crystal to light the way. It clearly awed his kinsmen to realize that their cousin had such a command of the Art—the Divine Art, he reminded himself.

Ironic. He had never, in his wildest dreams, thought of himself as Divine. Taminy was Divine. He knew that—could admit it. But he—he knew only that he was something beyond the frail, the human. What was he, if not Divine—he who pursued the Divine and sought to co-opt it?

Later, he would find an answer to that. Right now, he was faced with another doorway, its thick, oaken barrier an opaque face that pretended at disuse. Feich, disbelieving, bade one of his kinsmen open the door. It swung away into a gloom so intense even Coinich Mor's crystal made little impression upon it. He had the cleirach fetch a lamp and lit it himself without flint. His kinsmen's eyes gleamed.

A short but steep flight of stairs descended into the gloom. After a moment of hesitation, Feich sent one of his men down with the lamp. He followed, beckoning the second Feich guard to bring up the rear of the party. They were cautious, quiet. It hardly mattered. The dank chamber seemed as empty as the refectory, and the creeping feeling did not abate. They searched methodically among the kegs, crates and clay pots of goods. They even broke open random containers in case the Taminists had been that clever. They hadn't been; the crates contained only jars of preserved fruits and vegetables, the pots only flour and grain, the kegs only cider.

Cursing Osraed Fhada and Abbod Ladhar, cursing Taminy, Feich led his party back up to the ground floor, hoping the other searchers had had better luck than he. They hadn't, and though they searched even the private rooms, not one Taminist was found.

Furious, defeated, humiliated, Daimhin Feich retired to the courtyard and thence to Mertuile, taking his brooding cleirach, his smiling Wicke and his puzzled kinsmen with him.

He couldn't breathe. He could only stand with his back to the cold stone wall and let his terror suffocate him. His ears cringed from the sound of his breath rasping through his dry throat. He could hear the others breathing, too. Dear God, he could hear their *hearts* beating in their breasts and he found it impossible to believe the man standing not five feet from him could not also hear them . . . or see. Yet, Daimhin Feich's pale eyes swept the room, passing over the spot where he stood, again and again, each time looking right through him.

Saefren's breath caught in his throat, sweat started from every pore in his body. He wanted to glance at Aine, pressed to the wall beside him, and couldn't. He had done it once and found the blank spot where he knew she must be too unsettling to contemplate.

An invisible hand grasped his, pressing it, holding it against the cold stones of the refectory wall. He took a deep, painful breath. Humiliation washed over him, blanketing his fear. If he was invisible to Daimhin Feich, he was not to Aine-mac-Lorimer's *aidan*.

Not four feet away, now, Daimhin Feich snarled something to his men and turned on his heel. His entourage followed him to the refectory doors, trading uneasy glances. The skittish cleirach trailed after—it seemed he couldn't move quickly enough—but the Dearg Wicke lingered a moment to wander among the long tables, pondering the room with bemused eyes. Then she, too, was gone.

Saefren thought he might collapse, but could not, yet. The danger wasn't past and would not be until Feich and his party rode away. Minutes stretched. Sounds from the outer corridors continued, waned, ceased.

After long moments of listening to each other breathe, Aine loosed her grip on Saefren's hand and sagged back into the wall, becoming a solid and visible presence. "They're gone."

Saefren let his own body relax against the firm stones of Carehouse. "Thank God. I thought . . . "

"That they'd be able to see us?" asked Aine. Her face, too, was sheeny with sweat.

"Forgive me, Aine Red," he begged, mocking, "but I've never been caught in the midst of a Cloakweave before. It was an unsettling experience."

"Unsettling," repeated Leal, wiping perspiration from his brow. "I was terrified. I wasn't sure I could hold it that long. It's one thing to Cloak yourself, but to hide an entire roomful of people . . . " He shook his head, glancing around the room to where others stretched or slumped or shook themselves. "I'm exhausted."

"No time for that, I'm afraid." Osraed Fhada stood in the doorway of the cellar passage, a wide-eyed little girl attached to one arm. "We've got to get these people out of here."

"Do we?" Saefren asked. "Feich's searched and found nothing. Surely the place is safe now."

Fhada shook his head. "We don't dare take a chance, Saefren. He's Gifted. It could be only a matter of time before he realizes what we've done. Or he might put a watch on the place. We'd be in constant danger of being surprised. We can't stay cloaked forever."

So, they gathered up belongings and food and divided their number into small groups of five or six, the better to make clandestine journeys. Of the fifty or so people that had congregated at Carehouse, only a handful had mastered the Cloakweave. Those would be needed to ferry the refugees to safety.

When they had completed their plans for the exodus, Saefren gathered up his own belongings and loaded them onto his horse, thankful Feich hadn't seen fit to take the four-legged inmates of Carehouse's stable. He was tightening the cinch of his saddle when he sensed movement in the stable doorway. Nerves still fired, he whirled, hand finding his sword. But it was only Aine who stood in the broad aisle, her robust form silhouetted against the silvery haze of moonlight washing in from the courtyard.

"You're going to Mertuile?" she asked.

"I promised I would. A Claeg doesn't go back on a promise."

"I still think I should go with you."

"Feich's not stupid. He'll be expecting Taminists to try escaping him. You're one of the few here who can muster a Cloakweave. You'll be needed."

The silhouette shifted. "You speak of Weaving as if its something you now believe in."

"It saved my life. Have I a choice?"

"Then you believe the future of Caraid-land is in Taminy's hands."

"I believe the future of Caraid-land is in Daimhin Feich's hands, as frightening as that is. I also believe it's my duty to help pry it out again. I'll concede your . . . abilities and those of your Mistress, but that doesn't make me a Taminist."

She said nothing to that and, without further comment, Saefren led his horse from the stable and mounted. He'd

ridden halfway to the gate when Aine, following him, spoke
again.

"Are you just going to ride right out into the street?"

"Am I expected to fly?"

"Feich might have posted men in the streets. Had you
thought of that?"

He hadn't. But should have. He glanced up at the evening
sky with its undercoat of wood and peat smoke, and sighed.
"Have you a suggestion?"

"I can cloak you as far as the next block. Just in case."

"All right," he agreed. "As far as the next block, then."

She smiled, triumphantly, he thought, and faded from
sight as if obscured by a piece of the night sky.

I will never get used to that, he thought, and steered
his mount through the half-open gate and out into the
narrow street.

"And we can do nothing?" Airleas's eyes stung with tears
of futility and the snow-covered trees and houses blurred.

"We do what we do," Taminy answered him. "It's not
as little as you think."

Airleas thought he would explode with pent up rage.
The situation in Creiddylad grew worse by the day, and
yet he could do nothing but sit here, aloof on this
mountainside, praying and practicing inyx. He blinked into
the chill wind that roamed fitfully over the flank of Baenn-
an-ratha. "But when will we *act*?"

"We act already. We prepare our minds and souls for
the future. What more should we do?"

"We should go to Creiddylad, free Iseabal and throw
Daimhin Feich off of my father's throne and out of
Mertuile. Between the men The Claeg left here and the
ones camped in the lowlands, plus the Hillwild, we could
surely rout them." He turned to Taminy on a wave of pas-
sionate certainty and found her poking at a mound of snow
with the toe of her boot.

"Daimhin Feich hasn't mounted an attack on Hrofceaster
because he can't get to it right now. How do you propose
to get your forces down off the mountains?"

Airleas chewed on that momentarily. "We don't really need a force," he concluded. "We need only a handful of people—but all must be Artful. Then we could enter Mertuile by stealth, and deal with Feich. Maybe even force him to admit that he killed my father."

"I don't think Daimhin Feich will be at Mertuile much longer."

Airleas shivered. *Damn snow. Damn cold. Damn wind.* "Then he comes to Hrofceaster? Good! The allied Houses can sweep in behind him, squeeze him into the blocked passes and crush him against the mountain. Then I could lead the Claeg men and the Hillwild down to—"

"I thought we'd already covered that. Do you really think the Claeg and the Hillwild will follow you on a suicide mission?"

"I'm their Cyne."

"Cyneric, until you're set before the Stone."

"That's right. And I need to show leadership, don't I, if I'm to win their respect? If I lead my own defense—"

"You'd put yourself and your House at great risk."

"But Catahn says that taking risks is the mark of a great leader."

Taminy's breath appeared in a steamy sigh. "*Calculated* risks, Airleas. Well-reasoned and backed by steady intuition. There's more to leadership than taking troops into battle."

"Yes. Yes, I know, but how can I learn that here on this mountain? When will I have a chance to prove myself?"

"When you're ready to be proven, I suppose."

"But Daimhin Feich—"

"Is not your concern now, Airleas. He is mine." Her voice, always gentle, carried a new touch of iron.

"You don't think I'm ready, do you? Not ready to be Cyne—not even ready for Crask-an-duine."

She glanced at him out of the tail of her eye. "That's become very important to you hasn't it?" When he nodded emphatically, she told him, "I don't decide when you're ready for Crask-an-duine. The Aeldra and the Ren decide that."

"But you know—"

She turned to face him, laying her hands on his shoulders. "I know that you're being asked to grow up very quickly, Airleas. You're twelve years old and yet you must struggle toward manhood with every ounce of strength. I'll help you all I can, but I can't learn your lessons for you. You must learn them for yourself."

"But you won't even give me a crystal of my own to Weave with—just that tiny schooling stone. When will I have a crystal of my own, Taminy?" He was whining and he knew it. Abashed, he added, "It's just that there's so much I have to do."

"I know. And when you're ready to do it . . . " She left the rest unsaid.

Disappointed, Airleas turned away from her and continued down the trail to Airdnasheen.

CHAPTER 17

Gracious Spirit! If none strays from Your Path, how can Your children know mercy? If wrong is never committed, how can Your forgiveness be tasted? May I be a living sacrifice for those that err, for they shall know both Your mercy and Your forgiveness. God preserve them from Your justice.
—*Utterances of Taminy-Osmaer, Book of the Covenant*

He'd had no trouble gaining access to Mertuile and hadn't expected to. The gatekeep was hardly going to tell Iobert Claeg's nephew and aide he wasn't welcome in the Cyne's castle.

Daimhin Feich was not in the throneroom. Neither his House Elders nor his guards seemed to be aware of his whereabouts; Saefren thought intentionally so—they seemed strangely uneasy with the subject. He had to content himself with wandering the quiet halls. When Colfre was Cyne, the castle Mertuile had been a nest of activity—scurrying servants, visiting Eiric, Ministers, merchants, House Chieftains and Elders. The most purposeful activity he'd seen here took place in the outer ward around the Deasach cannon. The Feich and their allies did seem to be preparing for *some* action.

Smelling cooking food, Saefren at last made his way to the dining rooms. The larger one was unoccupied, but in the smaller private room, a fire burned in the far hearth and a screen had been drawn around the table there to help hold in the warmth. Here, Ruadh Feich ate a solitary meal, his shadow lying long across the floor. He glanced up as Saefren entered the room, his eyes widening in surprise.

"Saefren Claeg! Good-eve. Your presence . . . astonishes me. Is your uncle with you?"

"No. I was just in the city passing time, and I thought I might have a word with your cousin, the Regent."

Ruadh sipped hot cider, watching Saefren's approach over the rim of his cup. "About?"

"Uncle was concerned about your young hostage."

Ruadh's lips pursed and he peered into the depths of his cup. "Hostage?"

"The girl, Iseabal."

"Ah, the little Wicke, you mean. How did your uncle know about her? He'd left Nairne—"

"Surely her capture wasn't a state secret. That sort of intelligence does tend to slip out."

"To the concern of Iobert Claeg?"

"We delivered the girl to Halig-liath ourselves. We're concerned with her welfare."

"Ah. Most people around here are concerned about *Daimhin's* welfare. Consorting with Wicke has never been popular with the Feich Elders. It makes them nervous. Well, you've good reason to be concerned, I think."

Saefren tensed. "Has anything happened to her? Is she well?"

Ruadh's laughter was false. "My cousin happened to her. I haven't seen her for above a week, myself. But Daimhin sees her a good deal more than is probably good for her. Under the circumstances, I can't believe she's well. I only know she's not dead . . . yet."

Saefren tried to ignore the tight, cold lump that sat in the pit of his stomach. "Where is she?"

Ruadh gestured at the ceiling with his cup, which sloshed its contents down his arm. He seemed not to notice and Saefren realized he drank something stronger than cider. "Up there, somewhere."

"Somewhere."

"Her room adjoins my cousin's. I understand that's going to change soon."

"Can you take me to her?"

"*Should* I take you to her?"

"I only want to make sure of her health."

"You were looking for my cousin. If I take you to the girl, chances are you will find him."

So much the better, Saefren thought and caressed the hilt of his sword.

Ruadh did not miss the movement. "Or, he could be with our other auspicious prisoner. The Abbod Ladhar is a Taminist, did you know that?"

"I very much doubt *that*. Ladhar is ruthless when it comes to their persecution."

"Found one of their books on him."

"One he probably lifted from the hand of a dead Taminist."

Ruadh watched the firelight trace bright tracks in the etched silver surface of his cup. "I read some of it."

Saefren did not react.

"Have you, ever?"

"No. I've heard some of their . . . doctrine, if you will. But read, no."

Ruadh merely nodded.

"The girl?" Saefren prompted.

Ruadh rose from his chair, only a little unsteady, and led from the room.

"I noticed a lot of activity in the outer ward," Saefren remarked as they negotiated the chill halls. He didn't remember Mertuile being quite so cold and dark. "Are you still planning on trekking into the Gyldan-baenn?"

"Have to. Daimhin promised we'd get them back their little demi-god."

"Isn't that foolhardy?"

"Oh, but you forget—or perhaps you don't know—my cousin is fey. Kissed by the *aidan*, overflowing with Eibhilin energies sucked from his wickish lady-friends, his enemies, and probably every other living thing within a twenty-mile radius. Cousin Daimhin can now have whatever he wants, which makes it his right, I suppose."

That had an ominous sound even to Saefren's ears. He

forced a chuckle. "I see. Will he fly over the Gyldan-baenn, then?"

"Ah, yes. On the back of a raven, I believe," Ruadh said cryptically and fell into a thoughtful silence.

Saefren could think of nothing more to say to him, and wished he had Aine-mac-Lorimer's *aidan* so he could divine the other man's thoughts.

Once on the second floor, they traversed the Royal wing. The widely-spaced doors hinted at the size of the apartments behind the tapestried and paneled walls. At the end of the broad main corridor Ruadh stopped and nodded toward a heavily ornamented door. "That's it. He's not here. He usually posts guards when he's . . . consorting with one of his Wicke."

"Can you open it?"

"No key. Cousin wears it. Like a jewel. Around his neck."

Saefren stepped forward and tried the door. Indeed, it was locked. "Iseabal?" he called softly. "Iseabal-a-Nairnecirke, are you there? Are you all right? It's Saefren Claeg."

There was no answer and Saefren felt a chill of dread trickle like ice down his back. He put his ear to the door, ignoring Ruadh Feich's opaque stare.

"Daimhin isn't a very gentle man," Ruadh commented almost absently. "Never has been. Oh, he starts out that way—soft-spoken, caressing. But somewhere between wanting and having . . . it's as if a demon takes him. Demon-Daimhin. I've heard women call him that. And those were the willing ones."

Saefren rattled the door with no result. "Damn. Look, Ruadh, I need to talk to the Regent. Have you no idea where he is?"

"Behind you?"

Saefren turned. Daimhin Feich was indeed standing behind him, flanked by two armed men in Feich colors. He shook his head, made a clucking noise with his tongue. "I come to visit my lovely guest and what do I find—she's attracted other admirers."

"Saefren was merely concerned about the good health

of your lovely guest," said Ruadh dryly. "He seems to feel some personal responsibility for it."

"Uncle was concerned that the girl not come to any harm," Saefren offered.

Daimhin Feich smiled. "Charming. Concerned about the health of a virtual stranger—a Wicke, at that. Imagine how concerned he'll be about you."

Before Saefren could react to that obvious threat and draw his sword, Feich's men were all over him, forcing him against the wall and relieving him of his weapon.

Ruadh stumbled out of the way, a stunned expression on his face. "Cousin, what in the name of—!"

"Good work, Ruadh. You've helped me capture a traitor." Feich peered into Saefren's face. "All Claeg are traitors. All Jura, all Graegam, and all Gilleas. You, sir, are also insurance. If your uncle or any of his cronies put themselves in my way, I will have you dismantled, piece by piece, and the bits sent to your family." He glanced at the guards. "Take him to the first level dungeon. There's a little tiny cell there with his name on it."

Frozen in a moment of sheer terror, Aine watched Feich's men drag Saefren Claeg away down the corridor. It took all her will not to cry out, not to drop her Cloak, not to give in to desperation and division. But there was Saefren being taken away into the unknown, and there was Iseabal ebbing into aislinn silence just on the other side of that ornately carved door. She reached for Isha, frantic, wanting to shake her to awareness, but no awareness answered her.

In the instant she hesitated, Saefren was gone from sight and Aine could only stand and quake, desperately clutching her Cloakweave. Tears started from her eyes before she could stop them. She wanted nothing more than to lie down on the dusty floor and weep.

Aine . . .

She dropped the Cloak. *Isha?*

Aine, you shouldn't be here.

Aine crossed the hall in two strides to press herself against the door of Iseabal's room. *I came to see if you were all right. Oh, but Isha, you're not all right. I've got to get you out of here.*

The flash of relief from beyond the door was swiftly smothered in concern. *Saefren Claeg was with you? I felt . . . You're afraid for him. Where is he?*

Aine visualized Feich, Ruadh and the two guards who took Saefren away. Her knees began to tremble.

Aine, you must get him out of here. Feich will murder him! What he has done to Abbod Ladhar, to me, to others—

You first, Isha. Let me just unlock this door. Let me—

No! Aine heard that cry with her ears as well as her *aidan* senses. *Aine, no! You must get Saefren away from Feich. Now! Leave me. I can't come with you.*

Leave you! No! Why?

The answer was a flood of stinging physical and mental anguish that strangled the breath in Aine's throat.

I'll carry you out. Papa always said I was built like a horse. I'll carry you and cloak both of us.

Aine, leave me. Saefren can't be left here. He's innocent of anything but trying to help us, foolish as he thought it was. Leave me! As long as Feich believes I'm of some use to him, I'll be safe. And he'll waste his time trying to drain something from me that he can never use.

Aine cowered against the door, tears burning her eyes, heart twisting in her breast. *Oh, Isha, I can't!*

Don't ever say you can't.

Taminy's words. She had said them so long ago, it seemed, at Hrofceaster. Now they came, hauntingly, from Iseabal.

I can't find Saefren. I don't know where they've taken him.

You can sense him.

He has no aidan.

Aine, please! The anguish rolled over Aine again, battering her. *Taminy is watching over me. The Meri will care for me. She's put you here to care for Saefren.*

He didn't want me to come with him. He doesn't know I'm here.

Then he'll be that much happier to see you. Now, go. Please go! And God guard you.

Oh, Isha, don't—! she began to plead, but felt the connection between them sever.

In the silence of the broad corridor, Aine crouched against Iseabal's door, quivering with fear and loss and doubt. She was not good at praying; she tended to demand things of God rather than beg them humbly. But now, here in this alien place, in this nest of enemies, she pleaded pridelessly for Iseabal's protection, for her own courage, for some sense of where Saefren Claeg was. Then she willed herself to inner silence and got to her feet.

She followed the way the guards had taken and found herself at the top of a staircase. Simple enough; she descended and found herself on the landing of a crossing corridor. She paused in the darkness and made her mind and heart be still. *Saefren.* She'd divined his thoughts before, knew their texture and tenor. Knowing the dungeons must be somewhere beneath her feet, she turned her thoughts downward, seeing in her mind's eye an aislinn mist, drifting, settling, seeking.

It was Daimhin Feich she chanced on first—a hot, bright furnace of exultation. Shuddering away from his heat, she blocked Feich from her touch. Fear—she felt that next and reached for it, thinking it must be Saefren. But it was Ruadh Feich she found at the end of that thread. No time to ponder that. Aine searched further and dipped into a cold void. Thoughts were fevered here, flinging about like snow in a blizzard. He pondered neither life nor death, but the tiny closet of a cell his captors forced him into.

Aine moved then, ever downward, clasping the strand that now bound her to Saefren Claeg. It led her to a thick door three times the width of a man, half again as tall. It was ajar and voices came to her from beyond and below.

She closed her eyes. *Grey the veil, white the shroud, black the cloud that hides me.* The flush of *aidan* that swelled beneath the duan told her no eyes could see her. She waited in the hall as the door swung open and Daimhin Feich exited with his cousin and two other kinsmen.

" . . . found ourselves a perfect hostage," Feich was saying. "Iobert Claeg may be a heretic, but he's still a Claeg. He'll do nothing that will spill one drop of his nephew's precious Claeg blood." He laughed—an action shared by all but Ruadh Feich, who glanced uneasily at his cousin before following him away to the upper reaches of Mertuile.

When they were gone, Aine swung the great door open and slipped through onto a landing atop a short flight of steps. At the bottom of the steps, she stood in a nearly square anteroom, its torchlit walls broken by a series of doorways. Voices came to her from a doorway to her right— from that place, too, a path of firelight flickered across the rough stone floor. To the left, an arched portal gaped like a black, toothless mouth. Saefren was there.

She moved into the inky corridor, pausing only long enough to allow her eyes to grow accustomed to the gloom. She felt her way along the silken, *aidan* fiber until . . . She turned and knelt at a narrow, barred doorway. So black was it within she couldn't make out Saefren's form, but she could hear his breathing—heavy and rasping. And she could feel his fear now, sharp and chill—fear of this dark, stifling place, fear of strangling.

A chill shook Aine from head to toe. Glancing to make sure she could not be seen from the anteroom, she let go the Cloakweave and wove instead a tiny ball of light that sent soft illumination into the cell. What she saw made her gasp. In a deep niche no wider than a doorway, Saefren was forced to stand, caught about the neck by a thick iron collar. Joined to the frigid stone by only a few links of heavy chain, the collar kept him pinned, motionless, head up, neck at an unnatural angle.

"Aine!" he gasped. "What—?"

"Hush! Save your breath. I'll work on the lock."

He obeyed, a thing that Aine might have found smugly pleasing under other circumstances. She focused her attention on the heavily barred door with its mechanical lock. She'd never tried to manipulate a lock before. In theory, it should be like manipulating any physical object. The only problem was, she had no idea what the inner mechanism of the lock looked like. She could not visualize the metal gears, or tumblers or whatever lay within. So, she prodded and poked with aislinn fingers, her tongue caught between her teeth, listening to Saefren's labored breathing in the darkness.

The lock defied her every attempt to open it. Finally, with her head pounding and sweat chilling her body, she gave up in complete frustration. "I can't do this," she admitted. "The mechanism is too complicated."

There was a moment of silence from within the cell, then Saefren's strangled voice said, "Then you'll . . . have to . . . leave me here."

Aine laid her forehead against the bars and fought a moment of impotent rage. First Iseabal, now Saefren. "Never say you can't," she murmured and got to her feet. "If I can't open the door, then we need to get the gaoler to open it. And the collar as well."

"How?"

"Cry out. Pretend you're choking."

"I *am* choking," he returned wryly.

"Feich doesn't want you dead. If the gaoler thinks you're choking . . . "

"Then . . . what?"

Aine grinned fiercely in the dark. "You'll see . . . I hope. Just start yelling."

He did as told, giving a convincing portrayal of a man on the verge of suffocating. So convincing was he that the cloaked Aine cringed and covered her ears. In short order, torchlight spilled onto the corridor floor and two men appeared, keys and torch in hand. Aine all but held her breath as they took quick stock of the prisoner's red face and heaving chest.

He's choking to death, Aine suggested, hoping it might help.

The chief gaoler, a Malcuim regular, slipped the key into the lock and opened the cell door. Inside, he moved to check the collar. "Bring the torch in, Olery," he demanded when his shadow fell across the clasp. His partner did as commanded, squeezing into the narrow space behind him and flattening himself against the wall to his mate's right, arm raised to throw torchlight onto the collar. Smoke from the fiery wand curled along the ceiling making both men wheeze.

The gaoler took up another key and fitted it to the collar's lock. "You Claeg are a whiny lot," he observed, giving the panting Saefren a cruel shake. "I'd let you choke, if it was me calling the plan. You've caused the Malcuim House a damn lot of grief over time. But you're worth something to Regent Feich, so I suppose I've got to let you out of this collar, eh?"

"Oh, just do it!" muttered the other guard—a Dearg. "My arm's set to fall off."

The key turned, the iron band sprang open, Saefren sagged dramatically to his knees and the torch went out. In the chaos after, Aine draped her Cloakweave over Saefren and silently begged him to recall which way the door was. There was a mad scramble, thuds, a yelp of pain and the sound of a body falling heavily to the straw-covered stone.

A moment later, Aine felt someone brush by her on hands and knees, saw the faint shimmer of aislinn energy, and reached out a hand to grasp Saefren's shoulder as he scurried by. With the other hand, she pulled the cell door to and was gratified to hear the lock spring shut. Wordlessly, she dragged Saefren to his feet and hurried him out of the corridor.

He stopped her as they were crossing the anteroom. "What about the others?" he whispered, just making himself heard over the shouts of the captive gaolers. "There are other Taminists here in the next corridor."

"No time. When they find their keys—" The sharp clink of metal was followed by the feel of a ring and rods being pressed into her hand.

"I'm not entirely useless," Saefren told her.

"But if we free them, they may be killed trying to escape. I can't cloak them all."

"Can't, Aine Red? Can't? I didn't think you knew the word. And if we leave them here, they'll *surely* be killed."

They freed every prisoner in the Mertuile gaol block. And Aine did cloak them through lamplit halls and dark, past guards and guests and gatekeeps. She did not think about those left behind until she and Saefren and their two dozen or so charges were safe on the dark wharves above Saltbridge.

But later, as they took secret passage upriver in boats piloted by the father and brothers of a Carehouse Aelder Prentice, her mind and heart flew to them—Abbod Ladhar, whose secret dungeon they could not find, and Iseabal, whose own body now served as a prison. Sitting at the rail, staring sightlessly over the black flow of the Haligtyne, Aine did not even realize tears were falling till a hand brushed them from her cheek. She blinked and looked up into Saefren Claeg's face.

"For Iseabal?" he asked and she nodded. He crouched next to her at the rail. "She told you the Meri would take care of her, you said." Again, she nodded. "Then it seems to me you must believe her." He put a hand on her shoulder, its warmth melting through the fog-damp layers of her clothing. "Have faith, Aine." He gave the shoulder a squeeze, then turned his eyes out to the river.

She followed suit, wondering a little that he should be consoling her with advice on faith.

"Oh, and thank you," he murmured, eyes still on the water.

"Welcome," she whispered and laid her head wearily on the rail.

Sleep. Dear God, but he wanted sleep. Long ago he'd ceased to feel his legs and feet and the water had spread through his clothing like oil through a wick, chilling him to the marrow. What parts of him were not numb ached horribly.

When the water had risen to his chest he had been forced to stand. His legs had barely held him then; his sodden clothing freighted him down, the chains he wore tugged at him, there was no wall for him to lean against. It had been almost a relief when the water level reached his chest a second time—it had at least buoyed him up somewhat.

Now he sat as the icy liquid fled, knowing he could not survive another high tide. He had prayed much, wondered if the Taminists had had sufficient time to escape or hide, and strove to make his peace with God. He could now admit he did not understand all that had transpired since Taminy-a-Cuinn had been brought to Creiddylad. He now realized he had been swept along on the currents of events he could in no way control—like this insidious, freezing tide he was powerless to stop from sucking the life out of him. What a petty conceit to think he was master of his fate or anyone else's—he was not.

He pondered his own actions, realizing he had been at least in part responsible for Daimhin Feich's rise to power. Responsible, too, perhaps, for Cyne Colfre's death. A death he now suspected had been at Feich's hand. And he wondered if, in warning Fhada of Feich's intention to raid Carehouse, he had paid on his debt of sin or added to it.

"Do you doubt that choice, Ladhar?"

He looked up. The Osraed Bevol sat, not three feet away, perched, it seemed, on a jag of native rock—or perched above it in the ether. He shimmered within an Eibhilin veil, his Meri Kiss bright as the first evening star. And what surprised Ladhar most of all was his own lack of surprise at seeing him. "Ah, Shade, so you now haunt this spot, do you?"

"No more than you do."

"I'm chained here by these." Ladhar raised his wrist manacles, rattling the chains that anchored him to the floor. "What binds you here?" He glanced around, uneasily, certain the receding water would reveal Bevol's mouldering corpse.

"My body? You won't find it. It's gone the way of all flotsam." The spirit, if that's what it was, inclined its head toward the outer wall of the dungeon. "Well, there may be a few bits left. The grating down below is a bit clogged in places."

Ladhar blanched, though he doubted he could become

much more bloodless. "This is the effect of exposure, I suppose," he murmured, "or hunger. Perhaps both."

"You are what binds me here, as you put it," Bevol told him. "You're still uncertain that what you did for Fhada and his companions was the Meri's will and pleasure."

"Surely, you understand my uncertainty."

"I do. But be consoled, Ladhar. It was what you were purposed to do. And it was a great act of compassion and faith."

Ladhar's shivers were soul deep now and had nothing to do with the cold. "On your word, I'm to accept this? On the say-so of an apostate's ghost, I'm to believe that aiding Taminy-a-Cuinn and her brood of heretics is my Mistress's pleasure? And that, further—that Taminy is . . . the Sign of the Meri among us?"

"Not on *my* word, brother. On the word of the water." A spectral hand gestured at the smooth, dark expanse between them—a surface in which he cast no reflection, gleaming though he seemed to be.

Before Ladhar could respond—dear Meri, but his brain was slow—the ghostly Bevol was gone.

The word of the water? Ladhar shivered, yawned and peered down into the glassy flood. His own face peered up at him from the briny mirror. A face lit by its own light— an emerald star fixed at the center of its ample brow. He marveled. It was decades since it had been so bright. He recalled the words of the Taminist girl whose life he had spared—that she had known the Taminist Osraed by their Meri Kisses. "Like your own, sir," she'd said, "but golden."

Something warm and moist trickled down his cheek. He pressed numb fingers to his brow and remembered mornings he had looked in the mirror and barely been able to see it. He took a deep, pain-wracked breath. "A benediction?" he asked the darkness. "Am I absolved?"

The tide sucked at him, gurgled among the rocks, hissed through the grating. And when he had despaired of an answer, Bevol's voice came to him again: "Sleep, Ladhar. You've earned your rest."

"At dawn?" Ruadh wasn't sure he'd heard his cousin right. He blinked at him blearily and shivered in the cold of his room. "That's only hours away."

"I'm well aware," Daimhin told him. "I said dawn—I meant dawn. I trust you'll be fit enough to lead your men?"

"Yes, of course, I'll be fit. But . . . you can't have heard from Sorn Saba yet."

"We've no time and no choice, Ruadh. Ladhar is dead and that mewling cleirach hasn't been able to find the Stone at Ochanshrine, so I must assume the Taminists have it and it's on its way to Hrofceaster. I've lost Claeg—obviously through Taminist Weavings—and my pretty guest's Eibhilin powers seem to have dried up. We've no recourse but to go to El-Deasach."

"But the Banarigh—"

"Has either said 'yes' or 'no.' If it's 'yes,' we get on the trail with her reinforcements that much faster. If it's 'no,' then I can personally change her mind."

Ruadh grimaced. "So certain, are you?"

"I'm certain I've nothing to gain by hanging about here, waiting for the spring thaw. We ride to El-Deasach."

"And Creiddylad?"

"Will be held well enough by a minimum force. We'll leave most of the Malcuim men, about half the Dearg, and enough of our own to hold Mertuile. Put your best lieutenant in charge of the garrison here. Elder Maslin will be in residence, so he'll likely want some of his own men about as well." Daimhin quirked an eyebrow at his cousin. "Does that meet with your approval, Marschal?"

"Aye. Seems logical enough." Truth to tell, Ruadh was glad not to have had to think it out for himself.

"But . . . ?"

"I only wonder if . . . " Ruadh was reluctant to voice his thoughts. "I wonder if you shouldn't seek some compromise with the Taminists. Bring Airleas Malcuim home on their—"

"*No compromise!*" Daimhin smote the table where Ruadh sat huddled in his night clothes. "The Osmaer will be *mine*! Both the woman and her namesake."

Ruadh winced and rubbed his temples. "And when they are yours?"

Daimhin straightened and moved to warm his hands at the meager blaze in the chamber hearth. "I've been giving that much thought. It occurs to me that I might consolidate my hold on Mertuile if I were to marry the widowed Cwen."

Ruadh shook his head . . . slowly. "You think Toireasa will have you?"

"I think," Daimhin said, fingering Bloodheart's leather pouch, "she would be enchanted with the idea."

"I've heard she's barren."

"Taminy has healed worse conditions."

"You *have* been giving this thought, haven't you? Of course, once your heir is of educable age, I suppose Airleas Malcuim's life will be worthless."

Daimhin smiled at him over one shoulder. "I haven't thought quite that far ahead," he said, then let the smile fall. "See to it that your men are ready to march at dawn."

CHAPTER 18

And when my lovers ask you about Me, then know that I
am near. I hear the prayer of those that cry to Me. Let them
hear My Voice and trust in Me. And let them be led aright.
—*Osraed Ochan, Book of the Covenant, #99*

✦　　　✦　　　✦

Today Airleas's solitary walk fetched him up in Airdnasheen again, gazing around at the snow-covered roofs
of the clutter of houses and tiny shops. There were no
streets as such in the village, but only narrow avenues paved
with slate or granite block that converged on a central village
circle. In the warmer seasons there was an open air market here; now there was only a large patch of snow much
used by the village children.

Airleas watched them cavort among the drifts, building them up and exploding them gleefully in turns. They
glanced at him cautiously, never full on, making him feel
alien. He turned away, breathing deeply of the frosty,
smoke-laden air and caught a whiff of something baking.
The aroma drew him across the village circle to the
Backstere's shop, the carefree laughter of the children following him.

The shop was warm and smelled of cinnamon and nut-
meg and apples and . . . He gave up trying to catalogue
the smells and drank in the wonderful, if limited, array
of buns and breads and little cakes. From behind a long
table in the center of the front room, the Backstere smiled
at his visitor.

"Fresh cinnamon baps today, lad," he said.

Airleas liked that— "lad." It made him feel . . . normal. He grinned at the Backstere. "I'd like two of those, please. And a sugar cake." He held out a handful of coins, which the Backstere took after a moment of hesitation. Airleas gathered up his prizes, stuffed the baps in his pocket and began nibbling on the sugar cake. The door opened behind him, letting a draft of cold air into the shop and jingling the little silver bell tied to the latch. He turned to see Eyslk's mother, a basket on her arm.

Seeing him, the Mistress an-Caerluel smiled and inclined her head. "Good-day, lord."

"Good-day, mistress," he said and found that he also liked being called "lord."

Mistress an-Caerluel bid the Backstere good-day and conducted her business with him, trading eggs and herbs for baked goods. Then she turned her attention to Airleas once again. "Are you enjoying your stay here, lord?"

Enjoying? Airleas had never thought of his tenure here as something to be enjoyed as much as something to be suffered. "There are things I like about Airdnasheen," he admitted diplomatically. "But . . . I wish I could do more."

"Do more?" repeated Deardru, her dark eyes glinting humorously. "And what might a boy your age do more of?"

Airleas drew himself up, mustering his dignity. "I'm Cyneric, mistress. I should be doing more to . . . to take back my father's throne—to set things right in Caraid-land."

Deardru smiled and shook her head. "How like my first husband you are. Raenulf was ever ready to rise up and defend the land of his ancestors—single-handedly, if necessary."

"You speak of Raenulf Hageswode, mistress? The Ren Catahn's elder brother?"

"Aye. He was a brave man. A brave boy, too." She smiled again. "Like you."

Airleas flushed at the praise. "How old was he at his Crask-an-duine?"

Deardru began moving toward the door, drawing Airleas with her smile. "Well, let me see." She opened the door, letting in a gust of chill wind, and stepped out into the snow with Airleas at her heels. "I was thirteen at the time; I suppose he must have been almost fourteen. I'll never forget how proud of him I was. I knew he would be my husband even then."

"Almost fourteen," Airleas murmured. "Older than I am. Catahn was only twelve when he did it. I guess that's why he's Ren."

Deardru's face clouded momentarily. "Raenulf was . . . more headstrong than Catahn. He was a man of action. Where Catahn was inclined to sit and think and agonize over his decisions, Raenulf was impulsive, even as a boy. The village elders and the holt Council thought him brash, even cocky. But he wasn't. He was merely braver than they were, more willing to take chances for what he believed in." She glanced at Airleas obliquely. "I imagine you're a bit like that—ready and willing to fight for what you believe to be true. Ready to act on your beliefs."

"I am," said Airleas. "I *am* ready to fight—to take action, only . . ."

"Only?"

Airleas studied the sloping, snow-covered lane that led toward Deardru-an-Caerluel's house. How to put it into words . . . "Only I'm not really ready yet. Not for the kind of fight I'll need to wage."

Deardru's eyebrows rose. "And who tells you this?"

"Well, Catahn and Osraed Wyth and mother and . . . and Taminy."

She shook her head. "So little faith they have in you?"

"Oh no, it's not that. I'm *not* ready. I've so much to learn—from all of them. I used to think about . . . sneaking away. I even tried it once. I was going to make my way to Creiddylad—raise an army on my way." He laughed.

"Now, why do you laugh? I think that's very brave. That's the sort of thing Raenulf would have done. It's the sort of thing a Cyne might do."

"But, I didn't even have a sword, mistress! Or know how to use one."

"What matter? You have far greater strength than a sword arm—I can tell." She looked at him very directly, eyes assessing. "I have my share of the *aidan*, you know. And I can tell that you do too. You're a fountain of it, Cyneric Airleas. Strong, like Raenulf, and brave. You're more ready than you think. More man than many that have made the Crask-an-duine." They had come to Deardru's house by now and entered a small fenced yard. "I have something I want to give you, Cyneric Airleas, if you'll accept a gift from me."

"I . . . What sort of . . . ?"

"Wait a moment and I'll show you." She went ahead of him to the little house and disappeared within while he stood in the tiny front yard, wondering at how four people could live in a place that was no bigger than his mother's suite of rooms at Mertuile. He glanced up over the house's eaves at the stark castle molded to the mountainside. Even there, his world was extensive, if lacking in luxury.

The door swung wide and the Mistress an-Caerluel reappeared. She held out her hand and placed in his an amulet hung on a thong of braided hair.

"A catamount," he murmured. "That's the Hageswode totem."

"Aye. It belonged to Raenulf. It will draw courage to you and increase and preserve your valor."

He rubbed the hair between his fingers. "Whose is this?"

She smiled. "Mine. It will bind the protection to you while the amulet helps you focus your *aidan* and your courage."

"But it was your husband's, mistress. Are you—?"

She closed his fingers around the totem. "Take it. It should go to another young man so like Raenulf."

"But shouldn't Eyslk have it?"

"Eyslk is Catahn's daughter now, more than she is mine. Take it, with my blessing."

He thanked her, amazed by the gesture, bemused by her words, but feeling suddenly much older than his nearly thirteen years. And much closer to his Crask-an-duine.

He was standing there alone, studying his prize when someone called his name from the lane. He looked up to see Broran by the narrow gate and quickly settled the amulet over his head.

"'The Ren Catahn is looking all over for you," Broran informed him when he emerged into the road. "He wants to see what you've learned of swordsmanship. I think he's got a few things he wants to show you himself."

Airleas caught his breath. "Do you think I'm ready to learn from the Ren?"

Broran shrugged and began walking toward Hrofceaster. "Ready as you'll ever be, I reckon. You're not bad," he added. "You learn pretty fast. When you want to."

They walked for a while in silence, then Broran said, "So, what words did the Mistress an-Caerluel have for you?"

None of your business, was what he wanted to say, but he wanted Broran's good will and so, he said, "She told me about her husband, Raenulf. What a brave man he was . . ." He shrugged.

"What was it she gave you?"

Reluctantly, Airleas drew the amulet from beneath his jacket and was rewarded when Broran's tawny eyes nearly started out of his head.

"That's a Hageswode totem."

Airleas nodded. "I know. She said it would draw protection to me and focus my courage. She said I reminded her of Raenulf Hageswode."

Broran snorted. "You'd do better," he said, "to focus your brain. Courage is a grand thing, but a well-taught *aidan* is better and wisdom in using it better still."

Broran was right, of course, and Airleas could make no comeback.

"Raenulf Hageswode," Broran told him as if compelled to explain his advice, "was a wild man. He cared naught for wisdom or learning or patience or anything but danger and a good fight."

"Catahn never said that of him."

"Catahn wouldn't. But it's true. Catahn was always pulling him from the fire, but Raenulf liked the heat too well. Died because of it."

"You know so much," Airleas remarked, half-taunting.

"Ought to. My da served with Raenulf up at Moidart. They were cousins. Da was there when Raenulf died.

Brought his body back and all. Brought *that*—" He gestured at the amulet bobbing over Airleas's breast. "—back as well, to the brave man's widow."

Airleas swallowed. "Catahn said he was a brave man. That he died in battle."

"Oh, aye, he did that. And he started the battle that killed him. Took an encampment of Deasach corsairs in the foothills. Single-handed."

"Single—!" Airleas gasped. "But—"

"Sought out their camp in the middle of the night and slit two Deasach throats before the alarm was raised. Then off he ran—or tried to. Meant to lead the corsairs back to his comrades, Da figures, only he never made it. Of course his comrades tried to rescue him. Three of them died too."

Airleas bristled, not wanting Broran to be right about his newest hero. "Says your da."

"Says my da," Broran repeated emphatically. "You know you shouldn't wear that without showing it to Taminy. Mistress an-Caerluel is no special friend of hers . . . or Catahn's."

"Oh, and does your da know all about that as well?"

Broran reached out a hand and stopped him roughly, and Airleas expected the youth to mount some defense of his father. Instead, with an expression sober as any he'd ever seen on Osraed Wyth's face, Broran said, "Take the amulet to Taminy, Airleas. Let her decide whether it's a Weaving you should carry about you."

They had left before dawn, a long column of mounted men, silent amid the pale jingle of bits, the creak of leather, the muted *tack-tack* of cloth-wrapped hooves. Once on the beach outside Creiddylad's west-facing Sea Gate they had paused only long enough to unbind their horses' feet, then moved off smartly southward, the roar and rush of surf covering the thunder of their movement.

Now, as the Sun climbed in the sky, they were miles from the city, streaming south along the shore at a brisk trot. Very soon they would be crossing Madaidh land, and Daimhin Feich gave some thought to attempting to add

some Madaidh men to his forces. But the Madaidh, he
knew, were stubborn, loners. It was enough that they could
be counted on for their self-serving neutrality. They would
provide a physical buffer between his forces and the
Taminists in the hills beyond Creiddylad. The aislinn buffer
would be provided by Coinich Mor.

The sound of a horse moving at a gallop through moist
sand brought Feich's attention to the dunes along their
landward flank. Beside him, his cousin Ruadh roused himself from a near stupor and glanced away toward the rock-
strewn sands where a horseman in Feich colors had now
appeared.

He grunted. "It's Correch."

The rider was upon them in a moment, reining in his
mount alongside Ruadh. "The caravan is well away, lords,"
he reported. "It rolls over an hour behind on the cliff road.
The cannon slows things up a bit. Surely, we don't plan
to take it up into the mountains with us?"

"We won't need it in the mountains," Daimhin told his
kinsman. "We have stronger weapons. But I promised to
return the cannon to the Deasach, and I keep promises
to prospective allies, Correch. It shows good faith."

Correch shrugged. "It's nothing to me, I'm sure. As long
as it's not holding up the main column. It only seems we
might have needed it to defend Mertuile."

Ruadh chuckled, rubbing his eyes. "It's not a defensive
weapon, Correch. That cannon is intended for breaching
walls and laying waste to villages. Which makes me wonder a bit why the Deasach had it cast."

Daimhin raised his eyebrows. "To attack Caraid-land,
you suppose? You could be right. And with Colfre's mili-
taristic designs, they may have had reason to suspect they
needed it. But I have taken steps to see that they do not
need to fear us. We will not war with the Deasach when
it is better to be their allies. Better to be on the butt end
of that cannon than to stand before its muzzle." Glancing ahead, he caught sight of a rune post. "We're almost
within Madaidh lands. Prepare to run up the standards. I
want them to know who crosses their territory."

They did mount their standards shortly after that—the Feich's black raven on its field of yellow and, flanking it, the Malcuim and Dearg pennants—clasped hands on green, and a red hand on a white and yellow field respectively. But going before them was the standard Feich most wanted to catch the Taminist eyes when at last they reached Hrofceaster. There was no banner to play on the stiff breeze. At the top of the long, brass-jointed pole gleamed the Star Chalice—the Cup of Cynes—from which every legitimate ruler of Caraid-land had drunk his oath of office. Filled to the crystalline rim with sunlight, its delicate facets overflowed, spilling rainbows into the morning air. Beneath it in a gold and silver casket rode the false Osmaer. But only Daimhin Feich and a handful of his confidantes knew it was false, and they could be trusted not to speak of it. The Madaidh would not know, nor would the Deasach. He was riding to crown a Cyne at Airdnasheen; it remained to be seen whether the Cyne would be Malcuim or Feich.

By late afternoon it became obvious that the Madaidh were not interested in his train. Nor did anyone else seem to be, though they were watched after by fishermen and villagers at times during the day. Just before twilight, they bore inland, crossing the dunes and low hills to meet the shore road. Ahead, still at great distance, was the seaward tail of the Gyldan-baenn and the border between Caraid-land and El-Deasach.

They camped the night in the heart of Madaidh, but the only word from that House was a messenger sent to assure them safe passage and God-speed. It nettled Daimhin Feich that Rodri Madaidh could not be bothered to visit him face to face, but Coinich Mor was there to absorb his ill humor and offer comfort.

They were on the road the second day at dawn, and it was just shy of midday when riders were seen to be approaching from the south. It wasn't long before the flowing black robes of Deasach corsairs could be discerned. The handful of riders—a mere half-dozen—spurred their mounts forward along the road, advancing on the column at a gallop.

Ruadh drew his sword and started to call up a guard, but Daimhin stopped him with a leisurely hand.

"Stay cousin. It's our friend, Shak Saba."

"How can you be sure?"

Daimhin smiled, feeling the *aidan's* power ripple deliciously in his breast. "Simply know that I can. Halt the troops."

Ruadh shouted and raised his gloved hand. Behind him, the cavalcade came to a ragged halt. The advancing riders were upon them in moments. As Daimhin had said, they were lead by Sorn Saba, who pulled up beside them, a look of puzzlement on his face.

"Regent Daimhin! Why do you ride for El-Deasach? I expected to find you at Mertuile awaiting my return."

"Much has happened since you left, Sorn. Let us ride away a bit and I'll tell you of it." He reined his horse aside a measure of yards, Sorn Saba following him. When they were out of earshot of the men, Daimhin pulled up and turned to the Deasach. "Since you left Mertuile, the Osmaer Crystal has been taken from Creiddylad by Taminists."

"Your Great Crystal stolen?" murmured Sorn. "But how?"

"Our Abbod turned traitor and put it into their hands. He paid with his life, but that doesn't answer the fact that the Stone is gone—presumably on its way to Airdnasheen. I felt we could wait no longer. If your sister has refused our alliance, I must seek to change her mind personally. Tell me, Sorn, what is her answer?"

Sorn smiled. "As I suspected, she was eager to accept your plea for alliance once I explained your situation . . . and added my own plea. Of course, there is still the matter of the gifts . . . " His eyes swept the column, seeking sign of the tribute.

Daimhin smiled wryly. "Of course. A matter you may take charge of personally, if you wish. The caravan bearing my gifts to your sister . . . and yourself . . . is some distance behind us on this road."

The youth's eyes gleamed. "Some distance?"

"Half-day's ride, no more. The cannon determined their pace."

Sorn grinned. "I suppose I shall just have to take charge of the train and see if I can speed it up a bit. Half-day's journey, you say."

"Perhaps less."

"Then I shall be with the beautiful Iseabal tonight in my black tent. I will show her paradise," he promised.

Daimhin chuckled. "That ought to provide her a welcome change. I imagine she's weary of hell."

"Surely, you belittle your own charm, friend Daimhin."

"Charm? I made no attempt to show her any."

The boy made a clucking sound with his tongue. "An oversight, my friend. One may often have by charm what he cannot take by force."

The remark echoed in Daimhin Feich's head long after Sorn Saba and his men had galloped away toward Creiddylad with a Feich escort. Even now he felt suspicion curl in the back of his mind. Perhaps he had let the young Deasach fool him. Perhaps the boy had hidden fey powers of his own and had manipulated Feich into letting the Taminist girl go. Perhaps the boy would now draw from her the power he had been denied. And perhaps he was just overly full of suspicion. Sorn Saba's philosophical comment might have been just that—the romantic ruminations of a lusty young man. But Daimhin Feich could not help but hear words behind the words and wondered if the Deasach fancied himself able to charm from Iseabal-a-Nairnecirke something more than willing surrender to his lovemaking.

When they camped tonight, he decided, he would ask Coinich Mor if there was any way he could know for certain.

For two days Iseabal had slept, rocked in the luxurious confines of her gaudy little wagon. She had wakened hungry once and been given some corn cakes and honey with hot tea. Some part of her registered that the food was delicious and nourishing, but she didn't care. She was exhausted of mind and body, drained of spirit. On the second evening, early, she woke again, sensing the stillness of the wagon and the bustle of activity around it.

She gathered her senses, pulled them back from some half-lucid dream in which she walked the woods and hills of home, unfettered and cleansed. The wagon rocked gently and someone parted the rearward curtains and entered. It was not the solid Feich matron who had been tending her; the silhouette was too slender and decidedly male. She tensed, jerking upright on her fleece-covered mattress.

The figure raised a hand. "Please, don't take fright. It's only me—Sorn."

She relaxed, but only slightly. The young Deasach had visited her once at Mertuile. She had been terrified of him at first, but the warm voice had soothed her and she had sat with him at the fireside, drinking mulled cider and talking. He had told wonderful stories of his boyhood in the court of his father, of his sister's coronation upon the loss of their parents in a storm at sea, of his falcon and pet lynx. She, in turn, had spoken of Nairne and her family, of Taminy and Aine. He had seemed pleased to listen. The cider had the potency of wine and she carried no memory beyond the warm fire and Sorn's watchful black eyes.

"Poor child," he said. He'd called her that before, too, though he was not more than a year or two older than she. "Poor child, you look spent. Shall I leave you to sleep?"

"I only just woke," she said. "I've slept for days, I think."

"Then you must be hungry, yes?" At her nod, "I'll have dinner set out for you in my tent. But first, you must refresh yourself. A bath, yes? A hot bath. Scented with the petals of desert roses. Would you like that?"

"I would, thank you. Is . . . is Daimhin Feich . . . ?"

Sorn came closer to the edge of her pallet, his long, slender fingers prying hers from the fleece covering she unwittingly wrung. "No, no, dear Iseabal. I have saved you from Feich. He will trouble you no more—I swear it."

She didn't believe him for a moment. Surely there was nowhere in the universe where Daimhin Feich was not. He had been within her body, her mind; he was in her dreams. She had all but suffocated her *aidan* in fear of his loathsome touch—in fear that he could truly turn it to his own use. "You try to trick me. He's here."

He gripped her hands more tightly. "No! I promise you, he is not. Listen, Iseabal—I made a bargaining with Feich. The aid of the Deasach I made in part dependent on his granting me your care. You are in my keeping now, Iseabal. Feich is set on other aims. If you touch my mind, you'll see I tell the truth. Trust me, Iseabal. Am I not speaking truly?"

He sat beside her, silent for a moment and, at last, she put out a tiny feeler of sense. Feich . . . was ahead of them on the shore rode, riding post haste to El-Deasach.

She made herself relax. "Feich will reach El-Deasach before we do."

He nodded. "By days, perhaps. And by the time we reach my sister's capital, he will be so busy with his great plans he will not even notice you." He put a hand to her face. "He will not lay hands on you again."

She put her hand over his in a wave of gratitude. "Thank you. I'm in your debt."

"He terrifies you so?"

She shuddered. Terror was such a weak word when it came to Feich and his appetites. She had only just ceased to feel bruised and torn. Sorn was reading her face in the twilight leaking through the curtains behind him. He shook his head. "A monster, that one. I will try to help you exorcise his demon. You are an open wound. I promise you this: in my hands, you will heal."

She was bathed in scented water, dressed in a soft billowing gown of pale saffron silk with a warm felt overcoat of cinnamon, and taken to a black tent at the heart of the camp. It was a large tent. It was clearly intended for more than one person, yet Sorn Saba was its only occupant. Upon a carpet of thick fleeces, lay a single, low pallet, its mattress thick and soft. It was there they sat before a large, brass brazier and ate spicy Deasach food and drank spicy Deasach karfa. The tent was golden with lamplight and ornamentation—a mask and odd dancing figurines. The warmed air smelled pleasantly of food and spice and incense from the coals.

They spoke, at length, of many things. She asked about

the golden mask and figurines and Sorn told her of ancient ritual and belief. This was his father's death mask, and these, his family's patron spirit, Jamla, known for her grace and passion on the battlefield, in the dance, in love. Sorn had added this last, glancing at her shyly.

Fruit was brought, and wine, which Iseabal refused; the *waljan* did not drink intoxicants, she explained, but the karfa was lovely—wonderful. He ordered that a fresh pot be brought. The evening passed gently, pleasantly—but the honeyed fruit and hot karfa seemed to take its toll on Isha's reserves of energy. Heavy-eyed and heavy-headed she heard less and less of what Sorn said, understood her own answers not at all.

He, solicitous, massaged her hands, her neck and shoulders, speaking to her softly all the while in that sweet, warm, patient voice. His mother used to massage his aching muscles with scented oil, he told her, and then she was being so massaged.

She could name no point at which she realized she was naked in the golden glow of the brazier, her skin glistening with oils. No moment when she realized her senses were no longer hers to command, when she knew the fruit and the karfa—possibly all the food—had been laced with intoxicants, though none as potent as Sorn's voice, explaining this and that, gently ordering her body to comply with his. She knew only that in the end, what Sorn Saba coerced from her was no different than what Feich demanded. It was less painfully gotten, that was all.

Sometime in the black of night, she came back to herself and was lost immediately to confusion. Chaos broke like ocean waves beyond the black walls of the tent, bearing a flotsam of curses, cries and the metallic clash of swords.

Beside her, Sorn jerked to awareness, scrambling for clothing. His hand fell heavily on her shoulder. "Light!" he whispered urgently. "Make light! Now!" He shook her.

Shivering with fear, she cupped her hand and brought an inyx to mind; a tiny ball of light formed in the palm of her hand. In its glow, Sorn's eyes were huge and wild.

He had risen, pulled on his leggings and was scrabbling

about his saddle for a weapon when the tent flap parted, admitting a swarm of light and two men dressed in cloaks of deep crimson with edging of patterned yellow. One stood with sword drawn, the other carried a light-globe atop a wooden staff. Iseabal stared, trying to comprehend who these Weavers of light might be.

Sorn came up from a crouch, a sword in one hand and what looked like a tiny cannon in the other. The leader of the marauders raised his free hand. "Put down the weapon, boy. We've come only for the girl."

But far from pacifying Sorn Saba, the words inflamed him. His face twisted in a leer of rage, he fired the little cannon. It discharged with a roar and a flash of fire, shattering the light-globe and plunging the tent into darkness. Iseabal screamed as Sorn leapt upon her, pressing her to his side. She felt cold metal at her throat. "Hex them!" he cried. "Set a spell on them!"

Movement ceased and a voice out of the dark said, "Iseabal, I am Rodri Madaidh. I mean no harm to you. Here is my proof." From the place where the voice rose, a light appeared in the shape of a star—a *gytha*—on the palm of this stranger's hand.

Seeing it, Iseabal sobbed in relief. But it was a short-lived relief. Sorn's sword bit into her neck and his body shook with fear and rage. His intention was clear. She raised her marked palm to his face. A flash of Eibhilin fire flared from it and died. Sorn cried out and flinched, and Iseabal twisted away from him, purple flames dancing before her eyes. His sword lashed the darkness where she had been, and in a sudden flurry of motion, blade met blade.

Sobbing, Iseabal cringed by the tent wall, listening to the sounds of a battle that was over almost as soon as it had begun. When another light-globe was at last brought into the tent, Sorn Saba lay dead upon the floor of his tent, his blood soaking the fleeces.

Iseabal could only sit and stare at his body until Rodri Madaidh came to her side, his bloodied sword sheathed. He placed a cloak about her and knelt at her side. "I'm sorry, child," he said. "I hadn't meant to kill him."

"I thought he was a friend," Iseabal murmured irrelevantly.

The Madaidh encircled her trembling shoulders with his arm and brought her to her feet. "Even the *aidan* can be lied to," he observed, "as it also can lie. Now, we must be away from here. Your Mistress is anxious for your return."

CHAPTER 19

Beware, beware that you never seek revenge, even against those who cry for your life's blood. Beware, again, that you offend not anyone, even if he is wicked or wishes you harm. Never look upon the souls, turn your eyes to their Creator. Never look down at the dust; look upward, instead, and see the brilliance of the Sun, which causes even the darkest earth to gleam with light.

—*Utterances of the Osraed Gartain, #27*

❖   ❖   ❖

The city of Kansbar glittered like a jewel between beach and sandy hills. It was a city of light—polished stone of red, white, grey and gold gleamed from the facade of every major building. With evening, the streets warmed with illumination cast from bowls of liquid fire ensconced on the walls of buildings or hanging from metal posts. Daimhin Feich had been taken with its beauty for the first several hours he and his entourage gazed upon it from a balcony in the palace of Deasach's ruling family. But, as he awaited the presence of Lilias Saba, the beauty cloyed and he felt only impatience.

He and Ruadh and their contingent of elders had been ushered to a room of such alien opulence as to make Mertuile, sumptuous as it was, pale in comparison. And there they had been stabled for hours, fed on strange dishes by elegant servants, waiting for the Banarigh Lilias to greet them. When Feich was certain he must begin making rude demands or go mad, her castellan arrived to usher them into the throneroom—if it could be called that, for there

335

was no throne, only a dais with a billowing couch and an extravagance of pillows, all wildly colored. There was no one on the colorful cloud, and Feich found he once more had time to admire the chamber and take in its opulence.

It struck him then, as he eyed banners and streamers and garlands of rich-hued silk against snow white and sand walls, that this was exactly the sort of tactic he would use to deal with those he wished to impress with both his riches and his arrogance. The thought aroused equal parts irritation and amusement and he laughed aloud, drawing odd looks from his own party and the palace guards as well.

The Banarigh entered then, and Daimhin Feich's hilarity died in his throat. In this room of dancing color, she was a dark, mysterious jewel—a jet, an onyx. The gown she wore was the black of a starling's wing, shimmering from emerald to amethyst with her every move, making it appear that her waist-length hair carried the same shifting colors. And, as she mounted the dais and sat upon her couch, Feich realized that, through some artful use of dye, it did.

She was smiling at him, acknowledging the bold caress of his eyes. Her full lips parted in a gesture that suggested thirst and she said, in a voice like dark, red wine, "You are Daimhin Feich."

All others were excluded from that gaze and Feich gladly let them fade. "I am. And I have no need to assure myself that you are the Raven. Your portrait—I carry it with me—cannot but insult you. It lies in saying you are merely beautiful."

She laughed—a deep, throaty ripple of sound that heated Feich's ears. "Flatterer."

"I would love to flatter you more, Raven, but we have come on an errand of great urgency."

She held up one bronze hand. "Do you need these others to speak of your urgency, Regent Feich?"

He glanced at the Dearg Chieftain, the Malcuim Elder and Ruadh. "No. Not at all."

"Then come. Let us speak privately." She rose from her couch-throne and moved before him to a set of marvelous doors inset with panes of smooth, filmy crystal. None of the guards about the dais moved a muscle. She turned back at the glazen doors and looked to her castellan. "See to the comfort of my guests and their men. House the Elders in the palace, along with such private servants as they may require."

The man bowed smartly and moved to usher Feich's associates from the chamber.

Raven-Lilias was also moving again, through the doors into the corridor beyond. Feich followed, restraining an eagerness that made his innards tremble. The corridor into which he passed was extraordinary. Stone, cut to the thickness of a man's arm, formed arches of iridescent white that crossed and recrossed overhead as if woven by a giant's hands. Between the graceful arcs, through cunningly shaped glass, the night sky shone, alive with stars. The outer wall of the corridor was made of the same transparent stuff, and through it Feich could see the streets of Kansbar sloping away to the moonlit sea. Along the length of this incredible, gleaming tunnel, plants of verdant green, bearing huge, scented flowers, draped or billowed or grew stately from polished brass containers.

Lilias the Raven began to walk along the way, beckoning Feich to follow. "Now, speak to me, Daimhin Feich." Her accent was thicker than her brother's—a thing of great charm to her companion, who smiled at her and begged her to call him 'Daimhin.' She agreed with a slight inclination of her head, a shimmering rainbow ripple of hair.

"You know I have need of your aid."

She nodded. "You need men of war and safe passage. Explain this to me. Sorn has little grasp of statehood. He spoke of sorcery, of the kidnap of your Cyne."

"Then your brother told you about the Wicke, Taminy."

"Yes. An evil woman, from his account, who holds your Cyneric against his will . . . And I should grant you my help—why?"

Taken aback, Feich frowned. He hadn't expected to have to justify himself on the most basic of issues. "Taminy is also a grave danger to you, Raven, and to El-Deasach. She will not stop at Caraid-land. If she comes to power—"

"Oh, yes, yes. All this I see. But this is all politic. Why shall I, Lilias, aid you, Daimhin?"

He stopped and turned to her. "Raven, may I—?"

"Lilias, may I . . . " she corrected.

"Lilias . . . may I be honest with you?"

"I would prefer this."

"You are, without doubt, the most exotic, the most beautiful woman I have ever met. I feel . . . forgive me . . . a great attraction to you. An affinity. A connection. I can only pray you feel a similar bond, and hope you will aid me because of that."

She smiled, enigmatic, and said, "You, too, march beneath the banner of the Raven. There is a sign in that, I think. I *feel*."

"My family name in the old tongue means Raven."

"Clearly a sign." Her smile broadened and she moved ahead of him a little, crooking her finger. To the end of the hallway they traveled, side by side, and entered a round chamber with a ceiling as transparent as the air. Stars like chips of crystal studded the vault of sky beyond. Beneath the bowl of stars, lit subtly and draped in silks, was a nest of pillows.

Lilias stepped from her shoes and into the nest, turning to face Feich. Then, with a gesture subtle and elegant, she let fall her starling gown.

Suddenly inflamed, Feich was scarcely able to take her in. "Lilias . . . " he murmured, rooted to the polished floor.

She laughed at him. "Why do you hesitate?"

He needed no further invitation. An odd negotiation this, but one he craved.

"Ah . . . " she whispered against his kiss, "you answer well, Daimhin of the Raven. I wonder, will the rest of your tribute be as sweet as this?"

"If I answer so well, do you need more tribute than this?"

She laughed, churning his blood. "Not I. But I think you may not wish to make love to my Council. There must be fruit in this for them, as well."

"Their tribute arrives with your brother—a day, maybe a bit more. Can they wait?"

"They can. *I* cannot." She turned black eyes up to his. "My tribute, lord—"

He could barely speak. "And you . . . you will aid me? You will give me men, arms—?"

Again, the husky laugh. "So mercenary. I will give you more than that, lord Daimhin."

She was mesmerizing and he, willing to be mesmerized. Yet, as they sealed their pact, his mind wandered to the lacework corridor and the transparent vault overhead and he wondered how, with winter pressing in on them, the palace of the Banarigh Lilias was kept so warm.

The day of their departure for the Gyldan-baenn dawned clear and cool, the Sun shimmering off the sands of Kansbar's beaches as if reflected from the crushed remains of pearls. From the balcony outside Lilias's state salon, Daimhin Feich gazed up into the azure sky and took it as an augury. *The Sun shines on you, Regent Feich, and the way is clear. Clear to the Gyldan-baenn, clear to the Baenn-an-ratha, clear to Airdnasheen.* He set his eyes on the eastward track, gripping the balcony's tiled wall with eager fingers. "I'm coming for you, Taminy," he murmured. "Catahn Hillwild, prepare to give up your prize."

Arms slid sinuously about his waist. "Do you Weave, my dear Sorcerer?"

He chuckled. "I'm no sorcerer, Lilias."

"No? If not a sorcerer, then what?"

"What indeed?" He smiled. "Sometimes I wonder."

Lilias laughed and slid around into his embrace. From the courtyard below, where their combined forces gathered, all eyes could see them; she seemed not to care. "Less than a god," she murmured, "more than a man."

He accepted her flattery with a deep sense of wonder, feeling the truth of her words to his core. More than a man, indeed. His spirit, his soul, stretched to encompass power he had once doubted the existence of. He stood amazed at his own ability—at his own growth. "*Less* than a god," he teased. "That's not what you told me last night."

"Ah, well. In the dark, you *are* a god. And you make me a goddess."

He had lowered his head to her kiss when a commotion

within the palace unraveled the heavy Weave of desire. They parted and turned from the view of their gathering forces to see Loc Llywd enter the salon followed by a Deasach corsair in dirt-spattered clothing. Feich recognized him as one of the men Lilias had sent off in search of her brother and his caravan of gifts, now two days past their expected time of arrival.

Frowning, the Banarigh stepped from the balcony to meet them within. "You have a report? Speak. Where is the caravan?"

"The caravan is in the outer court," said Loc Llywd, his eyes on Feich. "But your brother . . . " He gestured at the corsair.

Lilias's attention turned to that quarter and she delivered a sharp demand in Deasach. In response the corsair rattled off some manner of report, the intelligible words of which were 'Shak Saba.'

The syllables that rolled from the man's tongue turned Lilias's bronze-gold skin to ash and shocked her graceful body into brittle rigidity. She asked several short, cutting questions in a voice that trembled with emotion, then dismissed the messenger with a slash of her hand. Loc Llywd hesitated to follow the corsair from the room, instead attempting to speak to Lilias in gentle tones. She raised her voice and her hand to him, and he bowed swiftly from the room.

She stood quivering for several minutes, her back to Feich—pike straight—hands gripping her upper arms. When she turned at last, fury and anguish burned in her dark eyes. "My brother is dead. Dead at the hands of your countrymen. While I have made you lover and ally."

Stunned, Feich could only hold out his arms to her and will her to feel his astonishment and outrage. She ignored his silent entreaty and flung herself past him to the balcony. He followed. "Tell me, Lilias. Tell me what happened."

Her eyes on the orderly chaos in the parade ground below, Lilias said, "Why should I not kill you, Feich? Tell me that."

"I can think of many reasons, not the least of which is that I have shared your bed these past nights."

"Sorn is *dead*."

"And I had nothing to do with his death, Lilias-Raven. I am as stunned as you are. Now, will you not tell me what your man reported?"

She drew a ragged breath, looking, for the first time, vulnerable, mortal—more woman than goddess. "He was bringing your caravan across Madaidh lands. The Madaidh attacked in the night. They killed Sorn. Some say it was the Madaidh, himself, that murdered him."

"And the tribute?"

She laughed—a sound like glass breaking. "They took nothing. Nothing but the girl my brother was so taken with . . . Iseabal of the White Skin."

The Wicke, they had taken, leaving priceless treasure. Why? Feich shook himself. "And the cannon?"

"They destroyed . . . *Why*, Daimhin? *Why* would they kill Sorn, yet leave others alive? Why would they take this girl and leave a treasure behind?"

Why indeed? He moved close to Lilias, holding her eyes by will. "Can't you guess? Rodri Madaidh, while pretending to me that he and his House were neutral, has all the while been under the sway of the Golden Wicke. The girl he liberated was herself a Wicke—a close confidante of Taminy-Osmaer. Your brother was murdered because he dared lay hands on one of Taminy's own."

"As you did, by Sorn's tell. Why are *you* not dead?"

"I am protected, Lilias, by my own *aidan*. Your brother possessed no such Gift."

"And yours did not show you what would happen to him?" she hissed.

He could feel her rage building, seeking an outlet. He must give her one. "Taminy is powerful. Even her acolyte was powerful. Even as I veiled us from the eyes of the Madaidh and the Taminists, so the Wicke and her minions lifted that veil to reveal Sorn to them. My only fault was that I did not stay behind to protect the caravan. I never imagined Sorn might become a target of the Wicke's wrath; though I knew myself to be such a target. No, Sorn was truly fond of the girl—was gentle with her. It was a gentleness she did not deserve."

"You could have left your woman behind."

"My—?"

Lilias's smile was joyless. "I know of Coinich Mor, my pale lover. And I know what place she has held in your pretty tent. You could have left her behind; you didn't because the Wicke, Taminy, willed you not to. You left Sorn behind because the Wicke willed him be left. Perhaps she could not avenge this Iseabal's honor on you because of your *aidan*. But she could wreak her revenge on my brother. And did."

"Lilias . . . " He reached for her yet again, but she stepped back from him.

"Truly, this woman is more powerful than I imagined. More deadly. Yet I, too, can be deadly. I would fight her."

Feich smiled fiercely into the searing blaze of her anger. "You are a goddess, Raven. Taminy is only a Wicke."

"Goddess of death, to her, I pray. Make ready your men."

He hurried to do that, full of exultation. What could have been defeat, he had transmuted to victory: Banarigh Lilias Saba was no longer a casual participant in Taminy's destruction.

He was mounted, ready to ride when he felt the eyes on him. Before he could turn and face their owner, Coinich Mor's dark voice struck his ears. "*You* veiled our party from the Taminists, did you?"

He jerked about to find her seated astride her white mare, yellow eyes jeering. "How did you—?"

She laughed at him. "Did you think you were alone with your Deasach Cwen just now, 'pale lover'? Do you imagine you have *ever* been alone with her?"

Feich's face blazed beneath the Dearg Wicke's steady gaze. He was outraged. He was aroused. Somehow the idea that Coinich Mor knew all that passed between him and the Deasach Banarigh was exhilarating. "You see more than I credit you for, Mistress Dearg."

"I *am* more than you credit me for, Regent Feich. Don't forget me."

"And will you make some jealous demand of me now? Would you have me leave off with Lilias?"

"Not at all, lord. I only remind you that your village cailin is gone. There is Lilias, but her Gift is small and her alien magics are full of superstition and ritual. One true partner in Weaving have you—Coinich Mor. Don't forget her."

"I promise I will not." He let his eyes feed passion to her for a moment, and though she now existed in Lilias Saba's shadow, it was a surprisingly honest passion. He reined his horse about, then paused and turned back. "Why did you not sense the danger to Sorn?"

"The same reason you did not. There was strong magic there—a wall of it."

"A wall built by whom?"

"By those we failed to veil ourselves from."

Feich twitched. "The Madaidh?"

"They are a wild people, lord Regent. It is said even their newborn are fey."

"I pray that is only superstition."

Coinich Mor threw back her head and laughed. "And what do you pray to, 'Demon' Feich? Some dark, unseen god or goddess?"

To whom did he pray? To whom *could* he pray? "To myself," he might have answered once. But his mind often turned to the idea that if Taminy represented some glorious Spirit of Light, must he not represent some opposing Spirit of Darkness—Caime Cadder's Evil One? Ironic.

Yet, he could not deny there were times when he felt a black power moving around him, through him, within him—in the throes of passion, in the clutches of rage, in the depths of his dreams. The fancy often took him that if he opened his eyes he might catch it, see it face to face. He could never quite bring himself to open his eyes in those moments. Perhaps he scorned his own suggestibility. Perhaps he was merely afraid.

Catahn loved the garden. Even in winter it was beautiful. The little pool was a misty mirror of water-crystal, icicles festooned the eaves of the castle and the bare limbs of the few deciduous trees; the conifers wore a furry mantle of snow. As he listened to Taminy singing, her gaggle of youthful disciples joining in close harmony, Catahn wished he had been granted the gift of song. He was too ashamed of his voice to do more than murmur duans. Like Wyth, he would only sit and keep silent time with the music.

Eyslk wielded the bodrun and Gwynet played a chanter, keeping less and less to the background. Today as she played, she danced and capered about the little high courtyard, her breath marking steamy trails in the crystalline air. Catahn could not help but smile.

Taminy sang of a fair maiden whose spiteful elder sister has insisted for so long that she is hideous, she never dares to look in a mirror. One day, a young woodman comes across her in the forest and, though she tries to hide herself, the young man takes her scarf and glimpses her face. Smitten, he declares her beautiful, but she refuses to believe him.

"She thought herself an ogre," Taminy sang. "She thought the boy a fool. Till she tumbled to the grassy bank and gazed into the pool." She fit action to verse and let herself down upon the rocks that ringed the little pond. But instead of continuing with the song, she leapt up again with a cry, her eyes on the icy water.

Catahn felt the tug of her sudden fear—for fear it was, sharp and thin and brittle. He came to his feet and rushed to Taminy's side, steadying her with an arm about her shoulders, his eyes following hers to the icy mirror.

A mist rode over the surface of the frozen pool, and beneath it shapes moved—shifting, splitting, recombining. Drawn to the movement, Catahn swore he could see men, horses, a cloud of billowing dust.

"They come," Taminy whispered. She looked up at him. "*He* comes."

And that, Catahn knew with certainty, was the cause of her fear—the approach of Daimhin Feich.

Airleas broke the ranks of those gathered around and peered into the pool. "Feich? Feich is coming? Can you see him? Where is he?"

"In El-Deasach."

"But how?" Airleas demanded.

"Alliances." She shook her head. "He plays with fire."

"Then I'll get to face him, after all," murmured the Cyneric, eyes distant. "The honor of my House—"

"Is not more important than your life," Taminy told him.

"What is life without honor?"

"What is honor without life?" countered Catahn.

Taminy turned her face up to his again, wounding him with her eyes. Her deep terror of Feich all but strangled him. Throat tight, he glanced at the others. "Taminy must be allowed time to meditate on this, to Weave for further knowledge. Perhaps you should all return to your duties and studies."

There was no argument, only anxious glances from Wyth and Eyslk and a muttered oath from Airleas. Subdued, they drifted away. Not until they were gone did Catahn move, turning Taminy to face him, taking her hands in his, all the while quivering with his own audacity. "Is there nothing I can do?"

She smiled wanly. "Can you guard my dreams?"

Her skin was so pale, her eyes so large and dark and bruised-looking, he nearly moaned in pain. "If I could only . . . But, *how*, Lady? How does he . . . enter your dreams?"

"I wish I knew. I don't. I don't even know if he does it willfully."

"Can you not deny him entry? You've taught your *waljan* to ward against another's Weaves. Is there no Wardweave for Daimhin Feich?"

"I thought there was. But my Wardweaves are useless. Somehow he breaks through them, slides past them, though I Weave them directly against him."

Catahn's frown deepened. "Cannot the Meri grant you more strength? Can She not shield you?"

Taminy shook her head. "This is a time of testing, Catahn. For me, for all of us. Already, I draw on the Meri's power. But *I* must determine how to direct it. Somehow, when I direct it at Daimhin Feich, he is not there. It's as if he . . . steps aside."

"Then there is nothing I can do? No way I can guard your dreams?"

Taminy squeezed his hands. "I'd not have you lose sleep, too."

"I do already. Mistress, must you face him?"

"Is that what you think I'm afraid of—coming face to face with Feich?"

"Is it not? I know I fear *for* you."

Taminy's eyelids slid downward as if suddenly too heavy to be borne up. "Daimhin Feich," she said, "does not face anyone or anything cleanly, squarely, honestly. He hides in dreams; he skulks in vapors." She shuddered, her voice falling to a whisper. "He touches me, Catahn. In the dark, in the aislinn vapors, in my dreams. His touch is like death, and I seem not to be able to turn his hand away."

There was such anguish flowing from her that Catahn forgot himself and gathered her into his arms. "I will find a way to guard your dreams, Lady," he told her. "I promise."

One moment he was asleep in his uncle's tent, the next he was wide awake, staring into the darkness, hearing rain whisper softly on the oiled fabric overhead. He sweated in the cold, heart pounding an uneven tattoo in his chest. Saefren Claeg gasped, shuddered and sat up. It was not a nightmare that woke him, but a sensation of pure cold panic.

"Uncle?" he panted. "Uncle Iobert?"

There was no answer, and indeed, when he put out his hand, he found his uncle's bedroll empty. He heard voices from beyond the tent flap—urgent murmurs, no words. As his world righted itself, he came out of his bedroll, pulled on his boots and stumbled outside.

His Uncle was there with The Jura and Aine, huddled under the boughs of a large pine, hoods pulled up against the fine drizzle. Aine was speaking, voice low, hands making emphatic gestures. As he approached, Saefren realized others had emerged from tents and lean-to's to join the circle beneath the tree—Leal and Fhada, Hethe Jura, others.

Iobert Claeg glanced up, noted his nephew's presence

with a raising of his brows and placed a hand on Aine's shoulder. "It seems others have had their sleep interrupted," he said. "Do I need to ask why you're here?"

Saefren swept damp hair out of his eyes and shivered. "I don't know why I'm here, Uncle. What's happened?"

Aine turned to him, her face a pale moon in the darkness. "Daimhin Feich has left Creiddylad this week past. He's crossed over into Deasach lands."

"And taken the bulk of his forces with him," added Iobert.

Saefren didn't bother to ask how they knew this. "To what purpose?"

"To gather allies, it would seem. Or so Rodri Madaidh has it. He overtook a tribute caravan bound for Kansbar with gifts for the Banarigh. The caravan drivers understood that their lord had forged an alliance with the Deasach Cwen and intended to march through El-Deasach to attack Airdnasheen from the east."

"But the Madaidh . . . " Saefren puzzled. "The Madaidh refused to—"

"As he said," commented Mortain Jura dryly, "there are advantages to neutrality. One of those advantages would seem to be invisibility. Feich completely overlooked him and, when the time was right . . . "

Aine grasped Saefren's arm. "He found Iseabal. He brought Iseabal away from there."

Saefren swum for a moment in overwhelming relief. He looked to his uncle and asked, "Now what do *we* do?"

"Alraed Aine believes we should attempt to reach Hrofceaster from the western side to offer reinforcement."

"But we couldn't hope to take enough troops through the high passes to do any good."

"We can't do *nothing*!" Aine erupted.

Saefren stayed her with a firm hand on her shoulder. "Uncle is right, Aine. To take our men into the Gyldanbaenn would be futile and hazardous."

"But—!"

"Our energies would be better spent elsewhere." He turned back to Iobert. "What forces has Feich left in Creiddylad?"

Iobert Claeg's eyes glinted. "Minimal, I would think, though a little reconnaissance should give the whole tell."

"Would the Madaidh join in an attack on Mertuile?"

Aine gasped. "Take Mertuile?"

"Our Cyneric will need a safe capital to return to," observed The Jura. "One emptied of traitors." He looked to Iobert. "Perhaps you and I should ride to the Madaidh."

Iobert nodded. "And perhaps our young bucks should gain some intelligence of Creiddylad."

Aine folded her arms and shifted impatiently. "And our refugees?"

"Would be welcome among the Graegam." That Chieftain stood at The Claeg's shoulder. "Graegam is the closest stronghold. From there, you could make your way to Halig-liath."

"We? You think I should go with them?"

"It would be safest for you, Alraed."

Aine glanced from one Chieftain to another, her eyes finally coming to rest on Iobert. "You also wish me to go up to Graegam with the others?"

"Karr Graegam is right, Alraed. It would be safest for you."

And for us as well, Saefren thought, watching Aine return to her tent. Anger and impatience radiated from her in waves he could almost see. *Firebrand*. No matter how acquiescent she might pretend to be, he suspected sending her to Graegam and *getting* her there were two different things.

CHAPTER 20

If I speak sweetly as an aingeal and have no wisdom, my speech is no more than the noise of a brass bell. And if I have the Sight of prophecy, and comprehend all secrets and all knowledge and hold the power to move mountains, and have no mercy, I am nothing.

—*Utterances of Taminy-Osmaer, Book of the Covenant*

In the arid foothills of the Southern Gyldan-baenn, the weather was brisk, but not chill. They slept comfortably by night and their breath did not hang on the air by day. Daimhin Feich found the journey exhilarating. Riding, he dreamed of holding the true Osmaer in his hands. Sleeping, he dreamed of other things.

He saw little of the Banarigh Lilias their first week on the trail. By day, she was a wind-blown wraith. Garbed in red (the color of mourning among the Deasach), she sat a black horse at the head of her corsairs, head and face obscured by yards of skillfully wrapped and draped cloth. By night, she took to her tent, alone. Feich Wove secretly to draw an invitation from her and consoled himself with Coinich Mor.

At the end of the week the invitation came, and he went to the tent of the alien goddess to receive her favors. He could not, somehow, make her become Taminy in his heated moments. She was Lilias, always, seductive and sultry. He had no complaints about that, but merely thought it odd that his *aidan* should be so circumscribed in her presence. He attributed it to her excessively strong will and accepted

349

her passion happily. There was, after all, always Coinich Mor, who left her husband's bedroll late nearly every night to seek out his. Their Weaving exhausted him, but she could always be bent to his whim. If it was Taminy he wanted, Taminy she became.

He had expected them to dislike or even hate each other, these two women who shared his attentions, but they seemed quite at ease in each other's company. They seemed, in fact, to like each other, and often rode side-by-side, chatting, laughing, even bathing together in the Raven's red tent. Feich chuckled over that development and decided he must have subconsciously willed it to be so. He might have been uneasy about their friendship had he given it much thought, but his thoughts had flown ahead to the passes south and east of Baenn-an-ratha and carefully worked out what he must do when they arrived there.

A fortnight, he figured. A fortnight and he would stand siege against the gates of Hrofceaster. And though he had arrayed about him many men, he knew it would be, first and foremost, a siege of spirit.

Aine-mac-Lorimer had no intention of going to Graegam, but she had pretended acquiescence anyway. So she was surprised when, on the day the Madaidh arrived with Iseabal, Saefren Claeg took her aside for a forest walk and asked a blunt question: "All right, Aine Red. What are you planning?"

"What do you mean?"

"You're not going to Graegam, I think."

She studiously avoided his gaze, staring instead at the leaf-strewn ground. "And where else would I go?"

"Hrofceaster."

"Ha! Now that'd be foolhardy . . . according to some."

"Aye. But you wouldn't let that stop you."

"All right." She stopped kicking acorns about and crossed her arms, tight, over her breasts. "Let's say I'm planning on going up to Hrofceaster. What then?"

"Who were you planning on taking with you?"

She chewed her lip, wondering how honest she could

afford to be. "Leal. Fhada wants to stay with the children. I think that's wise."

"Only Leal? And the Stone, of course."

"That's the whole purpose of the journey."

"And Iseabal?"

"I hadn't asked her. She's not well enough to make such a trek. She should go home to her family."

Saefren laughed, sending a family of magpies squawking to higher branches. "Aine, you hypocrite! How can you snarl at the Chieftains for making a decision for your safety, then turn about two-faced and make the same sort of arbitrary ruling for Iseabal?"

Aine flushed hot and cold. "Arbitrary, is it? Well, it's not! I'm up to this trek, by God. Isha's not. *That's* the difference. The Stone must be gotten to Taminy with all haste. We've already wasted enough time waiting on Rodri Madaidh to get here, and for your uncle and his cronies to come up with a strategy for Mertuile. Feich'll be halfway to Baenn-eigh by now."

His back against a gnarled oak, Saefren watched Aine with a gaze that only made her flush more prodigiously. "Are you finished?"

She clamped her mouth shut and glared at him.

"I agree that the Stone ought to go up to Taminy for safe-keeping, but you'll need a guide up that icy track. I'm coming with you."

She gaped now, unable to stifle her amazement. "But won't your uncle want you here?"

He shrugged. "I've done my bit of reconnaissance, and I'm no strategist. But I know my way through those mountains, having grown up at their feet."

Bluster deflated, Aine could only drop her defensive posture in head-shaking bemusement. "All right, Saefren Claeg. It's guide you are." She looked him square in the eye. "And thank you."

"Catahn says I'm not to study swordsmanship anymore." Airleas took the chair opposite Taminy at the huge eastern hearth of the Great Hall, his sword propped between

his knees, his chin resting on the hilt. He was bemused,
but there was no reproach in his voice or eyes, nor even
in his heart.

"We need the time, you and I, for other things."

The boy-Cyne sat up straighter, making Taminy realize
how much he had grown physically these last months. "Am
I to receive my own crystal now?"

"Not yet. Not quite yet. What you must learn now has
to do with Weaving only a little. You've heard the Tell of
Meredydd-a-Lagan."

"Of *course*, Mistress. She is now the Vessel of the Meri."

"And her Pilgrimage is known to you, too, of course."
He nodded.

"Recall the first task of her Pilgrimage to me."

"She was to choose, from among three amulets, the most
important one."

"And they were?"

"Healing, Clear Sight and Wisdom. She chose Wisdom."

"And why?"

"Because Wisdom is the foundation of all knowledge.
What good is either Healing or Clear Sight if you don't know
how to use it?" He grinned. "It's like when I first found this
sword. I had the thing, but not a clue how to wield it."

Taminy smiled back at him. "A good analogy. Your *aidan*,
Airleas, is like that sword. The might of Cyneship is like that
sword. Possession of either is only the beginning of things."

"I know this," he hastened to assure her. "I understand
the need for wisdom."

Taminy sat back in her fleece-covered chair, closing her
eyes for a moment and absorbing the movement and chatter
in the hall around them.

"Mistress, are you all right?"

She opened her eyes. "Tired, is all. But, better than yesterday." That was true, she realized. Yesterday, after weeks
of near sleepless nights, she had felt transparent, as if every
sluggish beat of her heart was visible to all eyes. Last night,
she had slept the night through and today she felt merely
translucent. Dear Catahn seemed to have found some way
to guard her dreams after all.

"Airleas, answer me this: Given a choice, would you choose wisdom . . . or the honor of your father's House?"

"My father . . . my father *dis*honored his House—*our* House. I realize that now. I'm the only one who can restore that honor."

"And how would you do that?"

"By stripping Daimhin Feich of any place or power and taking back the Throne."

Taminy gazed at her hands, folded upon her lap. "And?"

"Being a better Cyne than my father. I want to be as good a Cyne as Ciarda."

"You have powers Ciarda saw only in your grandmother, Brann Hillwild. They could make you an even better Cyne than he, or . . . they could make your every act of foolishness, weakness or selfishness a disaster."

The boy blanched. "I don't want to be weak or foolish or selfish."

"You didn't answer my question. Which would you choose, honor or wisdom?"

He looked very unhappy for a moment—consternated. Then his face cleared. "Why, that's a false choice, isn't it? For there can't be wisdom without honor or honor without wisdom."

"I suppose that depends on your definition of honor."

His brow furrowed. "I don't understand. How many definitions of honor can there be?"

"When you know, tell me," she said and sent him to study with Wyth.

No sooner had Airleas left the hearthside than Catahn took his place. He said nothing for a moment, but only studied her, eyes troubled. "You slept well, Lady?" he asked at last.

She nodded. "And you did not. Guarding my dreams?"

He shifted uncomfortably, turning his eyes to the flames within the cavernous fireplace. "I . . . Wove an inyx of my own device. I am pleased it worked."

She leaned toward him. "Catahn, you can't do that every night."

"And you cannot protect yourself as you sleep. Someone must guard you from such . . . horrors."

She glanced up at him sharply, sensing his uneasiness as something heavy and dark. "What have you done?"

"A simple channeling Weave. I thought that if the inyx could not be blocked at its beginning, it might be turned aside at its end."

Taminy's hands gripped the arms of her chair. "You took the nightmares upon yourself, you mean. *You* absorbed them."

His eyelids fluttered and swift color flooded his face. She put her hand on his to claim his attention, but he flinched away and rose, turning his back on her.

Stunned, wounded, she said, "Catahn, you can't do this. I won't have you . . . I wanted no one to know what those nightmares were. They were between me and him."

"There should be *nothing* between you and him!" Catahn growled, still not looking at her. "Nothing but six feet of earth." He strode away from her then, across the Hall, and would not let her call him back.

The air at this altitude was chill and brittle; it entered the nose and lungs sharply, as if made of invisible shards of frozen glass. A light powder of snow dusted the ground underfoot, but did not slow the advance of the multitude at Daimhin Feich's joint command. They climbed easily through the dry valleys, Feich blessing the rain-shadow each morning when he rose to clear skies.

"This won't continue indefinitely," Ruadh told him one morning, as he squinted up at the shrouded bulk of Baennghlo. To the east the so-called Wailing Mountain, Baenneigh, towered, flanks gleaming with snow. "When we get up there," —Ruadh nodded at the shadowy pass between the two giants— "we're going to have to fight the storms."

Feich let out a streamer of breath. "Then we'll fight the storms. Or perhaps I shall fight them myself. We will not be beaten."

"So certain?"

"Ruadh, you are such a pessimist. The pass is low and sheltered. We shall come upon Hrofceaster from the southeast—also sheltered. Only the last miles of the journey will be as dangerous as all that. And when it's over, we shall have the Ren Catahn's back to the ice. There will be nowhere for him to run."

Ruadh shook his head. "Sometimes I wonder if you know who or what it is you've come after out here, or what you hope to get out of all this. How hard would it have been for you to have compromised with Claeg and Jura? It would have put you close to Airleas, given you some control over him, over Creiddylad—"

"*Some* control? Not enough, Ruadh. Oh, for *you* perhaps, for my father, for all the other complacent elders of the House Feich. But I see a way to have complete control." He laughed. "My God, more control than any Cyne has ever wielded in Caraid-land. Not just temporal power, cousin, but *spiritual* power."

"You believe your . . . your *aidan* is that strong?"

Feich pointed a finger at his cousin's nose. "Colfre thought he was fey because of his Hillwild ancestry. I thought he was, too. It wasn't until the end—until just before his death that I realized the truth." He laughed again. "It was *me*, Ruadh. *I* was the one with the Gift. Oh, he had *some* ability, true enough, but it was weak. Enough for me to make use of, fortunately."

Ruadh made no reply to that, but only stared at him in wide-eyed amazement.

"You ask me why we come here. The reasons are not as simple as you would have them be. I've come here for Airleas, obviously. But yes, I want Taminy in my grasp, as well, for she is the key to spiritual power." He paused, wondering how honest he could be with his cousin, then said, "You've noticed my . . . ways with women."

"I'm not blind."

"Practice. For the time when I have Taminy-Osmaer at Mertuile. You understand, of course, that it's not mere physical gratification I seek—and get—from them."

Ruadh turned his gaze to the mists crawling their way up Baenn-an-ghlo. "You believe you draw power from them."

"I *do* draw power from them. A different kind of power

from each. It's like . . . like a banquet. I wish you could
know, could taste, this heady food, Ruadh."

"Why? Then we'd be in competition. I'd be a fool to
want that. Thank God, I'm not a fool. Nor am I 'gifted.'
But tell me, what will become of these other women when
you have Taminy?"

"I've given that a great deal of thought, actually, and I
think I will take the Banarigh Lilias as my wife. It would
seal the alliance between Caraid-land and El-Deasach, and
perhaps—who knows—give birth to a new nation."

"Provided you maintain control of the Throne."

Feich smiled. "Do you doubt that I can?" He clapped
a hand on Ruadh's shoulder. "Look, cousin, I know you
think I'm terribly foolhardy. But if you want something
badly enough, you *must* take chances. I want the House
Feich to be more to Caraid-land than a clan of court min-
strels and petty diplomats."

"There's nothing petty about being made Durweard to
the Cyne."

"No, but in comparison with being made Cyne—no, no,
not Cyne, Osric."

Ruadh gaped. *"Osric?* That title would have to be
bestowed by the Meri Herself. You're not even a believer—
never mind that you're not a Malcuim." He shook his head.
"When you spoke of marriage to the Raven, I thought you
shrewd and pragmatic, but . . . *Osric,* for God's sake . . .
An unbelieving Osric of Caraid-land, married to a heathen Cwen and sporting a stable of gifted, wickish paramours? Why do I not believe the Meri will so bless you?"

"She may not. But her Regent on dry land will."

"Taminy-Osmaer?"

Daimhin nodded. "Taminy-Osmaer."

"And why will she do this?"

"Because if she refuses, everyone she holds dear will
pay the ultimate price for her refusal."

"And you're not afraid of her power—of its Source? You
have no fear of God?"

"Less every day, cousin. Because every day I draw closer
to my own Source—my own god."

"*Your* god? Does our sanctimonious cleirach know you've brought your own god with you? I thought you'd won his allegiance by pretending to worship *his*."

"I won his allegiance by flagellating him as Ladhar did, as he flagellates himself. The pathetic creature spends every day in prayer and every night in self-loathing. He knows nothing. Sees nothing but his hatred of Taminy." He chuckled. "Ironic, isn't it? He who seeks only to preserve the flame of his religion has unwittingly allied himself with one whose purpose is to snuff it out."

Ruadh gave his elder cousin an awful glance. "I don't know whether you're powerful, shrewd and ruthless or the biggest fool in creation." He did not add, "or mad," but he thought it.

"I'm no fool, Ruadh. Let that assurance set your mind at rest. I'll do what's best for the House. And what is best for the House is what is best for me."

"This is taking too long," Aine complained. "It will take us weeks to get there if we keep angling south."

"Would you rather have to deal with the inclement weather in the foothills?" Saefren asked her.

"Rather that than deal with the Feich. If we head much farther south, we'll have to cross Feich land."

"My intent, lady, is to cross *Claeg* land, which can be done with complete safety."

"But we're over-riding the mouth of Baeg Cuillean pass. We'll have to turn north again when we reach the foothills."

"We're not going to take the Baeg Cuillean, Aine. That would be ridiculous. We're heading for the Vale of Orian."

"Orian? That all but borders on the Feich estates! We'll be riding right into—"

"Will you two please stop?"

Aine turned guilty eyes to Iseabal, who was regarding her with mixed exasperation and weariness. "I'm sorry, Isha. It's just taking so long."

"And Hrofceaster will still be there."

"Under siege, most likely, by the time we get there."

"And so?" said Iseabal mildly. "We can't fly, Aine. But we *can* pass unseen."

Isha was right, of course, but patience was something Aine had yet to master. Still, if Isha, having just visited hell, could be so patient . . . With three pairs of eyes on her, Aine felt foolish. "Sorry," she said, and put her horse in motion down the lowland track toward the Vale of Orian.

There was a place, a quiet streamside grove below the pool where the Gwyr was said to live, that Catahn Hageswode considered his own. Here, he had celebrated his Crask-an-duine—a late summer passage for him, beneath a full moon, sung of by cricket bards. The grass had been green and sweet-smelling, blending its perfume with the fragrance of the pines, and the grove had sparkled with the light of tiny candles.

Snow lay upon the sweet grass now, and ice sparkled from needle and branch. It was transformed—gleaming now, rather than verdant. Catahn, sitting on the same rock he had sat upon for that summer rite, tried not to find the place bleak or barren. But bleak, he felt. Bleak, ineffectual . . . evil.

In making Taminy's nightmares his own, in intercepting Feich's touch, he had uncovered his own weaknesses, laying them horribly bare to a self-condemning eye. Physical eyes closed, the sensations were an instant away—the silken slip of her hair between his fingers, the sweet, spicy fragrance of her skin, the warmth of her body. Her nightmares embraced his wildest, fondest, most impossible dreams.

He opened his eyes, letting the snow glare burn them to tears. The grove blurred. But he was not Daimhin Feich. He loved her. Did that not count for something? Did that not lessen his sin?

"Here is a troubled man."

Catahn jerked and brought his eyes up. Deardru-an-Caerluel stood before him at the center of the grove, a bright spot of blue on a field of white.

"I had meant to be alone here."

She put back the hood of her azure cloak, letting dark hair spill about her shoulders. "I recall you often came here *not* to be alone. Geatan told me she thought Desary was conceived in this spot." She glanced down at the snow about her feet. "Perhaps right where I stand. I always wished it had been me rolling in the summer grass with you."

Catahn rose and moved to leave, but she stepped forward, hands raised to stop him. "Stay, Catahn. I'm not here to seduce you."

"I would not be seduced."

"No. Most likely not. At least, not with *her* here." She looked at him shrewdly. "But, of course, one day she will leave. She will return to Creiddylad with her boy-Cyne and teach him how to govern."

"Perhaps. And perhaps I will go with them."

"You? At court? What a picture that paints! And who will lead the Hillwild in your stead? Your heir is one of her acolytes. Raenulf is dead."

"If you are not here to seduce me, then what is your purpose?"

"Eyslk has spoken to me often about how Taminy readies our Cyneric for his own Crask-an-duine." She smiled. "Our daughter very much wants me to like her goddess."

"Eyslk does not worship Taminy."

"Do you?"

"Your point, Deardru."

"Her reports disturb me. She tells of Airleas Malcuim's strong *aidan*. Of how Taminy schools him in its use. I've seen this myself. I've seen the child walk upon the water of the Gwyr's pool as if it were solid ground. I've overheard her lessons with him."

Catahn frowned. "Airleas is a boy who must quickly become a man. More than that, he must become Cyne—a Cyne with powers he must know how to—"

"Catahn, are you that passion-blind? She doesn't school a mere Cyne. She schools an Osric."

Catahn had to allow he'd never considered that. It made sense. With his strong Gift, Airleas Malcuim would be unique among the Cynes of Caraid-land. His appearance now, at the time of an equally unique Cusp was . . . all part of a Plan, surely. "I think you may be right. What disturbs you?"

She stared at him. "I tell you she would give us an Osric, and you *accept* it? No, wait. You needn't answer. You accept whatever she desires. But this? Catahn, think what this means. An absolute ruler. One who will determine law through revelation, one who will govern with another whispering in his ear."

"Cynes' ears have always been whispered into. Only now the whisperer will have the best interests of all Caraidin at heart."

"And this includes the Hillwild, you think? What faith you have. So, the Hillwild are now to be under the yoke of a lowlander?"

"We have long existed in willing cooperation with the Malcuim and the Hall. And I would remind you that there is Hillwild blood in Airleas Malcuim's veins—else he would likely not have his Gift."

Deardru shook her head, face eloquent with disgust. "You'd sell your soul for her. No, not only *your* soul, but your daughters' souls and the soul of every Hillwild, living or dead. Well, you may be willing to surrender your honor to a pretty Wicke and a lowland boy, but I am not." She put up her hood and turned away with a flourish of her cloak.

"What do you think you can do, Deardru?" Catahn asked, pausing her. "You're a gifted woman, surely. But she is the Osmaer."

"Oh, and what is that?"

"Something you should respect, if you weren't so blinded by . . . " He found himself unable to say it.

Deardru's eyes flashed wry anger at him. "By jealousy? Why not revenge? You took my husband from me, my daughter, my home, my pride. I offered you love and you rejected it. I would have given you more children—"

"Deardru," said Catahn wearily. "I never loved you. I loved only Geatan."

"Oh, yes? And yet, you bring *her* here with your worshipful lust—"

Catahn thought his face must peel away in the sudden blast of inner heat. "Don't—" he began, but Deardru was already laughing at him.

"Yes, you give yourself away. Does your tender virgin know how you burn for her? But of course she does. She's Osmaer." She walked away from him, back toward the village, her cloak brushing up a sparkling wake.

Catahn stood where she left him, a hulk of darkness—shadow stretched across the field of gleaming white. He was all shadow. All. In the midst of his despair, he sensed Taminy's call but could not bring himself to answer it.

Ice crystals, flung by a biting wind, tattooed Daimhin Feich's face with random patterns of red. They stung without his notice. Through the veil of snow, bright pinpoints of light glinted against the sky-eating flank of Baenn-anratha. Airdnasheen.

Feich turned triumphant eyes to Lilias Saba. "There. The holt of the Hillwild—Catahn. We have but to send our troops up to encircle it."

Lilias smiled, nodding. "Then I will soon avenge my brother's death. Do you think that girl, Iseabal, will be here?"

"Doubtful. I can't imagine the Madaidh would have consented to bring her here. And if they tried, they'd still be struggling through the foothills."

"Then I shall have to take my revenge upon her Mistress."

Feich glanced at her sharply. "Taminy is my affair."

"My brother's blood—"

"And my dead Cyne's. And the honor of Caraid-land's ruling House. And my own honor. All these cry for retribution as well." Seeing a hard look cross her face, he smiled and softened his voice. "Trust me, Lilias. The revenge I exact will satisfy all. Now . . . we will deploy our men to the west, along the mountain's flank and to the east through the gap." He gestured sweepingly.

To Feich's left, his cousin Ruadh nodded agreement. "My thoughts as well. The gap ought to take us around to their main access. Though, it will likely be a difficult climb."

"See to it, then. I want the siege troops to be in place by morning."

Ruadh gaped at him. "You can't be serious."

"Never more so."

"Daimhin, those maneuvers will be dangerous in daylight. In this dark and wind, this blowing snow—"

"You're afraid."

"Afraid? Yes, I'm afraid! Of losing men and horses to these God-forsaken crags. You're mad if you think I'd send our men up there now."

Daimhin twitched in irritation. "Then send Dearg to secure the positions and our kinsmen may follow them up after."

"No. Not even Dearg will I sacrifice to your . . . obsession."

"I am your superior, Ruadh," Feich reminded him blandly. "I speak with the authority of my father, The Feich."

"You're *not* The Feich, Daimhin. You're only his lieutenant. As Marschal of the Feich forces, it's up to me to decide as to their deployment. The Feich's Marschal is telling you, *Regent*, that to do as you plan would undermine the military success of this campaign you seem so attached to pursuing."

"I'm not sure military success is even necessary."

"Then why in the name of all that's holy are we here? Why have you dragged hundreds of men into this Spiritblasted wilderness? Why did you not simply wage your war from Creiddylad?"

"You mistake me. I didn't mean—"

"Are all Feich this argumentative?" Lilias's voice was tinted with laughter. The two men ceased their debate and turned to her, faces blank. "You argue needlessly. My corsairs know these mountains well by night or day. *They* will secure the siege positions and Hrofceaster will wake to find herself in the embrace of the Deasach."

CHAPTER 21

From the North, the South, the East, and the West, let the
Glory of the Spirit turn on this village sustenance, welfare
and ease.

Let the might of the Spirit free us from our enemies,
extinguishing all fear, averting all anger.

Above and beneath, behind and before, free us from our
enemies, O Glory of God.

—Traditional Hillwild prayer

Few were the denizens of Airdnasheen who were ignorant of the nighttime approach of the enemy. Those who
slept unaware were warned by their more gifted neighbors. Their reaction was unpanicked but swift.

By morning a legion of eyes was focused on the escarpment upon which the Hillwild village sat, prying at the
grey walls of her guardian fortress. In daylight, the own-
ers of those eyes could be seen; beneath red, raven-crested
banners, men in black flocked and fluttered. By late. morning, they had been joined by reinforcements wearing the
colors of the Dearg and Feich.. At midday, a handful of
horsemen rode to the gates of Hrofceaster beneath brilliant banners, while on the tallest standard among them,
the Star Chalice winked fire.

"Sacrilege," murmured Airleas, watching the approach
from the windows of the fortress' Great Hall. He turned
angry eyes to those watching with him—Catahn, Taminy,
the Cwen Toireasa. "Feich commits sacrilege. The Star
Chalice should not leave Creiddylad."

"The Chalice is a symbol," Taminy told him. "It's removal from Creiddylad is not so spiritually significant as Daimhin Feich's intent in removing it."

Cwen Toireasa gasped and pointed. "Look, Taminy! Below the Chalice—the casket there. Can Feich possibly have the Osmaer?"

Taminy shook her head. "No. The Stone of Ochan is not in his hands, but it's clear he wants all watchers to believe it is."

"He sends a courier," observed Catahn, watching a messenger slip through the well-guarded gates to scurry across the forecourt and disappear into the building below their vantage point.

"I want to hold parley with him," Airleas said. "I'm Cyneric. It's me he's come for. I should stand at the parley. I should speak on my own behalf."

Catahn started to object, but Taminy halted him, a firm hand on his arm. "He's right, Catahn. He should speak for himself. After all, it's his throne that's in question. All four of us should go. We'll take Osraed Wyth as scribe."

Catahn capitulated immediately and, when the courier arrived with his message that Feich requested a meeting outside the gates of Hrofceaster, he sent back an affirmative reply. The four donned coats and cloaks, neither hastily nor lazily, and went down to the forecourt where a nervous Osraed Wyth awaited them, scribe and pad in hand.

The gates of the fortress opened and their party moved to stand in the open arch, face to face with the adversary. Taminy could not help but be reminded of their last meeting at Halig-liath. This would not be negotiation, Taminy knew. This would be an attempt to manipulate.

Still astride his horse, flanked by the Dearg, the Deasach Cwen and Caime Cadder, Feich beckoned them forward. "Will you not come out on neutral ground?"

"We do not move beyond this gateway," said Catahn.

"Will you not dismount and meet *us*?" asked Airleas. "You need not fear deceit from us . . . as you well know."

Feich stared at the boy with obvious surprise, then smiled and dismounted. His party, save for the four standard bearers, followed suit. He did not waste time on diplomacy, but came directly to the point. "You know why I'm here. Airleas Malcuim must be returned to Creiddylad. As his Regent, I insist that he return with me."

"As his Regent?" echoed Taminy. "But you are not his *sole* Regent. The Chieftains of two noble Houses are co-Regents with you, according to an agreement which you signed and which the Abbod Ladhar witnessed. An agreement *this* man drafted." Her eyes moved to the cleirach at Daimhin Feich's side.

Caime Cadder started, eyes wide. "How can she—?"

"How can she know?" Feich finished for him. "You amaze me, Cadder. You know what she is, yet you doubt her powers. Unwise of you. In answer to your question, Mistress—yes, there was a compact drawn. But the other signatories—including the Abbod—proved to be traitors. Heretics. Much like yourself, Mistress. Much like this Cwen of yours."

Toireasa stirred. "I am not the traitor to Caraid-land, Durweard Feich. And I will fight you to the death rather than let you take my son from me."

"Regrettable, madam. But if those are your conditions . . ."

"I will not leave Hrofceaster as your prisoner," said Airleas. "Nor as your ward. I will leave here only with Taminy, for I have chosen her as my Durweard."

"You are a child, Airleas," Feich told him. "A child who has been mesmerized and bewicked. You *are* my ward, like it or not, and I am your legally appointed Regent—by your father's decree."

"A decree witnessed by Abbod Ladhar. You called him a traitor and a heretic, just now."

Feich's lips compressed. "Taminy-a-Cuinn has no place in your government. She is a danger to the established order and to the spiritual life of your country."

"I am Cyneric of Caraid-land and The Malcuim," answered Airleas. "And I'll not have a murderer and a traitor to be my Durweard. Take your men and weapons away, Daimhin Feich. I'm not going anywhere with you."

Feich's face reddened to the tips of his ears. He looked
to Taminy. "Mistress, do you expect me to believe that
this child speaks for himself? You have thoroughly bewicked
him."

"Airleas speaks freely, sir. Since he is what you've come
for, it's only right he should speak on his own behalf."

"No, Mistress. He is not all that I've come for. Caraid-
land is divided. Torn. And you are the cause. As much as
the people clamor for their Cyneric, they clamor for you.
The Osraed are powerless, barricaded in their Shrine; the
Assembly has not met; the Houses are in a roil; the streets
of Creiddylad are not safe for anyone—"

"Most especially *waljan*," murmured Catahn.

Feich did not so much as glance at him. "Mistress, we
cannot speak of such important matters like this. Before
Airleas can be considered, I must deal with you directly.
If we could but speak in private?"

"Without your allies and standard bearers?"

"Yes."

As Taminy inclined her head, Catahn objected sharply,
laying a protective hand on her shoulder. "Lady, no! You'll
go nowhere with him alone. I must be with you."

"*Lady*," echoed Feich, "I need to talk to you, not to
your guard dog. Let us go aside—where we can be seen
but not heard—and speak privately."

Taminy looked to Catahn, who reluctantly nodded his
agreement. "Away from all soldiers," he insisted.

Feich nodded. "As you wish. Shall we go sit upon that
rock?" He nodded toward a large flat boulder shaded
sparely by the bare branches of several trees.

They spoke no words as they moved to the spot. Taminy
brushed the snow from one end of the boulder and sat
upon it, her cloak beneath her. Feich sat opposite and
favored her with a long, appraising look.

"You fill out boys' clothing much too well to pass. You
don't dissuade me from finding you alluring, still. I admit,
I recall our time together at Mertuile with some fond-
ness . . . and frustration. You haunt my dreams, Lady
Taminy."

And you, mine, she thought, but did not speak it. Did he know he had reached her? She thought he must, and must take perverse delight in the fact. But now, facing him, looking into his eyes, she could not be sure. As always, he seemed . . . shielded from her in some way she had yet to comprehend. Here, now, face to face with him, she felt of his *aidan* and was puzzled by it. There was something . . . *uneven* about it. "You bring me here to offer me flattery? I thought you meant to speak of important things."

"These things are important to me. But let me be frank. I have resources and forces enough to hold Airdnasheen and lay siege to Hrofceaster indefinitely."

"We have the resources to withhold such a siege."

"Indeed? You have ample food? Water?"

"What do you think Hrofceaster is about, sir? It's a fortress. A stronghold. Intended to withstand the siege of seasons year after year."

"And Airdnasheen? Will it withstand the abuses of battle? The Feich and Dearg are civilized men. The Deasach corsairs are hardly that. Will you subject Catahn's citizens to their outrages?"

"What citizens are those, sir? The mice and owls?"

He started, feeling her amusement as a tickling veil drawn across his face, and looked away down the slope toward the village. Though it was broad daylight, it lay as if asleep. Nothing stirred in its streets, no smoke curled from its chimneys, no livestock moved through its paddocks. Feich swiveled his head back to Taminy, who continued to regard him expressionlessly. "It's empty."

"A Hillwild fortress is always ready to receive refugees from the holt," she said. "There was a time when Mertuile could take in all the citizens living outside her gates."

"I'll burn the village to the ground."

"You would not be the first to do that."

He fumed now. "I have other means of laying siege, Lady. I will not hesitate to use them. Against you, against your followers. I suspect an aislinn siege might be more effective here than a physical one. You may have observed my siege engine." He glanced up at the standard that bore the Chalice and casket.

"The Osraed Bevol's crystal, Aiffe?"

His face stilled. "You call my bluff. Very well. Then know that Ochan's Crystal is part of what I seek here. Don't imagine that because that box contains a lesser crystal, I am powerless. As I said, I have resources. I think you know this."

She refrained from answering, but waited for him to come to his point.

He leaned toward her, eyes intent, *aidan* focused. "I want Airleas—at Mertuile and with myself as Regent. *Sole* Regent. And I want you there, as well, to satisfy the people, to ensure Airleas's cooperation, to be my . . . confidante, my instructor."

"To be a trophy."

"Ah, more than that, dear Lady. Much more than that. Cyne Colfre was right in thinking you a superb symbol. I would make you a virtual goddess. Your word would be theological law."

"*My* word?"

He smiled. "When it agrees with mine. When it doesn't . . . " He shrugged.

"You would make us figureheads, then—Airleas and I."

"And I would spare the Cwen, your followers—who, by the way, are suffering greatly in Creiddylad—and your Hillwild protector." He turned a baleful eye on Catahn, who stood some yards away, watching. "Though I would take great pleasure in ending the nuisance he represents. I would even leave Halig-liath under your control. Of course, the Osraed must not be permitted to obtain the sort of power they've traditionally wielded."

"For my cooperation and Airleas's you would do all this."

"Aye. For that."

"Will your allies agree?"

"Eventually . . . Let me remind you again, that this will be more than a physical siege. Let me remind you of Iseabal."

The chill that Taminy had felt hovering about her now wrapped its frigid arms about her soul. She knew her face betrayed her.

Feich nodded. "Yes . . . I suspected you knew. Give in now, Lady. Save yourself."

"You attack at the wrong point, Regent Feich."

"I think not." He rose. "I *know* not."

He escorted her back to the gates of Hrofceaster, back to their hovering audience, and took his party back down the narrow, sloping road to his siege camp.

The fire was warm and, in its glow, Daimhin Feich basked and contemplated his situation, his options, his desires. Lilias Saba was seeing to the last of these, massaging him with scented oils while his mind turned in lazy spirals. He did not doubt that he would force Taminy to capitulate eventually. Then . . . then what? He had every intention of making her a spiritual figurehead. She would be able to keep the Osraed under control, quell their rebellious arrogance. And more, she would become his consort. No doubts had he about that either. Yet now, with his mind floating far afield, he realized he had a longer term goal at heart—that a son of his sit on the throne of Caraidland, binding it to the House Feich.

He saw his options for power in terms of women: a liaison with Lilias Saba would unite Caraid-land and El-Deasach. If he was exceedingly clever he might have two capitals at his command—Creiddylad in the north and Kansbar in the south—capitals his son would hold after him. Marriage to Toireasa Malcuim, on the other hand, offered the obvious benefit of consolidating his legal hold over Airleas, and he had no doubt that, through artful Weaving, her barrenness might be cured.

Yet, neither Lilias nor Toireasa could give him a son like himself—a son with the Gift. He realized his own *aidan* was a fluke and knew there was no guarantee a woman of little or no talent would bear him a Gifted child. Only one woman could be counted on to do that—Taminy-a-Cuinn, Osmaer.

He daydreamed of it. Fey son of a fey father and a divinely Wickish mother.

"I'm pleased my work delights you so."

Feich opened his eyes and gazed up into the face of Lilias and was struck again by her extreme beauty. An embarrassment of riches, he had. It was a shame Caraidin religious law didn't allow for polygamy. Perhaps he would wed Toireasa then have the Osraed allow for two extra wives. That, indeed, would be the best option of all.

"Or were you thinking about your Dearg Wicke?" Raven pouted prettily. "I know you will go to her later."

Feich reached up to run fingers through her glossy black hair. "Only to Weave, my darling. Only to send aislinn warriors against Hrofceaster."

"You believe that will work? That will cause the Sorceress to let loose of your little Cyneric?"

"I do believe that. Should I not?"

"There is much power there. In her, in the boy, in the Hillwild. Even that scarecrow of an Osraed who scribbled for them was powerfully Gifted."

Bemused, Feich framed her face with his hands and looked deeply into her eyes, probing. "Who told you that?"

"No one. I sensed it. I'm not without my own *aidan*, as you call it."

"You Weave?"

She shook her head. "Little. But I see. For many years I served my father as chief advisor. Only twice did he fail to take my advice. Once, it cost him a caravan. Once, it cost him his life." She shook herself visibly, peeling away the sudden melancholy that clouded her beauty. "Such sight is a useful talent for a ruler to have."

"Indeed. Still, I might teach you to Weave. Yes, I'm sure I could teach you that."

"When you are still learning from your Dearg?"

"'My Dearg,' as you call her, is only a focus and a source of energy for my own Weaving. I've learned all from her that I can. Now, she is merely a repository of useful energy—like a grain silo or a well." He chuckled at the image that evoked. "No, Lilias. Coinich Mor can teach me nothing. It is Taminy-Osmaer I must learn from now."

Lilias's brows winged upward. "Only learn? More than that, I wager."

He caressed her cheek. "And does this bother you, my love?"

"Not as long as you answer to my touch. But with me, you have no rivals. For your Golden Wicke's heart, you must compete with the Hillwild Ren." Her eyes held his with a satin grip that infused him with heat and sent his body, mind and spirit in conflicting directions. "He has her heart, Daimhin. More, I think he touches her spirit, as well."

Feich stiffened. "No, but he'd like to, I know. I see the way he looks at her, the way he guards her."

"Lusts for her," added Lilias, mouth curving, eyes glowing.

He shifted uncomfortably. "As well he might. She is, without doubt, the most beautiful woman in Airdnasheen."

Lilias traced his lips with her finger. "Ah, but it's more than lust, my demon. He loves her. And she, him."

"Pah!" He twitched away. "She loves only her Eibhilin Mistress, the Meri. You forget, I know the girl. She cannot be seduced."

Lilias laughed, a sound Feich found suddenly and unaccountably annoying. "Not by you, perhaps, but between her and that Hillwild savage there is a bond. I've seen it. Felt it."

Feich was suddenly in no mood to be petted. Passion dying, he set Lilias away from him. "I must see to my Weaving," he told her tersely and rolled up from her soft pallet.

Affronted, she hissed at him. "You are in love with her, yourself!"

"I am in love only with the Throne and Circlet," he returned, seeking his clothing.

She found it first and threw it at him. "You want her."

He gazed at her, even in his impatience, able to admire the way firelight painted shifting scenes on the gleaming bronze of her flesh. "I want many things, Lilias—you among them. But now, I must Weave or I shall not have what I want most—Caraid-land."

The Deasach was unappeased. Flipping back her tent flap, she summoned one of her young corsairs and, uncaring of her nakedness, invited him into the tent. If the young man was surprised by this, or embarrassed by Feich's half-clad presence, he hid it completely, and yielded to his Banarigh's sudden, fierce advances without comment. Before Feich could even remove himself from the tent, the two were locked in a fervid embrace.

For the moment, he hardly cared what Lilias Saba did in her petty disappointment, but hastened to his own tent to summon Coinich Mor. Tonight she would channel his *aidan* deep into Hrofceaster where he would strike at its heart.

It was pleasant by the fire. Warm. Taminy needed warmth just now—savored it. Hrofceaster had never seemed a cold place to her until now. But now *he* was camped at her gates. She despaired of being able to read him adequately, of being able to understand what she read. Daimhin Feich wore a thick facade of artful design beneath which nothing was apparent but a constant play of passions. His *aidan* flowed hot and cold and hot again. She could neither gauge its depth nor its direction. What he would do now . . .

Something shifted in the atmosphere of the room around her—dark ripples on an aislinn pool. She raised her head from her knees, glancing around. Did that shadow move? Had that curtain shifted? As she turned back to the fire, her eyes and *aidan* both caught the presence; motes of fire and blood spun in a vortex at the center of the room, struggling to unite.

Taminy faced it slowly, pulling herself to her knees, putting her back to the fire. As she moved, she described a Wardweave, keeping it tight, close to her, like an aislinn shield. Anger pulsed through the Weave—anger at having even this, her private sanctum, violated. Laying hold of her senses, she willed them to calm, to readiness, for the motes were describing a male form—a form she recognized.

In a burst of ruddy light and hot exultation it was complete and the Daimhin Feich of her nightmares stood before her, gloating. He was bigger than life, more vivid, vibrating with dark vitality. His pale eyes gleamed like the steel of a sword's blade, his shoulders and chest swelled beneath an aislinn fabric of crimson, blue fire made an aura about his head.

This is how he sees himself, she realized. *This is his mirror image.*

"I can see!" the effigy exclaimed. "My God, I can see as if—!" He broke off and stared at her, making her suddenly aware of her state of undress and she, in futile defense, clutched at the fabric of her soft robe.

Feich's image inclined its head. "Lady, as you see, I could not wait to behold you again. There is a matter of some importance I must discuss with you. A proposition I must set before you."

She said nothing, having nothing to say.

"My proposition, simply, is this: that we be allies. No, more than allies. That we be as one. Therefore, I offer you this—that we be wed for the greater good of Caraid-land."

She was stricken with the impulse to laugh, but incredulity overcame any amusement. "And how would our . . . our marriage work for the good of anyone—even yourself?"

"I'll refrain, for the moment, from speaking of my own needs and wants. Let me just say that it would put you in a position of influence and protection, and return you to Creiddylad, where you can best exert that influence. The Caraidin would benefit by your spiritual leadership. You would become . . . a focus."

"A figurehead, you mean. Yes, we've spoken of this."

"As my wife, you would be more than a figurehead." His smile was at once sweetly patronizing and repulsive. "You might even be Cwen, were you so inclined. And . . . it would guarantee Airleas Malcuim's continued existence."

The blood drained from Taminy's face, leaving her cheeks chill. "You make Airleas's life dependent on my capitulation?"

The aislinn Feich's teeth gleamed as if moonlit. "I prefer to think of it as cooperation. But yes, if you will. Airleas will most assuredly end up in my hands. His survival is now in yours."

"You assume much about where Airleas will end up.
But, I don't understand you. You have made your hatred
of me clear. How could marriage to me possibly benefit
you?"

The effigy moved closer to her. "First of all, dear Lady,
I have never hated you. You drive me to fury, to rage, to
violence. Must I explain to you how close to passion those
things are? Indeed, they are forms of passion. And second, is this: I will derive many benefits from marriage to
you, Taminy-Osmaer. Power, safety, satisfaction. But my
chief benefit will be the child you will bear me. A child
who will carry the might of our combined Gifts."

Taminy came to her feet on a surge of cold, sickening
outrage. "What you suggest is impossible. Unthinkable."

Feich's face blanked, a look that was almost distress flickering across it. A smile that was more snarl followed. "What
I am suggesting, Lady Osmaer, is your only means of
ensuring Airleas's return to his throne. That is your will,
is it not? And the will of your Mistress?"

"You know it is."

"And now you know my will—to possess you. I realize
now that has been at the root of my thoughts since . . . "

"Since I refused you."

The effigy's expression darkened. "Don't provoke me,
Taminy. Not now that you're within my reach. Not now
that your young disciples and your beloved little Cyneric
and your Hillwild Ren are *within my reach.*" He cocked
his head to one side, his eyes bright slits. "I assume you
care for your dog-faithful Hillwild. And I assume you realize
how the cur dotes on you. How he wants you. But he will
not have you. I will."

A spark of pure anger flared in Taminy's breast—a flame
of outrage that licked a hot tongue at her soul. "You assume
much about your power, Regent."

He spread aislinn hands and moved toward her with
steady steps. "I am here. Do I not seem substantial to you?
Would a touch prove my power?"

In the back of her mind, the hatred gained substance
and power; it coiled, straining to be unleashed, to destroy

him utterly. She considered it, fleetingly, a swift slash of fury—surely that's all it would take. He couldn't possibly be as strong as he believed himself. Someone so evil could never be that strong. She hefted the hatred as a sword, felt its weight and balance, looked into the aislinn Feich's pale eyes, prepared to strike.

The impulse died in a choking surge of panic, Taminy cowering before it—before her own hatred. "Be gone!" She edged backward, holding up a hand, restrained, the killing inyx clutched in her hand like a ball of flame. Feich watched the hand rise; was that fear in his eyes? Had he read her impulse to destroy him? Did he read her present shame? She let the destructive Weave unravel, leaving only the simple Shieldweave.

He laughed. "You'll have to do better than that, dear. I am stronger than you imagine."

"Leave me!" she told him, voice low, reining in rage. "If you'd have an answer from me, leave me!"

"I'd have more than an answer." He took another step, crowding her.

In the instant Taminy's shoulder pressed into the stone of the hearth mantel, in the instant fury threatened to engulf her, the door of her room thundered and flew open. In its black maw, Catahn poised, sword in hand. In a heart's beat he was in the room, face ashen, eyes struggling to take in what they saw. The false Feich turned, shedding bits of his aislinn stuff upon the floor to melt like fiery snow. With a roar of outrage, Catahn wielded his sword in a singing arc through the ephemeral figure. The blade passed clean through in a shower of sparks, the image exploding into a thousand fragments of gleaming, riotous laughter. Feich was gone, leaving only an echo and an after-image of ruddy flame.

"Taminy!" Catahn crossed the room to her in two strides, dropping his sword to pull her into his arms. "Lady! Dear God, how did he come to be here? Has he grown that strong? What did he say to you?"

She drew away from him, straightening her robe, willing herself to calm and self-possession. "In a moment," she said, turning her face to the fire. "In a moment, I'll tell you. Just now I need to pray. Wait for me here," she added, and withdrew to her bedroom.

It was more than a moment before she came to him where he paced, back and forth, back and forth across her parlor. And she told him, in a voice like icy water what Daimhin Feich had demanded of her.

Cold rage clawed at his gut. Cold rage and a desire to hack Daimhin Feich's smile from his face with a dull blade. How dare he contemplate marriage to Taminy? How dare he suggest that there could ever be a bond of any kind between them?

She was watching him. Watching him clench and unclench his fists, fight to control the breath that wanted to come out in a roar. Words flew from his mouth before he could drag them back: "You should be no man's wife."

She was silent for a long moment and, when she spoke, her words jolted him. "And why should I not? Can I not be loved?"

He sucked breath into his lungs. "Loved, yes. Adored. Obeyed. But *wanted*, never! To tie you in such a profane bond—!"

"How, profane? The Spirit made us this way—male, female, capable of generating new life through our union. He asks only that that union be one of love."

"You'll get no love from Feich. He desires only to conquer and possess. There is no love in that man. None."

"No. But there is love in another."

"What are you saying? Of whom do you speak?"

"What man loves me, Catahn? What man puts me before life itself? What man's life is tangled in mine so that we might never unentwine?"

She gazed at him with those extraordinary green eyes and he knew that none of his anguish, and none of his weakness, had gone unnoticed. Well, he should have known that. To be close to Taminy was to expose oneself completely. He was daft to have thought he could hide his feelings from her. Shamed to the depths of his soul, he lowered his eyes, unable to stand her scrutiny. "Forgive me," he said.

"Forgive you? Never."

His head jerked up and fear, abject and paralyzing, wrapped itself around his soul. Compared to this, he had never known fear. Now, it gutted him.

She came to him, then, taking his huge hands in hers, pulling his eyes down to her face, denying them escape. "I will never forgive you if you don't speak to me plainly from this moment on. What am I to you, Catahn?"

"You are my life," he moaned. "But the thoughts I have had. The dreams I have dreamed . . . " Tears started from his eyes.

"Feich's nightmares? Forget them."

He shook his head, miserable. "No, no! My own."

"I dreamed them with you," she said. "Every night praying that you would wake the next morning and bring them to me to share."

What was she saying? He shook his head and the bells braided into his hair whispered an unbelieving duan.

Taminy's grip on his hands tightened, feeling like fingers of flame. "Catahn, I love you. I would be *your* wife."

God, but he'd never been so cold—a column of ice with a soul of fire. He would melt. "You can't mean it."

"Why?"

"You're Osmaer. The Shadow of the Meri. Your purity—"

"I'm human, Catahn. A woman. I have a mission, but the mission is not *me*. And what is impure in our love?"

He groaned, finally tearing his eyes away from her perfect, gleaming face. "*I!*" he said. "I am impure. My hands are soiled. I've stolen, killed, betrayed my wife, fathered a child on a woman who was not my wife—"

"And you love me."

"I could be your father." He laughed—a sharp, humorless bark. "My own daughter is two months *older* than you are."

"Your love for me is not a father's love for a daughter," she observed, and he melted further. "My love for you is not a daughter's love for a father."

He closed his eyes and imagined flame danced behind them. "But to be your husband—"

He could feel her eyes on his face, feel her *aidan* probing his soul. She let go of his hands suddenly and released him, body and soul. He nearly collapsed in a swift agony of aloneness.

"I have laid myself open to you, Catahn Hageswode. Not as Taminy-Osmaer, but as Taminy-a-Cuinn. I have confessed my love for you—my desire for union with you. I cannot demand your heart or order your soul—"

"Lady, you have both my heart and my soul."

She put up her hands then, palms out, as if pressing at the invisible barrier between them. Her expression was agony itself. "Then why do you hide them from me behind this wall?"

His heart broke, and the wall with it. He swore he could hear the cracking of them as he bore through and pulled her up into his arms. His hands dared to tangle themselves in the long, golden banner of her hair; his lips dared to taste hers. He was consumed at once by glory and self-loathing. Then, the loathing was itself consumed in a swell of light and heat.

"I would be your husband," he murmured against the warmth of her neck, and shivered at the significance of the words.

"And I would be your wife," she answered, and turned her head for his kiss.

Deardru was part of the cold that emanated from the stones of Hrofceaster; her breath was the chill draft that eddied in its halls. But, no, the stones beneath her feet had never been and could never be as cold as her heart was this moment. Her eyes blurred, making chaos of the framed scene—the firelit sward of carpet, the massive hearth, the two forms melded in a haloed silhouette, their shadows lying suggestively across the floor.

Forcing down the bile that rose to her throat, Deardru backed silently away from the open doorway and lost herself to the darkness.

CHAPTER 22

How can a man banish hate if he thinks, "He mistreated me, he beat me, he defeated me, he dispossessed me?"

How can hate touch a man if he does not think, "He mistreated me, he beat me, he defeated me, he dispossessed me?"

Here is an eternal law: Hate does not defeat hate; only love does."

—The Corah, Book I, Verses 50-52

❖   ❖   ❖

"Ah, here you are, lord!"

Airleas left off his morose contemplation of the plumes of smoke from his enemy's campfires and turned from the narrow window to see Deardru-an-Caerluel step up into the small, dark alcove behind him. He couldn't hide his surprise at seeing her there; he'd thought himself well hidden. "Mistress an-Caerluel! How did you find me?"

She smiled. "You wear Raenulf's amulet. I can find you anywhere."

Airleas felt for the little stone catamount, warm beneath his woolen tunic. "I thank you for it, mistress. It helps me focus my thoughts."

"And what were your thoughts just now, Airleas?"

He turned his eyes back to the slitted window. "How near he is. I can feel him out there, scheming. Plotting how to lay hands on me and drag me back to Mertuile as his puppet."

Deardru's face darkened. "Aye. And plotting to lay hands on your poor Mistress, as well. God knows what he will make of her once he has got her."

Airleas glanced at her sharply. "He *won't* get her. She won't let him. He'd make her a prisoner."

"Nothing so simple as that, I fear. No, I overheard his plans for her, Airleas. He is a vile man. No, a monster."

"What plans? What have you heard?"

"He would force her to marry him to assure her submission."

"*Submission?*" Airleas cried. "She would never submit to him! How can he imagine she would? She's Osmaerl"

Deardru shook her head, eyes sad. "It pains me to see how your innocence will be sacrificed to this siege, child. Feich has made Taminy's submission to him the price for your life and freedom."

Airleas thought the entire fortress trembled about him. "No," he whispered. "Taminy must never have to make such a choice. She *won't* make it. Feich could never convince her. He hasn't the strength—"

"I pray you are right. But, in my heart—in my soul—I fear you're wrong. You are Taminy's greatest concern. She has made herself responsible for you. She loves you. I suppose, in a sense, she has taken the place of your father—watching over you as if you were her own child. And Feich . . . well, it seems he has more power than we had thought. There are rumors . . . "

Airleas prodded her with his eyes.

"There are rumors Feich has allied himself with some Dark Force, some evil spirit he has conjured."

"I don't believe in evil spirits. They're just excuses we make for our own evils."

She clucked at him in motherly concern. "It's never wise to taunt things we don't understand, child."

"I'm sick of being a child!" Airleas exploded. "I want to be a man! *I* should be watching over *her*! *I* should be protecting *her* from—from that demon!"

Deardru uttered a soft, sighing laugh. "How much like Raenulf you are. If he were alive, he'd call you a man. I call you one. Catahn should have required your Craskan-duine long ago."

Airleas was silent, fuming, impotent. God, how he hated

this feeling. If he were only a man—*truly* a man—*then* he would . . . he could . . .

"Aye. Raenulf would have felt the same, in your stead. Oh, he would have been aflame with the passion to act."

"But what would he *do*, in my stead?"

Deardru smiled wistfully. "A big question, that. Well, knowing my Raenulf, if he were here . . . I think he would sneak himself outside these walls, find his way to the rainbow colored tent of Daimhin Feich and kill him. Yes, I'm certain that's what he'd do. Raenulf was no more a coward than you are. I was right to give you his amulet."

Airleas glanced at her, found her black eyes on him, hot and intense. Did she expect him to—? A chill seized him—a chill of pure exhilaration. Hadn't he daydreamed of doing what Deardru suggested—of confronting Daimhin Feich on his own territory? But sneaking into his tent, killing him by stealth . . . "No. No, that wouldn't be right," he murmured. "I need to meet Feich face-on and not in secret."

"Noble," said Deardru. "But if you wait for that time, Taminy will fall into his hands. Can you allow that?"

"Maybe Raenulf would do as you say. Maybe he would seek Feich out and kill him. But I . . . I can't do that. If I did that, I'd be no better than Feich. I'd betray all Taminy has taught me. All she intends for me."

Deardru's eyes were shadowed now—guarded—Airleas could not read them, but only feel their pressure. "Yet, if you do nothing, do you not betray Taminy, herself? Do you not betray all those who look to you as their Cyne? Do you not betray the honor of your House? Feich spits at the Malcuim; he defiles your father's throne; he would defile your own dear Mistress. Are these not things that cry for vengeance? For sacrifice?"

Airleas pushed back against the weight of Deardru's regard. "But if I murdered Feich in such a way, I'd sacrifice my soul. Where would be honor then? Or vengeance? No. Taminy would never wish me to do that."

Deardru shook her head, spraying him with impatience and contempt. "Perhaps you are not so much like Raenulf as I thought—nor so ready for manhood. No, poor Airleas, you are still a little boy, after all."

When she was gone, he could still taste her disappointment as something bitter and acrid in the damp chill of the alcove. It seemed excessive and the excess bemused him. Why should her disappointment be so deep? Could she harbor such a hatred for Feich, a man she had never met, that she willed him dead?

He rubbed the little jet catamount between thumb and forefinger. Futile to wonder. Yet flowing back to him through the little effigy, he could still feel her anger, her contempt, and a cold current of resolve.

They were headed straight east through the foothills now, funneling up from the Vale of Orian. From the verdant lowlands patterned by crops and orchards, through forested grasslands, they had emerged at last onto a rocky heath— a place of twisted trees and patchy wetlands. The ground beneath them sloped increasingly upward and now their horses' hooves met the first dusting of snow. The setting Sun gleamed rose-gold on the mountains before them, showing the pass as a dusky violet slash. But sunlight was withdrawing rapidly from the floor of the narrow valley, leaving the travelers in a bowl of unrelieved grey.

Gazing up at the distant crags of Baenn-an-ratha, Aine thought she had never seen a more desolate setting. She had once thought Hrofceaster to be desolate, but now, it pulled at her, like home. And as she pictured the place, sitting high up on its craggy scarp, she saw tents scattered on the slopes below its walls. In their midst, a standard bore aloft an object that flashed fire into the violet bowl overhead and, near that standard, in a small, guarded tent . . .

"Aine, what is it?" asked Iseabal. "What's wrong?"

Aine shook the vision away, realizing she'd stopped her horse in the middle of the rock-strewn track and had frozen there, mouth and eyes agape. "Airleas," she whispered. "We must hurry, Isha. Airleas will be betrayed."

✧   ✧   ✧

Airleas stood on the parapet looking out over the forecourt of the fortress. Under a layer of moon-washed mist, the angles and planes of Airdnasheen glittered with a fine layer of frost. Odd, he felt no chill, nor did his breath cloud the frigid air.

Before he could contemplate that, his eyes were drawn to the courtyard below. Furtive movement roiled the mist—may have even been part of the mist. In moments, the movement took on form, coalescing to become colorless cloaked and hooded figures—a trio of satellites orbiting a central point. Airleas frowned. No, not satellites, shepherds, and the single charge was obviously captive. Cold panic flushed through him. He tensed to run, but found himself unable to move. He tried to cry out, but his throat failed him. His fingers gripped the parapet; they were numb to the freezing stone.

It could only be a Weave. But, dear God, so powerful?

The fleeing figures were almost to the gates when he remembered his own *aidan* and marshalled it. Though his body seemed incapable of movement, surely his spirit could fly. He barely had the thought when he found himself soaring over the parapet, swooping into the dark recesses of the forecourt.

Before the scurrying figures, he lit, bird-like, and braced himself for their attack. The wraith-forms did not even pause in their advance. It was as if he were invisible to them.

"Stop!" he shouted, but no sound came from his lips. The dark shepherds pressed on, and now the one they herded raised her head as if she alone had heard him. It was Taminy's face he stared into, Taminy's eyes that gazed blankly into his own.

Panicked and befuddled, he could only gape while sheep and shepherds bore through him as if he were composed of mist. Behind him the gates of Hrofceaster rattled and the invaders passed out into the night. Sluggish now, Airleas struggled to turn, to follow the men who had taken Taminy. Why had no one been aware of them? Why had no one raised the alarm or stopped them? Were all as bewicked as he was?

He floundered over the questions; his mind obeyed no better than his body had done. Clarity would not come. The grey world around him became black and close. He gasped, afraid he must suffocate.

He shocked to complete awareness in his bed, up to his ears in blankets and fleeces. Quaking, he struggled to orient himself. Had he been dreaming? Was he now awake? Then came fear. Had the dream been prophetic? Or had he been bewicked and seeing an aislinn vision from the midst of someone else's Weave?

Rattling. He could still hear the rattling of the fortress gates or . . . He sat up. No, it was his chamber door that rattled now. He rose unsteadily, pulled on a woolen cloak and stumbled to his door, yet unable to shake the vision. In the hallway, Deardru-an-Caerluel stood, trembling, muffled in an azure cloak.

"Lord!" she cried, seeing him. "Lord, Feich has taken your Mistress away by stealth and by inyx. He's befuddled Catahn and Desary—even Osraed Wyth. They all sleep as if dead. You must come!"

Airleas shook his head. Befuddled? He had certainly been that himself. How was he now awake? "Bewicked," he murmured. "But how have I—?"

"The amulet! I was awake when the Weave fell on the fortress. I could wake you only because we are linked by the amulet. Airleas—" She grasped his arm, bent to look into his eyes. "Airleas, you're the only one who can save her!"

Airleas's heart seemed to stop, trembling, in his breast. Taminy. Feich had taken Taminy. He had not dreamed. As he dressed, as he strapped on his sword, he flogged his mind, trying to clear it. Surely, there were questions he should ask. Things he must know before he went any-where. What should he do when he got outside the gates of Hrofceaster? Would he have to kill Feich? *Could* he kill Feich? How could he do what Taminy could not? How was it she was disarmed and not Eyslk's mother?

Head spinning, he followed the Hillwild woman from the room and through the chill corridors of Hrofceaster.

Perhaps it was the cold of the hemming stone, perhaps it was the dregs of his aislinn vision, but Airleas's mind at last grasped at one of the circling questions. "What must I do? I must know what to do," he murmured and realized his teeth were chattering. He began to pray, silently.

"You must kill Daimhin Feich," Deardru said. "You must rescue your Mistress."

"I . . . I *can't*! I can't kill Feich, I—"

"Don't be ridiculous, child. You can walk on water."

"No, I mean . . . " How could she know? Had she eavesdropped on his lesson by the Gwyr's pool? Why should she do that? He shook his head, wishing the effects of the enemy Weave would wear off. He grasped at a passing thought. "Taminy would despise me if I killed Daimhin Feich."

Deardru glanced back at him. "To save her life? Her honor? You are mistaken."

Even that, he thought, and fell silent, trying to decide what he could do now that he had decided what he *couldn't* do. Stopping, going back into the fortress, running to Taminy's room to see if she was there, none of these things occurred to him. His body followed Deardru as if on a tether, but his mind, pacing its narrow confines, came to a decision; he knew what he would do when he faced Daimhin Feich.

Outside the gates of Hrofceaster, Airleas took the initiative, moving ahead of Deardru down the rocky defile toward the trailhead from Airdnasheen. He had not quite drawn level with the village gate when he sensed the enemy presence and felt of the boundaries of their camp—physical boundaries and aislinn. The first he could circumvent, the second, he did not want to.

He announced himself to the watching, listening *aidan* and experienced a backwash of surprise. In the middle of the dark trail, he stopped and pulled his sword from its scabbard. Behind him, Deardru-an-Caerluel gasped, pulling up short. "Run," he told her. "Hide." And tossed the sword away from him onto the ground.

After a moment of hush, several figures arose before

him as if out of the ground. One of them picked up his
sword and moved to stand before him. In the dusky figure's
hands the sword blade flashed with sudden light, glowing a bright and silvery blue. By its light, Airleas could
see that the man he faced was Daimhin Feich.

"Is this surrender, Cyneric?" Feich asked him. "I rather
expected an attack."

"I've come to offer myself to stand as prisoner in Taminy's
place. Take me back to Creiddylad, but free my Lady."

Feich smiled. "Oh, I'll take you back to Creiddylad, rest
assured. But I can't possibly free 'your Lady.' I don't have
her." He glanced up over Airleas's head. "Thank you, Mistress, your help has been invaluable."

Airleas turned his spinning head. It came as no surprise
to see Deardru-an-Caerluel still standing on the trail behind
him.

She did not return the Regent's smile. "If you can force
Taminy-Osmaer out of Hrofceaster," she said, "I will consider my self well paid."

"I have the boy," he told his cousin, and Ruadh felt an
unaccountable surge of relief.

He settled himself before the brazier in Daimhin's gaudy
tent. "The Hillwild woman delivered him to you?"

"He practically delivered himself. I expected him to come
wielding his sword. Instead, he surrendered it."

"Because of your Weaving, you think."

"Mine, Coinich Mor's, and the Hillwild's. She gave him
an amulet that, according to her, amplified any inyx she
directed at him. Homey magic, that, don't you think?"

"I couldn't say. But we have what we came for, now.
We can return to Creiddylad."

"Not yet. There is one more thing I need to accomplish here."

Suddenly uneasy, Ruadh asked, "Surely, you don't intend
to try to take Hrofceaster?"

"Not Hrofceaster, itself. Only what it holds—Taminy-
Osmaer."

"Are you mad? The longer you stay here, the more time

you give her to retaliate. I know you think you and your Wickish consorts are very clever and powerful, but—"

"We are both clever and powerful. Taminy imagines that she is dealing with one power, but she is dealing with two—three if you count that traitorous Hillwild woman. And she is afraid of me."

"This awesome woman is afraid of you?"

"So Lilias tells me."

The uneasiness of Ruadh's soul increased. "Cousin, you have the Cyneric. You can return to Creiddylad and set yourself up as his Regent and Durweard. You can marry your Deasach Cwen, if you would. You can pacify the Houses and harness the Assembly. With Airleas in hand, you will have power in Caraid-land. And, if Taminy-Osmaer is, as you say, afraid of you, you can keep her at bay, as well. Why must we continue to put ourselves through this hardship? So you can avenge yourself on this woman for some former humiliation?"

Daimhin shook his head. "I don't want revenge, Ruadh. You scoff at my 'Wickish consorts,' as you call them. Well, you may be right in thinking them an inferior sort. Coinich Mor is certainly rough-cut and Lilias is a foreigner. But what of a Divine consort? Would you scoff at that?"

"A Divine consort? What do you mean?" Ruadh *knew* what he meant, but somehow hoped the words that came from Daimhin's mouth would prove his knowledge false. They did not.

"Taminy-Osmaer, cousin. That's who I would wed. Imagine it—Light and Darkness, the Divine and the Profane, the Blameless and the Wicked. The power, you see, is in the contrast."

Insanity. It wore his cousin's face. If he could, he would gather his men and leave this moment. Only honor prevented him. "How can you hope to harness that power? She is a minion of the Meri. Ultimately, the Meri will prevail."

"The beauty of her strength is that it is constrained, even confined, by a peculiar weakness. She could destroy me. I believe she *would* have destroyed me, once. But, you see, her nature prevents her. She is incapable of deviousness—I am deviousness itself. She abhors violence— I find it exhilarating. She is above lust—I am lust incarnate. She serves a Mistress of Light—I serve a Master of Darkness."

Ruadh could only sit and shiver with the cold that sat in the pit of his stomach. "You've spoken like this before— about your Dark Master. What Master do you mean? Surely, you don't believe in Cadder's Grand Demon?"

"What do you know of that?"

"Only what he's sniveled in his frequent moments of whining. Every evil thing in the world is the fault of this mighty Demon. Most especially, is Taminy-Osmaer the fault of this Demon. It would not occur to Minister Cadder that evil is a product of the human mind, born out of human weaknesses."

Daimhin smiled indulgently. "And would such a thing occur to you?"

"Yes."

"Then you don't believe the universe holds both the Spirit and Its Opposite, Its balance, Its undoing."

"No."

"Well, I *do* believe that. And moreover, I believe I am called to serve that Opposite. Coinich Mor tried to convince me that the power of my *aidan* arose within me. But she spoke in ignorance. Oh yes, of course, she instructed me in how to Weave by tapping my own energies and those of others. But I can feel something outside me, beyond me, feeding those energies. It is this that Caime Cadder fears and I exult in. A Being of Darkness. The Spirit's opposition."

"And in wedding Taminy, you expect to bring Light under the control of Darkness?"

Daimhin chuckled. "You misunderstand my intention. Let me share with you what I have come to understand. You see, the universe exists in a balance. If the balance is upset, chaos erupts. I now know that the Meri regenerates every hundred years or so. When this occurs, Light floods the world; the balance is upset. There is what the Osraed call a Cusp; there is a battle, if you will, between what the Osraed perceive as Good and what they perceive as Evil. There is chaos; blood is shed; the balance of power is upset in Creiddylad as elsewhere. But in this Cusp, the chaos will be short-lived because I have come to understand the need for balance. I will wed Taminy-Osmaer and there will be balance between Darkness and Light."

"And you expect to be in control of Light?"

Daimhin smiled. "I told you, Ruadh, Taminy lacks the strong qualities necessary for control. Therefore, I shall harness her powers as well as mine for the best interests of Caraid-land." His eyes brightened. "I shall bring about a confluence of good and evil. Think of it, Ruadh. For the first time in history, a balance shall be struck between the two."

"And there shall be peace and prosperity for all," said Ruadh facetiously.

"Exactly."

There was no talking to him, he was so full of himself—so full of his grandiose ideas. Ruadh had no recourse but to go to his cousin's allies, such as they were. They gathered in Lilias Saba's tent—the Banarigh, Coinich Mor, the Dearg, Caime Cadder and himself—and he told them of his cousin's intention to drag Taminy-a-Cuinn from Hrofceaster and wed her. He didn't mention Daimhin's prattle about Darkness and Light. He spoke in terms of a balance of power—of the logic of control.

"If he kills her, she becomes a martyr—someone for whom people will be willing to fight. Likewise, if he leaves her here and free, she continues to be a rallying point for every dissident and malcontent in Caraid-land. So, Daimhin has . . . come to believe that the only way he can control Taminy's allies is to control her. And to enlist her tacit support."

Caime Cadder's face was as white as the snow covering the ground outside. "But he *can't* control her. Doesn't he see that?"

"He thinks he's done a mighty good job of it so far. He believes his talent for subterfuge makes him inherently stronger. And, of course, his *aidan* and his fey allies." Ruadh bowed toward the Dearg and Deasach women, who glanced at each other in a way that made his skin crawl.

"He was to marry me," Lilias said. "He spoke to me of power and love." She smiled wryly. "And our common love of power. I will not share him with Taminy the Pure."

Eadrig Dearg made a rude noise. "I care little for that, mistress. But I do care that the man behind our Cyneric's throne not take this Wicke into his confidence. She'll taint him as surely as she draws air."

Ruadh declined to comment upon who would taint whom, but merely said, "Then are we agreed that he must be discouraged from this course? That he must be made to return to Creiddylad with Airleas, now?"

"At all costs," said Cadder. "He can have no idea how dangerous that woman is. He is swept up in a heady sense of his own power. He is naive. He cannot hope to control her. She Weaves to make him believe that he can." He glanced around at the others. "You see how insidious she is?"

"What do you put forth as a plan?" asked the Dearg.

"Withdraw your men. Threaten to leave him here with only the Deasach as allies."

Lilias Saba laughed. "He has no Deasach allies. He will not let me avenge my brother's death on this Osmaer woman and now he insults me by proposing to marry her. I've had enough of this gaming."

"Now, Raven," murmured Coinich Mor, "will you let your jealousy blind you? What better way to avenge your brother than to allow our Daimhin to get his hands on the Wicke so you can get your hands on her?"

Lilias pursed her generous lips. "You make a winning point."

Cadder scowled and glanced at Ruadh. "Where is he?"

"Visiting the Cyneric."

"I must speak to him."

"Speak to him," said the Raven, "of my decision to leave him alone on this mountain. Then perhaps your threats of Divine retribution may mean something to him."

She left the tent, swaggering, and Ruadh could not help but think how well-suited she and Daimhin were, albeit, she was not as mad.

✧ ✧ ✧

"Your cousin says you would marry the Caraidin Wicke."

Daimhin Feich glanced from Airleas Malcuim's pale face, flaccid with drugged sleep, to where Caime Cadder stood framed in the entrance of the tent that housed his prisoner. He had not wanted a confrontation with the cleirach just yet; he hadn't had a chance to formulate his plans fully. No matter, though. He found he thought quite well under pressure. "Coinich Mor?" he asked, deliberately dissembling. "My dear Minister, I wouldn't think of marrying such a coarse creature."

"Taminy-Osmaer. You mean to make her your captive wife."

Nettled by the sourly pious expression on the other man's face, Feich abandoned his previous caution. "Yes. And I mean to make the Banarigh Lilias Saba of El-Deasach my free wife. What have you to say to that?"

Cadder reddened. "What? You would marry both of them? Our laws will not permit such—such an immoral act."

"They will."

"They—? W—what you suggest is—is *blasphemy!*" He lifted his head, drew his shoulders back, showing that he did, after all, have a spine of sorts. "I won't countenance it. The Osraed—"

"The Osraed will be powerless before me once I have the Osmaer Crystal, once I have the Osmaer woman. They will be powerless before *us*."

Cadder's face blanched, then went deep crimson but for the braces of white that pinched his hawkish nose. "You'll not lay hands on her without your allies—and those you have lost. The Dearg and your foreign Cwen have both pledged to leave and strand you here." Quaking, Cadder folded his arms across his chest—a combative posture which Feich found both amusing and irritating. "I had come here to reason with you," the cleirach continued, managing to sound at once arch and timorous. "I had come to warn you of your allies' defection and to suggest that we should return to your capital at once to seal your victory. But now, I think I am too late. When the Dearg go, so shall I."

"They won't leave."

"You think they bluff? I assure you, Regent, they do not."

"I won't allow them to leave, Cadder. It's that simple. I need them, therefore they shall stay." He smiled at the stricken expression on the cleirach's thin face. "You don't understand yet, do you, Minister? You don't realize who I am or what I am capable of accomplishing."

"Well, Regent Feich, whatever it is you hope to accomplish, you will have to do it without the Dearg or the Deasach. Nor is the blessing of the Osraed any more with you. When Tarsuin hears of this—"

"Tarsuin be damned."

Shaking like a wind-blown sapling, Cadder swept out of the tent, vibrating the very air around him.

Feich laughed aloud. He turned back to the tethered boy. "So the little insect has a temper," he observed, though Airleas could not hear him. "I'd never have suspected."

From Airleas's tent, he returned to his own, there to carefully word his next dispatch to the fortress—a dispatch that would begin negotiations for Taminy's surrender. He drafted the message, his mind half-consumed with the desire for another aislinn visit to Taminy's rooms. He would see Coinich Mor when he had finished here, he decided. He would tender a more personal demand for Taminy's capitulation.

He did neither of those things—a heavy, sodden sleep caught him unawares and relegated thoughts of Taminy to his dreams.

Caime Cadder's universe had become a dark and terrifying place. He had always doubted Feich's quality of spirit, but he had at least been certain of one thing—that Taminy was the Enemy, was Evil incarnate. Therefore, allying himself with anyone less evil was justifiable. Now, he was certain of nothing. It was as if he'd wakened from a dream to find himself submerged in black water. There was no up, no down, neither left nor right, but only a vast and impenetrable darkness.

He recalled a nightmare from saner days at Ochanshrine—a place this dark, shared with Ochan's Crystal and Taminy-Osmaer. The threat to the Crystal was explicit in that dream; he'd assumed that threat was solely from the Cwen Wicke. Now . . .

But no, *that* he must still be sure of. Taminy-a-Cuinn was Evil incarnate, of that he must have no doubt. She had seduced an army of converts, seduced even the Abbod Ladhar at the end, but she would not have Caime Cadder. In this one thing, he would not fail.

Powerless before *us*, Feich had said. As if he and Taminy were not adversaries, after all, but allies. Very well. He had been grossly deceived about Daimhin Feich. But he had recovered from that deception, and now, surrounded by deceivers, he could be sure of no one but himself. His dream had foretold it; he was in a position to be the savior of the Stone. If Feich laid hands on it, took it to Creiddylad, then he would wrest it away and put it in the hands of the Osraed Tarsuin.

The thought gleamed before him as if it were, itself, crystalline. Yes, he would bide awhile, and by so doing he could manipulate the manipulator. Such a thing might wipe out every failure he had ever suffered.

It was like the popping of a bubble or the breaking of a wave; over the most Gifted citizen of Hrofceaster poured the sudden awareness that something was wrong, that Airleas Malcuim was now in the hands of his enemy. Awakened from a rare, sound sleep, Taminy felt of the peculiar energies in the afterwash of that wave. Aine. Aine-mac-Lorimer was on her way up the mountain with the Crystal. She would need to be shielded. Airleas was alive, but bound in a sleep so deep it could only be drug induced. Safer that way, perhaps, Taminy thought, and summoned her *waljan* to waking.

She couldn't reach Airleas to help him, but she could certainly reach the forces of Daimhin Feich.

✧   ✧   ✧

Chaos. Daimhin Feich was awash in it. He heard the
shouts of men and the shrill whinnies of frightened horses.
A dream? But no. The sound and confusion rose with maelstrom fury to batter at his sleep until he must open his
eyes or scream. Light gleamed redly through the slitted
panels of his tent flap, flickering like an unsteady lamp.
Dawn? Fire? He threw off blankets, dragged on boots and
coat and stumbled to sweep aside the tent flap.

What he saw was a scene from a nightmare. Liquid lightning the color of flame flowed from the high crags of Baenn-
eigh and down over the blocky columns of Baenn-an-ratha,
bloodying the bellies of the eternally hovering clouds.
Beneath the crawling crimson shroud, Hrofceaster's light-
blocking bulk threw a long, creeping shadow over Airdnasheen. The smoke from her fires fanned out below the
clouds, all but obscuring the banners flying atop her gates.
And from that smoke, wraiths unfurled, shredding away
like wisps of carded wool to take forms that boggled both
eye and mind. Huge wolves one moment, distorted riders upon deformed mounts, the next—silkies of the mountain mist, demons from frozen hell. And they swarmed
down the boulder-strewn trail from the Hillwild's stronghold into Feich's camp, demon eyes like flames dancing,
uttering obscene noises through lips meant for sucking the
life from souls. They met living men, Feich and Deasach
and Dearg alike and swooped around them, swaddled them.
Bodies fell right and left—molten lumps of flesh and cloth
under the red, red gleam of demon lightning.

His heart froze and his hair stood up on his head. Could
he reach his horse? Could he escape? No. There could
be no escape from this horror. Could this be Taminy? His
mind refused to accept that. She was a minion of the Meri;
this wholesale slaughter could not possibly be of her Weaving. Ah, who then? Coinich Mor? Lilias? The two of them
together? He had been a fool to laugh at Cadder, to underestimate Lilias and the Dearg Wicke, and these were the
wages of his foolishness.

He saw himself cowering beneath the canopy of his tent, wringing his hands, and was disgusted with the image. It was against every instinct he possessed to step out into the swell of red light, but he did it, and darted from shadow to shadow to the tent that held Airleas Malcuim. There, he would be safe.

It was an island of sanity, that tent, and others were there before him. His two women sat cross-legged on the ground-cover, the crystal Aiffe between them, their intent faces— the coarse and the refined—bathed in its golden glow. Behind them, Airleas Malcuim still slept the sleep of the drunken, oblivious. The sight froze him for a second as his mind flooded with the certain conviction that it was they who wove the destruction of every man about them.

"What are you doing?" he shrieked. "What are you doing?"

The women only smiled at him. He drew his sword and came toward them, arm raised to strike. A quick move of Coinich Mor's hand stopped him in his tracks as if he'd hit an invisible barrier.

"Calm yourself, Regent Feich," she told him. "We are not the Weavers of this inyx. Our Weaving is one you will celebrate."

"You . . . ?" He slanted a swift glance back at the tent flap. Bloody light crept along its inner edge, the din of death lapped through it in sickening waves. "Who, then? Who could—?"

"Your pretty Golden Wicke," said Lilias, wine-dark lips curved in a knowing smile. "She and her acolytes Weave this. Do you like it? Does it terrify you?"

He didn't answer. "Doesn't it terrify you?"

The women glanced at each other and laughed. "Come," said Coinich Mor, gesturing at their circle of calm golden light. "Come see what this sweet Raven has divined for you."

He sheathed his sword and moved to sit between them, facing Aiffe. To his surprise, the two joined hands so as to frame the stone, and gazed deep into its facets. Then Lilias's dark eyes seemed to roll back in their sockets and

Coinich Mor began to sing a duan. In the halo of light above Bevol's crystal an image formed. Four riders struggled through rocky fields of snow, leaning into a wind that Feich could neither feel nor hear. Four walkers led their mounts along the treacherous ledges of the Cauldron. Four travelers sheltered beneath the pines of Baenn-an-ratha miles below where his chances of capturing Taminy were being snuffed out.

"What am I seeing?"

"Look closely," whispered Coinich Mor, her gaze going to Lilias's flickering eyelids.

The scene shifted to the aislinn travelers huddled around a camp fire. Their faces revealed by the fire's warming glow. Feich gasped aloud.

"You know them?" asked Coinich Mor.

"Saefren Claeg, Iseabal-a-Nairnecirke, that idiot Osraed, Lealbhallain. The other girl I know only on sight."

The Dearg smiled. "They bring you a gift, Regent. The Osmaer Crystal is with them."

He gaped at her through the aislinn scene. "How do you know this?"

"Dear Lilias has a great gift for the Sight. I have merely added to it my own senses and this, the Osmaer's sister stone, cut from the same matrix. They are perhaps two days below us, Taminy shields them from more than observation. All this," —her gesture took in the turmoil without— "is her way of clouding your vision, lord. Of frightening you into retreat. Lucky you were to have us here."

"The Osmaer," he breathed. "But what must I do? How can I have it?"

"Attack Hrofceaster." The voice was Lilias Saba's. Feich turned his gaze to her, pulling it from the aislinn vision. "Distract them as they attempt to distract you. You have the forces at your command. Attack. And, when these children arrive, shielded though they be to outward eyes, I will see them. You will have them. You will have the Crystal. And I will have Iseabal-a-Nairnecirke and revenge."

Feich shook his head. "Don't you realize what's

happening out there? I have no more forces at my disposal. Those who have not fled in panic are dead and dying. Taminy is destroying my men and yours."

The women smiled secretly and rose and beckoned him back outside where red tongues of light and black tongues of smoke licked at the bodies of the fallen. He shuddered as Lilias Saba knelt by the body of a Deasach corsair and turned him over to reveal his face. He was little more than a boy and Feich was startled to recognize him as the young soldier his Deasach paramour had chosen to display her displeasure at him only nights ago.

"Look," she told him, holding a hand before the boy's face. "He has only swooned in fear. He will wake before long and wonder or run and hide."

"He's not dead?" Feich bent closer and saw that Lilias was right. Steam rose from the boy's nostrils. He had only fainted. Head raised, Feich looked out over the camp and realized that it was only the strange, squirming light that made the scene so horrible.

"Yes, you see?" asked Coinich Mor. "They've not melted away. It is all a trick of light and shadow. You are right about your Wicke. She is constrained to be harmless."

Feich felt laughter building in his throat. It bubbled out, sweeping him away on a tide of relieved hilarity. He let it take him, tumble him, steal his breath. "Shall I—" he gasped. "Shall I rally my fallen troops? Oh, but how shall they ride? How shall they fight?" He looked at the fallen bodies now and saw them as comic.

"Later," Coinich Mor told him, and together with her Deasach ally she led him back to his tent.

Deardru lived with a strange, tight, exhilarating dread clogging her throat. Around her, Taminy's followers scurried at their Mistress's beck and call, knowing that Airleas was missing or had been taken, but not knowing how or by whom. Reaching out through the catamount totem told her why they remained in the dark. Airleas slept, deeply and completely, dreamlessly, at Coinich Mor's Weaving.

Her first reaction to that realization had been relief; she'd

fully expected to return to Hrofceaster to be locked away
for her part in the boy's disappearance. But now she spent
every day in nervous anticipation that the boy would awake
and point an aislinn finger at her.

Alternately, she prayed that Feich would take his hostage
and run or that he would stay and fight and win. When
the *waljan* and their Mistress launched their aislinn attack
on the enemy camp, she was terrified. Corsairs and soldiers swooned away in terror or panicked and tried to run,
though there was nowhere to go with any speed. Unable
to do anything against the strength of that combined Weaving, she had reached out to Coinich Mor and been gratified to know that the Dearg Wicke already suspected what
she knew as fact—Taminy was loathe to kill even her worst
enemies. The attack was intended to induce fear, not bring
about death.

Yet, there was death. Fleeing down the steep, dangerous track on foot and on horseback, a number of terror-
stricken souls perished. She could see them, through the
eyes of the Deasach Banarigh, tossed like rag-dolls down
the toothed flanks of a pass known only as the Cut—Dearg
red, Feich yellow, even Deasach black.

She knew that Feich would attack once he'd regathered
his scattered and trembling troops. Still she held her breath,
awaiting that event, fearing that Airleas might awaken first
and reveal her as his betrayer, and went about her duties
at Hrofceaster—cooking, caring for the children. And all
the while she watched the bond between Catahn and
Taminy strengthen and grow. Like a living thing, it seemed,
eating away at her, growing fat on her anguish.

Yet so, her hatred of Taminy grew fat and flourished.

CHAPTER 23

Those who know God know none but God; those who fear God fear none but God, though the entire world be against them.

—from the Testament of Osraed Bevol

Between the three forces, they had lost less than twenty men to the canyon; another thirty or so had made their escape good and hid or fled back the way they had come toward El-Deasach. Most of them were Dearg. Daimhin Feich did not waste time with grief or anger. He left no one time to mourn the deaths—which were, after all, the result of cowardice—but had the men gathered before dawn, fed and ready to assault the Hillwild fortress. Here, he stepped aside; Ruadh would call the battle plan in consultation with Coinich Mor's slow but fierce husband and Lilias Saba. It amused Feich to think that the Deasach Banarigh actually commanded her own battle forces. He'd expected her to relinquish their control to a lieutenant, but she did not. He might have teased her for such a conceit if there had been time and opportunity . . . and if he had not such an appreciation of her pride.

They attacked Hrofceaster with the first faint reddening of the eastern sky—Ruadh with his troops, Daimhin with his *aidan*. Now, Taminy would taste of her own tactics.

Sunrise. The peaks to the east lit as if painted with fire. The mists of Baenn-iolair bled down her flanks and hung over Baenn-an-ratha in gaudy tatters. Still. It was too still on the mountainside, as if all things held their breath.

On the battlements, Catahn Hageswode watched as a strange mist rose from downslope and crept toward them—mist that didn't behave like mist. It billowed in the breezeless air, curled and fanned and obscured whatever might lie beyond it. Cover, Catahn realized. Cover for an attack. He summoned his lieutenants silently to preparation. A scent reached him, spicy, woody. Smoke, yes, but unnatural. Vaguely, he could feel the force behind it—a tickling on his skin, a prickling at the back of his neck.

Ready, ready, he thought to his men. _Be ready_. He glanced over his shoulder at the face of the fortress rising from the court, at the window of the Great Hall high in the facade. Taminy was there. He could see her only as a shadow against the thick glass. He could sense her as a flame, warm at his back. Reason enough to fight. Reason enough to die.

He turned back to the creeping smoke. It was below them now, had obscured the gate of Airdnasheen, rendered her empty houses and streets invisible. It rolled across the sloping access to Hrofceaster, spread east and west, blotting out the grove of Catahn's Crask-an-duine, the spring-fed mountain stream, the lonely stands of trees around and between. Concealing the ground, the sky . . . the enemy. It surrounded them and began to climb the walls. As the false mist flowed over Hrofceaster's battlements and into her forecourt, Catahn fought the tightness in his throat and took up his bow.

The assault came with lightning speed on the tips of flaming arrows and crossbow bolts. Pinned below the lip of her battlements, Hrofceaster's defenders could only await a cessation in the rain of weaponry. But there was none. Wave after wave of artillery rolled over them, preventing all but the most limited response. Catahn knelt in a narrow niche and brought his bow up, arrow notched. There was yet nothing to fire at. And now he heard someone cry out from the forecourt that a fire had sprung up there.

Chill clutched at his heart. If the arrows continued to fall, extinguishing the fires they caused could be impossible.

Above and behind him from within Hrofceaster's Great Hall, Taminy saw Feich's shield of smoke as the aislinn-molded thing it was. "Feel it?" she asked. "Feel the *aidan* behind it—within it?"

Arrayed around her, eyes on the lead-crystal windows of the big room, the *waljan* did indeed feel the presence behind the heavy billows that pressed against the panes.

"How?" Wyth Arundel asked, shaking his head. "How can a man like Feich have such a powerful Gift? I never sensed this in him before Cyne Colfre's death. Did you?"

Taminy shook her head. "I felt . . . something from him. But nothing like this."

"Yet he Weaves as one fully versed in the Art. He Weaves with the power of someone like Osraed Bevol."

Skeet, flanking him at the window, murmured, "He has Aiffe and he has allies."

"But a crystal is merely a focus. If he had no *aidan* . . ."

"He could do nothing," finished Taminy, her eyes never leaving the window.

"Then how has he been able to train such a strong Gift in such a short time?"

Taminy shook her head. "I wish I knew."

"The Deasach Cwen has the Sight," observed Desary. "Father says while you were talking with Feich, he felt her watching us. Watching you. But with Feich, he can sense nothing. It's as if—"

A muffled shriek pulled them from their murmured conversation. Eyslk had pulled back from the windows, one hand covering her mouth, the other pointing into the teeming mist. "Demons!" she cried, voice breaking. "They send demons in the mist!"

Taminy brought her eyes back to the glass. Black phantoms with flaming eyes assailed them. Spreading wings the color of midnight, carrying swords of flame, they hurled themselves against the windows of the Great Hall, rattling the iron frames.

"Oh, Mistress, they can fly!" whimpered Eyslk.

"No. They can't. They can only make us believe they can. There are only arrows set afire. Help me, all of you.

Help me disperse the smoke. Catahn's men can't see what
they're firing at."

The room fell silent as they Wove a wind—a cold,
relentless wind that rolled down from the crown of
Hrofceaster and blew Daimhin Feich's mist back into his
face. The hail of arrows did not stop, and now they could
see that there were fires in the courtyard. But the enemy
no longer had a place to hide. Caught on the shelf of rocky
ground beyond Hrofceaster's gates, they were forced to
flee or die as the Hillwild and their Claeg reserves at last
found targets. The arrow-storm lessened as the enemy was
forced to fire from concealment. Less than an hour later,
the fires in the court were out, but not without a loss of
livestock and fodder.

The battle continued on and off for the rest of the day.
By late afternoon, Taminy knew there were casualties on
both sides. The knowledge made her weep. Her only comfort was the promise that birth must be accompanied by
pain even in the Eibhilin realms. So, she wielded the *waljan*
and their talents like a shield and wondered what darkness would bring.

"They come." Lilias Saba's huge, luminous eyes opened,
light dancing across them—phantoms of fire and crystal.

Feich nodded, his own eyes on hers. "Yes, I see them."
And he *could* see them, slipping through the darkness below
Airdnasheen, imagining that they were concealed from him.
He smiled. Imagining that their Mistress would be the one
to greet them. "They'll try to hide themselves from us in
some way. But we will be more clever. We will make that
impossible." He rose, left his tent and the two women who
Wove there, and summoned a group of black-clad men
to him to issue them their orders. They moved swiftly away
toward the empty village.

In a narrow canyon mere miles below Airdnasheen, the
four travelers were forced to abandon their horses and
continue on foot. The night was dark and still and already
they could see the telltale glint of enemy fires above them

and to the north. Upward they moved, and southeast toward
Airdnasheen. Saefren figured on several hours of slow,
tedious travel—perhaps a bit less if they were able to slip
into the village rather than having to skirt it. He assumed,
as did Aine, that Catahn would have brought the villagers into his stronghold for safety's sake, leaving the place
empty. The question was, had Feich taken advantage of
that and stationed troops within the village itself?

In a little less than two hours the scarp upon which
Airdnasheen sat rose above them, close enough to blot
out a good part of the sky. Only by the enemy campfires
could they see the lowering mist; Airdnasheen itself was
dark and still. "I'll go up and take a closer look," Saefren
told his companions. "Wait here; I'll signal."

"I'll go with you." That was Aine, of course. "Then you
won't have to signal."

"Aine, there could be troops up there, hiding."

"And you'd have some advantage over them, alone? How
well can you Weave a Cloaking inyx, Saefren?" she asked,
when his mouth opened to reply.

He grimaced. "Not very well at all. Fine. I'll be glad of
your company, then, since you've offered to make yourself useful." He turned to Leal and Iseabal. "Wait here
until we see if it's clear."

They climbed, pushing through knee-high snow, using
rocks and brush for steps and handholds, up the flank of
the escarpment until they hunkered among a clump of
scrubby pines that grew at the northwest verge of the village. Darkness met them, a darkness so complete they could
see nothing of the village buildings save the most ghostly
wash of moonlight on the roofs of those closest to them.
For some minutes they sat, side by side, listening, watching, waiting. Aine, Saefren was certain, was scanning the
place with more than eyes and ears.

He turned to her, leaning his mouth close to her ear.
"Well?"

"It's empty. That is, the Hillwild aren't here, but . . .
Something's not right. *Someone's* here."

"Feich?"

"No, not Feich. No one with *aidan*."

"What do you feel?"

"Fear." She turned to look at him, her face gleaming like a dim moon. "I feel fear."

"Someone hiding out from Feich?"

"I don't know, but here. In Airdnasheen." She made a gesture upslope to where the southern reaches of the village huddled beneath the crags. "Up there."

"Do we dare travel through the village, then?"

"Do we have a choice?"

"We can move along the face of the scarp. But, we'd be exposed, hampered by the snow and the slope, and too damn close to Feich's camps."

"Well, then," Aine said and glanced back over her shoulder, though she could surely see nothing.

Saefren assumed she had just summoned the others. "My feet and hands are like ice," he told her. "Have you no Weaves for warmth?"

She chuckled. "Oh, aye," she said and took his gloved hands between her own gloveless ones.

In a moment, he felt warmth flood his finger tips, flow up his arms, invade his body, rush down his legs to his feet. It was an eerie sensation, for it felt like no fire he had ever sat before, no hot bath he had ever taken. This warmth moved from the inside out, from the red-haired girl to him. It was as if his bones had suddenly learned to conduct heat. He wished, for a moment, that he was not wearing gloves and could know if her hands were as hot as it seemed they must be. That thought led to one of a slightly more intimate nature. One Saefren dashed away with a charge of purely personal heat, only barely avoiding the guilty gesture of pulling his hands away. It was little more than a flash of feeling, not even a full-fledged thought, but it shamed him and he feared she may have caught it. Only when she didn't pull her own hands away, did he relax.

He was thoroughly warmed by the time the others reached them. They paused only long enough for Leal and Iseabal to taste of Airdnasheen's strange quiet, then they slipped silently down from the rocks and into the empty village. Within moments, Aine and Iseabal had oriented themselves and led the others toward the eastern perimeter and the trail to Hrofceaster.

In the river of mist, shops and houses loomed like shrouded islands. They kept to the shadows, eyes open for any other presence than their own. They were skirting the town circle when sudden light exploded across the snow-carpeted way, resolving into a billow of flame that exposed them utterly. In seconds, the roofs of three houses opposite them were afire. The flames leapt up in sheets, illuminating the rocky mountainside, washing across the circle along with a blast of heat. In a matter of seconds, they were spreading, racing to cut off the narrow lane that ran up to Hrofceaster.

Aine froze, staring at the inferno. She did not need to see the dark figures scurrying before the flames to know that they were being herded like sheep. The question was, where were they expected to go? She glanced over her shoulder, past the fire-washed startled faces of her companions. Back the way they'd come? She made a decision, praying it was the right one. "Come on! This way!" She slipped into a dark cut between two buildings, the others moving swiftly behind her.

Saefren moved to her shoulder. "Where are we going?"

"Out of the village."

"Are you sure—?"

"No, I'm not."

He followed without comment down the rough alley to the back of the row of buildings. They crossed a narrow strip of bare, rocky ground, stumbling over obstacles they couldn't see beneath the snow, Aine concentrating on the path, Saefren on Aine, Leal and Iseabal on a Cloakweave that would allow them to see themselves while shielding them from the eyes of others. Through the hemming rocks, they clambered, coming at last to the place where the escarpment fell away toward the canyon in a snowy roil of rock and frozen brush.

At the bottom of the track, Aine turned them eastward

and upward again, toward the fortress. Their only trail led between the burning village above and the enemy encampments below. She could only pray that the Cloakweave Leal and Isha supported would be enough to conceal them. She almost dared to stretch out her *aidan* to Taminy, but fear of discovery forestalled her.

The blaze of Airdnasheen lit up the snow and mist, bathing the mountainside in glory. Aine tried to accept its light and ignore its dangers, her attention ahead, her eyes on the narrow, rocky defile. They rounded a large outcropping and she saw them—the ramparts of Hrofceaster, gleaming in the fire-fed mist, tiny figures swarming along the top of its battlements. Her heart surged with relief so strong she nearly cried out. A second later a slim figure swaddled in red blocked their trail.

Aine stopped, weltering in confusion. Surely, this person couldn't *see* them. As she watched, quivering, others appeared, Caraidin soldiers, Deasach corsairs. The figure lifted an arm in a sweeping gesture and the soldiers deployed themselves. When they were surrounded, a man in Feich colors came to stand beside the red-robed figure—a man Aine had come to hate. He lifted a red crystal before him, balancing it on the palm of one hand. It glowed evilly in the orange wash of flame from the burning village. But more evil still, was the man behind the crystal, a man whose crimson face wore a smile of triumphant delight.

He had the Osmaer crystal, well she knew. He had Airleas Malcuim. And now he had Iseabal, Aine and Saefren Claeg. She was ready when he called her out, arrogantly demanding that she meet him before the gates of Hrofceaster to negotiate her surrender.

Catahn would not let her go, begged her to let the siege continue, to let the Hillwild at his command attempt to turn the tide. They had watched their homes burn, their village utterly destroyed, they were determined, they would prevail. But they could not prevail. Another day, another night, and Hrofceaster would crumble physically. Feich's forces were superior. With the capture of the Osmaer, there was a decision to be made and it was Taminy's, alone, to make.

She withdrew to her private chamber, leaving even Catahn behind in the Great Hall. On her knees before the fire, she sought the Touch of the Meri. She took herself to a place of light, a place beyond the room her body inhabited.

"What must I do?" she asked, and knew the answer in a breath.

"You wanted to strike him down."

Taminy raised her head, turning her eyes to the hazy shadows. Skeet stepped from them, seeming a hot, dancing flame in this Eibhilin chamber. Through the radiance that surrounded them, he seemed to wear two aspects, one overlapping the other like a translucent garment; a young boy, an old man with a beard of fire and snow and eyes like a summer sky.

"I thought of it," she admitted.

"And will you?"

"You know the answer to that. You were my example. Did you struggle against those who came for you at Mertuile? When Feich's men carried you off to die, did you lay them to waste?"

The half-aislinn half-corporeal being shook his head—a twinned movement.

"No more can I. It's part of the Pattern. To represent the Spirit, to lay claim to Its wisdom and wield Its power, I must reflect Its qualities. To do otherwise would destroy what I am consecrated to establish. The Tapestry would unravel. Six hundred years undone in a moment of vengeance and anger."

"So then, what will you do?" The voice was Skeet's, the soul-piercing gaze was Bevol's.

"I will surrender."

"I accede to your demand, Daimhin Feich."

He whirled, all but leaving his skin behind, and peered into the darkness of the hostage tent. She, the Divine Quarry, floated before him in the stygian gloom like a golden rose, watching him with grave, sad eyes. Forgetting the hostages he had been gloating over, he reached out a hand to the image—aislinn, of course—a mirage, but so real, so close. He groped after her. "You will meet me tomorrow, before the fortress gates?"

"I will."

"A wise choice. For their sake." He gestured at the drug-wrapt forms of Airleas, Aine, Iseabal and Leal. Saefren Claeg was Giftless as a post and so had been spared Coinich Mor's sleeping draught. He huddled in a corner of the tent, eyes glaring sullenly at his captor. Feich enjoyed his wakeful hatred. "You cannot withstand me, Taminy. Do you understand why?"

She grimaced. "I understand that there is a test in this for me; perhaps I have failed it."

"You fail because you are weak, dear Lady. Oh, I don't mean your powers or your wisdom. You are powerful enough. But your wisdom is based on a fallacy—that good is inherently more powerful than evil. You are wrong, of course." He smiled. "Shall I tell you why you are wrong?"

"I suppose you shall."

"Good cannot bring itself to perform the acts evil commits without conscience. I know you could wrest the Stone from me and use it to destroy me utterly. I even know you *want* to do that, but that *would* be failure, wouldn't it? So you do nothing. And that makes you weak—a sheep facing its shearer. The seeds of your undoing are within you, dear Taminy. They are inherent in your nature."

She seemed to consider that, her effigy's sea-green eyes never leaving his face. "The seeds of my undoing," she murmured.

Her voice was like the soughing of the wind or the surge of the sea, magical, musical. A sigh escaped his lips. "Unbind your hair." It was a demand, yet even he heard the raw pleading in his voice.

She studied him a moment, then reached up and tugged the leather thong from her braid, loosing it to fall about her shoulders in a pale gold cascade.

"You are exquisite," he told her. "A living analogy for Ochan's Crystal. When I have you—"

"You have Ochan's Crystal," she interrupted. "Why have you not tried to use it?"

"Ah, *that* I am saving so that all eyes may see my triumph complete. But most especially that *your* eyes may see it."

She nodded and, nodding, began to fade from view.

"Stay!" he cried.

"Tomorrow," she said and disappeared.

Feich blinked into the darkness of her passing and trembled. Desire pulsed through him, carried in his blood. He would go to Coinich Mor. No, to Lilias. But no. Neither of those poor substitutes would do now, not when he was so close to having the ultimate desire. A memory stirred in him of a long ago nightmare—a hunt, a chase, a Quarry he had been bent on destroying. He smiled at himself. How transparent all that was now. It was not Taminy's death he wanted, nor her destruction. It was her submission, perhaps even . . . her love?

Coinich Mor and Lilias both forgotten, he left the tent with its pair of guards and went to gaze upon the Osmaer Crystal, never noticing that a certain baleful pair of eyes no longer gleamed at him from the tent's darkest corner.

Saefren lay upon the ground behind the hostage tent, gathering his senses, letting the cold wet of the snow drive them into a tight, obedient, quivering herd. He didn't have time to ponder what he'd seen—Feich talking to a gossamer being, an aislinn projection of Taminy. She had given him the opportunity for escape, an opportunity he had only because Feich thought him Giftless and dull. He had to make good with it, somehow.

He wriggled his hands, bound tightly behind his back. Damn! If he had even a midge of Aine's Gift, he could untie himself and find a weapon. As it was, only his feet were free and so, with immense difficulty, he raised himself to his knees, then to his feet, desperate not to cry out or grunt with the exertion. He stood for a moment, trembling. The wind pirouetted playfully about him, poking icy fingers through the sodden weave of his clothing. It

was pitch black where he stood. A large boulder squatted
a few feet away at the edge of the tent's long shadow. He
shook himself and made for it with unsteady steps. From
there, each rock, each puff of scrub, each twist of tree
became the focus of his every thought and move. He floundered from one to another in silence, ignoring the cold,
the wet, the bruises and cuts of his passing. Closer to
Hrofceaster's walls. Closer. It was when he reached the
last vestige of cover that he realized how futile had been
his quest. Ruined Airdnasheen still cast a faint glow over
the snowy flat between the trail head and the fortress's
gates and, though no soldiers battered at them this moment,
a dozen or so men camped just outside. All his painstak-
ing struggle had been for naught. Giftless, he could not
hope to pass by Feich's men unseen.

Frustrated and exhausted he huddled in the lee of a
broad, twisted oak, staring up at the unreachable. He could
even see the shadows of the defenders walking the battlements for all the good it did him.

But wait. Perhaps his lack of *aidan* was not an issue.
Hadn't Aine found him in the bowels of Mertuile? He
trained his eyes on the towers behind and above the looming
walls and concentrated all his thought on Taminy, concentrated it there until he was sweating with the effort.
At length he lay back, exhausted. How easy they made it
look—speaking without words, touching across miles. He
focused his eyes on the gates. If someone came for him,
would he see them open? Would he see phantom foot-
prints in the snow? Shadows stretched across the firelit
surface?

His mind wandered and he found himself slipping toward
sleep. The realization shocked him awake. If he slept here,
he'd never wake again. Already his feet and hands were
beyond feeling. He scrambled to think of some way of staying awake until help came. *If* help came. He aimed another plea at the fortress. How long had he been here?
Minutes? Longer?

He squinted at the fortified walls until his eyes ached,
felt himself slipping again, and was shocked to full

consciousness by the touch of a hand on his shoulder. He jerked, nearly crying out. But the cry died in his throat; bending over him was a hooded figure. Within the recesses of the hood, the face was a young man's, lit by the glowing star between his brows. He attached a name to the face—Osraed Wyth. Another figure hovered, the face swaddled in darkness.

Hands moved him; voices prodded gently; he became aware that his hands were free, that he was on his feet, that he was moving across that yawning open area in clear sight of the enemy encampment. He watched their shadows stretch before the glow of their fires and wondered that no alarm was being raised behind them. They passed through the gates unmolested.

Some time later, before a roaring fire in Hrofceaster's Great Hall, Saefren sipped hot tea and tried not to betray the pain of returning sensation in his feet and hands. "I don't know what good I thought it might do," he murmured between swallows. "I probably should have stayed with them. But when the opportunity presented itself . . . "

Seated beside him, Taminy pressed a hand to his shoulder. "You could do little there but welter in frustration. He won't harm the others . . . not yet."

"He's given them a sleeping draught, you said," said Osraed Wyth. "Any idea what might have been in it?"

Saefren shook his head. "It was the Dearg woman who came up with it. I'm sure it was full of inyx."

Taminy's brow knit with puzzlement. "The Dearg woman? She wasn't the one who saw you on the trail . . . "

"No, that was the Deasach Banarigh."

"She must have the Sight," said Wyth.

"She has something," Saefren agreed. "She saw us. Iseabal and Leal were both Weaving and still she saw us. Then there was Daimhin Feich with that red crystal, and it seemed he could see us too."

Taminy nodded—absently, Saefren thought—her eyes not on anything in the room. "Yes, sometimes a person with a specialized Gift can enable other Gifted souls to share their ability . . . " Her eyes took on sudden clarity and moved to his face. "More than that. Iseabal and Leal were using a Cloakweave coming up the mountain and Aine used one to free you from Mertuile."

He nodded.

"You were very likely part of that Weave. Aine might very well have drawn on you to help her maintain the Cloak."

"Me? But I've no Gift. Not a shred."

"Everyone possesses a shred, Saefren. Everyone. And the more they possess, the more a talented Weaver such as Aine can draw on them." She rose from her chair. "Rest now. I should say you've earned that."

Saefren grimaced. "I haven't done anything."

"You got away from Daimhin Feich. Which shows me how distracted he is."

"He's a boiling pot, Mistress," Saefren told her. "A pot that thinks it contains the entire universe."

CHAPTER 24

Pay no heed to your frailty; keep your eyes, instead, on the invincibility of the Spirit. Did She not subject the militant Houses to the Divine discipline of the Meri through the first Osraed, Ochan? . . . Rise up in the name of the Spirit of this all, put your faith completely in Her, and let your soul be assured.

—*Book of Pilgrimages, Osraed Aodaghan*

✧   ✧   ✧

"And of course she will concede to your demands *this* time." Lilias did not seem convinced.

To Daimhin Feich that hardly mattered, she'd be convinced soon enough. He gestured up the trail toward Hrofceaster, hunkered balefully at the foot of her crags. "We will parade her beloved *waljan* before her; she will concede. Then Coinich Mor will bring the Stone of Ochan to me and I shall perform a great Weaving. Something that will put fear into the Hillwild and cause Taminy to recognize that I wield a power superior even to hers."

"Yet, her power is the Meri's, is it not? Do you believe yourself superior to that?"

He considered the question. Well, he had the upper hand, didn't he? The Meri hadn't struck him dead; Taminy hadn't lifted a violent hand against him. He had won. Simply and completely. Bested the Meri's viceregent, and therefore, bested the Meri Herself. The minion of some Dark Power, was he? Or perhaps—the thought excited him—perhaps he was, himself, the Power of Darkness, the anti-Meri, Her equal opposite and nemesis. "Yes. I do believe I have that power. Have I any choice?"

"And after your great Weaving?"

"I will take Taminy back to Creiddylad."

"But do you intend to set her disciples loose as you promised?"

"Why not? It hardly matters. If their Mistress can't stop me, what can they possibly do?"

Lilias laid a firm hand on the hilt of her sword. "I will not give up the girl, Iseabal. She will be made to pay for Sorn's death."

He opened his mouth to argue with her, then realized there was no point to the argument. Iseabal didn't matter. None of them mattered. Not even Airleas Malcuim mattered to him at that moment. "Very well, she's your responsibility. If Taminy ever asks after her, I'll refer her to you. But I might remind you that it was, to all accounts, Rodri Madaidh who put an end to your little brother's life."

"For her. He did it for her."

"Strictly speaking, he did it for Taminy. Of course, if you look at it another way, your dear brother would be alive today if he hadn't allowed himself to be smitten with the girl."

"Yes. And that, I am certain, was due only to a Weaving on *her* part. She made him become smitten with her. She used him to escape Creiddylad. And when she had brought her Madaidh rescuer to her, she had him slaughter Sorn as if he were a fatted sheep."

Daimhin considered telling Lilias just how ridiculous that sounded. After all, the Cirkemaster's daughter had not a mote of guile in her. The thought that she had engineered her own escape—no, it was ludicrous. She'd been barely aware of her surroundings when he'd packed her off in the tribute caravan. But again, telling Lilias Saba anything at all—besides that she was unutterably beautiful, of course—produced no result. And it didn't matter. "Believe what you will, my dear. Only now, it's nearly time for the fateful meeting. Where's Coinich Mor?"

"Near by, Regent," said the Dearg's voice practically in

his ear. "Always near by." Though they were several yards from the nearest tent, she appeared beside him as if she had but to take one step from concealment.

He nearly snapped at her that she had startled him, but didn't wish to admit he hadn't sensed her there. "Have you given our guests an antidote to the sleeping draught?"

"Aye. But, I've kept the inyx upon them—bound to that silly boy's cat amulet. Gullible, that one."

Feich frowned. "I want them to appreciate their predicament."

"Oh, they will, soon enough. By the way, the Claeg is gone."

"What do you mean, the Claeg is gone?"

"What I said. The nephew of Iobert Claeg has escaped."

"But how?"

She shrugged. "You would not have him be drugged."

"He was tied. I put an inyx on him."

Coinich Mor's dark brows rose. "Did you? And to what did you bind it, Regent?"

"Why to . . . to the ropes." He had, in fact, thought it particularly clever to have done that. Rather like an aislinn pun.

"Well, he isn't in the tent. Neither are his ropes. He must have taken your inyx with him."

Her eyes glinted with wry humor, making him despise her. "Taminy came to me last night in a vision. She must have aided him to unravel the Weave I set."

The Dearg Wicke nodded, her eyes gliding past him to Lilias. "Ah, yes. I can see that's what has happened. Well, it matters not a bit. There's no *aidan* in him. And it's likely we'll find his body wherever it was he froze to death."

"They're ready to go, then?"

She nodded.

He raised his eyes to the fortress and swept a gesture at it with one hand. "Behold, the gates of Hrofceaster open. Let us go to our parley."

Catahn to her right, Wyth Arundel and Saefren Claeg to her left, Taminy met Daimhin Feich before the gates of Hrofceaster. It was an oppressive morning, grey mist riding low over the clearing with trailing skirts, draping bits of them in tree and bush, entangling the battlements. The damp air reeked of ash.

Feich came alone, or nearly so. He left his cousin and the Deasach several yards behind him before a phalanx of Feich men. Now, in what he surely perceived as his moment of power, he did not smile or swagger. His pale eyes were alert, sharp as shards of crystal, his expression sober. He came to stand before her, only then allowing a smile to pass over his lips. "Lady," he said, "are you ready to surrender yourself to me?"

"Where are they?"

"My hostages?" He waved a hand into the air and the line of men behind him parted to allow the four hostages to move forward. They might have been sleepwalking— heads bowed, eyes glazed, feet shuffling through the snow.

Taminy wondered again at how Feich managed to control them so, though his attention seemed to be fully on herself. A boiling pot, Saefren had called him, and she knew him to be conflicted, a man of sometimes frenetic thought. That didn't tally with the discipline necessary to Weave as he had. She thought again of the Dearg woman and her inyx-laden sleeping potion, of the Deasach Banarigh and her sharing of her Gift of Sight. Was it just possible that Daimhin Feich was not the only Weaver at work here? Was he using one or both of them to amplify his powers? That was possible, but failed to explain why she could not smother his power at the source. The Deasach woman had, as Saefren had noted, the Sight. She was not using it now, and Taminy sensed nothing from her but bristling hatred and anticipation. The Dearg woman was nowhere in sight.

The hostages had stopped now, Airleas, Aine and Leal forming an uneven line to Feich's right. They were definitely mesmerized, looking like a set of particularly lifelike scarecrows propped in a farmer's vegetable garden. Iseabal remained beside Banarigh Lilias, her blue eyes fixed on nothing.

Taminy looked to Feich. "Let Iseabal come forward with the others."

Feich glanced over his shoulder. Lilias Saba had wrapped a gloved hand around the girl's arm. "Iseabal is no longer my affair. You'll have to discuss her fate with my ally."

Taminy didn't argue the point. "These three *are* your affair. Let them go, Regent. Loose the Weave. I promise no one will work any harm against you."

Feich smiled. "Oh, I can believe that." Again, he made an exaggerated gesture over his head with one hand.

It was as if a bubble had popped. The three drooping hostages jerked, then gazed around in confusion, realizing they were on the wrong side of an invisible line. Aine and Leal looked to Taminy, but Airleas's eyes were on Feich, a hatred born of humiliation burning deep in them.

"Welcome back to the waking world, Cyneric," Feich told him. "You are just in time to witness a most momentous event." He turned to Taminy then. "Here are your little ones, Lady. What will you surrender for them?"

"Myself."

Airleas's eyes flew wide open. "NO! Mistress, you *can't* surrender to this monster!"

Taminy shook her head. "Airleas, I must. For your sake. It's destined."

"No! I don't believe that. I *won't* believe it." He whirled to face Feich, eyes flaming. "I hate you!" He brought up his left hand, palm out, aimed toward Feich. A beam of emerald fire shot from the *gytha* there, catching the enemy between the eyes and flinging him backwards into the snow. The fingers of Airleas's upraised hand flexed and Feich shrieked with sudden agony.

Taminy longed to cry out, to stop the boy from giving in to his rage. But she knew, suddenly, she could not. This was the moment of testing—for both of them. She would not—*could* not—provide external controls for his *aidan* or his anger. She could only protect Feich from the results. Reluctantly, Taminy held up her own hand, ready to intercede, and wondered if it meant anything to Feich that neither his men nor his Deasach ally moved to protect

him from Airleas's attack. Only his cousin, Ruadh, his face
ashen with fear, did anything at all.

"Lady!" he cried, addressing Taminy. "Lady, please stop
him!"

Airleas stood over Feich's prone form now, face contorted with rage, hand clenched before him as if it held
his enemy's heart. Only then did he glance up at the party
from Hrofceaster, his eyes going to Taminy, then past her
to where Gwynet stared at him, her face white as the snow
about her feet. His expression went from crazed to stricken
and he straightened, relaxing his hand. He subsided to his
place between Leal and Aine as Daimhin Feich, choking
and breathing raggedly, clambered awkwardly to his feet.

His smile had vanished. With visible effort he slid it back
into place. "Weak. You are all weak. You could have killed
me, just then, boy, but a moment of indecision robbed
you of the chance, and I have once more proved myself
more powerful than any of you. And now, before all eyes,
I will reveal a glimpse of that power to you." He turned
his head back toward his line of troops and made a sweeping
gesture with one hand. "Behold, the Stone of Ochan."

The ranks behind him parted and a woman stepped forward, bearing an open gilt box. Even in the mist and smoke,
the gem it carried gleamed, painting the clinging tendrils
of brume rose-gold. It gleamed as if in the presence of a
strong *aidan*.

Taminy felt a cold shock run through her. Did the Dearg
woman have that kind of Gift? She might have doubted
it, but the Stone didn't lie. She watched as the woman
set the Crystal into Daimhin Feich's hands. The fire within
it wavered momentarily, then flared again. But now Taminy
realized it was not Feich's tremulous ability that lit it. It
was the Dearg who fueled the Stone; in handling it, she
had revealed herself.

Much became clear, then. Feich's grand gestures were
cues to the Dearg Wicke, for it was she who held the cap-
tives entranced, she who lifted the Sleepweave from them.
She was the source of the disciplined power Taminy had
found confronting her at every turn. Feich did not use

her, she used him, hiding herself behind his immature and inconsistent Gift. *And I was powerless to block it,* Taminy marveled, *because I was trying to defend myself against the wrong person. The real enemy was someone I couldn't even see.*

But now she saw, and couldn't help but wonder at the Dearg's motives. Was she in Feich's thrall? If so, why did she not work against Airleas when he attacked Feich? Or was it personal power she sought?

The woman was looking at her now, a smug smile on her full lips. "Shall we Weave now, my Lord Regent?" she asked Feich. "Shall we show them great wonders?"

He waved her off. "*I* shall Weave. You shall watch."

The dark look the woman gave him as she stepped aside was enough to answer all of Taminy's questions about her loyalties.

"Behold," Feich said, lifting the Crystal dramatically above his head. Behind him, his troops murmured, many flinching back a step. From Ochan's great Crystal a chaotic whirl of motes exploded like a festival fire show, painting the enshrouding pall of smoke and mist with carnival colors. Daimhin Feich himself was swaddled in an aura of paerie light and seemed, momentarily, to lift several inches from the ground. His men gasped and withdrew further.

Feich, his eyes gleaming, laughed aloud . . . and the light died. The fireshow ended as suddenly as it began; the aura drained away, the Crystal glowed dully in his upraised hand. He gaped at it, then turned his eyes to Taminy. "What is this? What have you done? *What have you done?*"

The Dearg woman was laughing, now, hands on her broad hips, head back. Her hilarity wound through the fog and echoed from the walls of Catahn's fortress. "You fool! *She* has done nothing! I'm the one you should ask. Go on, Regent. Ask me! Ask me what I have *not* done."

Feich glared at her, fury standing out in red relief on his face. "What are you talking about? What have you not done?"

"I have not aided you, Regent. I have not guided your

paltry powers and shored them up and supplemented them.
'Behold,'" she mocked him. "'Behold' what you are capable
of doing without Coinich Mor!"

"You lie! I have power. I have great power. I have used
it often since—"

"Since I tutored you? Since I held your hand and let you
believe you drew upon me for your Weaving? Behold *me*,
Regent Feich—the one who has been drawing upon *you*."

His face was the color of death and his eyes transparent as glass. "No. You lie. I Wove. *I* Wove. You've tricked
me. You've siphoned off my powers somehow. Are you in
league with her?" He jerked his chin toward Taminy. "Are
you one of her minions?"

"I am no one's minion, Regent. Least of all hers. I am
in league with no one but myself." She held out her hand.
"Give me the Crystal, and I'll prove what I say. I'll show
you power."

Feich shook his head and held the Crystal close to his
chest. "No. You'll not get your hands on this. You'll ruin
it. You'll defile it."

She laughed again, mocking. "And you won't? Come,
Regent. You're a good enough prentice, but a wretched
master. Give me the Stone."

He stepped back, prompting her to fling herself upon
him, locking her hands with his around the Crystal. "Let
go!" he shrieked. But she only laughed, crowing as the
Stone of Ochan caught fire, bathing their struggles in amber
radiance. Behind them, Feich's troops began to melt away
into the mist.

Sensing movement from the men near her, Taminy held
up her hand to them. *Do nothing.*

Their hands entwined around the glowing gem, Feich
and Coinich Mor continued their physical struggle, and
now, impatient, the Dearg assailed her opponent in other
ways, causing the Crystal to flare up so as to blind him,
causing it to grow cold enough to freeze his hands. Feich
fought back, flailing at the Wicke with random slashes of
thought. Aislinn sparks fell in a shower around them, and
now, Coinich Mor's cloak seemed to catch fire.

She cried out, but recovered quickly, recognizing trickery. Then she was laughing again. "Like heat, do we? Well, here's fire for you!"

The flames leapt between their fingers now, licking up Feich's arms, setting his clothes afire. He shrieked in agony. The fire was within him, around him. It was eating him alive. Rage soared with the pain. No! He would not let this woman best him with a lie. He would not let her prove her vile claims to be true. *He* was the Dark Power. It lived in him, walked with him, worked through him. He writhed, mouth forming meaningless sounds, trying to gather all his pain and fury for one great Weave. He turned his head to look at Taminy, found more reason for rage in the mute sadness of her eyes.

"Damn you!" he cried. "Damn you all!" He forced himself to look down into the Crystal past his burning, shriveled hands, past the smell of his own cooking flesh. He forced his mouth to form more words—a command of power. *"Destroy the enemy!"*

With a roar of sound like a thousand thunders, with a flash of light like a thousand Suns, the Stone of Ochan resounded with one great pulse of power. The mist and snow, the walls of Hrofceaster, the assembled troops, were lit more brightly than if the Sun had suddenly appeared in its noonday glory. Some cried out and shielded their eyes or covered their ears. Others simply turned and ran as all the light and sound and fury gathered itself into a mad whorl of flaming wind that rose from the place of struggle, catching up snow and mist into a scintillating storm of fire and ice.

A moment later it was over. The colorful maelstrom with its light and heat was gone. The world around the watchers faded back to grey. Where Daimhin Feich and Coinich Mor had stood there was only a circle of bare earth, naked of snow, steaming in the chill air. Of the two combatants, there was no sign.

For a long moment, the clearing before Hrofceaster was silent. Silent, save for the sounds of the hasty dispersal of Feich's loose alliance.

Catahn grasped Taminy's arm. "Lady! The Crystal!"

Lying in the sodden, snowless circle, the Osmaer glowed
fitfully as if lapping up the dregs of the aislinn explosion.
Taminy moved to pick it up. In her hands it caught fire
once again, making her a beacon in the morning gloom.

Caime Cadder's universe had come to a shattering,
explosive end, pieces of it falling down about him like snow.
In a blinding flash, his hopes of keeping Caraid-land out
of evil's hands failed. The Wicke had won. She had won.
And now her lovers flocked around her and her former
adversaries approached to grovel obsequiously—the Dearg,
Ruadh Feich, even the Deasach Banarigh.

How? How could evil prevail so utterly? How could the
Meri allow the Crystal to fall into *her* hands?

A small voice within him reminded him that Daimhin
Feich's hands had not been so very clean. He would not,
in his wildest dreams, have called Feich good. "Destroy
the enemy," he'd said, and had, himself been destroyed.
Taminy must have deflected the inyx, turned it back on
him. He wanted to believe that; the alternative was too
terrifying to contemplate. And yet, as he watched the
Golden Wicke, the Osmaer Crystal gleaming in her hands,
he couldn't keep his mind from wandering that path.

He scarcely realized he was moving, taking shuffling steps
backwards in the snow. The men who had stood around
him only moments ago had fled. Now, his feet found the
chaotic path of their flight and followed it. They had not
gone far—only returned to their camp, where they clustered in shivering, murmuring groups, eyes returning again
and again to the walls of Hrofceaster. Caime Cadder did
not join them. He pursued a stumbling track to the cor-
rals where he saddled his horse with fumbling hands,
mounted and rode away down the mountain.

The trail was steep, choked with snow, dangerous.
Cadder didn't stop to consider that, but spurred his mount
on with increasing speed. The mist was ungodly thick. The
Sun, which surely must be above the peaks by now, did
nothing to penetrate it. The horse skidded down the track,

belching steam into the air, a lather born of panic rising on its withers.

Without warning, Cadder found himself in an alien landscape. A mob of twisted shapes surrounded him as if they had leapt up from the frozen mountainside. Twisted and gaunt, they seemed to lean over him, threatening. He caught himself in mid gasp, realizing it was only a grove of winter-stripped trees; what he took for the arms of skeletal giants were only branches lifting to spear the ever-shifting fog. Still, the place reeked of Wicke Craft, stank of evil. Surely, it was a carefully woven snare.

Twigs whipped his face as the horse descended through the trees, stumbling over a concealed boulder and plunging into a snow drift. He tightened his grip on the reins and fought to pull the animal's head up, to help it lift its forequarters back up toward the trail. There, in the still, ghostly place of frozen trees and a sparkling veil of mist, the only sounds were those he and his horse made, blowing, grunting, thrashing the snow, regaining the main trail—if it could be called that—with great difficulty.

"Cadder."

He did not expect to hear his name called, but he heard it. Least of all did he expect to hear it called by a man he knew beyond doubt was dead. Jerking his mount around to face downslope, he saw—beyond belief!—the Abbod Ladhar blocking his escape. The animal beneath him danced sideways; he clutched the reins and choked out words. "You're dead. You're not there. You're not real."

"I am here." Translucent, he seemed, and faintly aglow.

Cadder pointed a shaking finger. "Be gone, foul spirit! You—you're a Weave meant to frighten me." He set his heels to the horse's flanks, but the stupid beast wouldn't move. It merely shuddered as if in some equine seizure, bobbing its head frenetically from side to side.

"You can't run away from Her, Cadder," Ladhar's ghost told him. "And there is no place to hide that She cannot find you."

"The Wicke? She's that powerful?"

"It's our Mistress I speak of. The Meri. She's the one

you flee. The only Wicke here was Coinich Mor of Dearg and she is dead."

"Lying spirit! Let me pass!" He raised the ends of his reins as if he might flog the apparition.

Ladhar's image laughed. "I am beyond lies, Cadder. Where I exist, they cannot."

"What are you?"

"A messenger of Light sent to offer you a choice. Turn back into light or flee into darkness."

"I don't comprehend you. Let me pass."

"To do what? To return to Creiddylad to try to raise the Osraed up against Taminy-Osmaer? You can't hope to succeed in doing anything more than slowing destiny. Turn back."

"Or what—she'll destroy me as she destroyed Daimhin Feich?" He felt tears pressing his eyes. His whole body quivered with terror.

"She didn't destroy Daimhin Feich, Cadder. He chose to destroy himself. He was given a choice, too. As I was."

"No! You try to mesmerize me. You try to trick me. I *was* tricked by you. Years, I spent, thinking you a saint, a visionary, my moral and spiritual superior."

Ladhar shook his head, shedding shreds of light from whitening hair. "I was never that. I was never your superior in anything but social rank."

"You were a traitor."

"I was . . . until the very end. Until someone offered me a choice. Then I realized what a traitor I had been to work against Taminy—to work *for* Daimhin Feich. That was a lesson hard learned."

Cadder could take no more. The horse was becoming increasingly maddened, as was he. What this Being said could simply not be true. He would not believe that he'd sold himself over to the wrong side of this. He would *not* believe it. And so, with one great effort, Caime Cadder shouted his prancing mount forward, intending to ride right through Ladhar's shade. But the horse whirled and bolted off the trail, flailing through drifting snow into a close-knit group of trees. Off balance, Cadder could do nothing more than cling to the saddle in desperation as the twining branches rushed to meet him.

He only barely saw the contorted limb that caught him about the throat. There was no time to dodge or cry out. Hands gripping the pommel, feet sunk in the stirrups, spirit buried in its own sick pride, Caime Cadder contributed as much to his death as did the ill-placed branch.

She could see herself through their eyes and knew she was a strange sight—sitting in Catahn's high-backed chair before the largest hearth in the Great Hall like a Cwen in boy's clothes, Skeet crouched at her feet like a loyal pup. The Stone of Ochan sat, glowing, in her lap; she glowed with it—as much from within as from its reflection or the fire's light. Each penitent arrived before her to bow, beg forgiveness and promise fealty with greater or lesser displays of trepidation.

The Dearg was first, with his several House Elders. He grovelled from real fear, laying his opposition to her at Coinich Mor's door, because he would never—no, never—have thought to make himself her enemy if he had not been befuddled by his brother's wicked wife and her Feich lover. But now the scales had been ripped from his eyes and he saw the truth. If she had but a midge of mercy in her heart . . . ?

And Taminy smiled and forgave him and his. It was a mightily relieved Eadrig Dearg who walked out of Hrofceaster to tell his men they would begin rebuilding the burned-out Hillwild village that very day—that very hour.

Lilias Saba was next, not nearly so terrified as the Dearg, but clearly awed. She had Iseabal brought out of her camp and returned her to Taminy's arms.

"You forego your revenge?" Taminy asked.

The Raven answered with a wry smile. "Well, I fancy myself a creature of honor. But my father didn't raise a fool. I imagine my little army is no match for the forces you command, Lady. And I've no desire to join my poor brother in death."

"You wouldn't die by my hand."

Lilias's black brows arched upward. "No?"

"No."

"And did my brother . . . die by your hand? Or by hers?"
She nodded toward Iseabal, now warming near the huge
central hearth in Aine's protective embrace.

"No. Be assured, Lilias Saba, your brother's true murderer is dead. It was Rodri Madaidh's sword that ended
his life, surely, and Iseabal was the reason for him falling
under that sword. But the man who put Iseabal into his
hands—*that* man is dead."

"Daimhin Feich." Lilias's brow furrowed as she considered that. "He was a fool. He might have had the Throne
of Caraid-land, had he been willing to settle for that."

Had he been willing to settle. Watching Ruadh Feich
approach her, sober and defensive, Taminy turned the
thought in her head. It was fruitless to wish for what might
have been—a virtuous Cyne Colfre; pure-hearted Osraed;
a Daimhin Feich who was, if unscrupulous, at least not
obsessive. How many lives had been blighted because of
Colfre's avarice, Ladhar's blindness and Feich's madness?

"The Banarigh was right," Ruadh told her. "My cousin
was a fool. He didn't believe you could destroy him—or
rather, that you *would* destroy him."

"Ruadh Feich," Taminy told him, equally solemn, "I did
not destroy your cousin."

"The Crystal, then?"

"No, not even Ochan's Crystal is responsible for his destruction. The Crystal is . . . a passive tool. Certainly, it's attuned to
Light as opposed to darkness. And perhaps, in that way, you
could say that the Crystal destroyed Daimhin Feich."

Ruadh shook his head, uncomprehending. "Then . . . ?"

"He demanded that it destroy the Enemy. Not *his*
enemy—at that moment, Coinich Mor—but *the* Enemy.
Its Enemy, the Enemy of Light."

Ruadh sucked in a sharp breath. "He destroyed himself,
that's what you're telling me. That for want of the right pro-
noun, he destroyed himself and his Dearg Wicke." The
corner of his mouth twitched. "You'll think me a barbarian,
Lady, but somehow, in my cousin's case, that seems . . .
fitting. He was more than a fool. He was mad. Every

morning, I would wake and wonder what new delusion he would seize on today. Would he be an aingeal of darkness, or darkness itself? Would he sit on the throne of Caraid-land, or of the entire world? Would he marry one powerful woman, or three? I began to consider whether The Feich would think me a traitor or a hero to our House if I abandoned him." He managed a wry smile. "You have saved me, Mistress, from a most difficult decision."

He made no protestations of lifelong loyalty after that, but merely pledged himself to help rebuild Airdnasheen and then to put his men at her disposal. "There will be chaos in Creiddylad," he added. "Perhaps the best thing I can do is to escort Cyneric Airleas back to Mertuile where he can be set before the Stone. A country shouldn't be so long without its Cyne."

"No, it shouldn't," Taminy agreed. "But it won't be Mertuile that sees the coronation of this Cyne. It would please me if you would escort Airleas to Halig-liath. *There* he will receive the Circlet."

She heard the murmur that went up among those who heard her. In an instant, she had changed a Rite of Succession that had been practiced for six centuries.

Ruadh Feich did not react to that, but only to the course the destination required they take. "You don't mean to leave here until spring, then? Surely, you must move sooner than that. Creiddylad—"

"Creiddylad is in the hands of Iobert Claeg and the Allied Houses. But yes, we shall move sooner than that. Within the week, I think."

"But, Lady, the weather! Surely, you can't mean to take mounted men along the Northern trail."

Taminy smiled, feeling suddenly giddy with the absence of Daimhin Feich's dark threat and Coinich Mor's secret presence. "Weather, Ruadh Feich? What is weather?" She rose and moved to the bank of windows that looked out into Hrofceaster's bustling forecourt. The mountain fog leaned close to the window, as if eavesdropping. Taminy dismissed it with a wave of her hand. It receded, lifting like a curtain, parting as if pulled by an invisible hand.

The stones of Hrofceaster turned from lead to gold, touches of snow-silver ornamenting the battlements.

"You order the weather," murmured Ruadh, and Taminy could feel in him, for the first time, unadulterated fear. She felt something else, too. She felt Skeet's eyes on her and blushed under their wry regard.

"Don't fear me, Ruadh Feich," she told him. "The weather has no mind of its own, unlike you. I may order a breeze now and again, but I can't order a man's destiny."

As Taminy had said, they prepared to leave for Nairne within the week. The Banarigh Lilias had departed already to her own home, the Dearg and Ruadh Feich both agreed to leave behind kinsmen who would continue to help rebuild tattered Airdnasheen. With a mixed contingent of Claeg, Dearg and Feich men under Catahn's command, they readied themselves for a long, careful descent to the river vale at the foot of Baenn-an-loc.

Taminy was alone in her parlor when the door slipped quietly open, admitting Deardru-an-Caerluel. Head high, the woman studied her in silence, arms folded across her breast, eyes dark with smug malice.

"So. I lose to you, after all."

"Lose to me?"

"Ah, I forget. You can't read my thoughts as you do other's. I speak of Catahn. He tells me you are to wed at Halig-liath."

Taminy nodded.

"Smug cat. Save your smiles for your lover and remind yourself, often, that he was *my* lover first."

"He was never that, Deardru."

"You think not? But what can you know? That much-vaunted Gift of yours can't even penetrate the simple Weaves of a villager. You think Daimhin Feich acted alone? That he was some powerful Wicke you might be proud to have defeated? He was—"

"A man with a strong, but unruly Gift that he never mastered. He played other people in a way he could never manipulate his own *aidan*. Coinich Mor stood behind him, hidden in his shadow. The Weaves were hers, not his—I know that."

Deardru's eyes revealed her disappointment. "So, you guessed a small part of the puzzle. But there's more you don't know."

Taminy sighed and pulled something from the pocket of her breeches, holding it out to the other woman on the palm of her hand.

Deardru frowned. "What—?"

"The amulet you gave Airleas. You used it to forge a Weaving bond with him, to create a link you might ride your *aidan* upon straight to his spirit. Yes, I knew it was you who betrayed him into Feich's hands. He knew it too . . . before he surrendered his sword."

Deardru fought to keep her face from betraying her sudden agitation. "Then why did he not flee? Why did he not Weave protection for himself?"

"He thought he might save me disgrace if he played himself into Feich's control. And you weren't the only one working at him. Like me, he armed himself against Daimhin Feich, not seeing that Coinich Mor wielded him like a shield."

"But if you knew—if you really knew—why did you do nothing to me? Why did you say nothing to Catahn?"

"I did say something to Catahn. I asked him to show you mercy. He wanted to throw you out into Feich's camp, since you had allied yourself with them."

Deardru's face was washed of all color. "And why did you not let him do that?"

"Because of what Feich would have done with you. He fed on people, Deardru. He devoured them, licking up every drop of their energies while, in turn, Coinich Mor fed on him, leaving him just enough power to sustain himself. Together, they would have drained you, the way they drained Iseabal. The way they drained others."

"I don't understand you. I betrayed Airleas Malcuim into his enemy's hands, but it was you I sought to wound. I wanted you out of Catahn Hageswode's life. Airleas was only a playing piece I might move to that end."

"Yes, I know that. But I'd condemn no one to Daimhin Feich's hands. No one. Not even someone who hates me as much as you do. And Airleas desires no revenge either. I think he pities you. I know I do."

"I don't care for your pity. I only want you gone."

"You'll get that wish. I *will* be gone from Hrofceaster, but so will Catahn and Eyslk. Your husband and sons may also be gone, in their own fashion."

"What do you mean?"

"I mean your husband knows what you did. He was here not five minutes ago, pleading mercy for you. He's a loyal man, Deardru. Which is, perhaps, more than you deserve."

"So, you told him, did you?"

"I told him nothing. Your youngest son saw you give the Hageswode amulet to Airleas and heard you speak to him. He told your husband, thinking it was a rather grand thing you did to give the Cyneric such a powerful totem. When Airleas was in Feich's hands, Garradh-an-Caerluel heard the tale again from Broran and saw it in another light altogether. You think your husband slow. He isn't. He sees much; he simply prefers not to speak of it."

"So, I shall lose everything I hold dear. Is that what you tell me?"

"Do you hold them dear, your husband and sons? I had wondered."

Deardru-an-Caerluel drew herself up to her full height. "If you think you can wound me, you're to be disappointed. You've no power to hurt me, Taminy-a-Cuinn."

"No. But you've all power to hurt yourself."

Flushed and furious, the Hillwild woman left the room in a swirl of skirts, charging the atmosphere with her frustration and anger. Taminy watched her go with sorrow, knowing that in the months and years ahead, Deardru-an-Caerluel *would* realize her losses and inevitably find someone else to blame for them— "Taminy did this to me," she would say, or "this is because Catahn Hageswode would not love me," or even "it was my doltish husband who kept me from what I could have had." She might even one day blame the long dead Raenulf for her woes.

"Don't let it pain you so, Mistress, please."

Taminy glanced up to see Airleas standing in the doorway. Was he taller, suddenly? Was his voice more the voice of a young man and less that of a child? He came into the room, his face eloquent with concern. Light from the windows gave it a frame of radiance and shadow, accenting planes and hollows that she had not noticed a day or a week ago. He moved into full light and became a child again, face boyishly round, wide eyes on her.

"You shouldn't grieve for her. She's woven her own Pattern."

She laid a hand to his shoulder. "It's her husband and her sons I think of mostly. They did nothing to be so disregarded, but Deardru is a woman caught up in her own self—in her own past."

Airleas nodded. "Catahn says we're ready to go. He thinks we can make the top of the Cauldron by nightfall." He glanced at the floor then, expression suddenly shy.

"In a moment. First, you've something you wish to ask me."

He glanced back up at her, determined, tentative, pleading. "You once said when I was ready, I'd have a rune crystal of my own to Weave with. I've done my Crask-an-duine,"—did he gain an inch or two in saying that?— "and I'm to be set before the Stone when we reach Halig-liath. Am I . . . ?" He frowned and set his shoulders. "When shall I be ready, Mistress? What must I do to be ready? Tell me, and I'll do it, learn it, *be* it."

She smiled and put her arms around him, felt him return the embrace. "You've done it, Airleas. You've learned it. You've become it." She took him by the shoulders and held him away that she might study his face. "You could have destroyed Daimhin Feich, but you didn't. You remained true to the Art, true to the nature of the Spirit. You gave him into the Spirit's hands."

Airleas's face flushed. "It wasn't my right to destroy him. *You* could have destroyed him, too. I wondered why you didn't. I was afraid, sometimes, that he was more powerful somehow. More powerful than you—than all of us. But

I realized that you had the power to do it—it was something else that prevented you. And then I knew that that something was what you just said—the nature of the Spirit. It wasn't your *nature* to destroy him, wicked as he was. And if it wasn't *your* nature, then it couldn't be mine either, not if I was to be the Cyne you wanted me to be."

She opened her mouth to comment and he flushed again and added, "That *I* wanted to be. Daimhin Feich's destruction," he said as if the thought was just now being born, "was written in *his* nature. It was inevitable . . . wasn't it?"

She nodded and told him, "When we reach Halig-liath, on the day of your coronation, you will receive your Weaving stone."

His smile was a little boy's, bright and jubilant. He gave her the biggest hug he had and ran to tell his mother, the Cwen.

EPILOGUE

And now, Malcuim, stand, and facing west, and taking up the Crystal, bow down. From this quarter, the Meri, the Firstborn of the Spirit, divine and enlightened, lives, abides, sustains Herself and teaches the Art. Pure in name, glorified in every corner of the world of being, the blessed Meri, Her manifestation equal to the sand of the Sea, giving the Tell of the Spirit, She answers the needs of men eternally. This Name you must honor, celebrate and glorify.

—*Rite of Coronation, Osraed Ochan
to Cyne Paeccs Malcuim*

Airleas let his gaze wander the great central courtyard of Halig-liath, taking in the brilliance of the day, the colors of sky and bright clothing and House banners snapping in the clean cold breeze. Beneath those banners the Houses gathered, Chieftains to the fore, their families about them, their people arrayed behind. *All* the Chieftains were here and all of their Elders. From Iobert Claeg, eyes like sun-kissed frost, to Leod Feich, still mourning the loss of his miscreant son.

Airleas shivered, but not with chill so much as excitement. This was his rite, his coronation, his moment of standing before the eyes of Chieftains and Elders, Osraed and Ministers, Eiric and citizens. All of Nairne was here, in this courtyard, and representatives from villages and settlements from all over Caraid-land. They were here from Creiddylad in the south, Eada to the west, Norder in the north, Cuinn holding and Moidart to the east. All were here to watch him stand before the Stone of Ochan, awesome in its splendor beneath the winter Sun. To watch Osraed Saxan, Apex, set the Malcuim Circlet on his brow. They had come to hear Taminy chant the words of ceremony that called upon him to respond as, six hundred years before, the first Malcuim Cyne had responded.

He glanced to where the *waljan* stood, his mother among them before the gallery. The look of loving pride in her eyes, the radiance of peace that smoothed her brow—that was the world to him. And in that glance Airleas fully realized that his perception was no longer limited to what he could see or hear or touch. He could *feel* the pride his mother's heart held, he could scent the perfume of affection that rippled to him on the crisp currents of river air from the others who had shared his exile. Even sad Iseabal smiled at him, even sober Wyth, even Taminy's new husband, the unreadable Catahn. Even bristly Aine's face was softer this morning—gone, the scowl that usually flirted between her garish brows. Of course, he realized, his eyes shifting to Saefren Claeg, who also stood among the *waljan*, he might not be entirely responsible for that miracle.

He found Gwynet Alheart, front and center. Felt her touch, warm and sweet, within his very soul. Playmate, sister, dearest friend, closest confidante. She smiled at him, tears glistening in her eyes. He returned the smile, not quite sure that was appropriate to this moment of moments, but not caring.

Lastly, he let his eyes and *aidan* go to Taminy, who stood with him upon the low gallery against Halig-liath's eastern wall. She did not block him, just now, and what he received from her made his heart swell almost to bursting. She had finished the verses and now waited for him to make the refrain.

Around him, the air stilled, anticipating, the only movement in the banners of cloth and breath that unfurled in the crisp air. He turned, facing the Western Sea, and removed the Osmaer Crystal from its pedestal. It woke to a blaze in his hands, brighter than the Sun or the clouds that framed it. He came to his knees on the stones of Halig-liath, and bowed his head to drink the stillness.

Then, raising his face to the sky, he spoke in a clear loud voice, wanting all of creation to hear him. "I look to the Meri, Firstborn of the Spirit, divine and enlightened. She who lives, abides, sustains Herself and teaches the Art. Pure in name, glorified in every corner of the world of being, the blessed Meri, Her manifestation equal to the sand of the Sea, gives the Tell of the Spirit and answers the needs of men eternally. Her Name I honor, celebrate and glorify."

Osraed Saxan moved then, stepping forward to place the Circlet on Airleas's head. Airleas smiled at him, unable to resist the gladness bubbling up from inside. Saxan re-turned the smile and bowed.

That was not part of the ceremony. Airleas turned his eyes to Taminy, but she was not looking at him. She now faced the great gathering spread out before the gallery and said, "I give you Airleas Malcuim, heir of the First Malcuim, Cyne of Caraid-land."

Airleas rose to the cheers of the crowd, some sincere, some perfunctory. *Soon*, he thought, *they will all be sin-cere. I will be a good Cyne.* He returned the Osmaer to its pedestal and faced his people, bowing to each quarter to make of himself a humble offering.

When he turned back to Taminy, his face beaming, he saw she had removed the Osmaer from its pedestal once again and cradled it in her hands. It was ablaze with Eibhilin light, making her seem bathed in the stuff, a creature of another world than this one. To his utter amazement, she held it out to him.

In the moment of chaotic thought that followed, he was vaguely aware that the crowd had, once again, stilled. Slowly, for he was sure Taminy would any moment shake her head to stop him, he raised his hands and placed them on the Crystal. She smiled at him, moving her fingers to cover his.

Looking to the assemblage, she said, "I give you Airleas Malcuim, Osric. Cyne by Divine right." And while the crowd around them reacted to her words, cheering, crying, gasping in astonishment or outrage, she leaned close to him and murmured, "You asked for a stone to focus your gift. Here it is. Use it with wisdom."

Hands quaking, Airleas held the Stone before his face and let it pull his gaze deep into its brilliant facets. "My first decision must be to appoint a Durweard," he said, and glanced at Taminy. "May I have two?"

Her mouth tilted with humor. "You can have as many as you please, Osric Airleas."

"Then I'll have two—you and Catahn. I doubt I could do better than that."

Taminy smiled. "Humility prevents me from commenting."

Airleas laughed, and raising the Osmaer Crystal over his head, turned back to the embrace of the people to whom he now belonged.

APPENDIX:

THE HOUSES OF CARAID-LAND AND THEIR BANNERS

Claeg   "House of Earth" — a midland House of traditional warriors represented by a sword-cleft rock on a field of red.

Cuillean   "House of the Bear" — a northern House represented by a brown bear on a green field.

Dearg   "House of the Red Man" — a midland House represented by a red hand on a white and yellow field.

Floinn   "House of the Red Child" — a breakaway Northern House related to the Dearg, represented by a dagger-bearing hand on a yellow and white field.

Feich   "House of the Raven" — southern neighbors of the Claeg represented by a raven on a yellow field.

Gilleas   "House of the Disciples (of the Meri)" — a midland House; traditionally strong allies of the Malcuim, represented by a golden star on a midnight blue field.

Glinne   "House of the White (One)" — a House traditionally dedicated to the worship of the Gwenwyvar (the White Wave), represented by a white wave cresting on a purple field.

Graegam   "House of the Grey Man" — western neighbors of the Feich represented by a castle keep on a red and white field.

Jura   "House of the Broken Heart" — the family of the martyred Osraed Gartain, represented by a twained heart on a white field with a red border.

Madaidh   "House of Wolves" — a sea-faring House thought to be descendants of Deasach immigrants to Caraid-land represented by a brown wolf on a yellow and blue field.

437

Malcuim   "House of the Sands" — the Royal House of Caraid-
            land represented by clasped hands on a gold and
            green field.
Skarf   "House of the Cormorant" — a House of fishermen
            and merchant seamen represented by a white cor-
            morant on a teal field.
Teallach   "House of Iron" — a Northern House represented by
            a sword on an orange field.

A GLOSSARY OF
CARAIDIN PRONOUNCIATIONS

Phonetics Keys:

<u>th</u> = "th" as in "the"
dh = a "d" with a slight aspirant
y = a long "i"
ay = "ay" as in "hay"
ey = "eye"
fh = the softest possible "f"
gh = a hard "h"

Names:

Aine   Ayn; "fiery one."
Airleas   Ayr'lee-às; a traditional Caraidin name meaning "a
            pledge" or "an oath."
Ardis   Ar'dis; "warm," "ardent."
Arundel   Ar-un-del'; "dwells at the eagle's grove"; family estate
            of the Osraed Wyth Arundel.
Bearach   Bay'rak; "spear carrier"; heroic Cyne of Caraid-land
            who won the First Battle of the Crystal against Buchan
            Claeg.
Bevol   Bay'vol; Hillwild name meaning "wind"; Osraed
            mentor of Taminy-Osmaer murdered at Daimhin
            Feich's order.
Bitan-ig   Bee-tan-eegh'; "preserving"; Cyne and hero of the
            Battle of the Chalice and the Skull.
Brys   Bryss; "quick" or "ambitious"; a prentice disciple of
            the Tradist Osraed Ealad-hach.
Caime   Kaym; "crooked."
Calach   Ka'lak; "companion."

Caraid-land Car-ayd'lànd; "land between the streams" hence, "friendly land."

Catahn Ca-tawn'; Hillwild name meaning "champion" or "warrior"; given name of the Hageswode Ren.

Ciaran Kee-ar'an; Hillwild name meaning "dark one"; the famous (or infamous) grandfather of Cyne Colfre.

Ciarda Kee-ar'da; a Hillwild name meaning "child of the dark one"; Cyne Colfre's father, also known as "Friend of All."

Claeg Clayg; "of the clay" or "from the earth"; one of the Caraidin Houses.

Colfre Kol'fray; Hillwild name meaning "a dove," hence, peaceful.

Creiddylad Creh-dee'lyah; "jewel of the sea"; traditional home of the Malcuims and capital of Caraid-land since the reign of Malcuim the Uniter.

Cuillean Kwi-layn'; "of the cub," one of the familial Houses of Caraid-land.

Cuinn Kwin; "wise"; family name of Taminy-a-Cuinn; from a small settlement east of Nairne.

Daimhin Day'min; "poet" or "savant."

Dearg Deerg; "the red," one of the Caraidin Houses.

Deasach Dee'sak; "southern"; the citizens of El-Deasach, the country beyond the southwest arm of the Gyldan-baenn.

Desary Deh'sa-ree; a Hillwild name meaning "longed for."

Eada Yah'da; "prosperity" or "blessedness"; large seaport to the north of Creiddylad situate on the mouth of the Ead-Tyne.

Ealad-hach Ay-lad-hak'; "ingenious" or "a scientist."

Feich Fyke; "a raven"; one of the Caraidin Houses.

Fhada Fha'dah; (the "f" is nearly silent) "long."

Floinn Floyn; "child of the red," one of the Caraidin Houses.

Gilleas Gil'lee-as; "noble" or "bold," one of the Caraidin Houses.

Glinne Glin; "dwellers in the white glen," one of the Caraidin Houses.

Goscelin Jos'e-lin; "the just"; a great Caraidin heroine.

Graegam Graym; "from the grey land" or "of the grey man," one of the Caraidin Houses.

Gwenwyvar Gwen'wy-var; "white wave" or "white phantom"; Eibhilin being associated closely with the Meri; often a bearer of Her messages.

Gwynet Gwi'net; "white" or "blessed."

Gyldan-baenn
Gil-dan-bayn'; "golden mountains"; chain of mountains that wraps from northeast to southwest about Caraid-land, forming a border with the Deasach lands.

Haefer
Hay'fer; "sanctuary," "safety"; given name of the great Hillwild Osraed and hero Haefer Hageswode.

Hageswode
Hag'es-wode; "from the high forest."

Halig-liath
Ha-lig-lee'ath; "holy fortress."

Halig-tyne
Ha-lig-tyne'; "holy river."

Haesel
Hay'sel; "hazel tree"; a follower of Taminy-Osmaer.

Hrofceaster
Rof'kays-ter; "sky fortress."

Iobert
Ee'o-bayrt; "glorious warrior"; Chieftan of the Claey.

Iseabal
Eesh'a-bal; "dedicated to God."

Lach
Lak; "by the water."

Ladhar
La-dar'; "path."

Ladmann
Lad'man; "guide."

Lealbhallain
Leel'bal-layn; "loyal champion."

Liusadhe
Lee'oo-sadh; "bringer of light."

Lufu
Loo'-foo; Hillwild name meaning "love."

Madaidh
Ma-dayth; "the fox."

Malcuim
Mal'kwim; "friend from the forest," ruling House of Caraidland.

Meredydd
Mer-e-dith; "guardian from the sea."

Meri
Me'ree; "star of the sea"; the Being through whom the teachings of the Spirit are conveyed to earth. The Meri is the firstborn of the Eibhilin beings of which the only the Gifted are truly aware.

Mertuile
Mer-tweel'; castle around which Creiddylad is built; ancestral home of the House Malcuim.

Nairne
Nayrn; "place by the river alder grove."

Ochan
O'kan; "boy" or "youth."

Orna
Or'nah; "pale."

Osmaer
Oz-mayr'; "divinely glorious"; station-name of the human Vessel of the Meri's spirit.

Paeccs
Payks; "peaceful"; second Cyne of Caraid-land; son of Malcuim the Uniter.

Phelan
Fay'lan; "little wolf."

Ruadhe
Roo'ath; "the red."

Ruanaidhe
Roo'an-aidh; Hillwild name meaning "red one"; treacherous nephew of Haefer Hageswode; said to have been turned into a river silkie after murdering Cyne Siolta.

Saxan
Sak'san; "swordsman."

Scandy   Skan'dee; "boisterer."

Siolta   Shee-ol'ta; "teal."

Skarf   Skarf; "of the cormorant," one of the Caraidin Houses

Taminy   Ta'mi-nee; "pure."

Teallach   Tee-lak; "of the anvil," one of the Caraidin Houses.

Thearl   Thayrl; "stern one"; Cyne of Caraid-land during the Blue Cusp; son of Cyne Siolta and Goscelin the Just.

Toireasa   Twa-ree-a'-sa; "reaper."

Wyth   Wythe; "dweller in the willows"; by implication, "a healer."

Wyvis   Wy'-vis; "determined."

Terms:

abbod   ab'od; the foremost Osraed at Ochanshrine.

aidan   ay'dan; Hillwild term for the aislinn Gift; literally "little fire"; indicates the touch of the Eibhilin realm.

aingeal   ayn-geel'; "messenger"; Eibhilin guardian spirit.

aislinn   ays'-lin; "vision" or "dream," a vision experienced either dreaming or waking which is a reflection of reality.

ambre   am'ber; "golden" unit of Caraidin currency minted in gold.

anwyl   an'weel; "beloved" or "dear."

backstere   bak'steer; a baker.

Cirke   Keerk; Caraidin place of worship.

cailin   kay'lin; "girl," "maiden."

claefer   clay'-fer; "clover"; small silver coin. There are four claefer to the ambre.

cleirach   clee'rak; "scholar," "teacher"; the cleirach is educator, administrator and adjudicator in the rural holdings and settlements. Trained in religion, he may also be called upon to lead worship.

cwen   kwen; "female ruler."

cyne   kyne; "ruler," "leader."

cyneric   kyne'erik; "lord ruler"; clear heir to the Throne and Circlet.

daeges-eage daygs-eeg'; "eye of the day"; a customary Caraidin greeting.

duan   doo-an'; the song that accompanies a Runeweave.

Durweard   Door'-weerd; literally a "gate keeper." The Cyne's chief steward and advisor. The Durweard may be deputized to speak for the Cyne or, with the Cyne's seal, to sign legal documents and make contracts on his behalf.

Eibhilin   Eye'vi-lin; "light"; of the spiritual realm or realm of light. Also, beings of this realm.

eiric   Eye'rik; "home ruler" or "master" or "lord," usually of an estate or holding.

inyx   ee'niks; "spell" or "magic"; combines with the duan to create the Runeweave.

jagger   jag'ger; "teamster," "wagon driver."

lorimer   lo'ri'mer; "saddle maker."

marschal   mar'shal'; "horse master," hence, a leader of troops.

mercer   mer'ser; "merchant," "shopkeeper."

moireach   mwa'reek; "mistress" or "lady"; as of an estate or holding.

oonagh   u'nah; "one," "single"; brazen coin, smallest monetary unit of Caraid-land. There are 100 oonagh to the ambre.

Osraed   Awz'rayd; "divine counselor"; chosen of the Meri to convey the teachings of the Spirit to society.

Osric   Awz'-rik; "divine ruler"; Cyne by Divine right as was Malcuim the Uniter.

ren   ren; foremost Hillwild Chieftain.

renic   re'nek; female Chieftain; the most famous of the Hillwild Renic was Garmorgan, an ally of Bearach Spearman during the First War of the Crystal.

riagan   ree'a-gan; "little cyne"; any male child of the House Malcuim.

saphir   sa'fir; "silver"; a tiny silver coin. There are ten saphir to the ambre.

sorcha   sor'sha; "bright"; half-ambre coin minted in pure silver.

steadman   sted'man; a farmer or stead owner.

tannere   ta'neer; a tanner of hides or leather worker.

tyne   tyne; "river."

weard   weerd; "watcher," "guardian"; in Caraidin religion, the weard accompanies a Pilgrim on his travels, providing food, shelter and assistance.

webber   web'ber; a weaver of cloth.